Praise for the novels of Rick Mofina

"*Six Seconds* should be Rick Mofina's breakout thriller. It moves like a tornado."
—James Patterson, *New York Times* bestselling author

"*Six Seconds* is a great read. Echoing Ludlum and Forsythe, author Mofina has penned a big, solid international thriller that grabs your gut—and your heart—in the opening scenes and never lets go."
—Jeffery Deaver, *New York Times* bestselling author

"*The Panic Zone* is a headlong rush toward Armageddon. Its brisk pace and tight focus remind me of early Michael Crichton."
—Dean Koontz, #1 *New York Times* bestselling author, on *The Panic Zone*

"Rick Mofina's tense, taut writing makes every thriller he writes an adrenaline-packed ride."
—*New York Times* bestselling author Tess Gerritsen

"Mofina's clipped prose reads like short bursts of gunfire."
—*Publishers Weekly* on *No Way Back*

"Mofina is one of the best thriller writers in the business."
—*Library Journal* (starred review) on *They Disappeared*

"*Vengeance Road* is a thriller with no speed limit! It's a great read!"
—Michael Connelly, *New York Times* bestselling author

RICK

MOFINA

FREE
FALL

MIRA

ISBN-13: 978-0-7783-1946-7

Free Fall

Recycling programs
for this product may
not exist in your area.

This book is for Barbara

One

You're not going to die today.

Kayla repeated her prayer as the boarding call for her flight at Buffalo Niagara International Airport was announced. Her thoughts raced as she clutched her boarding pass and ID while inching through the line to Gate 20. After the gate agent had cleared her, Kayla felt Logan's reassuring hand on her shoulder as they walked along the jetway to their plane.

"You're gonna be fine," he said.

She offered him a weak smile. Drawing on the advice she'd absorbed from her motivational books and recordings, she fought her fear of flying by repeating her mantra.

I can do this. I've faced worse.

The jet was a new-model regional aircraft with eighty-six passenger seats, and today's flight was full. Their seats were in the fourteenth row on the left side. Logan took the aisle. Kayla took the window.

After they'd stowed their bags overhead Kayla

buckled her belt and continued battling her anxiety by attacking her scariest thoughts.

This plane is not going to crash. I'm safe. My boyfriend's with me.

Logan took her hand in his and tried to calm her.

"Remember how important this trip is? Just think about that."

Kayla nodded, concentrating on the reason why she had to get on this plane: because her dream was within her grasp. Tomorrow morning in New York City, she'd be interviewed for a position with a rising new fashion designer, Maly Kriz-Janda. The house had offices in London, Paris and Milan. It had recently opened a Manhattan office and was hiring new designers.

The jet's door was shut and locked. An inboard chime sounded followed by an announcement.

"Flight attendants, prepare for departure."

The attendants ensured the overhead bin doors were closed and seats and trays were up as the plane pushed back from the gate. The cabin lights flickered as the engines came on and the plane taxied out.

"Logan, the wings are bouncing."

"It's okay. They're built to flex like that. It's normal."

As the attendants gave safety demonstrations about seat belts, flotation devices and emergency exits, for use "in the unlikely event..." Kayla heard the hydraulic moan of the flaps as they were adjusted by the pilot. The plane turned then stopped for several moments. As the engines whined louder another chime sounded.

"Attendants, prepare for takeoff."

The knot in Kayla's stomach tightened as the plane began rolling down the runway, slowly at first, gaining speed then accelerating faster, the ground blurring beneath them. Kayla struggled to control her breathing as the jet's nose rose before she heard a thud when the weight lifted from the landing gear and the plane left the ground.

The thrust was overwhelming as the force of the climb pushed her into her seat. Kayla heard the groan and bump of the landing gear's retraction. She squeezed Logan's hand, shutting her eyes for a moment. Somehow, she found the strength to peek down at the earth, the expressways, buildings and suburbs rapidly shrinking below.

I can do this. I can do this.

As the plane leveled off, Kayla took a deep breath to calm herself, and the flight attendant made a series of announcements about keeping seat belts fastened, using electronic devices and the upcoming in-flight refreshment service.

"How're you doing?" Logan asked.

Kayla nodded stiffly, smiling, still gripping his hand as he lowered his tray with his other hand.

"I'm getting some tomato juice," he said. "What about you?"

"A diet cola, whatever they have."

Not long after they'd received their drinks there was another announcement.

"This is Captain Raymond Matson with First Officer Roger Anderson. On behalf of our entire crew, welcome aboard EastCloud Flight Forty-nine Ninety. Very shortly we'll reach our cruising altitude of twenty-seven thousand feet. Everything's looking good. We have no weather ahead of us and no traffic jams at LaGuardia, so we expect a very smooth flight arriving on time. We should have you in New York at the gate in about an hour and ten minutes."

"There you go," Logan said. "It'll be over before you know it."

Kayla nodded and sipped her drink.

As the flight cut across Upstate New York, she tried to relax by focusing on the opportunity awaiting her in Manhattan. She'd studied fashion at Buffalo State where a professor, impressed with her designs, had done all he could to help her get noticed.

But nothing had happened.

After graduating Kayla had found a full-time position selling women's clothing at the mall in Cheektowaga, the Walden Galleria. While she was uncertain about her aspirations and her future, she was grateful to have a job so she could start paying off her student loans.

Then, three weeks ago, everything had changed when, through her professor's help, Kayla was short-listed for a position with Maly Kriz-Janda in Manhattan. They'd loved Kayla's designs and the position involved flying to Los Angeles, Miami and Toronto for major conferences with North American retailers. Kayla wanted the job with all of her heart and had begun working on overcoming her fear of flying. But her expected call for an interview never came. The other candidates had been stronger.

Heartbroken, Kayla had soldiered on at the mall.

Then, last week, her professor had learned that the two candidates ahead of her had dropped out of the running. One had accepted a job at Versace, and the other had gone to Givenchy. Two days ago, Maly Kriz-Janda had called Kayla, requesting she be in Manhattan for an interview as soon as possible. They'd pay all expenses—flight, hotel, meals and cabs.

Logan was thrilled for her. She'd asked him to go with her because she'd never flown before, and was terrified. He'd agreed, using his sister's points to cover his flight.

What if I get the job? Kayla had asked him. *I'd have to move to New York City. What would happen to us?*

Logan, who was still in law school, had told her not to worry.

I'll look into applying and transferring to a school there, he'd said. *But don't think about that. We'll cross that bridge later.*

Logan was good to her and she knew it. She took comfort in having him beside her now on what was her first—and maybe the most important—flight of her life.

"Hey, smile," he said, pointing his phone at her. "I'm making a documentary of your first flight."

Kayla waved.

"I'm really doing it. I'm flying. I'm nervous but I'm doing it."

Then she turned to her window to take in the view below.

"It's so pretty down there. Where are we?"

"I think we're over the Catskill Mountains," Logan said.

"Oh, I've got to take a picture."

Kayla held up her phone to the window but it flew from her hand and her seat belt cut deep into her as the plane suddenly rolled hard, the right wing tipping toward the ground as if the jet was flipping over.

Bodies bumped over seats as people not belted were tossed to the right wall, along with laptops, backpacks and purses amid shrieks and loud bangs as items thudded and hammered in the overhead bins. The service trolley crashed into passengers in the right rows, spilling hot coffee and raining down cans of soda and juice.

The jet froze with its wings in a twelve-and-six-o'clock position.

Kayla clawed at Logan, locking her arms around him as people screamed, cursed and prayed.

Then the plane lurched hard to the left with the left wing pointing directly to the earth. Again, bodies flew through the cabin, slamming against other passengers, the wall and the overhead luggage bins. The bin doors opened and luggage tumbled like boulders along the left row. Logan reached out to grab an older woman who'd fallen into them but she slipped from his grip as the jet suddenly rolled right until it was almost level.

Now it began dropping, banking downward, as if it would spiral out of control. Passengers yelled and screamed, some calling out to God before the crew regained control and finally leveled the plane.

"Please, please, let this be over," Kayla whispered through her tears.

In the aftermath, the attendants, despite being hurt and bleeding, took charge. Even as the sounds of crying and moaning passengers filled the plane, people began helping each other. Kayla thrust her face into Logan's chest, slid her arms around him and sobbed, feeling his heart beating rapidly against her face.

Logan held her tight as the jet resumed a smooth flight.

Kayla prayed for the plane to land.

Get us back on the ground! Please, God, get us back on the ground!

Her cheek twitched as something wet and warm splashed on her skin; one drop then another. As she pulled back, she saw blood dripping down on them from the little boy who'd been contorted into the open luggage bin above them.

Two

"New York, EastCloud Forty-nine Ninety…declar—an emer—"

"EastCloud Forty-nine Ninety, transmission garbled, say again…"

Kate Page, a reporter with Newslead, detected something in the chatter crackling from the news agency's emergency scanners. More than a dozen of them issued a constant stream of coded bursts across from where she sat in the newsroom. Kate stopped her current work, jotted down the name of the airline, the flight number and listened.

"…EastCloud Forty-nine Ninety…injur—request—medic—"

Sounds like "injuries" and a call for medical services.

She listened as the dispatches continued echoing in the news department.

It was Saturday and the newsroom was nearly empty.

Kate had a bad feeling about what she'd heard.

She went online. EastCloud 4990 was a commercial flight that had originated in Buffalo and was bound for LaGuardia. It was a new Richlon-TitanRT-86 with a capacity for eighty-six passengers. She quickly checked social media feeds. No one was tweeting about the flight.

Not so far, anyway.

She glanced at the corner and the glass-walled cubicle known as the scanner room. Reporters called it "the torture chamber," because if you were assigned to sit in it you had to endure and decipher the chaotic, simultaneous cross-talk flowing from metropolitan New York City's police, fire department, paramedics and other responders.

But no one was there.

The cubicle door was open, which is how Kate had been able to hear the chatter from the scanner.

What's going on? Why isn't someone listening?

This broke Newslead's cardinal rule: never, ever leave the scanners unattended. Emergency scanners were the lifeblood of any news operation, alerting the reporters to the first cries for help, pulling them into stories that would stop the heart of the city.

Or break it.

Kate's years of listening to police radios while working on crime desks in newsrooms across the country had given her the ability to pluck a key piece of data from dozens of staccato exchanges all happening at the same time. She knew the alphanumeric code systems. She could pick out a trace of emotion in a dispatcher's voice, the underlying tension in a transmission. This was a skill Newslead, the global wire service, demanded from every member of its reporting staff, especially here at its world headquarters in Manhattan, where the competition was fierce. But the incessant noise, the confusion and pressure not to miss anything was torturous for some reporters, making a shift on the scanners the most dreaded job in the newsroom.

Another transmission from air traffic control crackled.

"EastCloud Forty-nine Ninety, we can give you Teterboro or Newark."

The jet's response was overtaken by static.

Damn. There's a jetliner in trouble with injuries aboard and we don't know where it's headed.

Kate glared at the empty scanner room.

This is how we miss stories. This is how we get beat.

She made a quick check of the bank of flat-screen TV monitors tilted down from the ceiling over rows of empty desks. The sets were tuned to news channels with the volume turned low. Most newsrooms in New York subscribed to professional scanner-listening services that sent out alerts. Newslead had cut its subscription years ago to save money.

Nothing was breaking on TV, either. Kate picked up more dispatches.

"EastCloud Forty-nine Ninety, repeat—we can give you Teterboro or Newark."

"Thank you, New York. We've got a visual on the Verrazano Bridge. We'll keep LaGuardia."

"Forty-nine Ninety, stand by."

Kate did another online check. No one was tweeting anything.

This is all happening now.

Resentment bubbled in the pit of her stomach. She'd come in today on her own time to finish a feature about crime on the subways of the world's largest cities. She was pulling together files from Newslead's bureaus in Mexico City, Seoul and São Paulo. But she had to stop. The situation on the radios gnawed at her.

No way am I taking the blame for us missing a major breaking story because someone else failed to do their job.

Kate went to the scanner room, looking for the incident log, or at least a note from whoever was on duty. She found nothing. Again, she looked around the newsroom. One person was working in graphics. Other than that, no one was around. A portrait of an industry withering before the internet, she thought. When she'd started, one hundred and forty newspeople had worked here at headquarters.

That number was now seventy-one.

Kate went to the news assistant's desk, just in time to see a girl barely out of her teens returning while drinking from a thermos.

"Who're you?" Kate asked.

"Penny. I'm the new assistant. Todd was here but he went home sick."

"Who's on the scanners?"

"Sloane. I forget his last name."

"Parkman. Where is he?"

"He told me he was stepping out to get scones and would be right back. Is everything okay?"

Kate rolled her eyes.

Sloane was the worst person you could put on scanner duty. *All that crash-and-burn stuff is a bit too tabloid for me, but they say everybody has to do their time here,* she'd overheard him tell a friend on the phone.

He'd joined Newslead a year ago between rounds of layoffs. His family was one of New England's oldest. He had degrees from Harvard and Columbia, had worked at the *Washington Post* and *Forbes*, and had boasted about having political connections in Washington and corporate connections on Wall Street.

He always introduced himself as Sloane F. Parkman and assured you that he knew everyone and everything, right down to the best bars in Manhattan, the best shops and restaurants. He wore Brooks Brothers shirts, had a gleaming, white-toothed grin and never had a hair out of place.

How he'd gotten a job with Newslead in a time of cutbacks was no mystery. Kate knew that he'd been hired at the urging of her editor because of mutual family ties. There were no secrets in a newsroom. Sloane had half the news-reporting experience that Kate had yet he regarded her as he would an untested rookie, and as a latter-day-Dickensian working-class woman to be pitied.

I applaud you for what you've achieved in your life, he'd told her one day. *It's nothing short of heroic, putting yourself through that community college in Chicago the way you did—sorry I'd never heard of it. In any event, here you are. And raising a child alone. Bravo, Kate. Bravo.*

That was Sloane F. Parkman.

Kate entered the scanner room with Penny in tow as new transmissions came through clearly.

"Forty-nine Ninety, this is LaGuardia tower. Are you declaring an emergency?"

Kate took notes, motioning for Penny to sit in the empty chair and use the computer at the desk.

"Penny, did they teach you how to listen to the scanners?"

"No, not yet."

"Did Todd show you how to alert the photographers on duty and call freelancers?"

"Yes."

"Okay—wait—listen!"

More transmissions were coming through. Kate cranked up the volume and took notes.

"Affirmative. We're declaring an emergency. We have passenger and crew injuries aboard. Approximately thirty, some pretty bad. We'll need a lot of ambulances."

"Fatalities?"

"None to report."

"Forty-nine Ninety, do you have damage to your aircraft?"

Kate was writing as fast as she could, trying to make sure her notes were clear.

"Damage to the cabin, ceiling, galley, storage bins."

"Are you citing turbulence?"

"Negative. Negative on turbulence. We had a sys—" A burst of static drowned out part of the transmission, but the message ended clearly with "—malfunction."

"Repeating. You're reporting a—" more static "—malfunction?"

"Affirmative."

"Forty-nine Ninety, you have priority clearance

to land. Runway Four. Crash and Rescue will meet you at your gate."

"Roger...visual approach for Runway Four..."

Penny turned to seek direction from Kate but the older woman had already grabbed her bag and was rushing toward the elevators.

"Penny, I'm heading to LaGuardia!" Kate shouted. "Alert every photographer and let them know we have a plane in trouble landing now!"

Three

Queens, New York

As the taxi raced through the skyscraper-lined streets, Kate searched for updates on her phone.

Nothing so far.

She set up an alert for anything that broke on EastCloud Flight 4990.

Crosstown traffic was good; there were few double-parkers and unloaders blocking the street, and within minutes they'd entered the Midtown Tunnel. It smelled of exhaust and gleamed gold from headlights reflecting on the walls. As it curved under the East River to Queens, Kate found herself taking stock of her job and her life.

Wasn't she living her dream?

For as long as she could remember, she'd wanted to be a reporter and to get her life on track. In spite of all that she'd endured, she'd managed to work her way up the journalistic ladder to a position at Newslead, one of the world's top news organizations. The global newswire service had bureaus in every major city in the United States and in one hundred countries. Its reputation for excellence had been solidified by awards it had won throughout its history, including twenty-two Pulitzers. Newslead was respected and feared by its chief rivals, such as the Associated Press, Bloomberg and Reuters. Kate was proud to work for Newslead, but things were changing.

Fierce competition, the corrosive impact of the internet on the distribution of news and the melting number of subscribers continued to exact a toll.

Kate had to struggle not to pin her hopes on the rumor that Chuck Laneer, the editor who'd hired her at Newslead before he'd left to teach at Columbia after clashing with former management, was returning to help rebuild the news division. Chuck was gruff, wise and old-school. He could kick your butt and respect you at the same time.

But so far the news of Chuck's return was only gossip.

The reality was that anxiety had gripped the newsroom. Management weighed every financial decision extensively. Staff faced constant evaluation. Performance on every news story was scrutinized. Newslead had instituted a "staff efficiency process," linking story count and story pickup to individual performance assessments. It was championed by Kate's editor, Reeka Beck, a twenty-eight-year-old Ivy League management zealot.

Reeka had a cover-girl face, an insatiable ambition and was convinced that her news judgment was superior to that of seasoned journalists. Reeka had been a junior copy editor at Newslead's Boston bureau, whose collective work had been a finalist for a Pulitzer. In reality, she possessed little reporting experience. She'd never covered a homicide or asked an inconsolable parent for a picture of their dead child.

But her moneyed bloodline gave her an advantage. Reeka's uncle sat on Newslead's board of directors. However, most people strained to tolerate her—her dealings with reporters were often so curt and officious they bordered on rudeness. Conversations with her nearly became confrontations. Reeka had embraced the staff efficiency process even though it was killing morale.

Last month twenty people were let go from headquarters. Some were news veterans like Liz Cochrane, who'd covered wars, interviewed Mexican drug lords and escaped being kidnapped by terrorists in Iraq. Liz had sat near Kate and that day had been horrible.

She'd seen Liz falling apart at her desk while reading her severance letter then tenderly placing her belongings in a box for printing paper—*A cardboard coffin for my career,* she'd joked while saying goodbye.

Even though Kate had made it through the latest round of terminations, watching the funereal march of dismissed colleagues had been heart-wrenching. She'd been in their shoes; she was familiar with that soul-shattering feeling, for she'd struggled much of her life.

She was a thirty-two-year-old single mom with a nine-year-old daughter and she was living with her sister, Vanessa. There were days when Kate felt like she was hanging on by her fingertips but she was still here, doing the best that she could because she was a fighter who never gave up.

The cab left the tunnel and passed through the toll gates. As it accelerated on the Long Island Expressway, Kate's phone rang.

It was Reeka. "What're you doing, Kate?"

"Heading to LaGuardia. We've got a plane in trouble."

"You're not on today. Who assigned you to go to LaGuardia?"

"No one. I was in the newsroom working on my subway crime feat—"

"I just spoke with Sloane. He's on duty and he assures me that this Buffalo jet thing is minor. He's been listening to the scanners all day."

"No, he wasn't there when I was there, when things were popping!"

Sloane's trying to cover his ass by hanging me out to dry—

"Kate, were you in today hoping to collect overtime?"

"No. Reeka, listen, I was there on my own time working on my feature when this broke on the scanners. Sloane was out buying scones."

"I don't think so. I know Sloane and if he says—"

Anger bubbled in Kate just as her phone chimed with a news alert. The Associated Press had issued a bulletin: "Commuter jet with multiple injuries on board declares emergency landing at LaGuardia."

"Reeka, did you see what AP's just put out?"

A moment passed before Reeka responded.

"I see it. Okay, get to the airport and file as soon as you can."

Four

Queens, New York

Sirens wailed and emergency lights flashed as two ambulances sped by Kate's cab on the Grand Central Parkway near the airport.

"We need Terminal C, arrivals pickup area."

She directed the driver while keeping her phone to her ear. After four attempts, she'd finally reached Dwayne, somebody with EastCloud's public affairs. He'd put her on hold.

She'd already left messages with the National Transportation Safety Board, the Federal Aviation Administration, LaGuardia Airport, the Port Authority and several other agencies. No responses. Her taxi was on the ramp to the airport when the line clicked and Dwayne returned.

"Sorry, who've I got here?"

"Kate Page with Newslead. What happened to Flight Forty-nine Ninety? Why did it declare an emergency?"

"We're still assessing matters. We'll put out a statement soon."

"Are there fatalities? How many injur—?"

"I have to go."

"Can you estimate the number of injuries?"

"We'll put out a statement. I really have to go."

The call ended as Kate's cab slowed on the edge of havoc.

Red, white, orange and blue lights blinked from the police, fire and paramedic vehicles that were jammed outside the Terminal C arrivals area, backing up traffic. Kate paid her driver, who hastily scrawled a receipt.

Her phone was chiming with news alerts. She saw two news vans parked to the side. Up ahead, TV crews with shoulder-held cameras were shooting footage of people on stretchers being loaded into ambulances. Kate arrived to see one woman, her back raised on a gurney, her head bandaged and tears in her eyes. Microphones hovered near her and reporters hurled questions at her as paramedics placed her in an ambulance.

"Can you describe the flight?"

"It was horrible!" the woman said. "Just horrible!"

A cop inserted himself between the paramedics and cameras.

"Back off guys, back off!"

Kate's phone continued chiming with alerts. Bloomberg and Reuters had issued bulletins on Flight 4990. Finally, she saw one from Newslead. Someone on the desk must have woken up, Kate thought. It sure as hell couldn't have been Sloane.

Things were buzzing online, too.

Pictures were popping up everywhere. Twitter

had images of the aftermath in the cabin. Luggage, clothes, books, laptops, food containers and other items were strewn about the interior. In one clear photo she was certain she'd seen streaks of blood.

Kate scanned the crowd for a Newslead photographer. Not finding one, she went inside to the busy baggage-claim area where more news cameras had encircled passengers who were recounting their ordeal for reporters. She joined one group and extended her recorder.

"Could you please take us through it again?" someone asked.

"It was right after they'd served us drinks," a man with bloodied scrapes on his cheeks began. "Then bam, the plane tilts like we're going to roll upside down. Like this." He extended his arms, one hand pointed to the floor, the other to the ceiling as the woman beside him nodded.

"Everybody and everything not belted or bolted down flew," the woman said, her eyes still wide with shock.

"People were hurled like rag dolls. The service trolley smashed around. We were hanging on with all we had," the man said. "Then the plane rolled the opposite way, tossing people and things around like we were in a clothes drier. People were screaming and praying."

"The luggage bins opened," the woman said. "Suitcases and bags crashed on everyone. Then the jet just dropped and we were plunging, diving down. My stomach was in my mouth."

"What went through your mind at this point?" a reporter asked.

"That we weren't going to survive. That we were so helpless. That this was the end," she said.

"How long did it last?" another reporter asked.

"I don't know." The man shook his head. "Five, maybe eight minutes."

Kate glanced around and was relieved to see Stan Strobic, a Newslead photographer, had joined the group.

"When it was over," the woman said, "and they got things under control, it got quiet, except for the moans and sobs. People were trying to comfort those who were hurt. I think one lady was a nurse. But the pilot never came on and said what happened. Nobody has told us anything."

As the interview wound down, the couple— Connie and Carmine Delvecchio—spelled their names for the reporters. They ran a family towing business on Staten Island. Kate passed them her card.

Then she saw a woman across the baggage-claim area. She was near the baggage carousels, sitting alone on a bench, her back to the wall, her head raised with her eyes closed in anguish.

Kate nodded to Strobic to hang back as she approached her alone.

"Excuse me."

The woman looked to be in her mid-thirties. She had a pretty, fresh-scrubbed face and was gripping her phone in her lap with both hands.

"Yes?"

"I'm Kate Page. I'm a reporter with Newslead. Were you on EastCloud Forty-nine Ninety?"

The woman nodded.

"Can I get your name?"

"Diane Wilson."

"Would you talk to me for a story about what happened on the flight?"

The woman was trembling as she adjusted her hold on her phone. She swallowed hard.

"It was the worst thing you could imagine," she said.

Kate sat next to her. "Tell me about it."

"I was certain we were going to crash and I was going to die."

Kate took notes. "And at that moment, what went through your mind?"

"All I could think about was my family, that I'd never see them again, so I said goodbye."

Kate took a quick look around. "Your family was on the plane with you?"

"No. I was alone. I used my phone to make my last message to my children and my husband."

Diane lifted the phone slightly and lovingly from her lap.

"You texted them?"

"I made a video."

"Did you send it to them?"

"No."

"Has anyone seen it?"

"No."

"Would you let me see it?"

Diane considered Kate's request.

"I'm not sure. It's private and my family's coming to get me."

"I know, but it might help me to really understand

what you and the other passengers went through. It would help readers appreciate your ordeal."

Diane lowered her head to her phone, caught her bottom lip between her teeth and her face crumpled. She fought tears as she stared at her phone for a moment, then her fingers began working.

"You can look at it but I can't give it to you."

The screen came to life with Diane's face, a mask of fear. Through her tears she struggled to smile as her voice quivered in the cabin.

"It doesn't look good. The plane's in trouble and I don't think we're going to make it. No matter what happens, you know that Mommy absolutely loves you. Brandon, honey, take care of Melissa. Melissa, you help your brother take care of Daddy. Del, sweetheart, you're the love of my life. Be good to each other and remember how much I love you."

Kate caught her breath.

For a second the footage exploded in chaos as the jet tilted at a ninety-degree angle, the image froze before the screen went black.

Five

Manhattan, New York

Passengers and crew were tossed "like rag dolls" in the cabin of the EastCloud Airlines flight when it encountered severe turbulence, sources told Newslead.

What the—? That's not what I wrote and that's not what happened!

Kate had just returned to the Newslead building from LaGuardia and was in the elevator when her phone alerted her to Newslead's first full story on Flight 4990. She was incredulous as she read. Ninety percent of the item was her work but the story was topped with a single byline:

Sloane F. Parkman.

She was credited at the bottom in smaller font.

With files from Kate Page.

She cursed. And as the elevator rose, she seethed. *Calm down and think this through.*

Biting back her anger she checked her phone for responses to the repeated calls she'd put in to the official agencies. Not much had come back to her, except a text from LaGuardia Operations, with a short general timeline from when Flight 4990 first reported a problem to its emergency landing.

The doors opened to Newslead's fortieth-floor offices.

Kate swiped her ID at the security lock and swept through reception, with its wall of enlarged Newslead photos of pivotal points in history—immigrants gazing at the Statue of Liberty in 1901, a child in Africa comforted by an aid worker, a soldier weeping in Vietnam, and Martin Luther King at the Lincoln Memorial.

In the newsroom she saw no sign of Penny, the news assistant. But when Kate passed by the glass walls of the editors' offices, she noticed Reeka Beck's jacket and bag on her desk.

Reeka was not in her office as Kate went by.

But Sloane F. Parkman was in the scanner room, on the phone, working at the computer with the door closed. He was hanging up as Kate pulled it open to the onslaught of the radios.

"Hi, Kate. I've just confirmed that they took the injured passengers to hospitals in the area—Sinai, NYP/Queens and Forest Hills. We're pretty sure they're all minor injuries, one little boy with a concussion and broken arm, so no big deal on this incident. By the way, thank you for your help on my story. It wasn't necessary but nice work, much appreciated."

"What the hell do you think you're doing, Sloane?"

"Excuse me?"

"You know what I'm talking about. What's your name doing on my story, and why did you cite turbulence? It wasn't turbulence!"

"Sorry, but I'm on duty today, you're not. Didn't Reeka talk to you? She's come in. I think she's getting a coffee."

"Sloane, you weren't here when this story broke."

"I was."

"You weren't. You'd left the scanner room unattended to get scones. Where's the news assistant, where's Penny?"

"Her shift ended."

"Penny and I were both in this room when I caught the dispatches from Forty-nine Ninety. You weren't here."

"I was here, Kate, when I heard the dispatches—"

"What you heard—*when you came back*—was the aftermath!"

"I was here! Look, I'm trying to be diplomatic but the truth is you were trying to hijack my story."

"Bullsh—"

"What's going on?" Reeka stood behind Kate.

"I told you, Reeka, Sloane was not at the scanners when the story broke and he's inserted incorrect information into the story I filed."

"What's incorrect?"

"His unnamed sources said turbulence was the problem. It was not turbulence. It was a malfunction."

"What kind of malfunction?"

"I don't know."

Reeka looked at Sloane then at Kate.

"He has impeccable sources in the airline industry. Who's your source that contradicts his?"

"The pilot."

"You interviewed the pilot?" Reeka asked.

"No, it came over the scanner. There was static but I heard the crew say it was not turbulence, it was a malfunction."

Reeka looked to Sloane.

"Did you hear anything like that?"

He shook his head.

"He wasn't here!" Kate said.

"Kate, do you have an on-the-record source confirming it was a malfunction? The NTSB? East-Cloud? Any official?"

"Not yet."

"Kate," Reeka said, "we all know that the information we hear on police radios can often be wrong, especially with first reports. When I arrived Sloane was at his post and he had everything in hand."

"Oh my God." Kate shook her head in disbelief.

"What?" Reeka asked.

"You actually believe him. He's trying to downplay this story while taking credit for it and being wrong about it. He lied and you believe him. This could hurt Newslead."

"Excuse me," Sloane said. "I take umbrage at your accusation, particularly after you tried to secure overtime by hijacking a call I was handling."

Fury burned through Kate and as she battled to restrain herself she glimpsed the plastic trash can holding a white crumpled take-out bag. She retrieved it and flattened it out. The bag was from Miss Muffet's Café & Cakes and had "Sloane" scrawled on it in marker. A receipt was stapled to it. Kate circled the date and time of purchase.

Then she took a picture with her phone.

"What're you doing?" Reeka asked, as if Kate had lost her mind.

Sloane shook his head.

"This looks like yours, right? You're the only Sloane in the room," Kate said, scrolling on her phone, holding it out for Sloane and Reeka to see a text concerning Flight 4990. "And this is the timeline from LaGuardia, proof that when the plane was in trouble, you were at Miss Muffet's buying scones. Proof that you lied."

Sloane glared at Kate, saying nothing.

"I think," Reeka said, "given the circumstances, everybody needs to take a breath here." A long, uneasy moment passed before she continued. "Kate, if you can stay to help update the story, I'll authorize your overtime. Sloane, I'm assigning you to tie up loose ends and follow up the story tomorrow. We'll get the night desk to monitor for developments and top off with any updates. Okay?"

Reeka looked to Kate then Sloane before concluding.

"As for what happened here—we'll talk later and sort out what appears to be a misunderstanding. Is everybody clear?"

"Crystalline," Sloane said.

Kate said nothing, and left the room.

Misunderstanding.

Kate fumed as she worked at her desk.

There's no misunderstanding. I caught Sloane

failing at his job and lying about it. And Reeka pro-
tects him. This is how the one percenters get ahead.

One thing had been hammered home: Sloane was
not to be trusted. That guy was not a reporter—he
was somebody's favor. It was dangerous for Kate
and for Newslead but she had to shove it all aside
and get on with her work.

She went back to her subway feature and was
nearly finished when she received a text from East-
Cloud. The airline had just issued a news release on
Flight 4990.

The flight encountered an as-yet-undefined situation on its approach into New York and 28
passengers and 2 flight attendants received injuries ranging from fractures and concussions,
to minor cuts and bruising, to nausea. All were
evaluated by paramedics at the airport and were
transported to area hospitals for observation as
a precaution. None of the injuries are considered
life-threatening or critical at this time. EastCloud
will work closely with the National Transportation Safety Board to determine the nature of this
incident. The aircraft will be taken out of service
during the investigation.

As Kate digested EastCloud's statement, she
tapped her finger on her desk. "An as-yet-undefined
situation." What was that supposed to mean? Kate
began flipping through her notes from the scanner, looking for the original comments the crew
had made.

New York Center had clearly asked 4990 if it was citing turbulence.

The crew's response: *Negative on turbulence. We had a malfunction.*

Kate's phone rang.

"Paul Murther, spokesperson with the NTSB."

"Paul, what happened on EastCloud Forty-nine Ninety? Why did it declare an emergency?"

"We can't speculate on that. All we can say at this time is that we're gathering all the details. We're looking at the severity of the injuries and for any damage to the aircraft. We'll analyze the flight data."

"Was it turbulence or a malfunction?"

"We can't speculate but I can confirm that we're putting a team together to investigate."

Kate alerted Reeka to the new information she'd received then began updating the story with a new lede.

Mystery surrounds the cause of mayhem aboard an EastCloud Airlines flight that tossed some thirty passengers and crew "like rag dolls," injuring some seriously, officials indicated to Newslead.

More than once the Richlon-TitanRT-86 rolled to a ninety-degree angle, causing some passengers to prepare final messages to their loved ones.

"It doesn't look good. The plane's in trouble and I don't think we're going to make it," Diane Wilson told her children and husband in a farewell video she'd recorded on the stricken flight...

After she'd sent her story to Reeka, she went to the washroom to freshen up. Upon returning, she was glad the updated story had been issued with a solitary byline on top: "Kate Page."

She thought of Diane Wilson, the mother from Brooklyn, and her goodbye video. Then she looked at the faces of her daughter and sister smiling back at her from the framed photo next to her computer monitor. Grace and Vanessa.

What would I say to you in the final moments of my life?

Six

Jake Hooper kept pace with the rhythmic jingling of the leash as he and his German shepherd, Pax, trotted alongside the Lincoln Memorial Reflecting Pool at the National Mall.

Pax panted happily. He loved running here. But Hooper was running with a heavy heart. His dog was getting on and his arthritic pain and bone spurs had taken a toll. The vet didn't give Pax much time before the pain would be unbearable and he'd have to be put down.

Hooper and his wife, Gwen, couldn't have children. For them, Pax was a cherished family member who gave them nothing but unconditional love. Hooper was thinking about what life would be like without him when his phone rang and he stopped cold.

It was from the National Transportation Safety Board duty officer.

"Jake, it's Crawley at the comms center. We got one at LaGuardia, an EastCloud Richlon-TitanRT-86.

More than two dozen injured. No fatalities. Landed without incident."

"Thank God for that. Do we have a suspected cause?"

"Crew reports a flight control computer malfunction."

"A computer malfunction?" Hooper considered it.

"The RT-86 is a new model. That's why we're traveling on this one. I'm sending you a ticket now."

"Okay. I'll get home, grab my bag and get to National."

Hooper cupped Pax's head in his hands, reading the question in his big eyes.

"That's right. I gotta go, pal."

They caught a cab home to their porch-front row house in Glover Park. Hooper took a quick shower, called a cab and set out bowls of fresh water and food for Pax, who whined a goodbye as Hooper shouldered his prepacked bag and locked the house.

In the cab to the airport, he texted Gwen, who was at her sister's in Georgetown. Then he digested the information coming in about the aircraft and the occurrence.

EastCloud Flight 4990 had originated in Buffalo, bound for LaGuardia, with eighty passengers and five crew aboard. The plane had been twenty-seven thousand feet over the Catskills when it suddenly rolled ninety degrees right, then ninety degrees left, then dropped seven thousand feet before the crew regained control. Result: twenty-eight passengers and two attendants injured, some of them seriously. There was damage to the cabin.

The crew reported a flight-management systems

problem. But there are safety features to guard against that.

Hooper's years as an NTSB investigator had taught him that initial information on the circumstances of an incident was often incomplete. He always regarded preliminary data with caution. They had a long way to go yet and a lot to do, like analyze the cockpit voice recorder and the flight data recorder, and talk to the crew.

He considered the plane.

The RT-86 had come on stream about two years ago with few problems. The new model had a good safety record with no incidents with significant implications. Bottom line, Hooper thought the RT-86 was a very solid, state-of-the-art commercial jetliner.

So what could've caused the problem?

Don't overthink this. Wait until all the facts are known, he thought. But it was impossible not to consider theories. He was a detective. Probing crashes and incidents was all he'd done since he'd got his degree in aeronautical science from Arizona State University.

Hooper had been among the top graduates of his class. Right out of school he'd been hired as a civilian at Naval Air Systems Command in Virginia, where he'd examined United States Navy and Marine Corps aircraft accidents.

Along the way, he'd become a licensed pilot, then a flight instructor, and he'd obtained an engineering degree. He'd left Virginia when he'd been hired by the MacCalleb Aircraft Company in Wichita, Kansas, as a flight test engineer. He'd taken part in dozens of accident investigations, providing technical help to Federal Aviation Administration safety inspectors and the NTSB. He'd frequently and successfully challenged their findings.

Hooper's exceptional work led to a position as an NTSB regional investigator then, eventually, a job with Major Investigations Division at their headquarters in Washington. His insights impressed seasoned experts and he was not afraid to challenge supervisors. Hooper didn't care because he adhered to the belief, as did all investigators, that safety was paramount; that with each tragedy, each incident, his job was to find information that would prevent other accidents and enhance the safety of air travel.

He was obsessed, almost pathologically so, with ensuring that nothing in an investigation was ruled out without being triple-checked and triple-checked again.

Today, he was anxious because this was his last time on a Go Team as a senior air safety investigator. After this investigation, he'd be promoted to investigator-in-charge, the IIC, and would lead his own team.

Hooper's cab stopped at Departures and he headed for the American Airlines desk. The NTSB comms center had sent him an electronic ticket for the next flight to LaGuardia. Tapping his mobile boarding pass and showing his ID, Hooper made his way through security to the preboarding area of his gate, where he recognized members of the Go Team.

"Hey, Jake, you old tin-kicker." Swanson, the expert on power plants, shook his hand.

They were joined by Willet from maintenance.

From human performance, sitting off alone working on a laptop, was Irene Zimm. She was known as Good Night Irene, because if she found that a pilot had violated any aspect of safety procedures, it meant a world of pain.

The one man who didn't greet Hooper was on the phone: Bill Cashill, a case-hardened veteran. He had no love for Hooper, who'd once corrected Cashill at an investigation, something Cashill had never forgotten and never forgiven. Cashill was set to retire after thirty years as a leading investigator on some of the board's biggest crashes. He was the investigator-in-charge. He glanced at Hooper then resumed concentrating on his call before he finally stood and surveyed his team.

"What do you think about this EastCloud incident, Bill?" Willet asked.

"I think this is overkill, even with a partial team."

"But it's a new-generation aircraft," Swanson said.

"I'm aware of that, but my gut's telling me that this thing has all the indications of an overreaction by the crew to clear-air turbulence."

"But the crew said—" Hooper started.

"I know what the crew said, Jacob."

Hooper preferred to be called Jake, and Cashill knew it.

An uneasy moment passed before Irene Zimm broke it.

"Bill, would you come over for a second and look at this?"

Cashill went over to Zimm, who turned her computer so he could see the screen. They chatted quietly. A short time later, they boarded their jet for the one-hour flight to New York. As it leveled off, Hooper took stock, reflecting on Gwen. They'd been high school sweethearts and they had an anniversary coming up. He was going to surprise her with a pearl necklace and matching earrings.

The soft cry of a baby two rows ahead saddened him, not only because Hooper and Gwen would never have children, but because it pulled him back to the horrors of his job.

No matter how many investigations he'd done, it never got easier. He'd lost count of how many times he'd found charred remains, dead passengers holding each other at the moment of impact, victims entwined in metal debris, impaled in trees, buried in the ground.

He still had nightmares.

The baby in the seat ahead continued crying and pulled him back to last year, when a commuter jet had lost both engines on its approach to Memphis during a storm at night and plowed into a hillside. Forty-seven people had died. Walking alone in a wooded area among scattered pieces of twisted wreckage, Hooper had come upon a baby.

The only visible injury had been a tiny bloodied scrape on its head.

The child had been beautiful, a perfect angel, wearing pajamas with teddy bears and rabbits. Its eyes had been closed and it had appeared to be sleeping as a soft breeze lifted strands of its hair.

The baby had been dead.

Suddenly the wall Hooper had built to protect himself from the emotional toll of his work had crumbled and he'd been overcome. He'd dropped to his knees beside the baby and said a silent prayer, had removed his jacket and gently covered the child, then reached for his radio to call the medical examiner's staff.

Now, as his plane jetted to New York, he looked at the sky, relieved this incident had had no fatalities.

Seven

The next morning a vacuum cleaner hummed down the hall from a meeting room in LaGuardia's central terminal.

Outside the room's closed doors, Captain Raymond Matson waited alone to be interviewed by NTSB investigators. Nervous tension had dried his throat and he'd grown thirsty.

He hadn't slept well.

He thought of his passengers and crew—they'd suffered fractures and concussions. Rosalita Ortiz, one of the flight attendants, had broken her back.

Matson clenched his eyes tight.

He'd already given a verbal report to an FAA inspector who'd met him and the first officer yesterday at the gate, and he'd provided a blood sample for analysis.

After several seconds, Matson opened his eyes. He resumed reviewing his notes when his phone vibrated with a text from his lawyer.

Papers are ready to sign whenever you can drop by. That'll be it.

Matson stared at the message. With his signature, his sixteen-year marriage would be over. For a brief instant, he remembered a time when they'd been happy. He stared at a mural on the wall of Manhattan's skyline and his wife's accusations played through his thoughts:

You're never home. You've become a ghost to us and I'm so tired of being a single parent to three children.

She'd already taken the kids and moved back to Portland. She'd let him take care of the house in Westfield; a for-sale sign was on the front lawn. She'd get 60 percent when it sold, according to the settlement. It was true. He'd missed birthdays, Little League games, recitals and graduations. He was married to his job and now it was hanging by a thread. The doors opened.

"Captain Matson, we're ready to see you."

A woman invited him inside to an empty chair at one end of a large boardroom table. The woman, dressed in a burgundy jacket, white top and matching pants, took her seat at the opposite end.

"Thank you for coming in so early this morning, Captain. I'm Irene Zimm with NTSB. I'll be leading this session. To my right is Bill Cashill and Jake Hooper with the NTSB, then we have…"

She introduced the half dozen other officials who were seated at the table with notepads and pens poised. Small microphones rose from the table before each of them, as well as Matson himself. All eyes and a video camera were on him as Zimm proceeded.

"As we begin, you understand that this interview is being recorded, and anything you say will inform our investigation?"

"Yes, I understand."

"And you understand the rules and policies of the board, your airline and union, about talking to the media or public?"

"Yes, I understand."

"Very well, we'll go over some preliminary matters. We have a summary of your verbal report. You've been in contact with Gus Vitalley from the pilots' union, seated to your left."

"Yes, we spoke yesterday."

"And we have your blood sample."

"Yes."

Zimm tapped her pen on an open file folder she had before her and consulted a laptop next to it. "We'll confirm your personal background with you. You've been with EastCloud for approximately thirteen years, and have been a captain for six of those years, correct?"

"That is correct."

"You have over twelve thousand total flight hours, of which you were pilot-in-command for seven thousand flight hours."

"Yes."

"I see that you have no incidents and no failed check rides."

"Correct."

"As for the new Richlon-TitanRT-86, you have

approximately eight hundred flight hours as the pilot-in-command."

"Yes."

"Prior to this trip, you and the first officer, Roger Anderson, had flown together twice before?"

"Yes. Chicago to San Diego and Phoenix to Atlanta, both in RTs."

"Thank you. The aircraft has been taken out of service and moved to a maintenance hangar. The flight data recorder and the voice cockpit recorder have been removed and sent to our lab in Washington for analysis. We'll also be examining air traffic control radar and weather. Now, leading up to the incident, you reported the trip as routine with no weather issues."

"That's correct."

"Approximately twenty-five minutes into the flight, your course was one hundred fifteen degrees southeast, speed was four hundred ninety-one knots and your altitude was twenty-seven thousand feet, when you experienced a sudden, unintended series of roll oscillations, ninety degrees to the right then ninety degrees to the left, then a banked, unintended descent of seven thousand feet before you, Captain, regained control of the plane and alerted New York Center, then LaGuardia."

"That's correct."

Zimm looked to the experts around the table as a cue to begin questioning Matson.

"The autopilot was engaged prior to the incident?" Bill Cashill asked.

"It was."

"Did you at any time encounter turbulence?"

"No. And there was nothing of note on radar, and no reports of turbulence from earlier flights."

"Clear-air turbulence doesn't appear on radar, and the autopilot could make any needed adjustments for it," Cashill said.

"I'm aware of the characteristics of clear-air turbulence. We didn't encounter it."

"Captain Matson," Cashill said, "the Richlon-TitanRT-86 is a fly-by-wire model with an array of auto-detect safety systems to address any anomalies or problems that arise. The new design also has a provision that allows the pilot to disable those safety features so that in an emergency he or she can make control inputs that would not otherwise be permitted."

"I am absolutely aware of the features of the RT-86."

"Speaking strictly from a preliminary perspective, a strong theory would be that you encountered clear-air turbulence and did not feel the aircraft was responding to it, leading you to take the extreme step of disabling the safety features. In the process you overcontrolled the aircraft, causing the severe rolling, before you regained control."

"I'm telling you there was no turbulence and I'm telling you that I did not disable the safety features. For a time the aircraft just went crazy and when I intervened, it refused to respond to our inputs. After we got tossed around, the plane inexplicably allowed me to take control again. This was a flight control computer malfunction, not pilot error."

"No one said it was pilot error, Captain," Cashill said.

"That's what you're implying, *from a preliminary perspective*."

A few long, tense seconds passed before Jake Hooper spoke.

"Our analysis is not complete. We still need to download the data and conduct a full examination of the aircraft, along with other aspects."

Another moment passed as Irene Zimm flipped through pages of a file folder then looked over her glasses at Matson.

"Captain, I'm looking at the results of your blood analysis."

Matson met her gaze and braced himself.

"It shows traces of antidepressants."

"Yes, I'm taking medication prescribed by my doctor."

"Yes," Zimm said. "I see that, and in keeping with airline policy you've reported the prescription and that it arises from therapy you're undergoing as a result of divorce proceedings."

Matson cleared his throat and swallowed hard at having his life exposed to the painful core.

"Yes," he said.

"It's my job to be familiar with the impact of substances," Zimm said, "and I'm familiar with the adverse side effects of some antidepressants. Did your doctor tell you that the medication you're taking can, and I'm not saying this happened in your case, but can, in some instances, cause you to become agitated, emotional, suffer insomnia and confusion?"

"Yes, she did. But she indicated—and it should be in the file—that in my case, the medicine and dosage put me at a very low risk of exposure to those adverse effects and she green-lighted me to fly."

"Yes, I see that in your file."

Zimm tapped her pen and went around the table for follow-up questions.

Half an hour later, Matson was free to leave.

Since he was pulled from EastCloud's roster to fly for at least a week, he went to Manhattan and walked through Central Park until early afternoon. Amid the splendor of the trees, the ponds, the lawns and the gardens, he felt the walls of his world closing in on him.

He knew what was coming.

Matson went to Saddle River, ended his marriage and asked his divorce lawyer to recommend a criminal defense attorney.

Eight

Manhattan, New York

Kate woke up angry.

In the shower she scrubbed until her skin reddened, as if she could wash away yesterday's indignation.

I can't believe what Sloane and Reeka did. Are they setting me up to get rid of me?

Toweling off, she tried to calm down but it was futile.

Senior management knew about Reeka's incompetence, her arrogance and her mean-spiritedness, but they were afraid to do anything about her because of her family connection to the board. And now here she was building her own fiefdom with minion jerks like Sloane.

Kate had had enough.

I could leave Newslead.

Sure, news jobs were scarce, but she had friends at Bloomberg and Reuters who could help her land something.

I could call them today.

Still, the thought of walking away from a news agency she revered, a job she loved, of leaving behind all that she'd strived for, everything she'd invested, not only saddened her—it sickened her.

I'm not going to give it all up because of Reeka. I bled to get here.

As she wiped the steam from the mirror Kate looked back on the tragedies and triumphs of her life. After her parents had died in a hotel fire when she was seven, she and her little sister, Vanessa, had lived with relatives for a while, and then in foster homes. One summer, they'd been on vacation in British Columbia with their foster parents, driving through the Canadian Rockies, when their car went off the road and crashed into a river. That moment still burned in Kate's memory.

The car sinking...rolling...windows breaking... the icy water...grabbing Vanessa's hand...pulling her free...to the surface...the frigid current numbing her...fingers loosening...Vanessa slipping away... disappearing...

Kate survived.

The bodies of her foster parents had washed up on the riverbank, but Vanessa's body hadn't been found. Searchers had reasoned that it had got wedged in the rocks downstream, but Kate had never given up believing that Vanessa had somehow gotten out of the river.

In the time following the tragedy, Kate had bounced through the foster system until she'd eventually run away, spending most of her teen years on the street or in youth homes, while keeping a journal and wondering about the little sister she'd lost. Kate had managed to get back into school, and eventually pursued her love of writing. She took any job she could get to put herself through community college where she'd studied journalism, then found work in newsrooms across the country.

In San Francisco, she'd become pregnant by a man who'd lied to her about being married. He'd offered to pay for an abortion before dumping her. That had been the end of that. Kate had kept her baby, a girl she'd named Grace. She'd moved to Ohio and worked at a newspaper in Canton for several good years before downsizing cost her that job. But she never gave up. She got a short-term reporting position in Dallas with Newslead and did outstanding work there, which impressed Chuck Laneer. He offered her a job as a national correspondent at Newslead's world headquarters in Manhattan.

Kate knew how blessed she was to have the Newslead job, and to have her daughter and sister in her life.

We've all come a long way.

For some twenty years, Kate had never given up searching for Vanessa, even during her darkest moments. The day Vanessa was found after she'd been held captive, the day they were reunited, was a day that had changed them both forever.

Now it had been more than two years since her sister had been back in her life, living with her and Grace. Vanessa had proven to be unbreakable. Her therapy was helping her heal and she'd gotten her high school diploma. She was working as a waitress and taking business courses, determined to open her own restaurant one day.

The book that Kate and Vanessa had written together on their lost years had done well, providing
Vanessa with some savings and Kate with a college
fund for Grace.

We're hanging in there.

Kate glanced at the time. She was running late.

Pulling on her robe, she went down the hall to
Grace's room, taking in the stuffed bears and bun-
nies, the posters of Harry Styles and Justin Bieber.
The corkboard held Kate's favorite item: a drawing
of three stick people with enormous smiles entitled
"Mommy, Aunt Vanessa and Me." The newest was
a picture of Grace in the planetarium at the Vander-
bilt Museum. She'd written on the bottom: "I want
to live on a star." *She's growing up too fast,* Kate
thought, as she gazed upon her sleeping daughter.
She bent over the bed, gently brushed Grace's hair
aside and kissed her cheek, causing her to stir.

"Time to get up and get ready for school, kid."

Grace moaned and pulled the sheets over her
head.

"You better get moving, kiddo, or you're gonna
be late. Okay?"

Kate patted her leg. Grace's head nodded under
the covers and Kate returned to her room to get
dressed. But she paused. She needed to know how
the competition had done on EastCloud Flight 4990.
She checked the *New York Times*, the *Wall Street
Journal*, the *Post*, the *Daily News* and the other
wires.

I've been pushed off this story. Why do I care?

Because deep down it was her story.

She had an emotional connection to it. The image

of Diane Wilson's farewell video to her family burned in Kate's mind as she tried to imagine the horror of what the people on that flight had faced. One moment you're living your life. The next moment you're falling from the sky, expecting to die.

What happened to that plane?

No one had broken any new angles on the story. She put her phone down, finished dressing and went to the kitchen where Vanessa was working on her laptop, concentrating behind her glasses, hair curtained to one side. For a moment Kate acknowledged some facts of her sister's tragedy. She had not just been found, she'd been a prisoner before she was rescued, and the man who'd held her all those years had allowed her to read. In fact, he'd given her all kinds of books—novels, text books, encyclopedias and dictionaries. Books had become her lifeline. Her reading and comprehension skills were remarkable, the therapists had said. Despite her nightmare, her lost years and everything that she'd endured, Vanessa had emerged a poised, self-assured, beautiful young woman, Kate thought.

"You're up early," Kate said.

"Got a test coming. I need to study."

"Commerce?"

"Economics. I made some raspberry tea."

"Thanks. I could use it."

"You got back later than we expected. How'd things go for you yesterday?"

"Awful. I'm thinking of leaving Newslead. The place is falling apart."

Vanessa looked up from her work, pushed her hair back.

"But you love it there. You're devoted to that place."

Hands cupped around her mug, Kate shook her head, sipped some tea and told Vanessa about her ordeal. When Kate finished, Vanessa considered the matter then said, "You don't want to quit over this."

"Why not?"

"You're bigger than that."

"What do you mean?"

"Just let it go."

"But what happened is wrong on so many levels, and I don't see it getting better."

"It all comes down to bumper sticker clichés, Kate. 'What doesn't kill us makes us stronger.' Suck it up, step back and look at where we've been and where we are now. You're tougher than Sloane and Reeka and you know it."

Absorbing Vanessa's suggestion, Kate caressed the guardian angel necklace she always wore as she looked to the wall, at the framed cover of the book they'd written together: *Echo In My Heart: A Relentless Story of Love, Loss and Survival*. For years, Vanessa had been locked up by a madman, and Kate had helped rescue her. Through it all, neither of them had quit and neither of them had given up hope. Vanessa was Kate's inspiration.

"You make a good point," Kate said.

"Think it over. I've got to get dressed."

Vanessa smiled before she left. Alone in the kitchen, Kate couldn't suppress her need to know more about EastCloud Flight 4990. She got on her phone and again researched the plane. Again, as far as she could tell, the Richlon-TitanRT-86 was a new model, without any known history of major problems. The crew said it was a malfunction, not turbulence. And in its statement, EastCloud had said the flight had "encountered a situation on its approach into New York."

Kate was mulling over what she knew when her phone vibrated with a text from Tara Lawson, a reporter at Newslead.

OMG the rumors were true! Chuck Laneer is back!

What? This a joke, Tara?

I'm looking at him in his office now! Maybe he can save us all?

Kate's spirits soared. Chuck was back. This changed everything.

"Mom? Did you hear me?"

Kate looked from her phone to Grace.

"Can I get new shoes, pink ones like Amber got?"

"No, sweetie. The shoes you have are still new. Maybe in the fall."

"But Mom! Did you see Amber's shoes? They're so amazing!"

"Did you remember to clean the sink when you finished?"

"Yes."

"What do you want for breakfast, something quick?"

"Toast with honey."

"Okay, remember your chore today—you water the plants while I fix your toast. Want orange juice or milk?"

"Milk."

"Milk what?"

"Milk, please and thank you."

As Kate prepared her daughter's breakfast, her phone vibrated with another text. This one was from Chuck Laneer, and in typical Chuck fashion, he got straight to the point.

Hey Kate. As you no doubt heard, I'm back. Want to meet with you ASAP to discuss the Flight 4990 story.

I'll be there within an hour.

Sooner would be better.

Welcome back, Chuck.

Nine

Kate waited alone in Newslead's corner meeting room.

Looking out at the majestic view of Midtown's skyscrapers, the Chrysler and Empire State buildings, she reflected.

It had been three years since she'd started working at headquarters for Chuck and she thought about everything that she'd reported on in that time: all the crime, disasters, tragedies, investigations. And with most stories, especially those where she'd dealt face-to-face with victims and their anguished families—*I'm so sorry but would you have a picture of your son-daughter-wife-husband-brother-sister-loved-one you could share with us?*—she'd given a piece of her soul.

In her heart, she was honored to be part of Newslead because of its history of excellence in journalism, and it troubled her that its integrity was being eroded. But Chuck's return gave her hope and reason to reconsider leaving, because if anyone could restore morale and rebuild the newsroom it was Chuck Laneer.

A shadow fell across the room.

"Good morning, Kate."

She felt as if the air had suddenly been poisoned. Sloane flashed his brilliant grin, set his notebook and coffee down then took a seat across the table from her.

"What're you doing here?" she asked.

"I could ask you the same question."

He sipped his coffee casually. Reeka entered the room, wearing a navy power suit, her face focused on her phone, thumbs a blur. She completed a message, then looked at Kate.

"Did you send me your overtime sheet?"

"I'll do that today."

"Okay, everybody."

Chuck arrived and shut the door, prompting Sloane to paste on a smile, stand and extend his hand.

"Mr. Laneer, welcome. Sloane F. Parkman. We haven't met but I'm more than aware of your legendary status in the news craft."

"It's Chuck. Thanks."

"Hi." Kate smiled.

"Good to see you again, Kate."

Chuck smiled but his eyes betrayed a tinge of concern. His tie was slightly loosened and his shirt-sleeves were rolled up. He'd lost some weight, his hair was thinner and mussed, and the lines in his face had deepened.

"This won't take long. I wanted to get to the jetliner story before Hersh and I officially address the newsroom this morning about my return."

Chuck glanced at his watch.

"I've looked at our coverage of Flight Forty-nine Ninety, and we have an opportunity here to take command of this story and reassert Newslead's prominence. By all accounts, something went haywire and a plane nearly fell from the sky. The Richlon-TitanRT-86 is a new model that came into service about two years ago. There are about three hundred in operation around the world and it seems to have a good safety record. We need to know if this is an isolated incident or if there's a serious problem with that aircraft. Lives could be at risk and it's our duty to inform the public."

"My sources said it was not a technical problem but turbulence and pilot error," Sloane said.

"I heard the crew on the scanner report that it was not turbulence," Kate said. "That it was some sort of malfunction."

Chuck leaned forward. "The NTSB and East-Cloud haven't confirmed a damn thing yet," he said. "Until then, we're going to own this story and follow it until it's no longer a story. Now, I've spoken with Reeka and I've decided to put you both on this one."

"Both of us?" Kate was stunned.

"That's right. Both of you. Sloane, have you consulted FAA records on the airworthiness of this plane and the history of the model, or checked our legal databases for any civil action?"

"I was about to do just that, Chuck."

Shaking her head, Kate turned to the window to avoid screaming while watching hope fade away.

"Kate?" Chuck said.

She turned back.

"Kate, I want you to work every angle you can to get us out front and keep us there."

"Sure. I'm on it."

"Good. We're going to break news with solid, on-the-record reporting. Newslead will be the go-to source for this story and every story we cover. Is that understood?"

"Clearly," Sloane said.

"Abundantly," Kate said.

"Okay, that's it."

What's going on? I don't believe this.

Kate headed for her desk, reconsidered then went to Chuck's office.

Through his open door, she could see that he was standing with his back to her, looking at the empty bookshelves and credenza. Three cardboard boxes sitting on his desk were jammed with items: his baseball autographed by the Yankees, his Pulitzer and his framed photos. One of Chuck with his wife was already on the desk.

Kate was overcome with sadness, seeing him standing there alone, his life in those boxes. How long had it been since they'd talked, a year? She was angry at him for leaving Newslead after his blowout with previous spineless management. The fact he was dealing with his wife's illness at the same time had only complicated things. She rapped lightly on the door and he turned to her. This time his smile was from the heart.

"I'm glad you're back," she said. "It's been too long."

"The time got away from us. Look, when I left I had a helluva lot going on and, well—"

"It's all history now. It's okay. How's Audrey doing?"

"Still cancer-free. Thanks for asking."

"Good, I'm glad." Kate let a moment pass. She didn't have much time. "We need to talk about what just happened back there."

He ran a hand over his face.

"Shut the door."

Kate closed it.

"Chuck, let me go first. I don't want to scare you but this place is a mess. The cuts have taken a toll. The new management's dysfunctional. Morale here sucks. The quality of our work is slipping. The place is fueled by nepotism and cronyism."

"I know."

"As for Sloane. Oh. My. God. Chuck, I can't work with him. The guy's a freaking liar. It's a risk to have him in our newsroom and his name on News-lead stories."

"I know."

"You know?"

"Nothing leaves this room."

"Okay."

"I *need* you to work with him."

"What? Why? I don't get this. The guy should be fired."

"I can't do much about him. Not yet. It's complicated."

"Do you know what he did on this story? Shirking his duty?"

Chuck nodded.

"Word got to me. Before I came back, I called some people, did some due diligence. Listen, he's Reeka's hire and Reeka has pull with senior management. You know that. I can't touch Sloane. Not yet. She wanted him on this story alone. I pushed back to get you on it because I think it requires two people, even with our smaller stable of reporters. Truth is, I need you to watch over him, to keep him from hurting us."

"I can't do that!"

"Kate, I *need* you to do this, and break stories. We're under tremendous pressure. You know the song. We're losing subscribers. We're getting beat on stories. We're rushing down the river to irrelevance. From what I've learned, Sloane's not a reporter, at least not the caliber we need to work here, and he'll fail. Kate, I'm counting on you to prove your strength, like you did in Dallas, and like you did on your sister's story. I need you to help me fix Newslead."

Kate weighed the stakes as Chuck glanced at the time.

"Because it's you, I'll do it," she said. "But tell me, if you knew things were bad here, why did you come back?"

"The same reason you've stayed." Chuck glanced at the framed photo of his wife, then at Kate. "We've each given everything to this organization and we don't give up on the things we love and believe in."

Before Kate could react, a knock sounded at

the door. Kate opened it to Sloane and Reeka, who thrust her phone at Chuck.

"The *New York Times* is now reporting that Flight Forty-nine Ninety encountered severe clear-air turbulence and the pilot disabled the plane's safety features to deal with it and, in doing so, overreacted."

Adjusting his glasses, Chuck read the piece.

"See," Sloane said. "It was turbulence, just as I'd first reported. Looks like pilot error, not mechanical, just like my story said."

"They're using unnamed sources," Chuck said.

"It's the *Times*, Chuck," Reeka said. "I think everybody's just been killed on this story."

"We still don't have officially sourced confirmation," Chuck said. "Nobody does. Not yet. Sloane, did you check the FAA records and search court records?"

"Working on it."

"Good. Now, excuse us, if you'd give Kate and me a minute."

Reeka and Sloane left. Chuck loosened his tie more, then unknotted it and whipped it off.

"Dammit, Reeka's right. The *Times* just kicked our asses. We've got to get on top of this story."

"I'll do my best."

"We're going to need more than that, Kate."

Ten

Kate grabbed a strong coffee and ensconced herself at her desk, still reeling from the *New York Times* piece while grappling with Chuck's expectations.

It didn't help that she could sense Sloane gloating.

Kate shoved it all aside and knuckled down. She started with the key official organizations—texting, emailing and calling for reaction to the *Times* story and a chance to advance it.

"We don't comment on speculative press articles. We'll release a preliminary report in the coming days," Paul Murther, the spokesperson with the NTSB, told her.

EastCloud responded by sending Kate an updated news release which was light on actual news. The airline had noted what everyone already knew—that nearly all of Flight 4990's passengers who had been taken to hospital had been released and that East-Cloud continued to cooperate with investigators.

Kate called Richlon, the plane's manufacturer.

"I can confirm that we are participating in the

NTSB investigation. Other than that, we have no further comment," Molly Raskin, Richlon's deputy of public affairs, said from its Burbank, California, headquarters.

The FAA declined to comment, and so did most of the other agencies and groups she'd contacted. While waiting for responses Kate, in keeping with Chuck's request to be watchful of Sloane's work, reviewed news photos for the plane's registration information, known as the N-Number, then used that number to access FAA records on the specific aircraft's history.

No problems had emerged on that individual plane.

Kate then consulted federal records on the model, and found the Richlon-TitanRT-86 had experienced several incidents.

While taking off for Chicago from Omaha, an improperly secured front cabin door had come loose on an RT-86, forcing an emergency landing without incident. A flight from San Diego blew a tire on landing in Phoenix. No injuries were reported. A flight originating in Boston overshot the runway while landing in Atlanta during a storm. No injuries. There were several separate cases of various emergency-indicator lights automatically activating in the flight deck, for things such as landing gear, fuel supply, someone smoking in the restroom, a small fire in the galley. Emergency ground crews were alerted and in all instances the planes landed safely.

This is relatively standard.

Kate checked Newslead's legal database for

civil action against the airline, scouring the summaries from the list of lawsuits. They concerned lost luggage, job action, overbooked flights, missed flights, claims alleging civil rights abuses and racism. Again, all of it was relatively standard for an airline of EastCloud's size.

After rereading the *Times* story, Kate felt stirrings of self-doubt.

Am I wrong about hearing the crew insist there was no turbulence?

She paged through her notes. But it was there. She'd jotted it down the moment it had crackled over the scanner. Sure, there was static, but she'd clearly heard the crew say the problem was "not turbulence" but rather some sort of malfunction.

Kate called the news library and requested they look into possibly purchasing transcripts from one of the professional scanner listening services, even though they were not subscribed.

It was odd. If other news outlets, like the *Times* or the Associated Press, had possibly consulted transcripts of Flight 4990's transmissions before landing, wouldn't they have reported malfunction as the issue? But there had been so much static, maybe they'd missed it.

Kate tapped her pen.

The only way to know what the crew said is to talk to the crew.

But there was no way that was going to happen, she thought. Pilots rarely, if ever, talk to press about an incident while it's under investigation—way too many policies and too much at stake for them.

Did anyone reach out to the crew?

Kate tapped her pen faster.

She'd met a high-ranking official with the pilots' union a couple of months back at a security conference at the Grand Hyatt. What was his name? Kate searched her contacts until it came up.

Nick Benko.

He was middle-aged, silver-haired, smart and kind of flirty, but at his core, all business and union tough. They'd had a quick coffee and he'd said to call him if ever she needed help on a story.

Kate sent him a text, reminding him of their meeting and his offer. She asked him to call her. Six minutes later, her cell phone rang.

"Thanks for calling, Nick."

"No problem. Just stepped out of a meeting. What's up?"

"You know that EastCloud flight from Buffalo to LaGuardia?"

"Yes, it's in the news. I saw your name on one of the stories."

"What can you tell me about the investigation?"

"I'm not involved in that. Besides, I couldn't tell you, even if I was."

"I figured. Nick, I need help reaching the captain."

"No can do, Kate. There're policies, security, privacy, all that stuff."

"I understand, Nick, but if you were me, where would you look?"

Benko hesitated.

"You know I can't give you that name, Kate."

"Of course, but if you were looking, say for public sources, where would you look?"

Benko gave it some thought.

"Some airlines post milestone pages online," he said. "It's possible that if you looked deep into East-Cloud's site on the ten-year page, you might find something there."

"Where?"

"Under the *M*'s."

Kate jotted it down.

"What if there are other *M*'s?"

"I don't think you'll have a problem."

Kate's keyboard clicked and she'd found the site, went to the *M*'s and landed on a page with a photo and bio of Raymond Brian Matson. His was the only listing under *M* for ten years with EastCloud. The listing was about three years old.

"Nick, you know you have a friend here who owes you a favor."

"No favor, Kate." He chuckled. "Because I didn't give you any information that wasn't already public."

"Understood. Thanks."

Kate read the brief bio describing Matson's experience and time with EastCloud. Of course it didn't list his address or the city where he resided.

He could live anywhere in the country.

She tapped her pen again.

She had another source, Marsha Flood, a retired FBI agent she'd known since she'd been a reporter in California. Marsha ran a private-investigation firm and had quicker and better access to more databases than Kate, like the one containing driver's licenses. Kate sent her a text requesting help locating an address for Raymond Brian Matson. Then she sent a link to Matson's bio and pic to help her find the right Matson. Kate calculated the time zone difference, confident that Marsha would be up by now.

As she waited, she ran Raymond Matson's name through several of Newslead's archives and news information networks to see of he'd ever been the subject of a news story.

Nothing. She left a message on Marsha's voice mail.

She checked his name with several popular social media sites.

Nothing.

As she downed her coffee her phone rang.

"Hi, Kate, it's Marsha."

"Hey, Marsha."

"How're Vanessa and Grace doing?"

"Vanessa's doing great, and Grace—well, they grow up too fast, don't they? How's your son doing? Still posted overseas?"

"He comes home from South Korea next month."

"Oh, that's good. I'm happy for you."

"Now about your subject, Raymond Brian Matson. He's close to you. According to his valid state driver's license he resides in Westfield, New Jersey, Lamberts Mill Road."

"Thank you."

"I'll send you the address. Oh, I also saw that he's involved in divorce proceedings, so bear that in mind."

"I appreciate this, Marsha."

"Anytime."

Eleven

Lamberts Mill Road ran through a quiet, tree-lined section of Westfield.

The Matson house, a century-old two-story colonial with a screened side porch, sat back from the street. No vehicles were in the driveway when Kate pulled up.

It looked like no one was home.

She rang the bell but got no response.

Kate had been afraid this would happen—that no one would be home. The for-sale sign and the divorce were likely factors, she thought as she drove off and parked several doors down.

She adjusted the car's mirror and settled in to watch the address. Showing up cold was always a risk whenever you were pursuing a sensitive interview. When you emailed, or called, people were quick to delete or hang up. When you appeared at their door and looked them in the eye, the odds sometimes worked in your favor.

Not always but sometimes.

The air was tranquil with sounds of birdsong, the wind through the trees and the distant laughter of children. Traffic had been good. It had taken her about forty-five minutes using one of Newslead's leased cars to make the trip across the Hudson.

Kate worked on her phone, building a story based on the few updates she had from the people she'd reached earlier. Between sentences, she monitored her mirrors, noting that the for-sale sign could also mean that Matson no longer lived here.

She wasn't happy with the story; she didn't have much. The strongest stuff was the FAA records showing the incident history of the Richlon-TitanRT-86. She'd just finished folding the various reports into her piece when something blurred in her side mirror.

An SUV had rolled into the Matson driveway.

Kate gave it a moment. Then she collected her things, approached the house and rang the bell. A long moment passed before the door was opened by a man wearing a polo shirt and khaki pants. He was in his late forties with deep-set eyes that gave him a rugged look.

"Yes?"

"Raymond Matson?"

"Yes."

"Captain Raymond Matson with EastCloud Airlines?"

"Yes, who're you?"

"I'm Kate Page, a reporter with Newslead, the wire service."

The air tensed.

"Sir, I need to talk to you about what happened on Flight Forty-nine Ninety."

His jaw tightened then he moved to shut the door.

"I have no comment."

"Wait, Captain Matson, please. Is the *New York Times* accurate? Was it pilot error?"

"I haven't seen the *New York Times*."

"Hold on, I have it right here."

Kate displayed the story on her phone and passed it to him. As he read something flashed behind his eyes.

"No. That's wrong." He passed the phone back. "I don't have anything to say to the press."

"Are you going to let the *Times* story stand? Do you want to leave the impression that the crew over-reacted and caused the plane to roll?"

"I'm bound to a process."

"The NTSB can take a year to issue its official report. If you talk to me you can correct the record now, put the facts and the truth of what happened out there. Otherwise, this stands as human error for a year or longer. I understand that there may have been a malfunction?"

Matson arched an eyebrow as he absorbed Kate's argument. She gave him another point to consider.

"Who better than you to explain what really happened."

Matson considered for several moments. Worry clouded his eyes, and he adjusted his grip on the door. She sensed he was walking a mental tightrope before he came to a decision and pushed it open.

"Come in."

He indicated the living room.

"Have a seat. Want a soda? I think I also have orange juice."

"Water would be fine."

He left and returned, handing her a bottled water.

"Let me make a few calls and I'll be back," he said.

The house was fragrant and beautiful, suggesting it had been professionally staged for showings. Fresh flowers bloomed from vases on the mantel and end tables. The hardwood floors gleamed under gorgeous area rugs. Kate looked for telltale signs of family life but nothing was out of place. Still, she'd discerned an air of sadness, of finality.

While waiting, she checked for any breaking news, then reviewed her messages, wincing at one from Sloane.

The FAA and legal records show next to nothing on the plane and the model. I'll write it up for you.

What? Either Sloane never looked, or he's lying again.

She was about to respond but thought maybe she should inform Chuck instead. Matson returned.

"I called my lawyer and my union. If I talk to you I'm putting my head on the chopping block."

"But I think—"

"My head's already on the chopping block."

"I'm sorry?"

"You can't use that. I'll talk to you but this part you cannot use. You got that? This isn't for any story. It's completely off the record, okay?"

"Okay."

"I've met with the NTSB, my union, EastCloud and all the others who're investigating and I get the feeling they're going to put this on me. I can feel a noose tightening. What happens is the airline will try to blame the manufacturer, saying it was a technical issue, to avoid a negative impact on its operations. 'Hey, it's not us, it's the plane.' And the manufacturer will try to blame the airline, 'Hey, it's not our plane, it's your people, your pilots, your maintenance people,' to avoid a negative impact on their aircraft and costly litigation. Both players have millions at stake, so the best thing they can do is to ultimately put it on the pilot. 'Hey, it was this guy, he screwed up. He's gone so let's move on.' This is the context that I feel is at play here. You got that?"

"Yes."

"Okay, I want the truth out there, so I'll tell you what I told the NTSB and everyone else. This is what you can use."

"Wait." Kate switched on her recorder. "Okay, go ahead."

"There was no clear-air turbulence and I did not disable the safety system. The aircraft suddenly rolled. For a critical time, the plane refused to respond to our commands. I don't know what happened but I know something went wrong. This was a clear flight control computer malfunction."

"But if it's a malfunction, a safety issue, is the public at risk?"

"Until they find out the source of this system failure, I'd say yes."

For the next half hour Matson helped Kate with the timeline of the Buffalo–New York flight and the technical background. Matson said he was in agony for the passengers and his crew members who'd been injured.

"If we didn't fight for control of the plane the way we did, we would have lost it. And that's God's honest truth."

After Kate got everything down she confirmed with Matson that he hadn't spoken with any other reporters and that she would use his name and picture with her story.

"Agreed," he said.

"I'll be talking to other people for their response."

"That's expected, but remember, no matter who you talk to, I was on that flight deck. They weren't."

Kate thanked Matson, gave him her card and left.

Heading back to her car, she had to keep from running. She decided to go to a small park, where she sat at a picnic table in the shade of an oak tree and called Chuck Laneer.

"You got the captain?"

"Exclusively."

"What'd he say?"

"That it was a malfunction and the public is at risk."

"That's a helluva story. Get it to us as soon as you can. I'll alert subscribers telling them what's coming. Good work."

Kate stayed at the picnic table, made calls and sent messages requesting comment from EastCloud, the FAA, the NTSB and industry experts. Those who responded underscored that the NTSB had not yet issued a preliminary report and had so far found nothing that warranted grounding of the Richlon-TitanRT-86, or the issuance of safety alerts.

An industry expert in Seattle challenged Matson's account of the incident.

"The scenario as described by the pilot cannot happen with the type of fly-by-wire system installed in the TitanRT-86. It's that simple. For the plane to oscillate the way it did, according to the reports of passengers, the safety features would have to be manually switched off. This still sounds like a classic case of a bad response to clear-air turbulence."

Within two hours of her interview with Captain Raymond Matson, Kate's exclusive was released to Newslead's subscribers across the country and around the world.

Twelve

Clear River, North Dakota

A few miles beyond town, a lone wooden hangar rose defiantly from the badlands.

A faint clink of metal against metal signaled life as Robert Cole halted his work on the radial engine of an aging crop duster and climbed down the stepladder.

He dragged his sweaty, greasy forearm across his brow, tossed his wrench on his cluttered workbench next to where he'd left the *Minot Daily News*. His face was creased with concern over the back-page article he'd read that morning.

Worry pushed down on him as he moved outside the hangar's open doors to contemplate the earthen airstrip and search the eternal plain. But gazing at the horizon failed to ease his troubled mind about the news story and the direction of his life.

There was a time when he'd had everything. Now it was gone and he was alone with his sins, awash with guilt. A gust peppered him with dry dirt. In his mind, he heard his wife's laughter, felt her touch and saw her face.

Elizabeth.

Help me. Please. Tell me what I should do.

He thought of her every moment of every day and now, standing alone in the crying, aching wind, he rubbed his dry lips. The bottle in his lunch bucket called to him. It would numb his pain.

That's not the answer I need now.

He got into his pickup truck and drove through town, passed the strip malls, the municipal buildings, and the old storefronts that evoked the frontier days. Elizabeth had grown up here; her father was a doctor. This was her town and living here gave him some comfort.

He drove south over the rolling rangeland that stretched as far as he could see. Two miles later he turned onto a narrow, paved road that wound into a grove of trees overlooking a creek. A small sign identified the spot as the Riverbend Meadow Cemetery. He parked and made his way through the burial grounds, stopping at the headstone that read "Elizabeth Marie Cole, Beloved Wife and Mother. Died…"

He didn't need to read further.

The truth hit him as hard as the granite that marked his wife's grave.

I'm responsible for her death. I destroyed everything I had in this world.

He ran his fingers gently over her gravestone and a breeze rolled up from the river, carrying him through the moments of their lives.

They'd met at the University of Southern California in Los Angeles, where they'd bumped into each other at a bookstore, which had led to coffee and subsequent dates. She'd thought he was a looker, and he'd loved her smile. Her name was Elizabeth Hyde, and she'd had a scholarship to study medicine. He'd been in engineering. They'd both been reticent, nerdy bookworms.

After they'd graduated, Elizabeth had convinced him to take time off with a nonprofit international aid group. They'd spent a year helping people in poor parts of South America and Africa. When they'd returned, he'd taken her to a beach north of LA, and as the sun set, he'd given her an engagement ring. After they were married, they embarked on their careers. She became a doctor, and he became an engineer.

They got a house in Burbank and in the years that followed, they'd each put in long hours, dedicating themselves to their professions. They'd had trouble starting a family but after nearly a year of treatment, therapies and effort, Elizabeth had become pregnant with their only child, a daughter they'd named Veyda.

She was their miracle, their joy.

As busy professionals, the pressures of their jobs had been constant, but Elizabeth's priority had been Veyda. He remembered when Elizabeth had stayed up all night when Veyda had had a fever; or when Elizabeth had rushed Veyda to the hospital when she'd fallen from her bicycle; or that time they'd driven through Glendale, at three in the morning, Elizabeth frantic and desperately trying to reach her daughter, who'd passed out drunk after lying about going to a party and missing her ride home.

Yes, Elizabeth and Veyda had had their battles. But Elizabeth had been devoted to Veyda and Veyda had adored Elizabeth. Her mother had been her hero and theirs had been an unbreakable bond.

Yes, and Veyda had loved him, too, coming to him for advice or help solving a problem. But he had tended to be away often, working on projects that demanded his attention 24/7. Even at an early age, Veyda had understood and respected his job. He'd smiled when he'd overheard her telling a friend, *My dad's an engineer. Not the kind who drives trains but the kind who builds planes and makes them fly, which is a lot harder.*

Academically, Veyda had taken after her parents, excelling at school. She loved debating subjects, anything from veganism to eugenics, from politics to physics, from mathematics to rock-and-roll history. Her dream was to become a medical doctor, like her mother, and an aeronautical engineer, like her father.

First, I'll follow Dad's path and learn all about flight, Veyda had said.

They were so proud when she was accepted at Pepperdine then went on to UC Berkeley and then later to MIT.

But Elizabeth had missed her and lived for their visits, so she'd been ecstatic when Veyda surprised them with a call from Cambridge.

I've got a break. I'm coming home for a week!

Elizabeth had adjusted her schedule for the unexpected visit and had hoped he would do the same, but the timing couldn't have been worse for him. He'd been overwhelmed by the deadlines for a major project, one of the most challenging he'd ever faced. But he'd also wanted to see Veyda as much as possible, so he'd made what adjustments he could to get away from work.

Veyda's visit had been a happy time. It'd been months since they'd all been together. They'd decided to drive up the coast to a pretty restaurant they liked near Santa Barbara.

Before leaving, he'd checked with work. Serious problems with the project had arisen, but for the moment he'd believed they were manageable, although senior management had just launched a surprise in-depth review of a critical aspect.

Hang on to your hat, Bob, one of the other engineers had texted him just before they'd left.

During the drive, his phone had vibrated with texts, but he'd ignored them. When they got on the 101, his phone had begun to vibrate even more, which had concerned him.

Elizabeth and Veyda had been so deep in conversation that they'd never heard his phone, so he'd decided to do what Elizabeth had forbade: he checked it. He'd done it surreptitiously, taking it out of his left pocket and lowering it on his left side between his left leg and the door. He'd needed to know what management had been saying on the project. Carefully, he'd scrolled through the messages, and he remembered the moment Veyda had said, *Oh my God, Mom, the winters in Cambridge are absolutely cruel...* Then Elizabeth was shouting, *Robert!* They'd drifted across another lane and the rear of a slower-moving car had loomed instantly in their windshield, giving him less than a second to register it, twist the wheel violently and stomp on the brake... They'd missed the slower car, but suddenly theirs was lifting, rising and twisting in the air... The car had rolled. His seat belt had cut into him. He remembered Elizabeth and Veyda screaming then air bags exploding, and Elizabeth flying from the car amid glass shattering and metal crunching. The car had rolled and rolled, until it had finally come to a stop, and he'd heard a hissing and smelled gasoline. He'd crawled from the wreck, disoriented, unable to find Elizabeth or Veyda. The car had come to a stop on its roof, and he'd seen...Elizabeth's shoe... her hand... She'd been pinned under the car. He'd tried lifting, but the car wouldn't move... Elizabeth had been making gurgling sounds. He'd dropped to his knees, taking her hand the way he'd held it on their first dates...at their wedding...at their daughter's birth... As he'd held her hand...she'd cried out.

Veyda!

Mom! Veyda had been crawling to them, the whites of her eyes piercing him from between the blood webbing her face.

Elizabeth had squeezed his hand.

Stay with me, Elizabeth! I love you! Stay with me! Please!

Mom!

Veyda had collapsed some ten feet from her mother as he'd felt his wife's hand going limp... He'd heard sirens...shouting...a helicopter... His family was in pieces and everything was turning black...

Robert Cole was on his knees before his wife's headstone.

Elizabeth had wanted to be buried here. She'd

told him that, years before, when they'd made their wills. The aftermath of the accident and the funeral were a fog of agony. He remembered Veyda kissing her mother's casket, casting a single rose. She was still scarred and bandaged, standing like an apparition at the grave.

Her glare burned into him, an accusation.

It was all in the police report. He'd been negligent and had committed vehicular manslaughter. Elizabeth's seat belt had come undone as she'd turned from the passenger seat to talk to her daughter. The driver of the slower car ahead of them—a witness got the plate through dash cam video—had been driving without a license and with alcohol in his blood. Cole had been charged, but his lawyer had got the charge reduced to a misdemeanor and he'd received a light sentence. No jail time. *The defendant has suffered a monumental loss by his own hand and will live with the consequences all the days of his life, your honor,* his lawyer had said.

Cole never recovered from the tragedy. Elizabeth's death was like an amputation. Veyda had undergone therapy before returning to school in Massachusetts, but the accident had irrevocably changed both of them.

He'd sold their home in California and moved to North Dakota.

Something had pulled him here, something calling him to be near his wife, to watch over her and to find a path to redemption.

Maybe today he'd found it, he thought, driving back to the hangar.

He picked up the *Minot Daily News* and reread

the article with the interview of the captain of the troubled, New York–bound plane.

It was from one of the newswires.

Yes, this is it.

Cole mixed whiskey into his cold coffee.

The thing he'd feared, the secret thing that had tormented him in the seconds before the car wreck that destroyed his life had now become a reality.

Now he had his answer.

He knew what he had to do.

Thirteen

Manhattan, New York

The next afternoon Kate's subway train rumbled south out of the 125th Street station.

As it cleared the platform, she took a subtle inventory of her car's passengers, without staring, then focused on her reflection in the window.

As the drab tunnel walls raced by, her pulse quickened. Living here still excited her; the people, the smells—cologne to urine to grilled food from the street vendors. Even the traffic—she'd once seen a guy stomp right over a cab that was blocking a crosswalk—and the sirens. The power, the glory and the majesty that was New York—she loved it all.

Kate checked her phone.

This was her day off but Chuck wanted her to come in. He'd promised more time off later and said it was okay to be in by 1:00 p.m., but he needed her in to produce a follow-up to her exclusive interview with the captain.

We have to keep hitting this one, Kate, Chuck had texted.

The train swayed and grated. Station after station flashed by as Kate ran through some ideas. She could contact a lawyer she knew who specialized in aviation litigation. Maybe he was hearing something on the grapevine about the Richlon-TitanRTs.

The brakes creaked and her car lurched as they came to Penn Station, her stop. She threaded through the vast, low-ceilinged warren under Madison Square Garden. When she surfaced, she headed to the Newslead building, picked up a coffee and an oatmeal muffin in the main-floor food court. That was lunch.

At her desk, she reviewed Newslead's summary of the pickup of yesterday's story. The suggested headline from the copy desk had been: "Pilot of Troubled EastCloud Buffalo-to-NYC Flight: Malfunction Puts Passengers at Risk."

Pickup was rated "strong."

Her exclusive interview with Captain Matson was used by 1,149 English-language newspapers and websites in the United States, Canada, the UK, Australia, New Zealand, Hong Kong, parts of Africa, Europe, South America and the Caribbean.

The *Seattle Times*, the *Boston Globe*, the *Washington Post*, the *Toronto Star*, *The Times* of London, the *New Zealand Herald*, South Africa's *Daily Sun* and Hong Kong's *South China Morning Post* were among those who'd given it play.

This is pretty good, Kate thought.

She checked her public email box for the address tag at the end of her story. Readers could use the feature to contact a reporter directly. Most reporters

loathed it because, while much of the spam was filtered, what they nearly always received were emails
from political zealots, religious extremists, gram-
mar experts, scam artists, nut jobs and idiots. It was
rare that a story yielded a genuine lead.

*But you gotta check. You never know what you
can find there.*

Usually, for Kate, an article would result in
anywhere from a handful to more than a hundred
emails, depending on the story. She was skilled at
plowing through them quickly.

Like searching for buried treasure.

Her story had generated sixty emails so far and
she'd sorted through about a third of them, flagging
four to consider later.

"Why didn't you use my work in the story, Kate?"
Sloane F. Parkman stood over her desk, arms folded,
tie knotted, every hair in place. He was not wearing the grin today.

"Because it was wrong, Sloane."

"I wrote that according to litigation and FAA records. There was nothing of consequence regarding
the actual plane for Flight Forty-nine Ninety, or the
RT-86 in general."

"You editorialized. I checked those very records
and listed what the history was, what the facts are.
Then I contacted an industry expert who put that
history in context, saying all of the incidents and
civil actions were in keeping with what was to be
expected given the new model and EastCloud's size
as an airline. I put the facts on the record, Sloane.
You chose not to report them. Why is that?"

"There was nothing of significance to report!"

"You're not the expert to make that call! Why're you downplaying the facts, Sloane?"

"We're supposed to be working together on this story. Why did you remove my byline, Kate?"

"I didn't. I put it on the story—"

"I took it off." Chuck stared at them. "Let's take this into my office. Now."

They entered and Chuck closed the door.

"Nobody sits down. This will be quick," Chuck said.

"Where's Reeka?" Sloane asked.

"Got called to a meeting. Sloane, your effort was half-assed. Your contribution added nothing to the piece, so I removed your byline."

"But I did what you requested, Chuck. I consulted the records."

"What you submitted was akin to a street cop at a crime scene telling people there's nothing to see here. You kept facts from the light. End of discussion."

"But there was nothing—"

"End of discussion." Chuck put his hands on his hips. "Senior management liked the story, liked that we challenged the *New York Times*, got it on the record and got serious pickup. It shows subscribers are paying attention. Now I've asked our business reporters to dig into EastCloud and Richlon, to look into their histories. And I've asked our Washington bureau to start pumping members of the House Transportation Committee and the House Aviation Subcommittee. Maybe they're hearing something on the big players here. They'll feed whatever they get to us. We need to keep digging on this."

"Sounds good," Kate said.

"Want me to keep checking with my aviation sources, too, Chuck?"

"Yes. But Sloane, we need to be sure we can put names on the record, like Kate did with the pilot. Kate, I want you to keep pushing all the angles. Work with everybody and keep us out front. You know the drill."

Chuck let a few beats pass. His cell phone rang, but before answering it, he said, "Okay, that's it. Get to work."

Kate spent the next hour at her desk, putting out calls and messages to sources. Then she tried to reach Raymond Matson to see how he was doing in the wake of the story.

I hope he's okay.

But she got no response. In fact, not much was coming back from anybody. Kate remembered that she hadn't finished checking reader emails. The in-box showed there were now eighty. As expected, most were nothing.

That's the way it goes, she thought, coming to the end, pausing at the last one.

The subject line read:

I know what happened to 4990.

She opened it.

Your story's good, but it's wrong. What happened to that jet will happen again. I know because I made it happen and unless you announce my triumph, we'll make it happen again. This time it'll be worse. Watch the skies. We are Zarathustra, Lord of the Heavens.

Fourteen

Manhattan, New York

This can't be real.

Kate read the email again and a chill coiled slowly up her spine.

It's got to be a prankster or some nut.

Kate had encountered all kinds of people trying to insert themselves into stories: conspiracy types, people with agendas, people who were unbalanced, hoaxers, you name it. Yet she couldn't ignore the concern tightening around her. The phrase "I made it happen" gave Captain Matson's words new meaning: *I don't know what happened, but I know something went wrong.*

Kate bit her bottom lip as she continued rereading the message.

And they were threatening to do it again. Only God knows when.

"Hey, Mark, come over here and look at this."

Mark Reston, a rumpled hard-news reporter who sat near her, moaned, pulled himself to his feet and stood next to Kate, who tapped her monitor with her pen.

"What do you think of this? It's in response to my story."

Reston scratched his stubbled chin and drew his face closer.

"What's this Lord of the Heavens crap?"

"Mark, come on. What do you think?"

"Likely a lunatic is what I think."

"What if it isn't? We don't know what really happened on that flight."

"Likely someone with a tinfoil hat."

"But what if it's not a nutcase?"

"Did you respond, try to engage them in conversation?"

"Yes. I got the error message 'Permanent failure, unknown user' message."

"If this is real, you got a helluva story. Whatever it is, you should alert Chuck."

"That's the plan."

Kate printed the email and headed for Chuck Laneer's office. He wasn't there. She found him coming down the hall and handed him the email.

"Just got this."

Chuck pushed his glasses to the top of his forehead and read. He removed them when he'd finished and tapped one finger to his teeth, something he always did.

"Do you have any idea who sent this, Kate?"

"None. It's anonymous."

"Did you respond?"

"Yes and I got nothing, a failed-delivery message."

"Did you share it?"

"No."

"Make several paper copies and stand by. I'm calling a meeting on how we're going to handle this."

Fifteen minutes later, Kate, Chuck and several senior editors sat at the big polished table in the newsroom's main boardroom.

They'd reviewed the email and Kate briefed them on all she knew. "So it boils down to this," she said. "If we don't write a story crediting this person for EastCloud Forty-nine Ninety, they'll harm another flight."

"Have we had our IT security people try to track the source, verify it?" Marisa McDougal, head of world features, asked.

"Yes, I've got them on it," Chuck said, "but they're indicating that it'll likely be impossible, given our limited resources."

"So do we publish this or not?" Kate asked.

"I say we publish it," Reeka said. "It's our exclusive."

"Why come to us with this?" Dean Altman, chief of all domestic bureaus, asked. "Why not simply post it online?"

"If you get us to do it, it gives you credibility," Chuck said. "It gives the claim and the threat currency, and the advantage of our global reach. Our story would get redistributed online with authority, so it'd be a win-win."

"I say we run it," Reeka said. "It's our duty to report this."

"It's a little more complicated than that," said Howard Kehoe, who headed all foreign bureaus.

"Right now, we can't verify the validity of this thing. We run this with the threat and we'll cause havoc to air travel around the world."

"But our job is to inform the public," Marisa said. "There's a public safety issue here."

"That's just it," Kehoe said. "If we run this claim and this threat, will it make air travel any safer? If we don't run it, are we truly risking lives? We have the fact the captain said something went wrong on the flight, and now this person is claiming that somehow they took over the plane. How? Does the technology to do this sort of thing even exist? They're a bit short on details."

"I'm wondering why video from passengers in the cabin hasn't surfaced yet," Bruce Dabney, the business editor, said. "These days it's almost guaranteed somebody has shot something."

"That's right, and my point," Kehoe said, "is that we don't yet have any official, investigative confirmation from the NTSB, or the FAA, or anyone, on what happened. I think we need to be careful here."

"Could it be a terrorist threat?" Marisa asked.

"There's no indication in the note, no claim to affiliation, no demand or condemnation," Kehoe said.

"What about the name Zarathustra?" Reeka asked.

"That's the name of a Persian prophet from around seven or eight hundred BC," Chuck said. "As I recall, he taught about humanity following one God and the priority of living a moral life."

"You're dating yourself by a few centuries, Chuck." Marisa smiled.

"I took a few philosophy courses in school."

"So what would you like me to do?" Kate asked,

glimpsing something through the boardroom's floor-to-ceiling glass walls. Sloane was talking with Mark Reston, who was nodding to the meeting. Sloane looked uneasy.

"We're walking an ethical tightrope here," Graham Lincoln, Newslead's editor-in-chief, said. "If we run a story now and it turns out that the note is a practical joke, we open the floodgates to all sorts of crackpots and our credibility takes a hit. I think under the circumstances we're not going to publish it."

"Ever?" Kate asked.

"For now," Lincoln said. "Of course, we have a moral responsibility to protect public safety, so we'll alert the authorities, the FBI in this case. We'll ask them if we're the only news organization to receive this note, ask them not to share our note, and to keep us informed on their investigation of it. Above all, we'll investigate journalistically. That is our responsibility and our duty. That's what we'll do."

Lincoln let a moment pass for his direction to sink in around the table.

"I think we're done here. Chuck, Kate, contact the people at Federal Plaza straightaway, get the ball rolling. And remember, folks, everything said in this room remains confidential."

As the meeting broke and editors moved from the boardroom, Kate looked again at Sloane.

He was still talking with Reston and watching her.

Intensely.

Fifteen

"What's your information on EastCloud Flight Forty-nine Ninety?"

Special Agent Anne Bartell was unsmiling, as was her partner, Agent Phil Enroy, who'd clicked his pen and poised it over his pad. After Kate was cleared at security, they'd taken her to an interview room on the twenty-eighth floor of the FBI's New York Field Office in Lower Manhattan.

It was late afternoon and people were leaving for the day.

Kate didn't know Bartell and Enroy. She'd worked with agents at this office before; Nick Varner was one, but her call got bounced and had been assigned to agents who were new to her, so she was starting cold.

"You're aware of what happened to the flight?" Kate asked.

"We've followed the press reports, including yours," Enroy said.

"Is the FBI investigating in any way?"

"No cause has emerged for us to be involved. The NTSB leads the investigation. What's the nature of your information?" Enroy said.

Kate started by relating background on Newslead's public email for reader responses to stories, then reached into her bag and handed them printouts of the email. Upon reading it the agents made notes, and summoned Special Agent Ron Sanchez, a cyber analyst, who was also a senior member of the Joint Terrorism Task Force.

"Have you received any other communication from the sender?" Sanchez asked.

"Nothing."

"Would you be able to forward me the email to this address?" Sanchez took out a business card and jotted down an email address.

"I'll check with my editors."

"While you're at it, would Newslead allow our Computer Analysis and Response Team access to your system, if we need it?"

"I can't answer that. They may prefer you seek a warrant. Agent Sanchez, what do you think? Is the email legitimate?"

"Impossible to say at this stage. We'll have to assess it."

"Assess it for…?"

"Credibility and believability. We'll examine the identity given, this 'Zarathustra, Lord of the Heavens.' We don't know if this is simply a disturbed individual, a false alarm, or someone with the skills and resources to carry out the threat, or someone affiliated with a terrorist network. We'll assess it and run it through several databases to determine its validity. Those are the first steps."

"Then what?"

"There's a lot more after that. If we think it has substance, we'll pull in every resource we have. We'll alert the NTSB, work with them, call in other agencies if we have to. We'll track down the sender and secure the safety of travelers and bring forth the appropriate charges. As you know, just making the threat is a criminal act."

"Is the FBI aware of this person sending similar threats to other news organizations?"

"Not to our knowledge," Sanchez said. "You're the first to bring this to our attention at this office."

"Would you assure Newslead that you will not make this public, or share it with other news agencies?"

"We'll keep it confidential, unless circumstances change."

"But you'll keep us informed along the way?"

"We're getting into hypothetical areas. If an investigation is warranted, we'd need to protect its integrity."

"But would you respect the fact that it's Newslead's tip and we'd want to report on it exclusively if this goes anywhere?"

"You want an exclusivity deal."

"That's right."

"We'll leave that for the people here at a higher pay grade to sort out," Bartell said.

"What we'll do," Sanchez said, "is advise our supervisors that you came to us and you're cooperating. At this stage we'd ask that you not report on any aspect of this note."

"Newslead can't surrender editorial control to the FBI. But given that there's a public safety issue here, Newslead wants to take the proper approach."

"All right, then. Thank you for bringing this to our attention." Sanchez stood to leave.

"Wait, one last thing. What're the chances that this note is real?"

"It's anyone's guess at this point," Sanchez said. "The FBI receives upwards of a thousand tips a day. Everything from reports of a package left on the street, to an unstable person on a plane planning to do harm, to people overhearing someone plotting to assassinate the president. We review them all. This one will be no different. It could be someone trying to lay claim to the event. Or it could be an authentic communication from the person responsible for the problems with the flight, boasting that they have the means to carry out their threat. Until then, the truth about your sender remains a mystery."

"With time ticking down on us," Kate said.

Kate stepped off the elevator and was walking through the lobby when she heard someone say, "Kate? Kate Page?"

She turned to see FBI Special Agent Nick Varner pulling away from a group of people heading to the elevator doors.

"I'll catch up with you guys," Varner called to the group as he approached her. "It's been a long time. You're looking good. How've you been? Sorry, I've only got a moment, but what brings you here?"

Kate and Nick had worked together on a major kidnapping story nearly a year ago, and she trusted him completely. Varner looked good in his suit. He'd just hit forty and still had his Brad Pitt thing going strong, she thought. His eyes were sharp and he listened intensely as she related everything about the Zarathustra threat to him, telling him what she'd told the other agents.

"I know Ron Sanchez. I work with him." Varner reached into his pocket for a card and pen, making notes before passing it to her. "I'm strictly task force now. Here's my new number and private contact information. Keep me in the loop. Maybe I can help."

Elevator doors chimed and he turned.

"Gotta go," he said as he headed for the elevator. "Good seeing you. Keep in touch, Kate."

Sixteen

Logan Dunn studied the website for the *Buffalo News* on his phone while waiting at the Port Authority Bus Terminal in Midtown Manhattan.

He concentrated on a wire story the *News* had carried under the headline:

Pilot of Troubled EastCloud Buffalo-to-NYC Flight: Malfunction Puts Passengers at Risk.

He'd read it several times, coming back to the statements by Raymond Matson, the captain:

I don't know what happened but I know something went wrong. This was a clear flight control computer malfunction.

Damn right something went wrong.

Logan reached up to relieve an itch on his temple, touching the bandages covering the cuts he'd received on the flight. Then he went to the video he'd recorded.

It started with Kayla at her window seat, anxious but winning over her fear of flying, when the jetliner suddenly rolled hard, the right wing tipping toward the ground, passengers screaming for their lives as bodies and items were tossed like they were in a blender. The horror was repeated as the plane suddenly lurched to the left, throwing people to the opposite side as the jet leveled, then took a sudden death dive before the crew regained control.

Somehow, throughout the chaos and panic, Logan had managed to hang on to his phone and keep recording.

In the aftermath, when paramedics had taken him, Kayla and the other passengers to the hospital for observation, he'd alerted Kayla's parents, and his, that they'd been shaken but not seriously hurt.

Like the other passengers, Logan and Kayla had cooperated with the NTSB and EastCloud Airlines, providing statements. The NTSB and EastCloud wanted him to share his video and not make it public, stating that it would help with the investigation.

But Logan had refused to share it.

He wanted to help but he was hesitant. Word had circulated among the passengers that while many had still pictures and video taken *after* the incident, Logan was the only person whose footage had captured the entire event as it had happened. He'd called one of his law professors and told him about the flight with Kayla, his video and the circumstances.

The video is essentially your property, the professor had said. *I understand you'd want to help investigators because of the safety issues, but you might want to consider making your recording public first before sharing it with the NTSB and the airline. It would strengthen a civil case should you proceed with an action, and I would think you and Kayla have a very strong case.*

But that was the problem.

Kayla didn't want Logan to release the video.

Her reasoning ranged from *It's too frightening,* to *My screaming is embarrassing,* to *It could have an impact on my hope of ever getting a job with Maly Kriz-Janda.* Her opposition was irrational, but Logan understood. She'd been traumatized by the incident.

He looked down at Kayla now, her head resting on his chest as they waited at the bus terminal. Her chin was bandaged. Bruises dotted her neck and arm. He thought of how much the job at the fashion designer had meant to her, how hard she'd worked in school to pursue her dream. He thought of all she'd done to alleviate her fear of flying—the books, the recordings—and his heart ached for her.

While in the hospital, she'd called Maly Kriz-Janda, told them about the flight and canceled her interview.

I'm okay with it. Really, she'd told him.

But she wasn't okay. She'd cried in the aftermath. Then the designer called her back and very kindly offered to interview Kayla over the phone, if she was willing.

Kayla had gone ahead with a short, shaky interview in which she'd made it clear that she'd never again get on a plane. The designer had been upbeat, thanked her, called her brave and said they'd get back to her. But Kayla had given up on the job and wanted to get home to Buffalo.

And now here they were, awaiting a nine-hour bus trip across the state.

Logan's back and shoulders were sore from the items that had crashed into him, and he had to reposition himself on the bench, disturbing Kayla.

"I wasn't sleeping," she said. "I saw you looking at the video again."

"I know this is hard, and you've been through a lot, but we should release it. We can't be selfish about this, Kay. People have to know what happened on that plane."

"I know," she said.

"You know?"

She nodded.

"So you're okay to make it public?"

Tears came to her eyes as she nodded.

"I wouldn't want anyone else to go through this, and I know we're so lucky to be alive."

Tenderly, he pressed her head to his face and kissed her.

"It's okay. Everything's going to be okay."

They sat there for a moment. Then Logan scrolled through the newswire story. It was written by Kate Page. He searched for her email on the bottom then sent her a message.

After checking the time, he looked up Newslead's telephone number and called it.

Seventeen

By the time Kate had returned to the newsroom most of the day side staff had left, except Reeka, who approached her before she'd made it back to her desk.

"You're not on the schedule. What're you filing for us today?"

"Nothing."

"We need a follow."

"You know that I was with the FBI—" Kate glanced around to ensure nobody overheard "—discussing their response to the Zarathustra email. It's in the note I sent to Lincoln, you, Chuck and the other editors."

"Then give us a story saying the FBI is now investigating the flight."

"But they're not 'investigating.' Not yet."

"Your note said they've accepted our information, so write an exclusive saying Newslead has learned the FBI is investigating a claim that someone interfered with the near-fatal flight."

"What? No. That's disingenuous and runs counter to what Lincoln directed us to do at the meeting. You were there. Besides, the FBI hasn't even assessed the claim yet. Did you read my note?"

Kate searched the newsroom in vain for Chuck when Tyler Sharpe, a news assistant, trotted to them.

"Excuse me, Kate, but I've got a call for you that sounds important."

"What is it?" she asked.

"Got a guy on hold. Says he's got information on your story about the EastCloud flight."

"Put him through to me," Kate said, turning to Reeka. "I'll take this."

Striding to her desk Kate struggled to shake off the exchange. That Reeka was still working here was a constant source of trepidation, compounded by the fact Sloane remained an employee. Kate scanned the newsroom for him, happy she didn't see him.

Where's Chuck when I need him?

Kate seized her phone.

"Kate Page, Newslead."

"You're the reporter who wrote the story on the EastCloud flight?"

"That's me. How can I help you?"

"My girlfriend and I were passengers and I have some footage I took on my phone when it happened that no one has seen."

"Really? How can I be sure?"

"I'll send you a few seconds and our boarding passes, to show that this is the real deal."

"Okay, use this email."

Kate dictated the address and stayed on the line with the caller. A moment later the email came in.

She caught her breath as she viewed the frightening images.

"Can you send me the whole thing?"

"Not until we meet face-to-face. That's how I want to do it."

"Have you called other newsrooms?"

"No, just you. Your story was the best."

He just echoed Zarathustra. Kate tightened her hold on her phone. "Excuse me?"

"Your story had the most information, the interview with the captain. That's why I called."

"Are you seeking money? Because all we pay for images is spot news and freelance rates—a few hundred dollars—and that's it."

"I don't care about the money."

"Okay, can you come to our newsroom today? We'll make an appointment."

"No, we have to do this in one hour."

"Why?"

"That's when our bus leaves. We're at the Port Authority Bus Terminal."

Kate did a quick calculation of the distance and time, then traded descriptions with her caller before hanging up and collecting her bag.

"Tell Reeka I'm going to check out this caller," she told Tyler, before hurrying to the elevator.

The Port Authority Bus Terminal was in Times Square, an eight- or ten-block walk, depending on which direction Kate went. She headed north on Eighth Avenue, estimating that she could cover the distance within fifteen minutes.

Her breathing quickened at the prospect of securing unseen footage. She was glad that she'd told no one details about the call, sticking fast to her rule on tips: never tell an editor what you've got until you've nailed it. It was a rule that had kept her sane with every editor she'd ever dealt with, especially with Reeka, who overreacted to everything. Kate neared the terminal and the air grew heavy with the smell of diesel and the rush of air brakes.

She whispered a prayer for the caller to be there.

The Port Authority Bus Terminal was one of the busiest in the world. In keeping with her caller's directions, Kate went to the information booth and searched the nearest benches for a white man and woman in their twenties. They had two suitcases: a small red canvas one, and a large fluorescent green one. The man had short dark hair, and the woman's blond hair touched her shoulders. When Kate spotted a couple matching the description, she went to them.

"Logan?" she asked.

"Yes," the man answered, "and this is Kayla."

"Kate Page with Newslead." She held up her Newslead ID.

Their bandages reinforced the gravity of the matter. Logan pulled out his phone and pressed Play on the video. As Kate watched the events unfold, her hand flew to her mouth, for it was far more chilling than she could've imagined. Kate sat with the couple and interviewed them; they agreed to be photographed and identified for the story.

"We're thankful to be alive," Kayla said.

"We don't want anyone to ever have to go through what we went through on that flight," Logan said.

After they'd boarded their bus to Buffalo, Kate alerted Chuck, Reeka and the night desk to what she had and sent the video to Newslead's web team so they could post it on Newslead's website.

Adrenaline pumping, she sat down on a bench, blocked out the terminal's hubbub and focused her full concentration into crafting a story about Logan and Kayla's terrifying video.

Good work, Kate, Chuck wrote back after reading her story and viewing the footage.

Once the story went live, Kate sent individual messages about it to the NTSB, EastCloud, the FBI, Captain Matson and her friend with the pilots' union. For dinner, she bought an egg-salad sandwich, then headed to the nearest subway station for an uptown train to take her home. The day's events replayed in her mind as the train sped north.

Who is Zarathustra and how significant was the threat to disrupt another plane? Those images of what happened on 4990 were shocking. What are we really dealing with here?

Kate racked her brains for possible answers, but it was futile—she was exhausted. The train rumbled from station to station, calming her, and she almost drifted off before it reached her stop.

It was dark when she surfaced on 125th Street.

She lived a few blocks away in Morningside Heights, in a Victorian-era building where she'd sublet an affordable apartment from a Columbia University professor who was on an extended sabbatical in Europe.

With the exception of distant sirens, it was unusually quiet. Her neighborhood was a mix of small businesses—a deli, a check-cashing store, a florist, an electronics store, a hair salon—and small apartment buildings. Tonight, the streets were almost deserted, and she felt a sudden and inexplicable pang of unease. She stopped and looked behind her.

Nothing out of the ordinary.

I could've sworn someone was following along behind me.

Kate continued to her building.

She fished out her keys, let herself in through the secure lobby and summoned the elevator. The car was empty. She stepped in and it rose toward her floor. Then, without warning, it groaned to a halt.

"Great."

Kate pushed buttons, but to no avail. She rang the alarm button but nothing happened. *This is strange. We never have problems with the elevator here.* In the silence, she heard the echoing thud of someone rushing up a stairwell and called to them.

"Hello! Help! I'm stuck in the elevator! Can you push a button?"

Several moments passed without a response.

Kate then reached for the small door to the emergency phone when suddenly the elevator shuddered, resumed rising and stopped at her floor.

The doors opened and she stepped out.

That was weird.

She turned for her apartment then froze.

She heard the distinct sound of floorboards creaking around the corner. Thinking that it might be the person she'd called to for help, Kate went to the corner to thank them and tell them the elevator was now working.

She caught her breath.

No one was there.

Kate swallowed hard.

Attributing it all to the side effects of a busy day, she went to her door, entered her apartment, locked the locks and slammed home the dead bolts.

Eighteen

Tension was etched in the faces of the experts preparing to analyze Flight 4990's flight data recorder, or FDR.

They had met on the sixth floor of National Transportation Safety Board headquarters at L'Enfant Plaza. The room was devoid of the usual small talk, Jake Hooper thought, taking a sip of black coffee as the chair ran down meeting rules for the people at the table. They were from the FAA, the pilots' union, the airline, the recorder's maker, the plane's manufacturer and the NTSB.

Hooper knew the rules by rote. They were similar to those of the group that had met earlier to listen to twenty-five minutes of crew conversation downloaded from the plane's CVR, the cockpit voice recorder.

We're moving pieces into place but this case has twists.

The FBI had just advised the NTSB that a news agency had received an email from a party claiming responsibility for the flight's loss of control and was threatening to do it again with another plane. The message—whether a hoax or somehow credible—was unnerving.

The stakes had been raised.

There was also the captain's insistence that there had been no clear-air turbulence, and that the crew did not disable the safety features to make control inputs. And now the release of the dramatic video of the turmoil 4990's cabin had raised the profile of the incident.

"Shall we get started?" Ivor Carver, the NTSB's flight data recorder specialist, began by summarizing information on the digital flight data recorder, the model—a Sun-Signaler—and the parameters recorded.

"Data readouts have been circulated, and I want to underscore and remind everyone this is nonvalidated, preliminary data."

Pages were shuffled and throats cleared as Carver continued.

"As you can see, we've overlaid preliminary FDR plots with the characterizations of the text from the cockpit voice recorder, correlating them with radar and other data. Moving forward, we'll keep an eye to ranges, accuracies and resolutions. Okay, so let's look at the parameters."

The FDR recorded the aircraft's various systems, covering nearly one hundred aspects, from changes in altitude, thrust, control inputs and airspeed. One by one, the investigators read, interpreted and assessed each reading. Hooper took notes, concentrating on several areas he considered key, such as autopilot engagement, the automatic flight control system, the computer failure indicator, cockpit trim and all cockpit flight control input—the control wheel, control column and rudder pedal.

Hours later, as they concluded studying the last areas, Fred McCullers, Sun-Signaler's expert, offered his observation.

"It's clear the data recorder was functioning properly."

"And I don't see any issues with the fly-by-wire system," said Erna Valentine, the lead engineer with Richlon-Titan.

"You're absolutely certain there was no malfunction?" Hooper asked.

"Yes."

"What about an episodic failure?"

"No evidence of one here. It would've been recorded."

"What about system vulnerabilities?" Hooper said.

"You're alluding to the claim the FBI is investigating," Valentine said. "The suggestion that someone seized control of the aircraft from the crew?"

"We can't ignore it."

"That scenario is impossible. The claim's a prank. The system doesn't talk to the outside world."

"What about through the Aircraft Communications Addressing and Reporting System and the other wireless systems aboard? Perhaps they have vulnerabilities we're not aware of?"

"Absolutely not. Everyone at this table knows they're stand-alone systems that cannot be breached. Richlon-Titan designed and pioneered the new state-of-the-art, fly-by-wire systems for all the RTs and other aircraft around the world. They're absolutely secure."

"Let's come back to the pilots, who've stated that they encountered a system malfunction."

"Frankly, I don't buy it," Valentine said. "It had to be clear-air turbulence, which does not emerge on radar. It caused the captain to switch off the safety features, take control and overreact. You have to remember, this pilot's record shows that he's dealing with serious personal issues. An antidepressant was found in his blood. He was a prime candidate for distraction."

"For the purposes of this meeting—" Gus Vitalley of the pilots' union shot an icy glance to the chair "—we're required to stick to the facts concerning the flight data recorder and not veer into speculation."

"Those are facts, Gus," Valentine said. "Facts we need to consider in light of the preliminary evidence before us."

The meeting continued for another forty-five minutes before it concluded.

Alone in his office, Hooper flipped through his notes while consulting the FDR readout, mentally gnawing on the facts the way Pax went at a bone.

The plane had made two abrupt ninety-degree rolls. It shouldn't have done that. Something was up. Why had the safety features of the fly-by-wire system been disabled? That was only supposed to happen in an emergency, such as a situation involving severe clear-air turbulence. But Raymond Matson maintained that there had been no turbulence and that he hadn't disabled the safety system.

But there it was.

The records didn't lie.

Somehow that system had been turned off.

Nineteen

Clear River, North Dakota

Veyda was wearing a diaper and a T-shirt, and sucking on her bottle as she toddled into his study. He was working at his computer keyboard and she pressed against his knee, raising a tiny arm, forcing him to hoist her gently to his lap. She snuggled into his chest, falling asleep with her bottle as he worked with one hand while holding her with the other.

Elizabeth had captured the moment on video.

There were a few other videos and photos from their trips to Kitty Hawk and Cape Canaveral but he was often missing from ones taken at Christmas, birthdays and school events.

Looking at them now, on his computer in the gloom of his rented house, Robert Cole swallowed his pain with whiskey, letting the warmth of the alcohol flow through him. No matter how he steeled himself, no matter how much he drank, it tore him apart to look back at what he'd lost.

For not only was Elizabeth gone—he'd lost Veyda, too.

She'd been a brilliant child with an intuitive,

analytical mind, an exceptional little girl. In her adolescent years, she'd read her mother's medical textbooks, his engineering books, then their philosophy books. Plato, Nietzsche, Lao Tzu and Descartes had been her favorites. She'd forever been questioning them on subjects and concepts.

Have you ever seen a person's soul, Mom?

What is eternal consciousness?

How do jets fly, Dad?

Veyda had loved looking over their shoulders whenever they'd worked at home, absorbing whatever she could.

But those moments had been rare for him because he'd always been at the plant, never around to do normal dad things, like taking Veyda to a museum, or going with her and Elizabeth on a hike, or helping Veyda with the science projects she'd worked so hard on. His job had always come first and before he'd realized it, the years had slipped by and Veyda had left home for college.

Their time together had been all but gone.

As Veyda accumulated one academic achievement after another, he and Elizabeth had seen less of her, which had made the few visits they'd had more meaningful—until the day of the accident.

He drank more whiskey.

Veyda had suffered a serious head injury in the crash. For months after the tragedy she'd undergone treatment and therapy before returning to MIT, determined to get her PhD as her way of honoring her mother's memory, but in that time she'd grown distant and cold toward him. When he'd flown to Boston to spend time with her, she'd missed a dinner date with him, and had been late meeting him at his hotel. She'd behaved as if she'd resented his presence. It was as if she'd become a different person. Then, after he'd returned to California, she'd sent him an email.

I will never forgive you for what you've done. You loved your work more than us. In killing my mother you killed part of me. I no longer want you in my life. I never want to see you again. You are not my father and I am not your daughter. You're a sad, ordinary man who contributes nothing to this world and I hope you die knowing that.

Her words had pierced him.

Veyda couldn't have meant what she'd said, he'd thought, blaming it on her injury. In the days and weeks after her email, he'd tried to reach her through the school, her doctors, her therapists and, thinking she might harm herself, even police. But it had been futile. Veyda was an adult and not a threat to herself or others.

I'm afraid this is a private matter, sir, and not one for police, the officer had told him.

All of Cole's efforts to contact her, find her, speak to her and reconcile their relationship had been in vain. They'd become estranged and she'd vanished from his life, living on her trust fund and a portion of the insurance money they'd received from the crash. Cole had withdrawn into himself. Unable to function professionally, he'd lost his job, sold their house in Burbank and moved here to North Dakota where every day, haunted by her accusations, he tried to drown his guilt with alcohol.

But he failed because what Veyda had said was true.

The evidence stared back at him from the photos he'd saved. There were more pictures of him at work than with his family. At the time of the tragedy, he'd been one of Richlon-Titan's top quality-assurance engineers overseeing the fly-by-wire system. He'd been a highly regarded expert. He'd been asked to work with the US Air Force and national security organizations on system applications for classified projects, and he had often been called upon to provide technical help to the NTSB on crash investigations. Over the years, he'd developed professional friendships with NTSB and FAA people who'd respected his work.

He took another drink.

There was no denying it—he loved aviation and he'd loved his job. He'd enjoyed going to the RT plant each day in Burbank. Entering the massive hangar where they'd built planes, seeing the sections of fuselage, the scaffolding, the assembly jigs and hearing the *rat-a-tat-tat* of the riveting guns— he'd loved it all.

Moreover, he'd lived for the challenge of helping design, install and maintain RT's digital fly-by-wire system, an extraordinarily complex control system that enabled the aircraft to be controlled by electronic signals. The basic principle meant that pilot-initiated flight controls were converted to electronic signals that were then processed by flight control computers.

The system was programmed with flight control laws that provided hazardous flight envelope protection for such things as speed, bank, angle of attack and pitch attitude. The safety features essentially assured that the inputs made by the crew were within the limits of the plane's capability.

However, if the crew was suddenly confronted with an unusual emergency, RT's system provided for the safety features to be manually disabled, allowing the crew to manually direct the aircraft to perform beyond programmed safety limits.

Safe operation of RT's system was paramount. It was backed up five different ways to guard against problems such as a system failure, or the malfunction of any of the onboard computers, or loss of power.

Then there was the question of security.

Ah, yes, security.

He took another drink.

Was the fly-by-wire flight-management system vulnerable to interference by satellite transmissions or solar storms? Cole's team had ensured that it was protected against such occurrences.

Perhaps the most contentious concern had been the one about the system's vulnerability to a cyber attack. Was it possible for someone to seize control of the aircraft remotely? Again, based on several overarching facts, Cole's team had been confident the answer was no. Ultimately, the flight-management system and the autopilot were controlled by the crew. The avionics systems had been designed and built with extremely high levels of security.

From time to time, reports would emerge indicating that the computer systems used in commercial jetliners today could be hacked. But such claims were always baseless.

Then an assertion surfaced at a global IT security conference in Manila that had prompted Cole's team to reevaluate the security of the RT system. A former pilot and computer security consultant had told the conference that he'd purchased software online that he'd adapted to infiltrate the Aircraft Communications Addressing and Reporting System and the Automatic Dependent Surveillance-Broadcast System. These systems transmitted short messages between aircraft, satellites and ground stations. The consultant had said that by infiltrating the two systems, he had the capability to land or crash any plane in flight. He'd used a flight simulator and given an audiovisual presentation to demonstrate his findings.

The NTSB and the FAA, as well as several aviation bodies around the world, had refuted the consultant's claim, stating that it might work in theory on a flight simulator, but it was not possible to interfere with flight-certified hardware as he'd described. Initially Cole's team had agreed, but while they'd been reviewing RT's system, Cole had discovered something alarming.

Something that they'd missed.

There was a "back door" via a connection between the aircraft's computing systems that was unsecured and could be exploited by a skilled hacker to gain access to critical flight systems. All that was needed to exploit the weakness was to establish a framework of malicious codes to override the plane's security software.

Cole had alerted RT's senior engineers to the flaw in the flight-management system, clearly indicating that it could be hacked. It'd meant that they would have to ground the fleet for a retrofit. He'd worked on a proposal to redesign and install a more secure system at an additional cost of nine million dollars per aircraft.

Executive members of the company had been stunned. They'd disagreed with Cole's proposal. Under the direction of Hub Wolfeson, a powerful executive, and without Cole's knowledge, the board had used RT's European operations to launch a re-test of the existing system. That review concluded the existing system was secure and that Cole's theory was wrong. Cole had been angry, and after he'd managed to gain access to the European tests, he'd argued that the tests were inaccurate and therefore ineffective.

Again, he'd insisted the fleet be grounded and his proposal be implemented. Senior engineers and company board members, again led by Wolfeson, had been poised to review his request during the time Veyda had visited. Cole had been told that the board's response would take days. He'd tried to put it aside, when suddenly he'd received a text saying that upon review, the board had agreed with the European results and had denied his latest proposal to ground and retrofit the fleet.

Cole had been responding to those texts at the time of the car crash.

In that moment, the life he'd known had come to an end.

He swallowed more whiskey. A lot more.

And now we have the EastCloud incident. The fools. I told them. I warned them. They think they've got a safe airplane.

Cole reread the news stories on the mystery surrounding the horror of EastCloud Flight 4990 and replayed the video of the terrified passengers over and over.

I know what happened and it's going to happen again. I've got to do something. Washington. I know somebody in Washington. I know what happened to Forty-nine Ninety! It's going to happen again, I tell you!

Cole reached for his phone but heard the sound of clinking glass as he fell to the floor, drunk, and passed out.

He lay unconscious in the darkness, still gripping his phone, while on his computer monitor horrified passengers screamed for their lives.

Twenty

The sprawl of metropolitan London flowed under Shikra Airlines Flight 418 as it approached Heathrow.

The six-hour flight from Kuwait City had been a smooth one for Captain Fahad Al-Anjari, the crew, and for their two hundred passengers aboard the Starglide Blue Wing 250.

Al-Anjari was one of Shikra's top pilots with some twenty-five years' experience with the Kuwaiti airline. His seniority afforded him the Kuwait City–to– London route, considered one of the airline's plum assignments. Al-Anjari had flown it nearly a hundred times and had always enjoyed it.

He loved flying the Starglide Blue Wing 250. It was a modern plane, equipped with easy-to-use computers, and had an admirable safety record. It responded well in all conditions, and always gave a smooth ride.

He loved the views over London, starting with the Thames. Each time he saw it, he thought of

Joseph Conrad's passage in *Heart of Darkness* about the river evoking a large snake twisting deep into the country.

Flight 418 continued its descent and was minutes from landing. It was vectored for a visual approach to Heathrow's Runway 27L, the airport's southern runway. The autopilot and autothrottle were engaged. As the jetliner passed over the rows of homes crammed together in Hounslow, a suburb bordering the airport, it was ninety seconds from touchdown.

Al-Anjari had extended the landing gear.

The jet had now descended to one thousand feet and was fully configured for the landing. When the plane reached eight hundred feet Al-Anjari took manual control of the aircraft, instructing Khalid Marafi, the copilot, to disconnect the autopilot at seven hundred feet.

Marafi disengaged the autopilot.

At fifty seconds from landing, Al-Anjari, now in control, commanded more thrust from both engines. Both engines initially responded, but seemed disturbingly reduced to a trickle of power.

"What the hell's this?" Al-Anjari couldn't believe it. "What's going on?"

At thirty-five seconds from touchdown, Al-Anjari and Marafi scrambled to identify the cause for the loss of thrust.

"I don't know what's happening!" Marafi said. "Our speed is dropping fast! We're not going to reach the runway!" He scanned the instruments for the problem. The fuel level was okay, the pumps were okay, no fire indicators, no malfunctions.

"We've got a double engine failure! The engines have been switched off!"

"Switched off? How? We didn't do that! Try restarting!"

They commanded a restart without response. Nothing worked.

Al-Anjari's throat tightened as he scanned the rooftops of Hounslow and noticed a petrol station ahead.

Not here! Oh God, please, not here!

Now at twelve seconds before touchdown, a buzzer sounded and a robotic voice warned, "Air speed low! Air speed low!" Then the stick shaker activated and the control column physically vibrated, indicating that the aircraft was about to stall.

"We're going to crash!" Marafi shouted.

Al-Anjari reached for the cabin PA system and announced to the passengers, "Brace! Brace! Brace for hard landing!" Then he radioed the tower. "Four one eight, Mayday! Mayday!"

At five seconds before impact, the jet just cleared the houses of Hounslow and the petrol station, coming so low to traffic on the A30 motorway that ran along the airport's south side that vehicles swerved to avoid the airliner's landing gear.

In the moment before impact, Al-Anjari pulled back on the control column and thought of his wife and children, flying kites and picnicking amid the southern dunes, praying he would see them again.

The jet came down in the grassy undershoot of the runway about two hundred and fifty yards inside the airfield perimeter fence. The right wingtip hit the ground first, followed by the right main landing gear. The wing disintegrated and the landing gear broke away as the plane skidded, then lifted and rolled, cartwheeling to an inverted position.

As it tumbled down the right side of the runway, the plane broke up. The rear tail section separated, taking several rows with it. While most passengers were belted in their seats, others spilled from the plane to the ground as it bounced along.

The main fuselage, the large center section, remained intact. As it slid and rolled, passengers were rocked loose in the cabin, some catapulted through it and out of the gaping hole left by the separated tail section. The metallic grind was deafening as passengers in the cabin were jerked and shaken like toys. The section seemed to slide forever before coming to a stop upside down.

People still belted were hanging in their seats. Blood dripped everywhere, and severed legs, arms and hands were scattered about the cabin. In some areas, the fuselage had been crushed, trapping people in coffins of compacted metal, their bleeding hands reaching out. The air filled with screaming, moaning and the overpowering smell of jet fuel.

"I can't find my husband!" One woman cried. "Help me find my husband!"

As people began disentangling themselves and helping others, a ball of fire shot down the cabin, blasting it with heat and a kerosene smell. In the choking smoke, people fought to help each other, struggling to the daylight and away from the wreckage amid the wail of approaching sirens.

The crash track was clawed into the earth. It was strewn with passengers, some unconscious, some dazed, in a trail that led to the severed tail section. The people in that section who were able to helped others free themselves, then stumbled aimlessly, staring at the foul cloud of black smoke rising from the main fuselage.

The cockpit had separated and had come to rest some seventy yards down the runway.

Amid the dust and swirling smoke, rescuers pulled bleeding crew members from the wreckage. Captain Al-Anjari passed in and out of consciousness as he glimpsed the scene: his plane in smoldering pieces, passengers staggering through the carnage.

Amid the cries of victims and sirens, he turned his head to the sky, as if the answer to the horror was written there.

Twenty-One

Half a world away from the crash, Kate handed Grace her backpack and unlocked their apartment door. They started to leave for Grace's school when Vanessa called from the living room.

"Kate! You should see this!"

Vanessa was working on her laptop while watching a breakfast program. The TV showed burning pieces of a jetliner and the graphic at the bottom read, "Breaking News: Plane Crash."

"Turn it up, Vanessa," Kate said.

"…happening now in the UK. We're seeing live pictures of a Starglide Blue Wing 250, Shikra Airlines Flight 418, from Kuwait City to London. The plane crashed just short of the southern runway at London's Heathrow Airport. The airline has confirmed there were two hundred passengers and eight crew aboard and while we don't have verified figures, officials are confirming there are fatalities…"

A thousand thoughts blazed through Kate's mind. Her heart went out to the crash victims and their families, and she thought of the message she'd received, warning of another incident.

Oh my God, is this it? Is there a connection?

More questions swirled, but Kate had little time. She had to take care of her priorities.

"Let's go, honey." She turned to Grace. "Let's get you to school."

During the nine-block walk to the school, Kate made several calls and sent several texts, trying to get a handle on the new tragedy.

"Mom, you're walking too fast!"

"Sorry, sweetie."

"Does the plane crash mean you're going to work more?"

"Maybe. Maybe Nancy or Vanessa will have to pick you up today."

"We're still going to the zoo and the bubble show in the park this weekend, right?"

"That's the plan. But we'll have to see."

"Could we shop for my new shoes, too?"

"We talked about the shoes, honey. Did you get your report done?"

"Yes."

After hugs and kisses at the school, Kate called the newsroom. As she hurried to the subway, phone pressed to her ear, the news assistant put her through to an editor.

"Reeka Beck."

"Reeka, it's Kate. I'm trying to reach Chuck. He's not responding to my messages."

"He's in a meeting. Is this about the Heathrow crash?"

"Yes. I'm on my way in and I think we need to—"

"We're on the story. Our London bureau's dispatched people to Heathrow and I've got Sloane looking into any connections here."

"Sloane? Does he know about the warning message I got? At the meeting, Graham ordered the message be kept confidential."

"I know, but word gets around in a newsroom and I had to let Sloane know so he could work on the story. You two are teamed on it, or did you forget?"

Kate rolled her eyes. Where was Chuck when she needed him?

"I'm making calls, too, Reeka."

"You do that, but I think we're covered."

Anger boiled in Kate's gut as she reached the stairs leading down to the 125th Street station. She wanted to scream at Reeka.

"Kate? Kate, I think we need to—"

Kate ended the call.

Thirty-five minutes later Kate was at her desk, where she continued making calls, including a number to the offices of Shikra Airlines in Kuwait, London and New York. She also sent messages to a number of sources and kept up with the latest coverage on Heathrow.

The newsroom's large flat-screen monitors were tuned to 24/7 news channels, all of which were reporting on the crash.

Most networks had reached witnesses and experts to comment and speculate, while images of emergency vehicles and first responders working in the smoldering aftermath played live.

"We can now confirm at least nine fatalities,"

the anchor on Britain's Sky News reported. "That's nine dead in the crash of Shikra Airlines Flight 418 at Heathrow and that number is expected to rise."

The man at the desk for the BBC cupped a hand to his ear and said, "Our Miranda Foster reports that Scotland Yard is stating that so far nothing suggests this tragedy is terror related."

Kate kept track of the wire stories flowing in from AP and Reuters then went to the raw copy from Newslead's London bureau.

LONDON—A Shikra Airlines jet from Kuwait City carrying 208 people crashed while attempting to land, killing at least nine people and injuring dozens of others at one of the world's busiest airports.

National investigators will speak to surviving crew members and study the plane's flight data recorder and maintenance records to determine what caused the deadly crash landing at Heathrow Airport.

Nothing so far has surfaced to identify terrorism as the cause, a source at Scotland Yard said.

Nigel Ashworth, an aviation specialist, said the characteristics of impact would point to a total and sudden loss of engine power as a possible cause.

Upon impact the plane, a Starglide Blue Wing 250, broke into three pieces, with the tail, main fuselage and front cockpit sections strewn over several hundred yards. Some passengers spilled from the aircraft still strapped in their seats, while others remained in the wreckage.

Fire trucks responded by spraying fire-retardant

foam around the wreckage before paramedics could load the injured onto the thirty ambulances dispatched to the scene.

Kate thought the story was strong.

It went on with witness accounts from survivors Newslead staff had reached at Hillingdon Hospital, where most of the injured had been taken.

As Kate read to the bottom, something twigged in the back of her mind and she reread two paragraphs:

Harold Harker, editor of the Air Industry Network, an online specialty site, said the problem seemed to take place in the flight's final seconds.

"It's as if they encountered a sudden and major malfunction, as if a switch had been thrown to slam them into the earth," he said. "It is very odd."

Harker's comments made the tiny hairs at the back of Kate's neck stand up because they echoed what the captain of EastCloud Flight 4990 had told her.

Her phone rang.

"Paul Murther at the NTSB returning your call."

"Thanks for getting back to me, Paul. Is the NTSB going to take part in the investigation of today's Heathrow crash?"

"I can confirm that we're sending a team of investigators at the request of the UK's Air Accidents Investigation Branch because the aircraft involved was built in the US."

"Will you be looking for similarities with East-Cloud Flight Forty-nine Ninety?"

"We can't speculate on the focus of the investigation but we won't rule anything out. That's all I can tell you at this point."

As Murther disconnected, Kate went online to get contact information for Starglide's press office, which was at the company headquarters in Atlanta. While she was on hold, she researched the history of the plane. It seemed to have a good safety record, and she found an article in an aviation-industry magazine that noted the Starglide Blue Wing 250 had a state-of-the-art flight-management system.

Something pinged in the back of Kate's mind. She went back to her interview with Captain Raymond Matson, who'd said the problem with Flight 4990 was a "clear flight control computer malfunction."

"Chad Perkins, Starglide."

"Kate Page, Newslead. I'm calling for Starglide's response to the Heathrow crash."

"Of course, our thoughts go out to the families of those who were killed and injured. Air safety is our priority. Kate, we'll be issuing a full statement in about forty-five minutes."

"Any thoughts on what might have happened?"

"It's too early to speculate, but I assure you we'll cooperate fully with the investigation. Excuse me, I have other calls."

"Chad, one last question. Who's the maker of the fly-by-wire system installed in the Blue Wing?"

"That's a matter of public record."

"I know, but if you could confirm it."

"Richlon-Titan of California."

Kate sat up.

That's the same system as Flight 4990's.

She started writing fast, shaping her notes into a story to be inserted for updates on Newslead's Heathrow coverage. As she worked, she heard Chuck Laneer's voice, lifted her head and spotted him huddled across the newsroom with Reeka and Sloane.

Grabbing her notebook, Kate joined them just as Reeka was assuring Chuck that Newslead's London bureau had the crash well covered.

"Sloane's already checked and found it unlikely there's a link between Heathrow and the LaGuardia plane," Reeka said.

"Really?" Kate looked at Sloane. "You've confirmed that already, while the wreck is still burning? Before an investigation's even begun, you have the answer?"

"It's a different aircraft and different airline in London," Sloane said. "Most likely a coincidence. And, despite popular opinion, my sources and I are confident that the Buffalo incident was pilot error."

Kate shook her head.

"You know, Sloane, I just don't get why you're so quick to dismiss every unanswered aspect of these two cases," Kate said.

"Kate," Chuck said, "did you find anything, anything to add?"

"Yes. The NTSB is sending an investigative team to London."

"That's standard," Sloane said. "The Blue Wing's American-made."

"And—" ignoring him, Kate flipped pages of her notebook "—the flight-management system in the

Heathrow plane was made by Richlon-Titan. Both aircraft have the same system."

"You've confirmed this?" Reeka asked.

"Just now, on the record with Chad Perkins, Starglide's spokesperson in Atlanta. As you will recall, the captain of the Buffalo plane told us that he thought the problem was a system malfunction."

Chuck removed his glasses and stroked his chin.

"Remember," Kate said. "Our messenger warned of an incident if we didn't run a story crediting him for the EastCloud flight. We didn't run the story and now we have an incident with a plane that has the same flight-management system. Only now we have deaths. Chuck, we need to take a hard look at the Shikra flight."

Chuck folded his arms and tapped his glasses to his teeth.

"I don't want to gamble with this. I'll talk to Howard about alerting Heatley at the FBI. Kate, I want you on a plane to London as soon as possible."

Twenty-Two

Washington, DC

Robert Cole from North Dakota on hold for you, Jake. He says it's important.

Jake Hooper winced at the text message from reception, then texted his response.

Thanks. I'm tied up; tell him to leave a voice message.

For Hooper, the thought of Robert Cole always generated a wave of sadness—*such a tragic case*—but he returned to his notes as today's progress meeting on the investigation into Flight 4990 began.

This morning it was being run by Bill Cashill, the investigator-in-charge. All investigative team members were involved to assess progress, share key technical information and update recent findings.

"Evans—" Cashill kicked things off in his usual gruff way "—what d'you have on the ELMS?"

Drew Evans and his team oversaw examination of

the Electrical Load Management System, which distributed, monitored and protected electrical power to the aircraft. The system had the capability to record equipment failures and circuit faults going back some fifty flights.

"We're still reviewing all the fault logs."

"Did you find any anomalies?"

"Nothing so far."

Next, Cashill went to Scott Severs for an update on data. Severs was examining the quick access recorder, which kept track of far more information than the flight data and cockpit recorders. The QAR, as it was known, provided a comprehensive record of some fourteen hundred aspects of the aircraft, and it did so for a longer period of time.

"What's the QAR telling us, Severs?"

"Not a whole heck of a lot so far. We've looked at preflight, taxi and takeoff. All normal there. The initial climb was without incident. Autopilot and autothrottle presented no problems. While cruising, all systems functioned normally until the event began over the Catskills."

"That's when the safety features of the flight-management system were disabled," Cashill said, "and the captain took manual control of the aircraft."

"That's correct."

"Any indication of turbulence?" Cashill turned to Wendy Case, who handled weather systems.

"Nothing on radar and no flights in that sector within that window of time reported turbulence."

"Right, but we know that clear-air turbulence is not visible on radar."

Cashill turned to Irene Zimm.

"Irene, I understand you have an update. What can you tell us?"

"We've conducted more interviews. Roger Anderson, the first officer, is adamant he never saw Captain Matson disable the safety features and never commanded him to do so."

"Yet the record shows they were disabled," Cashill said. "Anything else?"

"In keeping with procedure, we reviewed crew phone records, conducted more interviews and studied crew activity seventy-two hours before the flight. One of the subjects we interviewed was Captain Matson's former wife. She indicated that less than twenty-four hours before the Buffalo–to–New York flight, she and Matson had several telephone conversations that she characterized as confrontational— that Matson was aggressive, agitated and despondent over their divorce, being separated from his children and the need to sell their house in New Jersey."

"This definitely puts his emotional state of mind into question," Cashill said. "I think we should consider Matson's psychological frame of mind a serious factor that warrants further investigation. What if, for a moment, Matson had decided to end his life, then changed his mind?"

"Hey." Gus Vitalley of the pilots' union pointed a finger at Cashill. "That's wild speculation. Our mandate is to consider only the facts."

"That's what we're doing, Gus. One by one we're ruling out what doesn't fit and compiling factors that do. It's a fact Matson's life was in crisis. It's a fact he was taking an antidepressant. It's a fact his divorce was being finalized. It's a fact he was not happy at that moment of his life."

"I think we're forgetting other factors," Hooper said.

Cashill stared at him. "Which are?"

"His denial of disabling the safety features of the flight-management system, which is backed up by the first officer. And now this claim that some outside force interfered with the aircraft."

Cashill waved Hooper's counterpoint off as if it were an annoyance.

"That threat is from a nut job," Cashill said. "First, there's no evidence to support it. Second, the FBI hasn't found anything of substance to it. Third, unlike what you see on TV or in movies and books, the flight-management system is secure against hacking, or cyber hijacking."

"Are we absolutely certain of that?" Hooper asked.

A knock sounded and Len Stelmach, a senior manager from the Major Investigations Division, entered.

"Bill, we've just received word of a crash at Heathrow. A Starglide Blue Wing 250, with two hundred eight people aboard, slammed into the ground just short of the runway. The Air Accidents Investigation Branch is requesting technical support from us. The chief recommends you go, Bill, along with Hooper and a few others. I'll send you the list."

Cashill made notes.

"Okay, Len, thanks." Cashill closed his binder, indicating the meeting had concluded. "Okay, people, we're done here. Keep going on Forty-nine Ninety and we'll reconvene when we get back."

"Excuse me, Len," Hooper said, "but do we know if there are fatalities?"

"At least nine, maybe more."

At his desk, Hooper sent his wife a text, letting her know that he had to get home, collect his bag and fly to London. As he set up his out-of-office email and voice mail, he accidentally heard the beginning of the message Robert Cole had left him.

"Jake, Jake, lishen, Jake, it's Cole zin in North Dakota. You hafta lishen…"

Hooper hung up. The sound of Cole's intoxicated voice filled him with sorrow, compounding the sadness over what awaited him in London.

As Hooper drove to Glover Park, he was haunted by what had happened to Robert Cole.

Bob had been a brilliant, legendary engineer who'd worked on Richlon-Titan's RTs, and had taken part in NTSB investigations over the years. Then there'd been the tragedy—that terrible accident, for which he blamed himself. He never overcame his guilt over the death of his wife.

It had broken him.

He'd lost his job, and had been reduced to being a delusional alcoholic who called the NTSB every time there was a crash or major incident with his views on the cause. He'd become a sad joke in aviation circles.

Hooper knew the man was trying to redeem himself.

It seemed like it was the only thing keeping him alive.

Twenty-Three

London, England

The British Airways 747 lifted off from JFK and the lights of greater New York City twinkled below.

As the big jet blasted upward, Kate's stomach fluttered, and she pressed her head back into her seat and blinked at the ceiling.

How long can I keep doing this?

It felt like her life was moving as fast as the jet. It was not that long ago when she'd overheard Flight 4990's dispatches on the emergency scanner and now she was bound for London at five hundred and fifty miles per hour. She'd already been working long days on this story but the look on Grace's face when she'd told her she had to leave had broken her heart.

Oh no, Mom, we're supposed to go to the zoo and the park.

I know, sweetie, but it's only for a few days. We'll go when I get back. I promise.

And then can we shop for my shoes?

Grace knew how to negotiate, especially since

she had leverage, given that Kate had been a pre-occupied, absent parent.

We'll see when I get back.

The jet climbed as Kate looked at her phone and traced her fingers over Grace's photo. In her years with Newslead, Kate had traveled on assignments across the United States, to Canada, Africa, Australia, the Caribbean and Europe. Being a reporter was in her DNA; it was who she was and how she'd made a life for herself. She was good at it. But the leaving part never got easier. In fact, it was getting harder and harder for her to take these trips. Kate was fortunate to have a friend like Nancy Clark, a retired nurse who lived alone on the floor above them. Nancy was like family, always ready and happy to look after Grace whenever she could. And now Kate had Vanessa.

I'm truly blessed to have them all in my life.

The jet leveled. Kate lowered her tray, switched on her laptop and reviewed her files. She began making notes on what she needed to do. One person she counted on for help was her friend Betty Yang. They'd worked together at the *San Francisco Star* before Betty had taken a job at the *Chronicle*, then moved to Kuwait, where she'd started a magazine for American expats living in the Gulf. Betty's father had been a diplomat. She'd grown up in the region and had a network of connections. Kate had kept in touch with Betty, and had reached out to her for help on the crash of the Kuwaiti jet at Heathrow.

But so far, she'd heard nothing.

Somewhere over Nova Scotia, Kate grew drowsy and yawned. The only available seat Newslead had been able to secure was on this later, overnight flight, which was due to land the next morning at 8:00 a.m. local time in London. Most passengers slept through it, and before they'd lifted off, Kate had swallowed two sleeping pills to ensure she'd be rested when she arrived.

The pills were working.

She shut off her laptop, snuggled under her blanket, gazed at the stars and fell asleep.

Kate was shaken awake.

The plane bumped like a pickup truck crossing a farmer's field. As wisps of memory assembled in her brain, a chime sounded.

"Ladies and gentlemen, this is your captain. Our apologies for this rough patch—we've come upon some turbulence in our descent into Heathrow. Please remain in your seats with your belts secure, and we'll endeavor to get around it. We should have you at the gate in thirty minutes' time."

Loud plastic creaking and crackling sounded from the overhead storage bins. The plane continued shaking and thudding. Some passengers gasped. Kate had no fear of flying but when she raised her window blind to the morning sun bathing the outskirts of London, she thought of the irony of her situation: a rough ride on a jetliner landing at the airport where one had crashed below—the very tragedy she was covering.

The turbulence ended some twenty minutes from landing and Kate watched the great city flow under her. As they began their approach for Heathrow's northern runway, which had remained open, the passengers became silent, almost reverent.

Runway 27L, the southern runway, was dotted with emergency vehicles; their lights flashed, and tarps covered the pieces of the Starglide Blue Wing 250 where Shikra Airlines Flight 418 had crashed. The impact tracks at the runway's threshold looked as if monstrous talons had clawed savagely into the earth to mark the tragedy.

Kate took a breath, let it out slowly and sat back in her seat as the 747 touched down to light applause for its soft, easy landing.

At Heathrow, a young British customs officer allowed Kate smooth entry into the country. She collected her bag and freshened up in a restroom. On her way to the transportation area, she passed a newsstand and the headlines of some of Britain's major national papers. The *Telegraph*: "Death Toll Rises to 15. What Caused Heathrow Tragedy?" *The Times*: "Heathrow Toll Now at 15 Dead. Investigation Searches for Answers." And the *Daily Mail*: "Why Did They Die? 15 Killed in Kuwait Air Disaster at Heathrow."

The dire reports conveyed the magnitude of the story, and once Kate was in a taxi bound for downtown, she began working. She got on her phone, but was disappointed that she'd received no new messages of any significance.

Nothing yet from Betty.

A couple months ago, Kate had helped Betty on a big United Nations scandal involving a Kuwaiti diplomat by tracking him down and privately sharing information with her.

Come on, girl. I need your help, you owe me.

As London rolled by, her stomach knotted from the pressure she was under. She had to go beyond what was already known, to answer the most serious question.

Is the crash at Heathrow tied to the Buffalo flight and the threatening email?

The assignment was not easy.

How am I going to get inside the investigation?

Kate would need help and getting it would be a challenge. As was the case with foreign assignments, journalists at local bureaus were protective of their turf. While they may help, they considered intrusions by people like Kate, parachuted in from headquarters, an affront to their expertise and performance.

Kate sent out more messages, including one to Clive Dromey, a British security consultant and former airline pilot she'd met at a conference in Washington, DC. She'd been in touch with Dromey before she'd left New York. He'd responded to her with the promise that he had solid sources inside the investigation.

Contact me when you get to London, Kate. I'll help you.

But Dromey still hadn't gotten back to her. She began following up on other messages and calls she'd placed to other contacts before she'd departed New York.

It took a little under an hour to slice through London's morning traffic and get to Newslead's London bureau on Norwich Street.

It was situated in a granite building constructed

on the site of a hat factory that had been destroyed by Nazi bombs during the Second World War. It was a short walk from Fleet Street, now the address of more financial, business and law offices than news organizations. But Bloomberg, the Associated Press and other foreign wire services were close to Newslead's bureau, reminding Kate that the competition was always near and that the risk of losing the story increased as time ticked by.

Newslead's fourth-floor office was classic newsroom décor, largely open with eight desks, each with a monitor and keyboard. It looked empty. Each station was in disarray, with files, newspapers and empty coffee and tea cups. Three large flat-screen TVs were anchored to the far wall and tuned to news channels.

The wall near the reception desk featured enlarged news photos of London during World War Two, royal weddings, Princess Diana's funeral, Beatlemania, the London subway bombings and others.

The woman at reception was tapping her pen and talking on the phone. She halted her conversation when Kate stood before her.

"Yes, how may I assist you?"

"Kate Page from headquarters in New York. I'm here to see the bureau chief, Noah Heatley, or the deputy, Ethan Clancy."

"Oh yes, just one moment, please."

The woman left for a small office and Kate set her bags aside. A moment later a man in his forties, not very tall, average build, stepped forward and shook her hand.

"Noah Heatley. Welcome to London, Kate. Howard Kehoe and Chuck Laneer advised us that you were coming. I trust you had a good flight?"

"A bit of turbulence, but otherwise fine. Have there been any developments?"

"Not much I'm afraid, though we're expecting official statements of condolences from the prime minister and from the State of Kuwait."

Kate nodded. "Noah, I was told that you'd have a hotel room, cash and other things for me?"

"All arranged, but let me be clear, Kate. We didn't request help, and we have things covered on all fronts. As you know, the Air Accidents Investigation Branch, Scotland Yard, the anti-terrorism branch, the International Civil Aviation Organization, the airline, and foreign investigators from Kuwait and the US are all extremely tight-lipped."

"I know."

"But most major UK national news outlets are based here in London, making this one of the most competitive cities for news on the planet, and everyone has their sources."

"I'm aware."

"Yet you're here from New York. Chuck Laneer was not entirely clear what it is you're going to do that we can't."

"I'm following a lead we have based on extremely confidential information."

"Is this the so-called Zarathustra email you'd received?"

Kate hesitated and stared at Heatley.

"Yes, but headquarters had wanted this kept quiet."

"Reeka Beck told me—let it slip on a call, actually," Heatley said. "I have to say, that New York would attempt to keep us in the dark about information related to one of the biggest air tragedies in the world is confounding."

"I'm sorry, Noah."

"It makes no sense at all. If we're unaware, we could miss key facts that relate to the story. I'm puzzled by management's thinking. These internecine wars don't help morale."

"I know, but that's how Graham Lincoln wanted it."

"Graham Lincoln." Heatley shook his head. "Most of Newslead's executives have never been journalists, a fact I find troubling. I think our news agency is due for an overhaul, wouldn't you agree?"

"Absolutely."

"Well, so be it. We'll still help you in any way we can, Kate."

"Thank you."

Heatley searched the top of the reception desk, found an envelope with Kate's name on it and passed it to her.

"My apologies. Your hotel is not as close to the bureau as we'd hoped, but they have us watching expenses."

"Thank you." Kate put the envelope into her bag.

"Call us if there's anything we can do," Heatley said. "Good luck."

Kate caught a taxi at the street corner.

She was frustrated that no one had responded to her messages and continued making calls until her taxi reached her stop. The Regal Oakmont Inn was a townhome hotel, a four-level building attached to other four-level buildings that, together, resembled pretty wedding-cake layers where Penywern Road led to the gentle curves of Eardley Crescent.

Kate's room was no bigger than a closet. It was on the third floor, overlooking the street. She turned on her laptop and sent out more messages. Then she showered. Afterward, as she unpacked, her anxiety began to grow with her exhaustion, just as her phone chimed with a message. Her spirits rose. It was from Clive Dromey.

This could be the break I need.

Kate. Welcome to London. Hope your flight was uneventful. Unfortunately I must apologize. Everyone involved in the Heathrow crash is understandably silent. None of my people will talk to me. I'm so dreadfully sorry but I'm unable to help you.

Kate's stomach tightened.

She refused to give up.

Again, she called the Air Accidents Investigation Branch, and this time she was put through to a recording at the press office. She called Scotland Yard and got through to the anti-terrorism branch, but they had nothing to share. She called Shikra Airlines and was read a statement she already had. She called the International Civil Aviation Organization to no avail.

Three hours had passed.

Exhaustion was taking hold and the trip began to smell like failure. Struggling to think of anything she'd overlooked, Kate drifted off. She didn't know for how long she'd slept when her phone rang and she answered.

"Kate, it's Betty in Kuwait City."

"Oh my God! I'm so happy to hear your voice! Betty, can you help me?"

"I think so."

Twenty-Four

The graceful curved-glass facade of the St. Rose's Gate Hotel reflected the sky and a jetliner lifting off when Kate's taxi stopped at the entrance.

St. Rose's was among the new airport hotels clustered around Heathrow. The front driveway was hectic with shuttles, taxis and buses for travelers coming and going. Kate scanned the parking lot, relieved she didn't see any news vehicles.

I need this to work. This is my only shot.

Betty had told her that engineers from Shikra Airlines and experts from Kuwait's Aviation Safety Department, the ASD, who were part of the investigation into the crash, were staying at St. Rose's. Betty, apologetic for taking so long to get back to Kate, had arranged for one of ASD's investigators to meet Kate privately.

His name is Talal Nasser. He's a friend of mine, Betty had said. *I had to set this up. That's why it took so long to get back to you.*

Thanks, Betty. You're a lifesaver.

I owe you big-time for helping me, Kate. Good luck.

The reception area opened to an inner atrium overlooking a courtyard garden and waterfall. The Kuwaitis were gathered in one of the hotel's fifty meeting rooms, but Betty had instructed Kate to be alone at the bar in the Seven Seas Lounge at 3:00 p.m. to wait for Nasser. Betty had sent him a picture of Kate and he would find her.

Kate was fifteen minutes early. She ordered a Coke and checked her phone for new messages. She had two. The first was from Chuck in New York, where it was midmorning.

How's it going?

I've got a possible lead.

Good, keep us posted.

The second message was from Reeka.

Have you got anything for today for me to list on the story schedule?

Give me a break, Reeka.
Shaking her head, Kate bit her bottom lip as she typed.

Not yet but I'm working on it.

Kate began reading the latest online reports on the crash. Not much new had surfaced in the British press, and nothing from the Associated Press, Reuters or Bloomberg had linked it to EastCloud.

Kate went back to the warning message.

Your story's good, but it's wrong. What happened to that jet will happen again. I know because I made it happen and unless you announce my triumph, we'll make it happen again. This time it'll be worse. Watch the skies. We are Zarathustra, Lord of the Heavens.

Again, Kate began weighing the factors of the EastCloud flight and the tragedy at Heathrow when a man approached her at the bar. She guessed him to be in his late forties. He had a neatly trimmed beard that accentuated his dark eyes. He was above-average height and wore a well-cut suit that flattered his build. He had a leather-bound binder tucked under one arm.

"Excuse me, are you Kate Page?"

"Yes, I'm Kate Page."

"Talal Nasser. We have a mutual friend who suggested I talk with you."

"Yes. Thank you for meeting with me."

"Perhaps we'd be more comfortable over there." He nodded to a booth that had just become available. Kate reached into her bag to pay her tab. "I've taken care of it," Nasser said.

"Thank you."

A moment after they were seated a server appeared.

"Would you like another drink?" Nasser asked.

"Sure." Then to the server, "I'll have another Coke, please."

Nasser ordered water. When they were alone they

exchanged business cards. He studied Kate's briefly before slipping it inside his pocket.

"I'm here as a courtesy to Betty," he said. "My father's one of Kuwait's more progressive businessmen. She wrote a nice story on him, and my family considers her a very good friend."

"I understand." Kate glanced at his card. "You're a lead technician with the ASD?"

"That's correct, and in meeting with you, I'm violating the protocol for air-accident investigation. Therefore you must never use my name or any information that might identify me. This is strictly confidential."

"Agreed."

Nasser glanced at his watch.

"I'm afraid I have little time. We're meeting at AAIB headquarters with the NTSB and other officials, so we should come to the point."

"May I take notes?"

Nasser nodded.

"What do you suspect is the cause?"

"We're too early into the investigation to know. The crew is in stable condition in the hospital. The AAIB recovered the flight data recorder yesterday."

"Did you listen to it?"

Nasser nodded.

"Does it give you an indication?"

"It might point to a systems issue or it could be a human factor. It's too soon."

"Are you aware of a recent incident with EastCloud Flight Forty-nine Ninety from Buffalo to New York City?"

"Yes."

"It was a Richlon-Titan aircraft with the same fly-by-wire system as the Shikra Blue Wing."

"We're aware."

"Will you be looking for a link?"

He hesitated for a moment, rubbing his chin in concentration.

Kate remained silent, waiting for him to answer.

"I shouldn't tell you this," he said.

Tell me, Kate thought. *Tell me.*

Nasser looked as if he was reappraising her.

"Betty spoke highly of you. She said you could be trusted to be responsible with sensitive information."

Kate nodded, inviting him to continue.

"You're aware," he said, "that the International Civil Aviation Organization encourages countries to share risk advisories and information about threats?"

"Yes, I picked that up in my research."

"Recently, there was a threat against an aircraft."

"You're talking about the threat I received at Newslead?"

"We've been advised of that, through the ICAO and the NTSB, but no, I'm talking about a threat that came to us."

"What?"

"Our embassy here in London received an anonymous email suggesting unspecified harm to an aircraft."

Kate froze. This was huge.

"Was the Shikra flight targeted?" she asked. "Were there any demands? Can you share a copy?"

"Hold on, please."

"Was it from Zarathustra? Do you have the details?"

"No, I didn't see it. I was only briefed on it."

"Was it sent before or after the crash?"

"I believe it was after. But I'm not clear on that."

"Can you get a copy and share it with me?"

"I don't think that's possible." He glanced at his watch. "I know it was with Kuwaiti security, who were assessing its credibility with British authorities and the FBI."

"Do they have any suspects?"

"No, we've not heard anything like that."

"Isn't the airline industry concerned? Shouldn't you be taking some sort of action or warning the public?"

"We take these matters most seriously—safety is our top priority. But allow me to give you some context. I'm told that the email we received was vague, with no specific details. This kind of threat is not uncommon. Whenever we have details in these matters, such as an implied action against a specific flight, or information that could make a threat more credible, then we take immediate action by alerting the public and investigating. If needed, we'll ground a fleet or halt operations, but that's a major undertaking."

"But you cannot rule out the possibility that the two emails are linked and that someone may have caused the problems to both flights?"

"That's a dangerous, hypothetical leap, Ms. Page."

"But you can't rule it out, can you?"

"No, at this stage, nothing can be ruled out." Nasser leaned forward. "I shared this information with you as background with context. I'm being forthright out of respect for our mutual friend who assured me you could be trusted to handle information with the appropriate sensitivity."

"Of course."

"We have fifteen deaths and nearly one hundred injured passengers and crew. Let me emphasize to you that our responsibility as investigators is to determine what caused this disaster. To do so we'll focus on indisputable evidence, not speculation and wild claims." He held Kate in his gaze until it was nearly uncomfortable, then shook her hand. "A pleasure to meet you. Now, if you'll excuse me, I must leave."

For several moments after Talal Nasser left, Kate sat quietly, digesting the enormity of what had just been revealed to her.

She had just landed one of the biggest stories in the world.

After ordering a coffee, she collected her thoughts, then began writing an exclusive on the link between the tragedy of Shikra Airlines Flight 418 in London and the terrifying EastCloud flight in New York. To protect Nasser, she was careful to leave out references to sources connected to Kuwait, or specifics about an email.

Investigators are assessing the emergence of a thread common to both ill-fated flights, Newslead has learned...

Kate then pulled in all the current background, public, on-the-record statements from the airlines and investigative agencies. Upon completing her piece, she sent it to New York.

"Here is good," Kate told her cabdriver.

Shops and businesses stood on both sides of the street of the commercial section, a few blocks from Kate's hotel in Earls Court.

It was late afternoon as she returned from meeting Nasser. She was hungry and pumped about her story, but a bit concerned.

Why am I not getting any feedback on it from New York?

She entered the Six Bells Pub, let her eyes adjust to the dim light and found a small booth. After ordering fish and chips and a Coke, she took in the two large TV screens above the bar. One was tuned to soccer, the other to a news channel. Kate checked her phone; still nothing from Newslead, so she texted Grace.

Miss you like crazy, sweetie.

She then sent messages to Vanessa and Nancy just before her order arrived. The plate was heaping, the food was good, and she'd managed to eat half when her phone rang with a call from Chuck Laneer.

"Great story, Kate, but we can't use it."

"Why not?"

"We're not there yet."

"What do you mean, 'We're not there yet'? We have the link. It's why you sent me here. Chuck, it's a world exclusive."

"I know, but we have to nail it down. We need on-the-record confirmation on the link."

"But we *can* confirm this. We received the first email. We know that's a fact. We know both jets have the same RT fly-by-wire systems and I trust my source on the threat the Kuwaitis received."

"Do you? Did you see that email?"

"No."

"Do you know exactly what it says? Do you know what language it's written in?"

"No."

"Then how do you know it exists?"

She had nothing to say. Chuck was right.

"Kate," he said, "we need to be on the money. We can't be wrong with so much at stake. Remember your journalism history. News outlets thought they'd identified the Boston bombers and they were wrong. One of the networks based a story critical of President Bush's military service on false records someone supplied them and they were wrong. The press identified a security guard as the Atlanta Olympic bomber, and they were wrong. Before that, Chicago news agencies identified a Middle Eastern man as the suspect in the Oklahoma City bombing and they were wrong. We cannot risk damaging our credibility on what is a global story."

Silence passed between them.

"Kate, you've done good work. I'll weave some of your story with the copy we've got coming out of London and give you a byline. But we're not touching the link until you have it nailed. You're on the right track. You just need to take it the rest of the way. All right?"

She didn't respond, her disappointment registering in the silence.

"All right, Kate?" Chuck repeated.

"Sure."

After the call, defeat and fatigue washed over her. To tend to her despair, she moved to the bar, ordered a tea and stared at the TV. For the next few hours, as the bar filled, she struggled to rescue her work. She put in a call to Nick Varner at the FBI and got his voice mail, but didn't leave a message. She texted him but he didn't respond.

Soon she saw the Newslead stories filed from London, including one with her byline. It was straightforward with nothing about the link, and she felt another stab of failure.

"Allo, what's this?" A red-faced man in about his late forties, thick curly hair mussed, tied loosened, a beer in his hand, stood next to Kate, smiling. "Aye been watching you. You're lookin' dreadfully forlorn for such a pretty bird. My name's Dick. Can I be of service?"

Kate looked at him and grinned.

"Why yes, Dick, you can."

"You name it. Anything you want, luv." He smiled back.

"I want you to piss off."

Dick's smile vanished. He turned, cursing her as he staggered off.

Kate shook her head and stared at the TV. News reports showed footage of victims of the Heathrow crash in body bags, or covered with tarps, then cut to relatives in London and Kuwait. The agony in their faces was unbearable.

Never, ever, forget what this is really about.

Kate whispered a prayer for them, paid her bill and left.

The sun had set but it was not yet full night as she walked to her hotel. Parked cars lined the quiet street. At one point a shout echoed, and Kate turned, thinking she saw a distant shadow behind her.

Is it that drunk from the bar?

She reached into her bag and checked the address for her hotel. It wasn't far. She crossed the street between parked cars and picked up her pace. She felt relieved a few minutes later when she entered the lobby and took the elevator to her floor.

That was crazy.

She was tired and began to undress for bed when a tiny knot of unease tightened in her stomach.

That's strange.

Earlier, she'd unpacked a sweater and set it on the seat of the desk chair, atop a file folder that held story clips and NTSB reports. Now the sweater was draped over the chair's backrest and the pages were peeking from the folder.

I don't remember doing that.

She looked at her suitcase in the corner. It had been moved slightly, as well.

That's not how I left it.

She blinked, thinking back to the moment before she'd left the room for her meeting at Heathrow. Something was amiss. Seconds later the phone was in her hand.

"Front desk, how may I assist you?"

"Kate Page in three twenty. Was there service in my room today?"

Kate heard the clicking of a keyboard.

"Checking for you… Nothing showing. Do you require service?"

"No, thanks. But can you tell me if anyone was in my room? Maintenance? Any staff for any reason?"

More clicking on the keyboard, then the clerk said, "One moment." Kate was put on hold to Elton John singing "Tiny Dancer." Then the clerk came back. "We have no indication that anyone was in your room. Is there a problem, Ms. Page?"

Kate hesitated.

"No. Thank you."

Exhaustion from the flight, as well as the stresses and challenges of the story, pushed down hard on her as she got undressed.

Maybe it's all in my head?

She reached for her phone, looked at news footage of the Shikra crash, then fell asleep with questions unanswered and mysteries unresolved.

Twenty-Five

Deep inside the FBI's New York Field Office at 26 Federal Plaza in Lower Manhattan, Special Agent Nick Varner headed for the Cyber Crimes floor with guilt flickering in the back of his mind.

He hated that he had to ignore the latest plea for help from Kate Page, especially since he'd invited her to keep him posted on matters concerning the Zarathustra threat.

Sorry, Kate, I just can't get back to you right now.

Varner closed her most recent message on his phone and studied other information. The cyber team had not yet identified the source of the Zarathustra email. He was concerned because by this time, in the majority of cases, the FBI's cyber experts would have yielded the information needed to provide a suspect, a physical address, a warrant and an arrest.

They had nothing like that so far.

But are they close? That's what I need to know.

Varner's concern had mounted since he'd been

advised of the email the Kuwaitis had received shortly after the Shikra crash in London.

He read it again on his phone.

Sorrow and pain for one of your planes –Z

It lacked details. It was written in Kuwaiti Arabic but signed with a plain *Z* and it had been sent to a general public email comment box at the Kuwaiti Embassy in London some twenty-four hours after the crash. The *Z*—it could represent "Zarathustra." In the wake of the Shikra crash, Kuwaiti intelligence had shared it with Scotland Yard and the UK's National Crime Agency, and the FBI through its legal attachés at the US Embassies in London and Kuwait City. Investigators were working on determining the source, its credibility and any connection to the previous threat.

Varner stepped off the elevator into rows of white-topped desks that took up half the floor. Each was occupied with agents and cyber experts working nonstop on analyzing every type of suspected cyber activity imaginable.

Ron Sanchez's face was bathed in the blue glow of the monitors at his desk, a portrait of sober concentration as he worked. The top button of his crisp white shirt was undone; his tie was loosened.

"Got anything for me?" Varner said.

Sanchez reached for his ceramic coffee mug and sipped from it without pulling his eyes from the three monitors at his station. He shook his head slowly.

"What do you make of the Kuwaiti email, Ron?"

"We've got Paplinksi and Wong on it and they're in touch with the Brits and Kuwaitis."

"Great. So where are we with Zarathustra?"

Sanchez's shoulders rose as he inhaled, let his breath out slowly and turned to Varner.

"The sender of the email is using onion router technology. That is, they're attempting to ensure secrecy by randomly routing the message through a multitude of places online, wrapped in layer upon layer of encryption."

"We know that pattern's been used before."

"It's standard on the Darknet, but in this case it looks like they may have custom-built their own software and written their own codes to create even more layers, possibly hundreds, that result in even more encrypted connections through relays on any given network."

"So a little different than a run-of-the-mill hacker?"

"Yes, more sophisticated. And they're using hidden servers."

"Isn't that how the child porn industry does it? And we've defeated them and tracked people down."

"Correct, but what may be at work here is people who're using off-the-grid servers, or servers that may be rented through third and fourth parties. Those servers could be anywhere—Latvia, Thailand, Romania, anywhere. Remember your basics, Nick. Our suspect pool is anybody with a computer and access to the internet."

"So where are we, Ron?"

"We're pulling in help from the National Cyber Investigative Joint Task Force. We're hoping the Department of Defense, the CIA and the NSA might be able to give us a hand."

"So we don't yet have any names, any addresses, or anything for the foundation of a warrant?"

Sanchez shook his head.

"Ron, if they're that good with email, do you think they have the skill to hack into a flight system and take control of a jetliner?"

"It's our job to find out," Sanchez said. "Look, Nick, I'm not going to sugarcoat this—whoever is behind the Zarathustra email is very smart and very good."

Twenty-Six

At the site on Mesa Mota Mountain, the young American tourist Veyda Hyde shaded her eyes and took in the sweeping view of the city below, the airport and the Atlantic Ocean.

Breezes with a hint of sea salt rolled up the mountainside and lifted strands of her hair.

"It's so glorious up here, so tranquil."

"Calming, almost spiritual. As it should be." Seth, her boyfriend, turned to photograph the monument again. The couple was traveling with a local sightseeing bus, and the memorial on Mesa Mota was its most solemn stop. Seth marveled at the structure, a modern piece of artwork depicting a towering spiral staircase that ascended sixty feet, representing the connection between the earth and the sky.

The memorial plaque at its base said that it was erected in memory of the people killed in the aircraft accident at the Los Rodeos Airport below, where, in 1977, two 747 jumbo jets collided in the world's worst aviation accident. Veyda and Seth were familiar with the history. Events leading up to the tragedy had unfolded when a bomb planted by a separatist terror group had exploded at Gran Canaria Airport on a nearby island. It had forced the diversion of a number of large international jetliners to the smaller Los Rodeos Airport at Tenerife. A sudden fog had enshrouded the area, reducing visibility as an airliner from Los Angeles taxied and another from Amsterdam prepared to lift off on the same runway. The poor weather and problematic radio communications with the air traffic control tower resulted in the two jets colliding on the runway, killing 583 people.

Veyda and Seth had joined the other tourists, studying the plaque, running their fingers over it, then touching the staircase and admiring the memorial wreathes, some of which were in various stages of decay.

Veyda covered a yawn with her hand.

Their pilgrimage to Tenerife was the latest among several others they'd made.

In recent weeks, they'd traveled to Japan, where they'd visited the site of the world's second-worst aviation disaster, that of Japan Airlines Flight 123.

The aircraft, a 747 jumbo jet, was doomed some ten minutes after the plane had lifted off from Tokyo International Airport for Osaka, when the rear pressure bulkhead tore open due to a maintenance error. The incident had ruptured the hydraulic lines and led to the failure of the vertical stabilizer, making the plane impossible to control. The jet stayed aloft for half an hour before it crashed into Mount Takamagahara, some sixty miles northeast of Tokyo, killing 520 people.

As part of their pilgrimage to Japan, Veyda and Seth had rented a car and navigated their way to the village of Ueno-mura in Gunma Prefecture. Then they'd trekked to Osutaka, the mountainous crash site. There, they'd observed the memorial stone, the bell and the religious statue representing mercy. They'd also taken in the metal-wood-and-stone memorial posts that had been erected by victims' families. The structures held the remains of those victims. Veyda had crouched for a closer look at the photographs, toys and notes families had left at the posts.

Afterward, they'd gone to Tokyo International Airport and visited the Safety Promotion Center, which housed a memorial to the tragedy. It displayed pieces of the wreckage and a history of events leading up to the accident. From the moment the bulkhead tore open, sealing the flight's fate, it had remained airborne for half an hour before it crashed, giving some passengers time to write final messages to their families.

These were respectfully presented for viewing at the memorial.

"I don't think we will survive. Thank you for a good life," one note had read, while another passenger had written, "Always take care of each other. I'll always love you. Please don't forget me."

Tears had rolled down Veyda's face as she'd read more notes.

She was intimate with loss.

After their visit to Japan, Veyda and Seth had

flown to India and made their way to the location of the world's third-worst air accident—in 1996, a Kazakhstan Airlines Ilyushin Il-76 had struck a Saudi Arabian Airlines 747.

The Kazakh charter flight, with twenty-seven passengers and ten crew, had originated in Kazakhstan. It had been on its descent to Delhi's Indira Gandhi International Airport where the Saudi jumbo jet, with 289 passengers and twenty-three crew, had departed for Dhahran, Saudi Arabia. The Kazakh jet had wrongly descended lower than its assigned altitude and had collided midair with the Saudi plane, killing 349 people.

Wreckage had fallen from the skies to the fields below, nearly one hundred miles west of Delhi. Pieces of the charter jet had scattered near the village of Birohar, while remains of the Saudi 747 had fallen to the earth near the village of Charkhi Dadri. Enduring the heat, Veyda and Seth had walked among the fields where debris and bodies had rained down from the heavens.

They were aware that upon recovering the cockpit voice recorder from the Saudi plane, investigators had learned that the pilots had recited the Islamic prayer for believers when they face death.

Veyda was well acquainted with death.

She felt a deep, spiritual connection to the disaster sites in Japan, India and the Canary Islands, and was glad that she and Seth had seen them, *felt them, breathed them*, firsthand.

I need to bear witness to what we're doing.

She tugged at Seth and they stepped away from the Tenerife memorial at Mesa Mota to be alone.

While Seth took pictures, Veyda checked her phone. She took a fast look at Newslead's stories on East-Cloud Flight 4990, and then reviewed Newslead's stories filed from London on the Shikra Airlines tragedy.

"Have you read them, Seth?"

"I have. I'm disappointed, because she's by far the best."

"Still nothing, nothing showing reverence to Zarathustra." Veyda shook her head. "Does this Kate Page realize the gravity of her failure?"

"Perhaps she needs to be enlightened?"

"This entire sad world needs to be enlightened."

Veyda tapped her phone to her chin as she took in the airport below, her face stone-cold behind her dark glasses.

"What happened on this island was a tragedy," she said.

"An epic tragedy. A record number of deaths."

"Records are made to be broken."

Twenty-Seven

Farnborough, England

Shikra Airlines Flight 418's right wing disintegrated and the landing gear ripped away as the jet piled into the ground, scraping, lifting, cartwheeling, breaking into pieces, spilling passengers, catching fire.

Jittery footage of the crash had been captured by an amateur plane spotter, perched outside the perimeter of Heathrow's southern runway.

Jake Hooper made notes as the video was replayed several times in slow motion by an engineer with the Air Accidents Investigation Branch. Hooper was among the investigators gathered at the AAIB's headquarters, located amid lush woodland at Farnborough Airport, a forty-five minute drive southwest of London.

In keeping with international agreements, Hooper, Bill Cashill and other American experts, along with a contingent from Kuwait's Aviation Safety Department and Shikra Airlines, were there to support the British investigation of Shikra Flight 418, which had crashed after its engines had shut down.

The people around the table viewed the tragedy on the flat-screen that covered one wall. The silence that fell over the room was broken by the flipping of pages and the impatient tapping of Bill Cashill's pen.

"All right, colleagues, shall we continue, then?"

A slide presentation on the crash replaced the video on the screen as Evan Taylor, a lead AAIB engineer, continued. The AAIB's overview included a timeline, the aircraft's flight history, summaries of the readouts from 418's flight data recorder and transcripts from the cockpit voice recorder, as well as the email sent to the Kuwaiti Embassy in London.

"Of course this is all unverified," Taylor said. "We've yet to interview the crew, who are in serious but stable condition in hospital. You all have copies of the currently available information in your folders. Let's go through it, shall we?"

The group studied every aspect of the preliminary data, looking for the key piece to point them to the cause. Hooper examined factors like the automatic flight control system, autopilot engagement and disengagement, all cockpit flight control input, the control wheel, control column and rudder pedal, and the computer failure indicator.

Other investigators concentrated on the performance of the crew. But they found nothing noteworthy on that front. All crew members were experienced with exemplary records. Blood testing showed no indication of drugs or alcohol. The crew was rested before the flight.

Nothing had emerged as a potential preliminary

explanation of the jet's sudden shutdown of its engines. No reports of wind gusts, no early evidence of a bird strike; a simultaneous dual-engine failure was highly unlikely. Investigators scrutinized readouts for the power plants, and key factors such as fuel levels, fuel pumps and fuel flow. No problems had surfaced, and no evidence had emerged pointing to a system failure or malfunction of the aircraft's digital fly-by-wire system, an extraordinarily complex control system built by Richlon-Titan.

After several hours of intense work by the group, Taylor opened up the meeting and encouraged brainstorming on possible causes.

"We believe we must give serious consideration to the email received by our Embassy in London," said Waleed Al-Rashid, lead engineer for Shikra Airlines.

"Why?" Bill Cashill's head snapped up.

"We think it is a factor, this anonymous communication." Al-Rashid read from the page: "'Sorrow and pain for one of your planes —Z.' We cannot rule out the possibility that somehow, someone interfered with the operation of the aircraft."

"I think you're grasping at straws," Cashill said. "We've seen nothing to give this claim an ounce of weight, given it came after the incident."

"But Mr. Cashill," Al-Rashid said, "the message is signed clearly with an English letter, *Z*. It is our understanding that American authorities also received a similar email concerning the incident with EastCloud Airlines Flight Forty-nine Ninety, the so-called Zarathustra email. Given that both flights involve aircraft with Richlon-Titan flight systems,

I think we have a commonality worth considering, an avenue of investigation worth pursuing, wouldn't you agree?"

Hooper saw Cashill's jaw muscles bunching.

"Absolutely not!" Cashill said. "Everyone in this room is aware that the air industry receives groundless 'threats' daily, both in-flight and on the ground. And in ninety-nine percent of cases, they are unsubstantiated. Make no mistake, I'm not being cavalier about this. Yes, the FBI, British officials and your own security authorities are investigating both emails but so far, to our knowledge, they've found nothing concrete. If they had, they'd be leading both of our investigations right now."

"Mr. Cashill, I point you to line one twenty-three and those that follow in the transcript—the conversation between Captain Fahad Al-Anjari and copilot, Khalid Marafi, the line starting with Marafi." Everyone turned to the transcript and read.

Copilot: "We've got a double engine failure! The engines have been switched off!"
Captain: "Switched off? How? We didn't do that! Try restarting!"

"My concern," Al-Rashid said, "is that aspect about the switching off of the engines—specifically when the captain says, 'We didn't do that.' This might point to a problem linked to the threat."

Cashill stabbed the table with the end of his pen.

"This is nothing but a distraction. Look, our preliminary review of EastCloud points to clear-air turbulence and a pilot disabling the flight-management's safety features to deal with it, resulting in the over-control of the aircraft. The pilot had an antidepressant in his blood and was embroiled in a personal family crisis at the time of the flight. Those are facts, and an absurd claim by Zarathustra, Lord of the Heavens, to a reporter in an email has no bearing on them."

"But, sir—" Al-Rashid said.

"Let me finish. These emails are a distraction diverting us from the real facts here with your airline. And let's be candid, your maintenance history with this plane has been sloppy. For starters…" Cashill tapped his pen to the table to underscore each point. "Tools left in the aircraft. Rivets improperly replaced in the underbelly. Maintenance logs incomplete. And the topper here everyone seems to have missed—improper replacement parts used in the flight-management electrical system."

"Mr. Cashill, without question, we—" Al-Rashid nodded to the other Kuwaiti experts "—accept and acknowledge your observations. However, my point, in relation to the two emails, is we must take into account the history of assertions by cyber experts that the computer systems used by new commercial jetliners can be hacked."

Cashill shook his head.

"We've all been over this a hundred times. Those claims have been knocked down before by the NTSB, the FAA, the AAIB, the International Civil Aviation Organization, the European Aviation Safety Agency and many others, because it's not possible to wirelessly interfere with flight-certified hardware. And we know the Richlon-Titan system has safety features that can be manually disabled, allowing the crew to manually direct the aircraft to perform beyond programmed safety limits. However, that system has some half a dozen safeguards to protect against a system failure, the loss of electrical power, or the malfunction of any of the onboard computers, which run on a stand-alone network. They can't be hacked. We really need to move on here."

In the tense moment that passed, investigators made notes or studied pages from their folders.

"Thank you, Bill and Waleed, for the informative debate. I think all points have to be considered as we move forward," Taylor said.

The AAIB engineers turned to the topic of engines. As they debated theories, Hooper could not silence the alarm ringing in a back corner of his mind because he agreed one hundred percent with the Kuwaitis.

The threats raise real concerns.

And Hooper couldn't dismiss them. With both the Shikra and EastCloud flights there had been a sudden malfunction and a sudden failure. In both cases, they appeared to have surprised the crew.

That formed the basis of a disturbing pattern.

Was it interference?

Hooper flipped through his folder, and began drawing circles on his pad, something he did as he fell into a deep thought.

What if, just for a moment, we consider that somehow, somewhere, someone discovered a point of vulnerability in Richlon-Titan's fly-by-wire system? What if they found a wireless jump point or a back door into the system? Was it possible to over-

ride the plane's security software and gain access to the flight-critical system?

Hooper felt a chill coil up his spine.

What if it is possible?

Twenty-Eight

Old men played Chinese chess at the tables of Columbus Park in Manhattan's Chinatown while not far off, a group of senior citizens practiced Tai Chi.

Strategy and strength. That's what I need.

As Kate watched, she felt her story slipping away.

It had been two days since she'd returned from London. In that time, she'd reconnected with her family, giving Grace, Vanessa and Nancy the souvenirs she'd bought for them in England. Kate had kept her promise and had taken Grace shopping for her new pink shoes.

Wait 'til Amber sees these! Thank you, Mommy! Thank you!

But with each passing moment since she'd got back, the story spun through Kate's subconscious. Gut instinct told her that the London tragedy, the EastCloud flight and the Zarathustra email were connected. But she couldn't go with the story until she could get an official to acknowledge it.

Or could prove it herself.

Chuck was right to demand on-the-record confirmation. Given the magnitude of the story, more was at stake than Newslead's credibility. The impact it would have on the airline industry would be huge. It was clear to Kate that Newslead could not risk anything short of an airtight item.

But since London, she was getting nowhere, and her frustration was growing, a problem exacerbated after her encounters in the newsroom this morning—first, with Sloane.

"Welcome back, Kate. Read your stuff out of London. Looks like your jaunt there was a bust," he'd said. "It's like I told you, there's no link between Heathrow and the LaGuardia plane. Different aircraft and different airline. Just a tragic coincidence."

"On what grounds do you come to that conclusion?"

"My sources in the industry and my read of things," he said. "Look, now the British tabloids are reporting that Shikra Airlines had a history of maintenance issues with its doomed jet."

"So? That's speculation."

"And let's face it, it looks more and more like that Buffalo incident was pilot error and your fan mail was from a whack job."

"What I don't get, Sloane, is why you're so quick to dismiss these events."

Before he answered, Reeka approached them and addressed Kate.

"I'm going to talk to Chuck. If your airline story's fizzled I'm going to give you other assignments. We can't be wasting time and resources."

Fortunately, Chuck had come over, picked up the tail end of Reeka's comment and intervened.

"I think we need to keep Kate on this. We're a long way from folding the tent on this one."

When Reeka left, Chuck turned to Kate and said, "You've done good work, but I need you to break something on this soon. Build on what you learned in London. I know you can do it."

At that point Kate launched another offensive, sending urgent, desperate messages to every source she had, begging them for help. It was Nick Varner who'd finally responded and suggested a private meeting at Columbus Park.

But he was already twenty minutes late and Kate's heart was sinking.

Come on, Nick. Don't leave me hanging like this.

She scanned the park and her phone vibrated with a text from Erich, one of her sources, a brilliant young cyber consultant. She only knew him by his first name, although she was aware he was known as "Viper" in his world. Erich was a cryptic, shadowy figure who'd done contract work for the CIA and the NSA. He'd helped her in the past and he was good.

Just finished a job in New Zealand. Been reading your stories and will help if I can when I get back to NY.

Encouraged, Kate exhaled.

This is good. I could use his expertise.

Kate thanked him, took solace in his promise and watched the fluid, calming ballet of the Tai Chi group.

"Hey, Kate."

She turned to Nick Varner, who sat beside her.

"Sorry. I'm late and short on time."

"I need help."

"This is on your airline story with the email?"

"Yes."

"What did you learn in London?"

"I learned that Shikra Airlines received an email concerning the crash at Heathrow. I think it's linked to my Zarathustra email, the crash and the East-Cloud flight." Nick nodded, saying nothing, and Kate continued. "I was told the Shikra email was shared with the FBI. Is that right?"

Nick took his time before answering.

"Kate, give me your assurance that you won't use anything I tell you."

"You know you have it."

"All right. The task force is looking at both emails as potential threats, and we're assessing their veracity."

"What about the connection to the flights? They're linked, right?"

"I didn't say that. First we have to find the sources of the threats and assess them."

"Do you believe it's the same source?"

"Too soon to say."

"Can I get the FBI spokesperson on the record saying you are investigating the emails in relation to the two flights?"

Nick shook his head.

"Why not, Nick? We nearly lost the EastCloud flight. We've got fifteen dead people in London and somebody claiming responsibility in each case. The public has a right to know what's going on."

"They also have a right not to be unduly panicked and a right to a thorough investigation. Yes, making a threat is a criminal act, but we don't have enough to shut down the airline industry based on two vague, unsubstantiated emails. We don't know what we're looking for yet. We have no solid evidence. You realize what would happen if this turned out to be a false alarm but got out the wrong way? People wouldn't get on a plane. The economy would take a serious blow. And we'd be inundated with copycat threats."

Kate cupped her face in her hands.

"Nick, can you give me an idea how close you are? How much longer before you have something?"

"I can't answer that but I'll tell you this. We're using every resource we can because indications are that whoever is behind these messages is extremely skilled and intelligent." Varner looked at his watch and patted Kate's hand. "I have to leave but we'll keep in touch."

Kate sat for a moment alone, watching the old men play chess and the seniors continue with Tai Chi, as a jetliner roared over the East River.

Twenty-Nine

Hyattsville, Maryland

The stone bungalow sat back at the end of a dead-end street, sheltered by stands of oak and maples, not far from the University of Maryland.

"Baba O'Riley" thudded from the small, battered Chevy sedan that squeaked to a stop in the driveway. Setting the parking brake and leaving the motor running, the driver collected the insulated pizza bag, trotted to the door and rang the bell.

Veyda Hyde answered.

"That'll be twenty-five seventy." The driver slid the box from the bag.

"The pizza's free." She held up her phone. "You're late."

"No way! There was traffic and the offer says—"

"Delivered in thirty-three minutes or it's free. You took thirty-nine minutes. I tracked your time from your call center."

"I know, but the time rule says—"

"Any first-year law student could tell you that your advertised terms and conditions on the time rule are so sloppy they're invalid. You're late. The pizza's free. Don't argue with me. I've just taught you and your company a lesson. Consider *that* my tip."

Veyda seized the pizza and shut the door just as the driver raised his middle finger.

Trailing the aroma of baked cheese, onions and pepperoni, she entered the living room where Seth waited on the sofa before a hundred-inch flat-screen TV. She set the pizza down on the coffee table, went to the kitchen and returned with paper plates, sodas and napkins. They pulled the tabs on the cans then dug into the pizza.

"Ready?" Seth chewed on his first bite.

"Okay."

Seth wiped his fingers on his jeans and grabbed his phone, which he'd programmed to use as the TV's remote control.

The screen came to life with Newslead's footage showing the cabin of EastCloud Flight 4990 twisting out of control. Passengers were tossed violently like toys as the jet rolled. Bodies bounced over seats, smashed against walls. People screamed for their lives.

Images cut to news reports and the river of emergency lights in front of LaGuardia's Terminal C. TV crews jostled with police to crowd around injured passengers on gurneys being loaded into ambulances.

"It was horrible!" one woman told reporters.

Seth finished off his pizza and picked up another slice.

Next, there came footage of the terminal's baggage claim area, where news cameras had encircled passengers recounting their ordeal.

"People were hurled like rag dolls," one man said.

With her eyes on the TV, Veyda sipped her ginger ale.

Seth belched and tapped his phone, and new footage ran, showing Shikra Flight 418 plowing into the ground at Heathrow. The right wing and landing gear broke up as the jet cartwheeled. The tail, fuselage and cockpit separated into pieces, scattering passengers before the wreckage ignited. Emergency vehicles sped to the disaster with lights flashing as rescuers worked to save lives, while others draped canvas over the dead.

Then there came news reports showing agonized relatives in Heathrow's arrival area; some were inconsolable and collapsed.

"And now," a British news anchor staring into the camera said, "authorities begin their long investigation to determine the cause of this horrific tragedy, the crash of Shikra Airlines Flight Four Eighteen."

Veyda raised her palm to Seth, who slapped it in a high five.

"I told you we would do it," she said. "Kate Page disappointed us. We selected her because her work was the best. We thought she was worthy to honor Zarathustra, to be part of history."

"Her silence was a colossal failure."

"Shikra was the price to be paid." Veyda laughed to herself. "We'll teach her a lesson. Soon she'll be shouting Zarathustra's praises to an awestruck world and we will rule the heavens."

"This is our time, our destiny, baby. Everything's in motion. For yours is the power…"

Veyda gave Seth a victory kiss, pulled away and said, "And the glory."

Seth cued more news reports on Heathrow and they continued eating.

As images of the tragedy played out before them, Veyda basked in the knowledge that she and Seth were extraordinary humans who were in the process of making history and enlightening the world. She took quick stock of the bookcase and their new souvenirs: candles from Japan, an incense burner from India, a carving from the Canary Islands. She looked at their worktables across the room with the laptops, large computer monitors and the small desktop flight simulator they'd built. Through the patio doors, she saw the array of satellite dishes in the backyard, which was enclosed by a ten-foot hedge. They'd bought all the things they needed online.

Veyda reached for her ginger ale, reflecting on the triumphs and tragedies of her life.

She'd been six and her mother had been brushing her hair, telling her that she had an exceptionally high IQ. *You're our miracle. You're going to accomplish monumental things when you grow up, sweetie. I know it in my heart.*

Veyda let the memories flow.

Her mother's teary smile when she'd applauded her from the audience, as she'd taken the auditorium stage to accept another academic award. As Mom had taken pictures, Veyda had searched for Dad, finding his empty chair.

Her father's work had always come first, but her mother, a busy doctor, had always been there, like the sun in Veyda's life. Ever encouraging, ever nurturing, ever loving, and always rationalizing her dad's absences.

Well, he's working on an important project and they need him at the plant. We'll do something together next time, honey.

Veyda had been a solitary child. She hadn't cared much for other kids. Her books and computers had been her friends. Her craving to learn had been insatiable. At times her father, when he'd been home, would explain theories and solve the mysteries behind the abstract concepts that had puzzled her.

Yes, she'd loved him then.

School had been easy for Veyda. She'd studied first at Pepperdine, then received a master's degree in computer science from UC Berkeley. From there she'd gone on to the Massachusetts Institute of Technology to pursue her PhD in aeronautic computer systems engineering. Her doctoral thesis was going to be about advanced computer engineering. She had been working on it when she'd taken a break to return home to California to visit her parents. She'd ached to see them. The brutal New England winter had deepened her loneliness and isolation.

That visit home had been the last moment of happiness Veyda would know. It had been a beautiful time, right up to the point when her father had decided messages about his work were more important than her mother's life.

In the quiet of the night she'd heard crumpling metal, breaking glass, seen the sky spinning...

Through a curtain of blood, she'd seen her mother's shoe. She'd been pinned under the car... Her father had been on his knees holding her mother's hand as she'd cried *Veyda!* with her dying breath...

The world Veyda had known ended that day because of her father.

Vehicular manslaughter. That's what he'd been charged with, but his lawyer had had it reduced to a misdemeanor and kept him out of prison.

In the forty-eight hours after the crash, doctors had been uncertain Veyda would survive. Her skull had fractured in four places and she'd suffered a concussion. But somehow she'd fought back, beating the odds, regaining enough strength to demand she be allowed to attend her mother's funeral in Clear River.

Standing at her mother's gravesite, Veyda's thoughts had swirled in a maelstrom of medicated anguish. She'd kissed her mother's coffin and placed a rose upon it before it descended into the North Dakota ground. But it had been the sight of her broken father, peering into the hole with his tear-soaked face, that had crystallized one clear thought.

You killed my mother.

Veyda had grown to hate her father more with each passing day, hating him for sacrificing his family incrementally over the years, until it culminated in their final, life-altering tragedy.

What was worth more to you than my mother's life?

She'd hurled that question at him one night as he'd sat alone in the dark, drinking. She'd blud-

geoned him with it until he'd fallen to his knees
before her.

*I am in hell because of what I did. Nothing will
ever change that. I will never ask for your forgiveness, Veyda, because I have no right to it.*

After the tragedy she'd lived in California with
him—the doctors had thought it best—while she'd
recovered. A nurse had visited regularly. For weeks
Veyda had endured jackhammer headaches so severe they'd brought on spasms and hallucinations.
Then there'd been the nightmares. She'd undergone
drug therapy and counseling, telling her psychia-
trist that she had changed, that she was no longer
Veyda Cole.

I don't know who I am anymore.

Months after the crash she'd achieved a degree of
recovery. On the outside, she'd appeared to be coping with her loss and her injuries. Yet in her heart
something had cleaved. She'd barely been able to
stand looking at her father, let alone speak to him.
She'd wanted to return to MIT and finish her PhD
as her way of honoring her mother's memory.

The estate had been settled, with Veyda receiving
a large sum of money from a trust her parents had
established and additional money from her mother's life insurance policy. Veyda had been planning
to move back to Cambridge, when one day she noticed her father gathering her mother's belongings
to donate to charity.

Don't you dare touch her things! I'll do that,
Veyda had told him.

She'd waited for a time when he was out of the
house then, through tears, began boxing up her

mother's clothes, jewelry, pictures and other items, selecting what to donate and what to keep. Touching a favorite sweater, holding it to her face, breathing in her mother's scent, tracing her fingers over her rings…it had all been so hard, and the more she'd tried, the angrier she'd got, until she'd been consumed again with rage.

Why, why, why did he do this?

Her fury had boiled over, and she'd stridden into her father's study and to his computer. He was careless with his passwords. She'd known where he'd kept them. She'd begun opening his folders, files, his emails, going to those dated around the time of the crash. Her university studies and her research had enabled her to understand his work easily—there were times they'd discussed it—but she hadn't known what specifically had consumed him that day until then.

Flight-management systems.

That's it? A debate over the interpretation of a security review? That's what couldn't wait? This is why my mother died?

Suddenly, Veyda's brain had spasmed, pain knifing through her skull, so excruciating and piercing she'd found herself on the floor in a fetal position, her head clasped in her hands to keep it from tearing apart.

Her screams had resounded in the dark, empty house.

Veyda felt a hand on her shoulder, jolting her out of her reverie. She turned and looked at Seth.

"Everything okay?" he asked. "Do you want that last piece of pizza, babe?"

Thirty

Seth stopped the video, concern rising on his face.

"You're sure you're okay?"

"I'm fine."

He looked at her long enough to ease his worry before putting the last slice of pizza on his plate.

"Okay, then, I'm getting another soda. Want one?"

"No, thanks."

Seth went to the kitchen and Veyda returned to her thoughts of that dark time after her mother's death and how she'd rejected her father's offer—more like a plea—to drive her to LAX. She'd taken a cab in the predawn light, leaving the house in darkness, knowing that she'd never return.

The life I knew is dead. It's gone.

Her heart in turmoil, she'd been unable to sleep on her flight.

Veyda had read, finding comfort in her mother's favorite philosophers. Then she'd turned to her own—Hegel and Nietzsche.

As her jet flew over America, she'd read nonstop.

She'd read with ferocity and yearning, squeezing meaning out of every word, sentence, concept and idea with desperation because somehow, at that moment, she'd felt like her life depended upon it.

At one point in the flight, she'd been hit with a severe headache, and took medication. As it did its work, Veyda had gazed down at the world below and had an epiphany.

I'm with the gods now and my purpose is true.

She'd continued reading, and as the hours melted away, Veyda realized that she had undergone a metamorphosis. By the time she'd landed at Logan, she'd known two things. Number one: she was no longer Veyda Cole. She would no longer bear the name of her mother's killer. From then on she'd honor her mother by taking her mother's family name, Hyde. Number two: she was going to change her thesis topic from aircraft systems engineering, computational engineering, controls, communications and networks, to blaze a path far more important. One that would elevate the world.

The day after she'd landed, Veyda had met with her research advisor, who'd been aware of her family tragedy and had offered her heartfelt condolences. Veyda had brushed them aside and alerted her to her name change and that, while she was in the final stages of completing her thesis, she'd wanted to switch topics.

Veyda had intended to spike all of her research, which had involved new perspectives on transmission probability, independent Gamma random variables, innovative methods on employing the infinite-horizon LQR control in satellite systems; her new ideas on approaches on the stochastic first-order system with linear dynamics and nonlinear measurements. She would cast aside her new work on Gaussian white noise processes.

I'm going to surprise you with my new subject. It's going to blow your mind.

Alarmed, her advisor had reminded her of procedure and rules on dissertation requirements, but Veyda had demanded the change.

For the next few weeks, she'd worked eighteen to twenty hours a day on her new thesis while her advisor, the members of her thesis committee and the graduate officer had waited with trepidation.

When Veyda finished, she'd delivered her report to her committee.

Her advisor and the committee had been concerned about her sudden switch in academic disciplines and disturbed by the subject matter and her handling of it.

Her new thesis championed the real-life application of German philosophers Hegel and Nietzsche as being critical to the betterment of mankind. Like the Russian novelist Dostoevsky, Veyda had refined their theories on the Superman to encompass "extraordinary humans."

Veyda had argued that the extraordinary being embodied the highest passion and creativity of all humanity and would exist beyond the conventions of good and evil.

This was absolute.

She'd written that extraordinary humans possessed skills, gifts and talents that elevated them above ordinary humans. Extraordinary humans possessed the *God-given duty and right* to take any action, commit any crime or immoral act, without conscience or consequence because it is the extraordinary human whose achievements take civilization to unprecedented heights, lighting the way forward for all of human existence.

Less than a week after Veyda's submission, her thesis committee had called her to a critical meeting.

Your paper sanctions bloodshed in the name of progress, articulating that if the ends are noble, the means are justified, one professor had observed. *How can you possibly defend this idea?*

Easily, Veyda had said. *As noted in my section on use of weapons of mass destruction, Hiroshima and Nagasaki ended war, but also advanced nuclear technology for the betterment of civilization. Look at the uses in nuclear medicine, the uses in energy.*

But Veyda, you applaud research conducted by the Nazis in the Second World War, another professor had said.

We cannot deny that Nazi advances in rocketry put us on the moon. In both cases, atomic weaponry and rudimentary aerospace technology, much blood was shed for what ultimately benefited mankind. Look at space travel, satellite technology, telecommunications—the benefits are endless. My work clearly demonstrates a fundamental law of nature—without pain, without blood, there is no birth, no advancement for humanity.

I have to admit your paper is not only disturbing, it's long, rambling and in many parts incomprehensible, another professor had said.

Troubled by her thesis, Veyda's committee had concluded that she'd experienced a breakdown stemming from her family tragedy and injuries. In their report to the graduate program chair, her thesis committee had rejected her work and recommended she seek counseling and take a sabbatical.

Veyda had done neither.

She'd quit MIT and drifted to back California, where she'd met Seth Hagen.

The only child of Silicon Valley computer scientists, he was a genius who, throughout his childhood, had been ignored by his parents. Seth had become a multimillionaire in his teens after designing cutting-edge video game programs while getting his first degree at Carnegie Mellon University. Later, he'd received his master's degree from the University of Washington, and his PhD in computer systems from Stanford University.

But Seth had soon grown bored and had lived as a recluse until he'd met Veyda through an online comments section on an article about a NASA breakthrough. Their friendly exchanges had led to a meeting at a Starbucks in Pasadena, then subsequent meetings and walks on the beach.

Seth had been so impressed with Veyda's "extraordinary people," thesis, he'd deemed them fated to be together, destined to put her theory to work.

We are exceptional people, he'd said. *We're destined to advance mankind. We must expose weaknesses and failures in order to enlighten and advance understanding. We must teach people to learn from their failings in our digital age. It's the only way to elevate human understanding.*

Together they'd moved into the house Seth owned in Maryland.

It's quiet there. We can get a lot done.

They'd begun by defeating the cybersecurity systems of banks, retailers, internet providers, broadcasters and an array of corporations. It had been fun and easy; nothing was ever traced back to them, but they'd received little recognition—no glorious headlines affirming their advancing of understanding.

That's because no blood was shed, Veyda had said, and proposed commercial aviation as an effective target. *Nothing seizes the world's attention like an aircraft tragedy.*

The bigger, the better, Seth had agreed.

So, several months ago, they'd employed their combined and formidable skills to test the safety of air travel, starting first with the New York and London planes.

If my father thought his work important enough to sacrifice my mother to it, then it's my duty to expose the flaws of his system, no matter the cost. It must be done, for it will ultimately advance our technology.

Now, after finishing the pizza and before they resumed their research planning for further operations, Seth played a documentary on the 1977 crash at Tenerife.

As Veyda watched the flames of the tragedy, she heard her dying mother scream her name. She clenched her eyes shut and willed her memory to return her to better times when...

She'd been six and her mother had been brushing her hair, telling her that she had an exceptionally high IQ. *You're our miracle. You're going to accomplish monumental things when you grow up, sweetie. I know it in my heart.*

Thirty-One

Clear River, North Dakota

The earth had shifted under Robert Cole as he'd watched the slow-motion swan song of Shikra Flight 418.

Ice tinkled against glass as he lifted his drink.

No, stop! It won't help. Be strong. Keep your mind clear.

He set the drink down without tasting it.

Still, the images of the crash haunted him and guilt crept into a frightened corner of his heart.

Fifteen people dead.

In the days that had followed since the Heathrow crash, he'd gone online, scrutinizing every news report he could find, examining every image, absorbing every published detail.

Speculation in the British press on the cause had ruled out a terrorist act, pointing instead to a double engine failure, even though such occurrences were rare. Some reports referred to an earlier incident—the crash landing of a Shanghai-to-London charter jetliner at Heathrow sixteen months ago. In that case, ice buildup had choked fuel flow to both engines on landing, resulting in loss of power. Dozens had been injured, but no one killed. In that incident, the route had taken the jet over mountainous regions of China and Russia, where temperatures plunged, which had caused ice to form in the fuel system. But Cole knew that ice couldn't be a factor in the Kuwaiti flight because its path presented warmer temperatures, and fuel mixtures in the industry had been adjusted since.

The key factor in both the Kuwait flight and the EastCloud flight was that each aircraft had the same Richlon-Titan fly-by-wire system, the one he had created and helped build.

My flawed system. And now fifteen people are dead.

The Times of London had just published excerpts of transcripts from the Shikra crew, and one segment leaped from Cole's monitor.

Copilot: "We've got a double engine failure! The engines have been switched off!"
Captain: "Switched off? How? We didn't do that! Try restarting!"

There, that part.

"Switched off? How? We didn't do that."

Cole clicked to an earlier story from Newslead that quoted EastCloud's Captain Raymond Matson.

"There was no clear-air turbulence and I did not disable the safety system. The aircraft suddenly rolled. For a critical time, the plane refused to respond to our commands. I don't know what happened but I know something went wrong. This was a clear flight control computer malfunction."

Cole dragged his hands over his face.

It was evident to him that what he had feared was now a reality, a horrible reality. He was staring at the telltale signs of the system's vulnerability—an external breach of the system's security system.

I have to tell them that someone is hacking into RT's system.

Cole took in a long breath, let it out slowly, reached for his phone and called Jake Hooper at his NTSB office in Washington, DC.

"NTSB, Major Investigations Division," the receptionist said.

"Robert Cole calling for Jake Hooper."

"Oh, hello, Mr. Cole. We've passed your message to Jake."

"I haven't heard back, and my emails to him keep bouncing back. Could you give me a number where he can be reached?"

"No, I'm not permitted to do that. As I mentioned when you called an hour ago, and the hour before that, he's overseas assisting on an investigation."

"Listen, this is very important. He needs to know that there's a security issue with the RT flight-management system."

"I'm sure he's aware and that the team is looking into all aspects."

"You know that I used to participate in investigations with the NTSB."

"Yes, we're aware of who you are, Mr. Cole." He thought her tone condescending and dismissive. "We no longer have you listed. That's why your emails are rejected. As I've mentioned in your previous calls, you don't have party status on any ongoing investigation, which restricts us from doing much more than relaying your message to Jake. I'm sorry."

Cole squeezed his phone hard before hanging up.

He knew what they thought of him but he couldn't give up. The reasons stared back at him from his laptop, picture after picture of the Heathrow tragedy—burning wreckage, anguished relatives and body bags dotting the grass near the runway.

I know what I have to do.

Cole had to go beyond alerting the NTSB to the problem. He had to give them the solution, the one he'd developed, to retrofit RT's fleet and every aircraft with the RT flight-management system.

I know what I have to do but I don't know if I can do it.

He felt as though an enormous weight were pushing down on him, because even if he found the solution, he'd have to adapt it to what RT had actually installed in planes now in service. Cole was unsure he had the skill, the thinking power he needed. Not after all these years. Not after what he'd become.

I have to try. If it's the last thing I do, I have to try.

He got up, poured his drink into the kitchen sink and made himself a sandwich and black coffee. Then he showered, put on fresh clothes, grabbed his keys and got into his pickup truck. Driving across town, he sorted through his thoughts.

When he'd sold the house in California and moved to North Dakota, he'd considered destroying all of his personal records and material from his work at Richlon-Titan. But something—a distant voice, an impulse or an instinct, he'd never know— had told him to keep the material.

Cole couldn't bear to have it with him, so he'd put it away in self-storage along with furniture, keepsakes and other items he couldn't let go of, but couldn't stand having with him in his small house in Clear River.

Now more than ever, he was relieved that he'd kept his RT files.

If he was going to develop a solution, he'd need to review the corrective work he'd developed for the system. He had put into storage two file cabinets jammed with manuals, schematic drawings, equations and USB flash drives, all invaluable.

Now he had a starting point.

What I don't have is time. Who knows how much longer before we see another tragedy?

He turned onto Wagon Road at the edge of town, following it until he came to a cluster of low-rise buildings enclosed within a ten-foot-high chain-link fence topped with barbed wire.

The sign at the gate read Riverwind Self-Storage.

Cole inserted his key and turned it in the entry post and the fence gate automatically opened, giving him access to the complex. He went to the structure marked Building 2 and used another key to enter.

He walked down the long, straight corridor that

divided into rows of uniform storage units, each about the size of a small garage. He picked through the keys of his key ring, coming to a silver key with "108, Riverwind, Bldg 2" scrawled on a piece of paper that was taped to it.

Cole passed units 105, 106 and 107, then froze in his tracks.

The door to 108 was unlocked.

He opened it.

Everything was gone.

Thirty-Two

Manhattan, New York

Sirens howled in the twilight as Kate entered the bar where she'd arranged to meet her source.

It was seven blocks from her building in Morningside Heights, sandwiched between Aunt Dottie's Pie Shop and Loving Care Alterations. This was a region of Harlem and the Upper West Side that locals considered an extension of Columbia University's campus.

Kate threaded through coveys of grad students, making her way to an empty booth. The air was heavy with the smells of beer and deep-fried food. The place was dark, the floor was sticky and the walls were aging brick. Each wooden table had a flickering lamp. The menu was on the chalkboard behind the bar, above the mirror that hung between the muted flat-screen TVs, which were tuned to sports. Thankfully, the music was played at a level that invited conversation.

"I'm waiting for a friend. I'll just have a Diet Coke," she told her server.

Kate checked her phone for messages, then marveled at how time had flown. It'd been a year since she'd last seen Erich. Sipping her drink, she inventoried the crowd, wondering what young Erich, or "Viper," looked like now, and, more important, if he could help her.

"Hello, Kate," said a voice behind her.

"Erich."

"I was in the corner when I saw you." He slid into her booth.

The lamplight reflected his intense, deep-set eyes. His hair was cut short; he still had a stubbled goatee and a stud in his left earlobe. She detected a pleasant hint of cologne.

"What're you, twenty-three now?" she asked.

"Twenty-four. You're looking well, Kate."

"Thank you. So are you. Are you still doing your top secret consulting work as one of the world's best hackers?" She smiled.

"Cyber specialist."

"So what was the job in New Zealand? Did you have to eliminate anyone?"

He tugged at his ear, smiling.

"Well, keeping this between friends, I was contracted to help with Stone Ghost."

"Stone Ghost?"

"It's a classified network that shares defense intelligence among the US, the UK, Canada, Australia and New Zealand."

"But if it's secret…"

"You can read a summary of Stone Ghost online." Erich turned to the server. "I'll have a tomato juice with ice, please." Then to Kate: "So, how are your daughter and sister doing?"

"Both good."

Sipping her Coke, Kate caught the reflection of a woman at the bar. She seemed to be watching them. *More likely Erich.* Dishwater blonde, tight T-shirt, jeans, red bag. She was older than the students, and had a hardness about her. Divorced? A cougar? A hooker, maybe?

"Kate?"

She returned her attention to Erich.

"I've been reading your stories on the airliners. Is there any way I can help?"

She ran down the history for him, from the beginning when she'd first heard the EastCloud crew on the newsroom scanners to her current quandary.

"I believe the cause of these two flights' issues is linked to the email. I need help confirming it and I need help determining the source of the email."

Kate unfolded printouts of the Zarathustra email and passed it to Erich. He studied it, rubbing his stubble thoughtfully.

"I tried to respond but got this." She tapped her finger on the printout with the error message reading "permanent failure, unknown user" and a long string of technical text. "What d'you think?"

"Off the top, it looks basic, but smart. Your sender is likely routing the message through a multitude of places online, using layers of encryption, characteristic of an onion router. Good chance they're using hidden servers on the Darknet."

"Can you help me?"

"No guarantees, but there are things I can try, people I can talk to."

"Thank you. Anything you could do would be great."

Kate heard a soft vibration. Erich reached into his pocket for his phone and scrolled along the screen, reading a message.

"I'm sorry, Kate, I have to go."

After Erich left, Kate stayed, finished her Coke, and paid the bill.

The night was warm and pleasant. Buoyed by Erich's promise to help, Kate decided she'd walk the seven blocks to her building. Along the way she searched her phone and reread the Zarathustra email.

One way or another I'm going to find you.

The sudden growl of a motor prompted Kate to look quickly behind her at a passing motorcycle. She did a double take. Half a block back, she saw a woman window-shopping.

Dishwater blonde, open jacket over a tight T-shirt, jeans, red bag.

The woman from the bar.

Kate continued walking, thinking hard. Something troubled her about the stranger. She was familiar. Why?

Kate crossed the street, throwing her a backward glance. The woman continued window-shopping. As Kate kept walking, she scoured her memory, trying to recall anything familiar about the woman's hairstyle or the shape of her face. As details swam into focus, it hit her.

I saw that woman in the grocery store near my building just before I left for London!

Kate kept walking and glanced back. The woman was still behind her but was now on her side of the street. Maybe she lived in the neighborhood.

No, because I saw her again when I got back from London and took Grace to Central Park. She was on a bench reading a book. She was always in the distance. I remember her. She can't be following me.

Kate walked faster.

I'm going to find out.

Kate stopped in front of a closed jewelry store and gazed through the steel bars of its storefront. All the while, she watched for the woman. The stranger crossed the street and rounded a corner. Kate resumed walking, rounding the opposite corner. A short time later, she spotted the woman in the distance. Kate thought quickly, deciding to go around the entire block.

With every turn of every corner, the woman had stayed with her.

Kate stepped into an alcove. Her breathing quickened.

Why am I being followed?

Kate peered from the alcove. The woman was at the end of the block, across the street. Kate waited to confront her, unafraid.

She could handle herself.

She'd taken firearms courses, although she hated guns and never carried one. She'd taken self-defense courses. She'd taken courses with private investigators. She had a can of pepper spray and a personal alarm in her bag.

The stranger lingered at the end of the street.

Come on, come on.

Kate wanted her to get closer. She reached into her bag and slid her fingers around the pepper spray canister.

Come on. I'm ready for you.

The woman kept her distance.

Kate stepped from the alcove and walked in the stranger's direction. The woman turned and began walking away. Kate bolted after her, glad she'd worn flat shoes. The woman ran around the corner. Kate ran after her as fast as she could, rounding the corner, glimpsing her crossing the street and running to the next corner. Kate darted through traffic, adrenaline and anger giving her speed.

When Kate took the next corner the woman had vanished.

Kate stopped in her tracks and scanned the street. A car door shut. An ignition turned. She was near. Kate tore off in the direction of the sound and spotted the woman in a sedan, hearing the transmission shift. As she got closer, the engine revved, the car lurched, tires squealed and it pulled away.

Kate stood on the sidewalk, reciting the license plate as she wrote it down in her notebook.

"Gotcha!"

Thirty-Three

The fresh coffee Kate gulped at her desk scorched her throat.

She'd gone to the newsroom early that morning, riding a wave of anger and hammering at her keyboard.

Who was following me and why?

She had to cool off and think clearly. She looked at her notebook again, thankful she'd gotten the stranger's New York license plate and gone on the offensive. Before leaving her building for the subway that morning, she'd taken action.

One of her sources was Ivan Vestrannicki, an NYPD detective, who'd had twenty-one years on the job before his squad took down an armored-car heist in the Bronx. Ivan had taken two bullets in his left leg. It'd left him with a limp and a cynical view of the world. After he'd retired he'd set up his own PI agency. Kate had interviewed him for a series on the challenges cops who'd been wounded on the job faced with disability payments. Ivan never forgot that.

You got a friend here, he'd told her.

This morning Kate had reached out to him for help with the plate.

Leave it with me. I'll get back to you.

While waiting, Kate had searched the plate on-line, but struck out. Then she'd thought of Grace and Vanessa. Without revealing that she'd been followed, Kate had questioned them at breakfast. They'd said that they hadn't received any strange calls or hang-ups, or seen anything odd. They hadn't seen any-one following them. Nothing appeared to be out of the ordinary.

She'd considered all of the recent stories she'd written.

Who would do this?

Twice in the past she'd been the target of private investigations. A corrupt millionaire stockbroker who'd been scamming seniors had hired an agency to follow her. It had also happened with a story she'd done on people trying to break away from a cult. In both cases they'd tried to find dirt on Kate to scare her off the story. In both cases they'd failed. Their tactics had become part of the story. Her line rang.

"Kate, it's Ivan."

"Hey, what'd you find out?"

"The plate belongs to a woman who works for a private investigation agency, who subcontracts for a larger one."

"Any idea who her client is and why she was hired?"

"I won't be able to get that info. It'd be like ask-ing you to name your sources. I can tell you the larger agency is Infinite Guardian Shield, a global security operation."

"Really? Do they have offices in London, England?"

"Yup. Say, aren't you working on that airline story?"

"You think it could be related to that?"

"Maybe, maybe not. Could always be something you wrote about prior to that. Hard to say."

Kate glanced around the newsroom.

"Ivan, could they bug my phone, intercept my emails?"

"It wouldn't be easy, given your office environment, but it wouldn't be impossible, either."

"What about at home?"

"Quite possible."

"Holy crap."

"Look, Kate, the fact you challenged this woman and made it clear to her that you knew what she was doing means her surveillance of you was blown. That could end the case right there."

"Think so?"

"Again, anything's possible. Let me do a little digging and see what I can find out. Meanwhile, try not to piss off anybody."

"Very funny."

"Thought you'd like that."

Kate took another sip of coffee and pulled her thoughts together. She had to tell Chuck what was going on. She went to his office. His jacket was draped over his chair but he wasn't there. On her way back to her desk she saw Sharlese Givens from the news library.

"Oh, Kate, I've got those printouts of the articles you requested on airline security. I just dropped them off at your desk."

"Thanks."

The clippings were in a yellow legal-size folder. Kate had just sat down and opened the thick bundle when her phone rang.

"Newslead. Kate Page."

"Kate, Tim Yardley at the Washington bureau. Got a minute?"

"Hi, Tim. Sure."

"I didn't want to put this in an email. You know Chuck assigned us to help out on your EastCloud stuff, look into the companies involved and any political connections, anything we could find."

"Right, but I thought nothing came up."

"It was looking that way until we got an interesting lead. It concerns Sloane Parkman, who's working at headquarters with you."

"What about him?" Kate looked across the newsroom just as Sloane was arriving at his desk. "I can see him now."

"Are you good to talk?"

"I am. Go ahead."

"It turns out Hub Wolfeson, who sits on Richlon-Titan's board of directors, is Sloane's uncle."

"What?"

"That puts Sloane in a serious conflict of interest when working on stories concerning Richlon-Titan. Newslead policy states that you cannot report on issues or subjects where you, or your family, have a direct personal or financial interest, or can be perceived as having one."

Looking more closely at Sloane, Kate saw that he was wearing a jacket over his Brooks Brothers shirt.

Every hair was in place but there was no gleaming white-toothed grin today. In fact, he looked somber.

"Does Chuck know?" Kate asked.

"He does. This all came up last night. Very few other people know and since you were working with him, I wanted to give you a heads-up, Kate."

Sloane had placed an empty cardboard box on his desk and was putting personal items in it.

What's going on?

At that moment, Chuck Laneer stepped into the newsroom, which was still largely empty because it was so early. He gestured for Kate to come into his office.

"Kate?" Yardley said on the phone. "You still there?"

"Yes, Tim, thanks. I appreciate the heads-up, but I have to go."

"Shut the door," Chuck said. "Have a seat."

His collar button was undone and his tie was loosened. He remained standing and rolled up his sleeves.

"I just met with Lincoln and Fitzgerald in Human Resources. We've let Sloane go this morning."

"He's fired?"

"Yes, for violating Newslead policy. He not only failed to disclose his direct family connection to Richlon-Titan, he tried to direct coverage in a manner that deflected any criticism of the company. We'll post a memo to staff underscoring Newslead policy on conflicts of interest."

Chuck tossed his pen on his desk and put his hands on his hips. Stress lines cut deep into his face.

"I can't tell you how much this sickens me," he said. "Sloane's uncle is a senior board member at RT."

"How's Reeka taking this? Sloane was her hire."

"She was advised to take some time off and reflect," he said. "We can't afford this kind of bullshit at a time when we're trying to strengthen our credibility. That's why I was pushing you hard on getting confirmation."

"I get that."

"So where are you at on the story? We could use a big score right now."

"I've reached out to my best sources, but something's come up."

"What?"

"I was followed last night."

"Followed? By whom? Have you been threatened?"

"No, nothing like that."

Kate brought Chuck up to speed on what had happened the night before. While listening, he ran his hand over his face. Then he interrupted her several times to ask questions, staring hard at her when she finished.

"Are you sure you're okay?" he asked.

"Yes. I've been through this before."

"This is what we're going to do. We're going to talk with Newslead's lawyers and you're going to report this to the NYPD. I doubt there's much they can do, but I want this on the record. Okay?"

"Okay."

"If, at any time, you want off this story, or want help of any sort—"

"Thanks, I'll let you know."

Kate went downstairs for a fresh coffee.

The morning had barely started, but she felt as if a week's worth of stress had washed over her. Back at her desk, she resumed reading the batch of articles the librarian had left for her. Kate tried to push her concerns aside and focus on her research. She paged through story after story, but she was familiar with many of the reports. *Not much here,* she thought, but then she came to one story that was written shortly after September 11, 2001, and froze.

"Oh my God! How did we miss this?"

Thirty-Four

North Dakota

Robert Cole pounded on the door of the double-wide trailer that served as the office for Riverwind Self-Storage before reading the hours-of-operation sign in the window.

The office was closed.

He cursed then saw the number to call in case of emergency, took out his phone and called it. He got a voice mail, left a message, then called the Clear River police.

"I want to report a robbery. A break-in and theft of property." Cole gave the police operator details. Then he sat down and waited on the wooden steps in front of the office and battled the panic surging through him.

He struggled to fathom why his belongings had been taken, while contending with the chilling fact that it was now hopeless for him to even attempt a solution to prevent another airline tragedy.

Some fifteen minutes later, a Clear River police car, along with a pickup truck, rolled up to the gate.

Officer Ken Bropton and Chester Yakawich, the owner of Riverwind, had arrived. Yakawich, who had an unlit cigar in the corner of his mouth, retrieved a clipboard and keys from the office. The three men walked quickly to unit 108, Yakawich's keys jingling as Cole recounted his shock and anger. Bropton immediately inspected the door.

"Doesn't look like forced entry," he said.

"That's because it wasn't." Yakawich pulled out his cigar and snapped through pages of his clipboard. "Nothing was stolen. All the contents were auctioned on the weekend."

"Auctioned?" Cole repeated. "Who gave you permission to auction my property?"

"You did, sir."

Cole shook his head.

"I certainly did not."

Bropton shot a glance to Yakawich, who suggested they go to the office. Once they were in the trailer, Yakawich went to the steel cabinets against one paneled wall. He sifted through files, removed one and consulted it.

"Yeah," Yakawich said, "it's what I thought. You called us on the twenty-sixth of last month, Mr. Cole, and told us to auction the contents of your unit. I sent Becky to your place. You signed the paperwork and gave us your spare key." Yakawich handed a contract to Bropton, who gave it a quick read and passed it to Cole. "She said you weren't feeling so good that day." Yakawich gave Bropton a subtle look. "And, I'm sorry, but we found a lot of empty liquor bottles in your unit."

"I don't think this is a police matter," Bropton said.

Cole stared disbelievingly at his signature and traveled across a wasteland of fog-shrouded memories.

It was true. In a fit of booze-drenched emotional pain he'd decided to jettison all his belongings, but he'd been too drunk to remember.

"In any event—" Yakawich went to his desk and passed an envelope to Cole "—we've just processed your check. Here it is, four-hundred and fifty, after our fees. The invoice and list of items are in there."

"Who bought my property? There's something of value I need to retrieve. Where is it?"

"It's on your invoice, but I can tell you that it went to Kord Pitman. He's a second-hand dealer in Bismarck."

"Would he still have it? It was only last weekend."

"I'll give him a call for you right now if you like, sir."

"Please, it's urgent."

The distance to Bismarck from Clear River was over three hundred miles and was usually a four-hour drive. Cole made it in a little over three and a half, heading directly to the High Plains Vintage Emporium.

The business was in the northeast fringe of Bismarck, on a stretch of flatland with an aging farmhouse and an enormous metal Quonset hut. Behind it, there was an array of used cars, trucks, farm vehicles and heavy equipment. Three large German shepherds roamed the grounds freely.

"Well, like I said on the phone, Mr. Cole—" Liz Pitman led him into the massive Quonset hut

"—you're more than welcome to take a look. See if you can find what you want. Then we can talk."

The hut was crammed with rows of huge storage shelves groaning under the weight of beds, tables, dressers, stoves, fridges, sofas, TVs, desks, paintings, driers, washers, clothing, books, toasters, blenders, it went on and on. Dust mites danced in the columns of sunlight leaking through the tiny rooftop windows. The place had an air of discarded dreams.

"The load from Clear River was recent and hasn't been processed."

"Processed?"

"As you can see, we distribute items to the proper area," Liz said. "Kord's in Idaho, so Jess and Dwight were working on it this morning. All the new items are near the back. So what was it you were most concerned about?"

"The contents of two metal file cabinets."

"There you go and there they are." Liz pointed.

Cole's cabinets stood alone in an area near all the other material from his storage unit.

"Now we'll be happy to sell it back to you."

Cole opened the first cabinet. It was empty. So was the second.

"These were filled with files and material. Where is it?"

"Hold on." Liz reached for her phone.

She made a call, then turned away from Cole to talk privately, which he took as a bad sign, as he searched among the other items. He touched things that had belonged to his wife and to his daughter. In this place, it made him realize how short and fragile life was.

"Sir?"

Cole turned to her. His heart skipped.

"We usually recycle all paper material, and that's where my sons are now, at the recycling plant. They had a large load and added your material to it."

"So it's gone?"

"No. I stopped them, but if they bring the load back, that'll be an additional cost."

"I'll pay it! Get them back here as soon as possible, please!"

For thirty-five tense minutes Cole waited with Liz, until the dogs barked and a five-ton truck grinded up to the hut's back door. As country music leaked from the truck—Johnny Cash—Liz and her sons helped Cole locate his property. After he'd agreed to a payment of four hundred dollars, they'd helped him load his pickup truck.

During the long, lonely drive back to Clear River, Cole considered all of his items bundled in the bed of his truck.

I don't know if I still have the skill to develop an answer to the system's weakness. His hands tightened on the wheel. *And do I have the time before the next tragedy?*

Thirty-Five

Manhattan, New York

Kate worked at her desk, mining the article for useable information.

It was a report in the *Chicago Tribune* on a speech President Bush had given to air industry workers at O'Hare International Airport a few weeks after the terrorist attacks on September 11, 2001.

The president's remarks had focused on strengthening air safety and security. Kate went to the link for the White House archives and printed off the full speech. In it, the president had promised action on a number of fronts.

Kate underlined one key section.

"We will look at all kinds of technologies to make sure that our airlines are safe," the president had said, "including technology to enable controllers to take over distressed aircraft and land it by remote control."

Remote control? What happened to this technology? Was it ever used? Kate chided herself for not finding this piece of information earlier and using it in her reports on EastCloud and Shikra.

It was there all this time and I missed it.

Chuck Laneer was not at his desk when she placed her printouts of her research on his chair. "I think we could have a story here," she wrote in the yellow note she stuck to the package.

Thirty minutes later, Chuck called her.

"This will work," he said. "And I have an idea on what we can do."

He called Kate into his office, along with Hugh Davidson from the business section. Hugh reported on computer technology and was known as Newslead's Emperor Nerd. He was partial to bow ties and pastel shirts.

Chuck had Tim Yardley with Newslead's Washington bureau and Noah Heatley with the London bureau on the line. He turned on his speaker.

"You've all had a chance to look at the older clips. We're going to build a story on this. Kate will lead. Hugh and Tim and Noah, I want you to feed whatever you can find on the subject to Kate."

"Excuse me, but this issue's been around," Hugh said. "What exactly is new here? What's the context?"

"We'll build our story in relation to the questions surrounding Shikra's crash in London and the near disaster with EastCloud at LaGuardia," Chuck said. "Whatever happened to this remote-control technology the president promised? Does it exist? Could it have helped, or could it have somehow been in play and abused by some criminal group? We'll come at the story fresh."

"Why didn't we do this earlier?" Noah asked from London. "Why didn't we, or anyone else for that matter, pick up on this? I mean, there have been long-standing arguments in the aviation industry about the possibility of cyber hijacking, and conspiracy theories, all of these things."

Chuck hesitated, glanced at Kate, thought for a moment.

"Besides," Noah continued, "everyone here thinks Shikra was caused by a double engine failure due to an electrical malfunction arising from poor maintenance. Why is there such a desperate push for this odd angle? Is it because of the Zarathustra message Newslead received?"

"What Zarathustra message?" Hugh asked.

"All right, some background," Chuck said. "This is confidential, but I'm not surprised that some of you know this. Newslead's aware of two threats, emails, by someone claiming responsibility for Shikra and EastCloud. The one Kate received after the East-Cloud story broke was from someone identifying themselves as Zarathustra. They claimed responsibility and wanted us to do a story crediting them or they'd cause harm to another aircraft."

No one spoke as Chuck provided more context on the Zarathustra and Kuwait emails. When he'd finished, silence followed.

"If you were already aware, fine," Chuck said. "If you weren't, my apologies. We had to keep this tight. So consider yourself informed. None of this has been reported because the emails are unsubstantiated and we don't want to create alarm in the commercial airline industry. We've alerted the FBI, which is assessing them."

Chuck paused, inviting any comments, before he continued.

"There's a strategic reason I want to proceed this way with this story."

"Are you going to share that with us?" Hugh asked.

"Later. For now, we'll take this one step at a time and we will make no mention of the emails unless we have confirmation of their credibility. Any questions?"

None were voiced.

"All right, let's get busy."

Kate drafted a list of sources and experts she intended to go to for the story. She reached out to Nick Varner at the FBI for any updates. There were none. She called the NTSB, the FAA, EastCloud, Richlon-Titan, Shikra and Talal Nasser, her source with Kuwait's Aviation Safety Department. Kate also called Erich, asking if he had any updates. He said he was working on it.

Soon, copy came in from London and Washington.

Noah Heatley's team filed chilling commentary from cyber experts from around the world claiming they could—in theory—hijack a jetliner remotely. Industry officials refuted those claims.

Yardley in Washington confirmed that Congress had approved five hundred million dollars for the fiscal year 2002 to go to the Transportation Department, to allow the air industry to fortify cockpit doors, ensure continuous operation of aircraft transponders in an emergency, and to provide "other innovative technologies to enhance aircraft security," which many industry insiders interpreted as remote-control technology.

Working with Hugh, Kate interviewed leading aviation experts. She hit pay dirt when she reached Fred Winston, who headed an airline industry consulting firm in Los Angeles.

"That technology the president discussed evolved into the Continuous Autopilot System," Winston told her. "It works like this—should the crew feel the plane is under threat of being hijacked physically, they throw a switch, allowing remote control of the plane by the ground, traffic control, which can remotely employ other auto features to land the plane safely. That system cannot be interrupted by anyone or anything in the cockpit or on the ground."

"So what happened to the technology?" Kate asked.

"Several major airlines hold patents on variations of it," Winston said. "But it was never applied, installed, or used in the commercial air industry."

"Why not?"

"Safety issues," Winston said. "Chief among them is the fear that somehow someone could hack the system—override and take control of a jetliner."

"Could that happen?"

"I know a lot of experts might disagree, but I wouldn't rule out the possibility," Winston said. "In fact, there were rumors that the military, which can control aircraft remotely, had also developed a top secret remote auto-control system for landing distressed commercial jets, but that it somehow got leaked, or was stolen, creating fears it had fallen into the wrong hands and would be used to crash airliners."

"What?"

"That's the rumor, and many credible experts place it in the realm of conspiracy theories, so I don't know how you would confirm that."

Taking careful notes, Kate talked with Winston for several more minutes before thanking him and ending the call.

Pen clamped in her teeth, she began typing up the significant points of her interviews. As she weaved in the copy coming to her from Hugh, Washington and London, her heart raced.

This is shaping up to be a hell of a story.

Thirty-Six

Manhattan, New York

Kate's face swam in and out of focus on the big screens throughout CTNB's New York studio in the Time Warner Center at Columbus Circle.

She was perched on a stool at the desk, shoulder-to-shoulder with two other panelists, Cal Marshall, a former NTSB investigator, and Stuart Shore, a retired commercial airline pilot, now an air security consultant.

"We're just four people discussing commercial air security," said Reese Baker, the CTNB moderator, after glancing up from the monitor under the glass desktop. "Forget the cameras and talk to me like you're talking to neighbors over the back fence."

"Twenty seconds, everyone!" a voice called out.

"Kate, that was a great article yesterday. Excellent." Reese smiled.

Kate's story had explored the president's security promise of remote-control technology, but it had also raised the fear of its use against commercial airliners. She'd set it within the context of the

Shikra crash at Heathrow and the EastCloud incident at LaGuardia.

Working closely with Chuck, and never mentioning the two threatening emails they believed were sent by Zarathustra, Kate had produced a nuanced article, a "situational," on the theory that the two flights could have been targets of cyber hijacking. She'd backed it up with balanced, on-the-record comments from experts and built it on the president's pledge.

Let's see what happens, Chuck had said.

Interest in the story had been strong, yielding a high level of pickup by subscribers across the US, in Europe, South America, the Middle East and Asia. It had prompted CTNB producers to request that Kate be a panelist the next day on *Beyond the Headlines* with Reese Baker.

The show's guests had gone through makeup and a sound level test; camera angles had been checked and set. The theme music played, seconds were counted down and the program went live.

"Good afternoon. Mystery still envelops the Shikra Airlines crash at Heathrow, which claimed fifteen lives, and the chilling close call with an EastCloud flight to New York's LaGuardia Airport. Could these two incidents be linked to potential hacking and a presidential promise to introduce remote-control technology in jetliners? That's the subject of today's panel. I'm Reese Baker and this is *Beyond the Headlines*."

Reese turned from one camera and introduced a setup segment of CTNB news reports on the London and New York cases that ran for four minutes.

When the producer threw it back to Reese, she introduced Cal Marshall, Stuart Shore and Kate.

"Let me take you back to September 27, 2001, two weeks after the terrorist attacks. President Bush, in a speech on aviation safety to air industry workers at O'Hare in Chicago, promised to introduce technology that would enable controllers on the ground—I'm quoting the president—'to take over distressed aircraft and land it by remote control.' Stuart, I'll start with you. As a former commercial pilot and expert on airline security, does this technology exist?"

"Yes and no. Several airlines have the patents for it, but it hasn't been applied in the commercial airline industry. Military applications are another issue, with drones and other types of aircraft, but the technology we're talking about here, for commercial aircraft, is not employed today."

"Cal, you're a former investigator with the NTSB, a highly qualified expert. Tell us, could this technology somehow have been developed surreptitiously and used to take control of the Shikra and East-Cloud planes?"

"Reese, first I want to stress that at this time we don't know what happened in the cases of the Shikra and EastCloud flights. We're not privy to all the evidence, data and facts. Only the people investigating are. And I can assure you that these investigations are meticulous and they take time. To be honest, to theorize about them, sitting here with no information at a desk in your studio, is a fool's game."

Reese smiled, acknowledging his point.

"Absolutely, but we're free to address the implications of the type of technology promised by the president."

"Let's be clear," Cal said. "The aim of the technology we're talking about is the safe landing of a troubled plane by remote control."

"Could it conceivably make a plane 'hijack-proof'?" Reese asked.

"If we're talking in-flight, then yes, I'd say it could," Cal said.

"Could such technology be hacked?"

"No," Cal said. "The design and the systems in aircraft make it impossible for a hacker to gain entry to the flight-management system to engage and control the aircraft. It's just not possible."

"But Cal," Stuart said, "you can't rule out all possibilities. If you could control a plane remotely from the ground, then your system is vulnerable to attack."

The panel debated the subject until the show neared its end.

"I'm afraid we're running out of time," Reese said. "I'd like to close with you, Kate. You touched on this with your story. Why has this technology not been put into use? Let's look at the Japanese airliner that disappeared over the Pacific a year ago, and the Argentine jetliner that crashed into the Andes. Some theories hold that they were hacked."

"Well, in researching the story, we found a number of reasons why the system has not been installed."

Kate explained that pilots had objected to it. In some cases, there were concerns that controllers couldn't see all that pilots see in the cockpit, which could create a hazard. There were arguments that the skies were too crowded to make remote navigation safe.

"And there's the fear that the system could be hacked?" Reese added.

"Yes, the fear that the system could be hacked was a major concern. However—" Kate looked directly to the camera "—while there are many conspiracy theories, claims and debates, there has yet to be a single confirmed case of a commercial aircraft being cyber hacked."

"And that's our time," Reese said. "Thank you all for joining us. News is next."

Thirty-Seven

San Francisco, California

Veyda Hyde and Seth Hagen worked on their laptops at San Francisco International Airport while awaiting their return flight to Washington National.

Veyda suddenly seized her computer because their seats had shaken violently. Her first thought was: *Earthquake.* Wrong. The force was a boy who'd slammed his body into the seat beside her.

"Here! Mom! I wanna sit right here!" He smashed his fists repeatedly into the seat, causing Veyda's to bounce.

"We made it just in time." The boy's mother sighed as she arrived, struggling with their bags. The preboarding area for Washington, DC, passengers was next to the gate for an Atlanta-bound flight. The mother was either oblivious or indifferent to her son's behavior.

"Give me a cookie, now!" The boy jumped up and down, knocking over Veyda's take-out coffee cup, which emptied around her feet. Aware of his crime, the boy met Veyda's ice-cold glare, considered his situation, then pointed at her and said, "You made a mess!"

"No, *you* made a mess. Now, what do you say for being so rude?"

The boy's eyes narrowed in defiance.

"Mom! That strange lady's talking to me!"

"Oh, just look away, Billy. We'll be leaving in a minute."

The boy stuck out his tongue at Veyda, who glared back with such intensity the boy recoiled, retreating under his mother's arm.

"Mom! That lady's scaring me!"

The mother turned to Veyda, assessed her then pulled her son closer.

"Excuse me," the woman said, "do you have a problem with my child?"

"Was your son deprived of oxygen at birth?"

The mother's jaw dropped and Veyda stared at her for an uneasy moment, until the Atlanta flight was called.

"That's us, Billy." The mother stood. "Let's get away from here."

"I'll pray for you," Veyda said.

"What?" The mother stopped. "What did you say?"

"I'll pray." Veyda smiled. "That your plane doesn't crash."

Puzzled and unable to discern the full meaning of Veyda's comment, the woman scowled and left with her cookie-eating offspring. Veyda shot the woman and her spawn a parting glare.

Some people shouldn't be permitted to breed.

Veyda resumed her work, pleased that Seth had

possessed the wisdom not to intervene. They'd come to the Bay Area to pick up a critical component they needed to complete the next phase of their operation, a highly advanced integrated circuit that was in the final stages of development. Seth knew people in Mountain View with access to one and had arranged to buy it. He'd concealed it in a small case that resembled a USB key, which he was now admiring.

"This will guarantee our success, babe," he said before he zipped the key into a pocket of his carrying case.

Their return flight had been delayed, and they'd found a quiet corner in which to work. Seth was studying commercial air routes when Veyda nudged him to look at the TV suspended from the ceiling. It was tuned to CTNB's *Beyond the Headlines* with Reese Baker.

"Look, it's our reporter." Veyda moved closer to the TV, but kept her distance from other people. "This could be it. Kate Page could make the revelation now, live on network news."

Seth joined Veyda in watching, and the show began with footage of the Shikra and EastCloud incidents, after which Reese Baker introduced the subject and her panelists.

So this is Kate Page, Veyda thought. *She's pretty and she seems intelligent. She'd better do what's expected of her.*

Veyda and Seth focused on the panelists as they debated airline security, betraying a rudimentary understanding of what was and wasn't reality.

They know so little.

The minutes rolled by and Veyda's frustration evolved into anger.

When? When is she going to announce it? We selected her.

It soon became clear that Kate Page had missed every opportunity to acknowledge Zarathustra's triumphant work.

Look at her, prattling on. Why does she refuse to recognize our achievements in the name of Zarathustra? We selected her. We communicated with her specifically because she was the best reporter. We handed her the story of a lifetime. Now she's hogging the glory for herself.

Then Kate Page made her closing remarks.

"While there are many conspiracy theories, claims and debates, there has yet to be a single confirmed case of a commercial aircraft being cyber hacked."

Zarathustra! Zarathustra! We gave you confirmation! Veyda gritted her teeth. "This is insulting!"

Seth hushed her.

"Who does she think she is, Seth? She's done nothing extraordinary. We selected her to be part of history."

He took her back to the corner out of earshot of other passengers.

"She's nothing more than a lower-caste human," Veyda said. "Straight out of *Brave New World*. A lowly Gamma girl. Who does she think she is? Does she know how dangerous it is to defy us?"

Veyda burned to take action against Kate Page. Seth began working on his laptop, digging fast into her life, softly reciting to Veyda Kate Page's address, her Social Security number, her height, weight, her income, her shoe size, and he went on.

"I'll find out whatever you want," he said.

"Good. She needs to be taught a lesson. She needs to be punished!"

Thirty-Eight

Clear River, North Dakota

Scotch, bourbon and then Canadian whiskey gurgled down Robert Cole's kitchen drain as he emptied bottle after bottle.

Pungent alcoholic waves wafted from the sink, filling his nostrils. He licked his dry lips, contending with the powerful urge to keep one bottle.

Just one, a voice called from his well of sorrow. *One. Please.*

No, get rid of them all. It has to be done.

He needed a clear, strong mind because he had to do more than alert the NTSB to the fatal flaw of Richlon-Titan's system, and more than just providing them with the solution. Cole's supreme challenge would be convincing them that he was sober and sane enough to be believed.

And I've got to do this before more people are killed.

After he took the bottles to the trash outside his house, he made scrambled eggs, shaved and showered. Needles of hot water pricked his skin and his thoughts pulled him back across a wasteland of pain to his work on the system before the crash that took Elizabeth from him.

We'd discovered the vulnerability in RT's fly-by-wire system and we developed a solution. They rejected our findings, retested and said the existing system was secure. But did they make any changes to the system that I'm not aware of?

That was the critical question.

He dressed then stood in his dining room surveying the files he'd recovered from the second-hand dealer in Bismarck, relieved that he'd plucked them from destruction. He had folders with printed data, manuals, schematic drawings, equations and flash drives. He'd worked late the night before, painstakingly organizing the material by subject into neat stacks.

Bittersweet memories washed over him when he discovered that some of Elizabeth's and Veyda's papers, books and pictures had gotten mixed up with his work. There was one of him holding Veyda when she was three weeks old, another of him helping Veyda learn to ride a bike, and another of her with her first car. Cole missed them both, ached for them both.

Where are you, Veyda? Is it too late to repair our lives?

He didn't have time to dwell on the answers. He shifted his focus to the task before him. He read the reports arising from the Manila security conference and the claim that cyber infiltration of the Aircraft Communications Addressing and Reporting System and the Automatic Dependent Surveillance-

Broadcast System was possible, affording a hacker the capability to land, or crash, any plane in flight.

Official aviation bodies around the world had dismissed the claim as only a theoretical possibility but it had prompted Cole's team to review RT's system. That's when they'd discovered an unsecured back door at a connection between the aircraft's computing systems. It was vulnerable to attack. A skilled hacker could gain access to critical flight systems.

Cole spread a number of schematic drawings on the large table in the dining room. Here was his proposed remedy, the one he'd submitted that had been rejected. They'd said his analysis had been incorrect, that they'd retested the system in Europe.

But they'd been wrong.

He consulted a pile of reports concerning the European tests. Cole knew that they were inaccurate, that the results couldn't be trusted. He knew the issue for RT, especially Hub Wolfeson, was money. The retrofit needed to make the system secure would cost nine million dollars per aircraft. Wolfeson didn't think the risk was worth the expenditure and had persuaded the board to support him.

Cole studied other reports that a colleague at RT had sent him in the weeks after Elizabeth was killed.

"Cole—for when you're in shape to care. These are the changes Wolfeson approved. They cost nothing and they're a quick fix that fails to rectify the situation," read the note affixed to the reports.

Cole had never read the reports or looked at the schematic drawings showing the changes. He placed the drawings on the table and pored over them. As time passed, realization dawned on him. The system had been altered. It remained vulnerable but it also meant the solution he'd originally designed was now ineffective.

I have to design an entirely new solution.

A knot tightened in his gut. He'd have to do it without the help of his team, without the airline's resources.

I'm completely alone.

Cole stared at the schematics, seeing challenges at every turn.

The difficulties began swirling before him on the table.

This is too much for me.

Overwhelmed, he dragged the back of his hand across his mouth, feeling a craving coming to life like a wild force awakening in a cage, thrashing, roaring, demanding to be satisfied.

The hangar. There's still a few bottles of bourbon at the hangar. I could drive out there and... No!

Cole gripped his head with his hands.

Images of Shikra Airlines Flight 418 burning at Heathrow, of screaming passengers tossed about EastCloud Flight 4990, streaked through his brain.

I've got to do this before it happens again!

Thirty-Nine

Manhattan, New York

"There she is, crackerjack investigative reporter and celebrity panelist!"

Mark Reston, Kate's newsroom neighbor, ducked when she threw a crumpled news release at him as she settled in at her desk.

"Knock it off, Reston."

"Seriously, you done us proud there, Ms. Kate. I'm sure you riled up the crazies who'll want some of your stardust."

"Leave me alone—" her keyboard clicked "—I've got work to do."

"I'm grabbing a coffee." He stood. "Want one?"

"Sure, if you're buying."

Kate shook her head at Reston and at the whole CTNB thing. *My teacher said she saw you on TV, Mom,* Grace had said at breakfast that morning. *So did my friends at work,* Vanessa had added, forcing Kate to acknowledge the reach network news still held in the digital age.

After scanning the competition online, Kate determined that no one had hit on any new developments with the London or New York incidents. She was annoyed that no new leads had emerged for her in the wake of her CTNB panel—other than messages from friends and former colleagues across the country and around the globe who'd seen it.

Kate checked her public email box for the address tag that was affixed at the end of the story she wrote. The email count following the show was one hundred and ten. Thankfully, much of the spam had been filtered but, as usual, the crazies and idiots had weighed in.

"Nice job yesterday on the show." Chuck stopped at her desk.

"Thanks."

"It went well. You got anything new in the way of a concrete lead?"

She shook her head. When her phone rang, she looked at Chuck.

"Go ahead, take it. We'll talk some more later," he said, leaving her to answer her call. The number was blocked.

"Newslead, Kate Page."

"Hi, it's Erich."

"Hey, what's up? Got anything?"

"Not at the moment, but I wanted you to know that your TV panel has generated some chatter on the Darknet."

"Really? What kind of chatter?"

"Let's call it freestyle debate on myths, conspiratorial beliefs and the president's statement."

"Sounds weird."

"Listen, Kate, I've got to leave the country again.

But I've reached out to a guy I know who may be intimate with some classified initiatives in this area."

"Really? What's his code name?"

"Very funny. This guy's extremely sensitive about the press, but I've urged him to talk to you and he'll deny knowing me. That's our thing."

"I'll take any help I can get."

"I gotta go."

After hanging up, Kate found herself gazing across the newsroom at the empty workstation where Sloane F. Parkman used to sit.

"Chuck sure is cleaning house." Reston placed a coffee on Kate's desk.

"Thanks. Yeah, well, Sloane was no great loss."

"You heard the latest on Reeka?"

"That she's taking time off."

"Word is she's been told not to come back."

"Are you serious?"

"I heard they're working out terms of her departure and keeping it low-key. I'm telling you, little by little, step by step, Chuck Laneer is restoring the integrity of this place."

Reston's phone rang and he answered with "Be right there."

"Gotta go," he said to Kate.

"Thanks for the coffee."

It didn't take long before Kate had disposed of half the emails in her inbox. She'd flagged two to consider later. Before resuming, she reached for her coffee and locked onto the subject line of one email:

YOU FAILED ZARATHUSTRA—A TOLL WILL BE EXACTED

She opened it and read:

We offered you a place in history. We selected you because we regarded only you and your work worthy of the honor. We chose you to announce our triumph with Flight 4990 but you failed. The cost was 15 innocents from Flight 418. Then you insulted our victory with your televised lies. Why did you deny that we have taken control of the skies? Why did you lie? Like Peter's denial of Christ, it was preordained. We warn you now to tell the ordinary masses that we are extraordinary people destined to soon achieve a monumental victory on a colossal scale, the likes of which the world has never seen. We will take civilization to unprecedented heights, lighting the way forward for all of human existence. We are Zarathustra, Lord of the Heavens.

Kate felt the tiny hairs on the back of her neck stand up as she read the postscript:

Do not doubt the seriousness of our intentions. We know you live with your daughter and sister in Morningside Heights.

Forty

They know where we live!

Fear raged through Kate like a wildfire as seconds ticked down and buildings rushed by her cab's window.

Frantic, she'd shown Zarathustra's new threat to Chuck. He'd tried to calm her, and he'd made calls, but Kate hadn't waited. She'd torn out of the building, flagged a taxi and demanded the driver get her uptown to Grace's school on 115th Street as fast as possible.

Now, as her cab zigzagged through traffic, Kate made her second call to Grace's school.

"As I've said, Ms. Page, we've sent an assistant to Mrs. Blake's class. I assure you that we have nothing unusual to report. Your daughter's fine."

"Thank you. I'll be there to pick her up shortly."

"Is there something we need to be aware of, Ms. Page?"

Kate didn't want to alarm the entire school.

"No, I'm sorry. A family emergency's come up."

Catching her breath, Kate ended the call then pressed the number for Big Tony DiRenaldo's Grill, the diner where Vanessa worked. Kate needed to hear her sister's voice. Needed to know she was safe. The sounds of cutlery and dishes clanking amid the din of conversations spilled into the phone before Vanessa came to the phone.

"Are you okay?" Kate asked.

"Of course I'm okay. Why wouldn't I be okay? What's going on?"

"I'll tell you when I get to the diner with Grace."

"You're coming here with Grace? Kate, what's going on?"

"I'll explain it all when I see you."

Kate had to think, had to keep calm. Yes, she'd already been followed by a private investigator. That was one thing, but she'd handled that.

Or had she?

Then there was her feeling that someone had been in her hotel room while she'd been in London.

Could the Zarathustra messages be related? The emails are the bigger issue, a greater unknown. If it's all real, if Zarathustra has the ability to crash jetliners, then imagine what they could do to us.

Her mind swirled with scenarios and sweat trickled down her back as the cab halted at Grace's school. Kate told the driver to wait. Her hands trembled as she waited at the school office where a staff member eyed Kate closely over her bifocals.

"Is everything all right, Ms. Page?"

"Yes, a family matter." Kate turned when Grace arrived.

"Hi, Mom. What's wrong? Why're you here? Am I in trouble?"

"No, no, sweetie. I just need to have you with me for the day." Kate took her hand and then, for the benefit of the staff member, said, "I'll have you back in school tomorrow."

Big Tony DiRenaldo's Grill was on 130th Street.

Again, Kate told the driver to wait knowing she was facing a huge cab fare. The diner was busy, and it took a minute before Vanessa saw them. She led them to a booth and gave Grace a glass of chocolate milk, her favorite.

Kate took Vanessa aside, so Grace couldn't hear.

"What's going on, Kate?"

Kate pulled the printed email from her bag. Vanessa read it quickly.

"This isn't good, Kate."

"I know."

"You told me this story was giving you problems. Now someone is trying to scare you."

"I want you to know because I don't want to take any risks, okay?"

"I get that, but after all we've been through, you know that we don't scare easily. I don't like this. It makes me nervous, but I'm not going to let this idiot control my life."

"Yes, but we're not taking chances. I want you to text me all the time, where you're going and when you get there. Be vigilant, be careful, okay?"

Vanessa touched the back of her hand to her moist brow as a bell rang.

"Vanessa!" a man dressed in white called through

the small opening to the kitchen after setting two plates on the shelf. "Pick up!"

"Okay?" Kate repeated.

"Okay. I gotta work."

Kate sat down with Grace, who was blowing chocolaty bubbles through her straw just as Kate's phone rang.

"It's Chuck. We need you back in the newsroom."

Forty-One

Manhattan, New York

The air held traces of men's cologne in the glass-walled boardroom at Newslead's headquarters, where Kate joined Chuck Laneer, Graham Lincoln and five other people.

"Everyone, this is Kate Page," Chuck said. "Kate, I believe you know Nick Varner with the FBI from some of your previous stories. With him, also from the FBI, is Leonard Brock."

Nick and Brock, an older balding man, nodded, then Kate turned to the two men in rumpled jackets who sat across the table.

"We also have detectives Karl Steiger and Ted Malone of the NYPD."

Both men wore grim faces. The woman near them wore a dark blazer.

"And we have Helen Swayne, with our legal team."

Swayne opened her leather-bound notebook, clicked her pen and gave Kate a professional smile. Kate looked beyond the glass at the newsroom, where she'd left Grace at the copy editor's empty desk. She was doing her homework on her tablet.

Grace was safe.

"To bring you up to speed," Chuck began, "everyone's seen both emails, and everyone's been briefed. Now they have questions and thoughts to share. Nick, if you want to start."

"Right. There are multiple aspects to today's email—the implicit threat to take action against the airline industry, the demand for publication and the personal threat against you, Kate."

Kate nodded.

"Our first question," Varner said, "is have you experienced anything unusual that you might consider a result of your stories, or connected to the emails in question?"

"Nothing other than being followed, and I've reported that to the NYPD."

"That's right, and that's with us," Steiger said. "Kate informed us that a woman had followed her, and she managed to get the woman's license plate. We've determined the woman was a private investigator working for Infinite Guardian Shield, an international private firm."

"Any idea who hired her and why?" Lincoln asked.

"We've spoken with the firm. They're not required to give us that information. What they did was legal, but in light of this latest development, we'll continue to pursue the matter."

"Can you think of anyone who might have an ax to grind?" Varner asked. "Either with the airline, with your news agency, or with you?"

"One person comes to mind." Kate looked at Chuck and Lincoln.

"Who?"

"Sloane F. Parkman," Chuck said. "A reporter we recently terminated for violating company policy in relation to this story."

"A caution," Swayne said. "You don't have to volunteer this information."

"Given the circumstances," Lincoln said, "we will. Continue, Chuck."

The investigators took notes as Chuck recounted Sloane's history with Newslead, his relationship with Richlon-Titan and his behavior.

"We'll talk to him," Varner said, more to Swayne. "As you know, with the first email, it was your preference that we use a search warrant for our Computer Analysis and Response Team to gain access to all your servers and networks in order to identify the source of the email."

"Yes," Swayne said. "That's what we prefer, so we're not perceived as being police informants or an extension of a police agency."

"Expect us to issue another warrant for us to search everything related to Sloane Parkman."

"What's the status of your investigation into the source of the threats?" Chuck asked.

"Our work continues. We've yet to deem the threat either credible or a hoax by someone seeking attention in relation to the London and New York air incidents. We know that the sender is skilled, intelligent and is using sophisticated means to keep themselves anonymous. But this new email, with more content, may prove to be helpful and work to our advantage."

"Let's hope so," Lincoln said.

"With these threats, this person has committed

a felony, and they will be charged and prosecuted," Varner said. "Are you going to publish this email as demanded, or any part of it?"

Chuck and Kate looked at Lincoln to answer.

"As was the case with the first email," Lincoln said, "our position is unchanged. We have no plans to publish this demand."

"Good. That will give us time to assess and analyze the new content," Varner said.

"And it will give us time to pursue the private investigation launched against you, Kate," Steiger said.

"Sounds like we can wrap this up," Chuck said.

"One last matter." Varner looked at Kate. "We don't take the threat lightly. Let us know if you don't feel safe and the FBI can arrange for someone to stay with you and your family."

Images streaked through Kate's mind, memories of her being followed, of a sense of being watched in New York and London. *And that time I felt someone was in our building.*

She looked at Grace.

Then she looked at Varner.

"Yes, maybe for tonight."

Over lunch in the food court downstairs, Kate tried to explain the situation to Grace.

"You know how sometimes a bully will say 'I'm going to follow you and get you'?"

Grace nodded as she chewed.

"They say it but they never do it," Grace said. "They just want you to be afraid."

"That's right. Well, a bully said that to me because they didn't like my story, so the FBI is going to have an agent stay with us for tonight, just to be safe, okay? That's what this is all about today, okay?"

"I guess so. Maybe we should get a pizza, then?"

"That's a good idea." Kate smiled.

Kate called Vanessa to update her.

"You really think we need it, Kate?"

"Just for tonight. I need the peace of mind."

What Vanessa had said before was true, Kate thought. Because of all they'd endured, especially Vanessa, they weren't easily frightened. But Kate wasn't thinking about herself. She was thinking of Grace and Vanessa, and she needed to do something to ease her anxiety.

That afternoon, the FBI's Office for Victim Assistance called to make arrangements. A couple of hours later, Hank Bradley, an FBI agent, arrived in an SUV with two other agents to pick up Kate and Grace. Then they picked up Vanessa and drove to their building in Morningside Heights.

Bradley, a gentle giant of a man, along with the other two agents, inspected Kate's apartment before allowing Kate and her family inside. Satisfied it was secure, the two agents left and Bradley, who had an overnight bag, stayed. They had pizza and ice cream, then Kate set him up in Grace's room. Grace would spend the night with her.

Kate collected extra blankets for Bradley and knocked on his door. He opened it, wearing sweatpants and an FBI T-shirt. She saw his gun on Grace's nightstand, but also noticed scars on his arms. He noticed her looking at them.

"Sorry for staring."

"Don't apologize. I was wounded when I was on the SWAT team."

Bradley was in his fifties. He had a kind face, and Kate liked the way his eyes crinkled when he smiled. He reminded her of her dad.

"Thanks for being here," she said.

Despite Bradley's presence, Kate still had trouble sleeping.

She got up several times in the night, stood at her window and looked out at the darkened street and a sliver of the city's skyline.

Who are you, Zarathustra, and what are you planning?

Forty-Two

Manhattan, New York

Sloane F. Parkman gazed at the Brooklyn Bridge from the 28th floor of FBI's New York office in Lower Manhattan, where he sat at a table in a small room.

A file folder, thick with printed copies of emails, texts and cell phone records, was dropped before him.

"You've been busy," NYPD Detective Karl Steiger said.

Steiger and FBI Special Agent Nick Varner faced Sloane and Myron Gold, his attorney, across the polished table. It had been forty-eight hours since the FBI and NYPD had met with Newslead editors.

"Why did you ask me down here?" Sloane asked. "What's this about?"

"You know what this is about," Varner said.

"No, to be quite frank with you, I don't."

Sloane jumped when Steiger smacked the table with his hand.

"Don't play dumb with us! You know we've been

serving warrants. You know we've been talking to a lot of people. You're in a world of trouble."

Sloane's Adam's apple rose and fell as he adjusted the tie of his shirt. He'd tried to project cool confidence but the emergence of tiny beads of sweat on his upper lip had betrayed him.

"Are you Zarathustra?" Varner asked.

"You don't have to answer that," Gold said.

"I'll answer. The answer is no."

"We went through all of your emails at Newslead, at your home, all of your phone records," Varner said. "This is not the time to mislead us."

"I'm not misleading you."

"You threatened the air industry," Steiger said. "That's a criminal offence. You threatened Kate Page and her family, and that's a criminal offence."

"Hold on," Gold said. "I object to this line of questioning."

"Your client agreed to cooperate. He agreed to be interviewed." Varner turned to Sloane. "Your response?"

"I didn't threaten anybody."

"You knew about the Zarathustra communication," Varner said.

"You're talking about the email sent to Kate Page?"

"Yes."

"A lot of people knew about Zarathustra. Word got around the newsroom."

"You were working with Kate Page on stories concerning the plane that crashed in London and the plane that had problems before landing at La-Guardia," Steiger said.

"Yeah, so?"

"You were at odds with Kate Page and your editor about the stories. You tried to dissuade her from pursuing them. You tried to downplay them. Why's that?" Varner asked.

Silence.

"Did it have anything to do with your family connection to Richlon-Titan?"

Sloane licked his lips but said nothing.

"You were fired for violating Newslead's rules, weren't you?"

"So what?"

"Agent Varner," Gold said, "we are contesting Newslead's dismissal of my client."

"You're not being very cooperative, Sloane," Steiger said. "You'd better rethink your strategy, pal."

"I'm answering questions."

"Do you know who Connie Lopilla is?" Varner asked.

"No."

"Are you familiar with Infinite Guardian Shield?"

Sloane didn't answer.

"Infinite Guardian Shield is a private investigation agency and Connie Lopilla is a private investigator who was hired to conduct surveillance on Kate Page. Tell us, who wanted Kate Page followed?"

"I don't know."

"You don't know?" Steiger reached into the folder and plucked out pages bearing text underlined in red. "See this?" Steiger jabbed his finger on the pages. "You sent Infinite Guardian Shield Kate Page's address, information about her daughter, her sister and other private data you took from Newslead's employee contact list, which you had access to. Now, why would you do that?"

Sloane didn't answer.

"You can't keep pretending not to know," Varner said. "The evidence is sitting in front of you. We've studied these emails, especially those between you and your uncle, Hub Wolfeson, who sits on Richlon-Titan's board. Your uncle wanted you to do anything possible to prevent RT from looking bad. Isn't that right?"

Sloane said nothing.

"And, as luck would have it, you were in a perfect position to take care of it, weren't you?"

Sloane remained silent.

"You went to Harvard, didn't you?" Varner said. "We obtained your school records. Seems you took a philosophy course that included the study of Friedrich Nietzsche's work."

Varner slid him a page showing a photo of one of Nietzsche's most famous works, *Thus Spake Zarathustra*. "We found this on a shelf in your apartment."

"Agent Varner," Gold said, "I'd say many college graduates across the country have that book."

"I'm asking Sloane. Now, I'll ask you again. Did you make the communication to Kate Page as Zarathustra?"

Sloane said nothing.

"Threatening harm to an airliner is a felony," Varner said. "Now's the time to come clean, because in about five minutes we'll be talking to the US Attorney, and what you tell us will have an impact on what we tell her." Varner looked hard into

Sloane's eyes. "And I gotta tell you, she lost people in 9/11, so she won't be taking any of this lightly."

Sloane cupped his hands in his face, then looked to Gold, telegraphing that the interview had not gone as he had been told it would go.

A moment passed before Gold nodded for his client to answer.

Sloane exhaled.

"All right. Not long after the EastCloud thing happened, my uncle contacted me. I don't hear from him for months and suddenly Hub Wolfeson is talking to me."

"What did he want?" Varner asked.

"He wanted me to see if I could influence Newslead's coverage of the incident by ensuring that anything reported about Richlon-Titan was not damaging. The stock was shaky. He promised me a position with the corporation if I succeeded. So yes, I tried to downplay the story and deflect attention from RT, to get a different story out there, another version."

"Was it your idea to follow Kate Page?"

"No. It was requested through Richlon-Titan's corporate security, at my uncle's insistence. He wanted to know who Kate was talking to. I just passed on information."

"Why go to these lengths?"

"Several deals with airlines in India, Saudi Arabia, Brazil and Japan, amounting to two hundred new RT jetliners, or jets with RT systems, were pending. A lot was at stake."

"So you created Zarathustra in a further effort to

draw attention from the company after the crash in London and the incident with the EastCloud plane?"

"No. I had nothing to do with that."

"Don't start lying now."

"I admit to what I've just told you, but I swear I'm not Zarathustra."

"Would you agree to submit to a polygraph examination as soon as possible?"

"I would."

Forty-Three

"**D**amn. So close," Keith Dorling whispered to himself, his chair creaking as he leaned back to think in the subdued light of his workstation.

He'd shifted his focus from his three monitors to the faces of his wife, Eve, and their little girls, Hayley and Ariel, smiling back from the framed photo beside his keyboard, taken during last summer's trip to Cape Cod.

What I do here keeps them safe.

Dorling worked at the Defense Cyber Crime Center. Known as DC3, it operated under the Air Force Office of Special Investigations. He was a civilian analyst, an expert in cyber crime, and he held top secret security clearance with DC3's Analytical Group.

The group was a member agency of the National Cyber Investigative Joint Task Force and was helping the FBI. Dorling, regarded as one of the center's best investigators, had been tasked to help investigate the Zarathustra emails.

For the past several days, he'd been attempting to track the source of the potential threat arising from emails sent to Newslead, a news agency in New York, and the Kuwaiti Embassy in London. This case was unlike any he'd pursued. The subject was remarkably skilled. Dorling had marveled at the beauty of the encryption work that the sender, Zarathustra, had employed. It reflected a level of sophistication and understanding that Dorling had rarely encountered in his work. His target had used rented servers in Thailand and Romania. Dorling had been tight on the trail, discovering that Zarathustra's path then went to Sweden, and then to servers in Estonia.

With the Kuwaiti email, he'd found a glimmer of something that took the trail to the United States, suggesting that the end point—or source—was here.

But it had vanished.

That's where I lost it. I can't find the source. Not yet.

Dorling exhaled, reviewed the logs and dates, then rechecked all the notes supplied by analysts in the UK who were also pursuing Zarathustra.

I must've missed something. Okay, back to square one.

He shook his head and resumed working.

Forty-Four

Sloane F. Parkman's polygraph results were consistent with the truth.

"It's unlikely he's responsible for creating and sending the Zarathustra emails," Nick Varner wrote at his desk.

Varner was updating his case notes with everything he, Special Agent Leonard Brock, Karl Steiger and Ted Malone of the NYPD had so far.

The United States Attorney was reviewing their evidence against Sloane concerning the passing of information to a private investigation agency for the purpose of surveilling Kate Page. Probably not much of a case there, Varner thought.

Then he consulted status reports from Scotland Yard in London.

Little news had emerged.

No progress had been made by British investigators on the origin of the emails. To date, authorities in the United States, the UK and Kuwait had failed to uncover any evidence suggesting the

Shikra crash was a criminal action, or linked to the EastCloud flight.

Varner turned to the latest from Ron Sanchez with Cyber Crimes and the National Cyber Investigative Joint Task Force. While Ron and the task force had reported that they'd gotten close to the source of the email, their investigation was ongoing.

Still untraceable.

Varner shook his head.

The task force had experts from something like twenty intelligence and law enforcement agencies, including the best from the industry, yet Zarathustra had thwarted them all so far. If this person was that good, then was it possible that their claims that they could remotely control aircraft were true?

We need a break here.

A knock sounded at his workstation.

"Ready for the call, Nick?" Leonard Brock asked.

"Yup." Varner gathered his notes.

Varner and Brock were joined by Trent Hollis, their supervisory agent, Steiger, Malone, Sanchez and a few others in a boardroom for a short teleconference call on the case with the Behavioral Analysis Unit.

Joanne Foley of the BAU led the call from Quantico, Virginia.

After a round of introductions, Foley, an analyst who'd studied the Zarathustra emails and the known case facts, presented her findings.

"I have to tell you—" her voice crackled on the line "—there's not a lot here, so put whatever BAU offers into that context."

"Of course," Varner said. "We're interested in anything you can provide or recommend."

"All right. Again, it's pretty thin, and much of it is obvious."

Varner's pen was poised over his yellow pad as Foley began.

"For our purposes, I'll refer to your subject as Z. Your subject is on a mission. Z is clearly egocentric and craves attention for their mission. The reference to the German philosopher Friedrich Nietzsche suggests an above-average intelligence, someone with maybe one or two degrees."

"What about the threat?" Hollis asked. "How do you weigh that?"

"With some difficulty. There is no technical information, nothing specific that would give it credibility. And, based on what I can deduce from the information you sent me, there's no evidence that links Z's messages to the cases at issue. Still, I would not rule out the potential. Again, you have nothing concrete on which to act."

"Do you have any recommendations?" Varner asked.

"Publish the emails."

"Really?" Hollis asked. "Wouldn't that create problems, inspire copycats and invite unstable people to make demands for attention?"

"Yes, you would run that risk. However, with this case, even with these short messages, the syntax, the language, the content and subject are rather distinctive. Putting it out to the public creates the possibility that the nature of the content could be identified by someone who could point you to your subject."

Soft murmuring rippled around the table before Foley continued.

"I'm suggesting you go to the press and request they publish an excerpt, but with a story that is framed in a way that limits panic in the airline industry. You could present it as an FBI appeal to the public for help locating a person of interest. The advantage is that you appear to be meeting Z's demand for attention while turning the table on them. It's not without risks, though."

"Yes, we could anger Z," Varner said, "or open the floodgates to false leads, dead ends and other unstable people. Or, by feeding Z's ego, we could inspire more threats and demands."

"Correct on all fronts."

"And there's no guarantee the press would agree to such a request," Steiger said. "That could be a challenge."

"Correct again," Foley said. "But I could help you with points on how to frame it and how to pitch it to the media. Also, you could hold some information back in order to help you quickly eliminate any false claims or leads."

Varner looked to Hollis, who was deep in thought.

"Unless you've got other avenues of investigation, or are absolutely certain Z is not a danger to commercial air travel," Foley said, "this is one strategy to consider. Honestly, it appears to be your best option."

"I agree," Hollis said. "Let me talk to some people."

Within two and a half hours, Varner and Hollis, with Foley on the line, were at Newslead's headquarters in the same boardroom where they'd met earlier.

Graham Lincoln, Chuck Laneer and Kate Page listened as Varner provided updates.

Because of Newslead's involvement, the FBI was sharing more information than they normally would on the status of the investigation. They updated them on Sloane, and on how they'd yet to identify the origin of the emails. Once they'd outlined the full context, they requested that Newslead publish Zarathustra's email.

The request was met with silent, sober concern until finally, Lincoln responded.

"This raises significant ethical issues," he said. "We need to give this very careful consideration. Give us some time to think this through and we'll get back to you."

Forty-Five

Eyeglasses were repositioned, pens were tapped and sections of text underlined as Newslead's senior editors studied the three Zarathustra emails and the FBI's request to publish them.

Everything was on one page, provided by the FBI.

The FBI had also given Newslead a short timeline of events and the edited email text they'd wanted published. Additionally, they'd provided notes on the hold-back information that would help authenticate any tips, should people call the news service.

"Absolutely nothing leaves this room," Lincoln began. For the next several minutes he, Chuck and Kate recounted all Newslead had uncovered on the London and New York incidents.

"You have the facts as we know them," Lincoln said. "Since we received the first email, we've been mindful of our journalistic duty and respectful of the roles of law enforcement and federal aviation investigators. But the story has intensified with the latest email. The FBI's request raises ethical concerns. The question we need to answer is do we publish or not. Let's go around the table. Jerry?"

"I say no," Jerry Lemothe, deputy national editor and a perpetual gum chewer, said. "This is meant more for this Zarathustra than the FBI, but nobody should dictate what we write. We can't allow stories to be extorted from us. If we did this, we'd set a precedent, and we'd open the floodgates to every malcontented crazy out there."

National features editor Ellen Markon pushed her glasses to the top of her head and turned to Lemothe.

"But Jerry, it's our job to inform the public," she said. "And to protect the public's right to know."

"True," Howard Kehoe said, "but we'd run the risk of being perceived as a branch of the police, an investigative tool. It's not our job to aid police. We shouldn't do it."

"What about when we publish most-wanted info for police?" Marisa McDougal asked. "We certainly aided police last month in their search for the convicts who'd escaped from prison in Texas, and last week when that mother and her child were abducted in Los Angeles. I don't see how this is much different."

"Marisa makes a good point," Markon said. "There's an overriding safety concern, a real possibility this person can do what they claim."

"Is there?" Lemothe asked. "So far the NTSB and the FAA have not indicated any such thing."

"Jerry's right," Kehoe said. "Nothing's been proven to show this disturbed person has the resources to control airplanes. We shouldn't rush to cede editorial control. If we feed this nut job's ego, then we'll run the risk of copycats and more demands."

Ellen Markon shook her head.

"No, I say we publish it. We have an obligation to do all we can to help identify this person," she said. "I'm concerned about what we've seen here—the EastCloud incident, the Shikra tragedy with fifteen deaths. Look at Sloane, his ties to Richlon-Titan and the unbelievable aspect of Kate being followed. There's so much we don't know, so much at risk."

"That's right," Marisa added.

"No, the more I think of it," Ellen said, "the more I believe we need to expose the facts and see where they take us."

"Chuck, what do you think?" Lincoln asked.

"Everyone's made solid arguments," he said. "But we have to look at the bigger picture. Newslead knows more about what's at stake than any other news outlet. We're not bending to the will of Zarathustra. We're not publishing a manifesto, and the FBI isn't asking for editorial control. They want us to agree to use the portion of the Zarathustra email they've edited so as not to alarm the public.

"The FBI needs to identify Zarathustra to assess the validity of the threat. At the same time, to the best of our knowledge, aviation experts have yet to report anything that would confirm, or even suggest, that a cyber hijack was behind the two incidents. We've told the FBI how we would frame the story, and it is our story. Remember, we went to them first and since then the relationship on this has been respectful. But if we say no to publishing this excerpt, there's nothing to stop the FBI from arranging some deal with a news competitor."

Chuck waited for his comments to sink in.

"So far, this information is exclusive to us. It could yield a tip that would be exclusive to us. A reader may recognize the writing, the phraseology. The peculiarity of the sentence construction of the message might ring a bell that leads to an arrest, or something more."

"Chuck, are you leaning toward publishing?" Lincoln asked.

"Yes, I say publish."

"And you, Kate?"

"Publish."

Lincoln removed his glasses and massaged the bridge of his nose.

"Well, I think we should publish and it appears we have a consensus to do so. Kate, pull a story together, go as long as you like with it, and we'll get this thing moving. Chuck, when we're ready I'll take a look at it. Then we'll alert subscribers to what's coming.

Kate grabbed a coffee, returned to her desk, got into her zone and began writing.

Within five minutes, she'd crafted her lede:

A potential puzzle piece has emerged in the mystery surrounding the horrific crash of a jetliner at London's Heathrow airport and the near-tragic incident experienced by a New York–bound commuter plane.

She then drafted what was known in journalism as "nut grafs"—a few tight paragraphs containing the news facts and background details of Shikra Flight 418 and EastCloud Flight 4990. She followed them with:

But in a new twist, Newslead has learned that the FBI is examining cryptic communications made by someone claiming to have knowledge of what is behind both events.

Assertions of responsibility are not uncommon during the course of an investigation. And while American and British investigators have stated that nothing has yet surfaced to suggest terrorism or even criminality is behind the incidents, the FBI is attempting to locate "a person or persons of interest."

She provided a timeline on the two cases, interspersing the section with comments she'd obtained from aviation experts, and referencing the emails sent to Newslead and the Kuwaiti Embassy in London by a person using the name Zarathustra.

Using the section of Zarathustra's email that had been edited by the FBI, Kate wrote that in one message, the sender had said:

"...tell the ordinary masses that we are extraordinary people destined to soon achieve a monumental victory of a colossal scale, the likes of which the world has never seen. We will take civilization to unprecedented heights, lighting the way forward for all of human existence. We are Zarathustra, Lord of the Heavens."

Kate had called a professor of literature at Columbia University, requesting his thoughts concerning Zarathustra, and the connection to German philosopher Friedrich Nietzsche.

Kate then quoted official spokespeople from the NTSB, the FAA, and British and Kuwaiti agencies, who'd stated that their investigations were ongoing and that they could not elaborate or comment on the Zarathustra emails.

She ended the story with a closing quote from an aviation expert.

"It's not possible to hack into a system and take remote control of a commercial airliner, a so-called cyber hijack," he said. "In the end you'll find the boasts and wild claims made in the cryptic messages stem from a troubled and fantasy-driven mind. It's a sad fact that disturbed individuals who have such delusions create this sort of widespread, groundless fear."

After polishing her story, she proofread it, then sent it to Chuck.

Kate then finished her coffee and texted Grace and Vanessa. She needed to hear from them.

All was fine.

Then, to cope with her anxiety, she went to Chuck's office, where he'd just finished reviewing her article. He'd passed it along to Lincoln, who would send it to the news desk to handle and send out.

"It's going global," Chuck said. "Good job, Kate. Good storytelling."

"Yeah, well, I don't feel good about it."

"Why's that?"

"It leaves me wondering if we've eroded the line between a free press and the police, and in the process, have we just given a criminal the world stage that they'd craved?"

"Time will tell, Kate. Time will tell."

Forty-Six

Hyattsville, Maryland

Seth opened another can of "Shark's Blood" energy drink, took a big gulp and belched before he resumed working.

Ensconced at his desk amid his high-powered laptops, he looked over the material piled around him—studies, drawings and manuals. He glanced at Veyda, who was on the sofa across the room. She was still undecided on what action they'd take against Kate Page for her failings.

For now, Veyda was working on her laptop, nodding her head while listening to music. Florence and the Machine's "Dog Days Are Over"—he could hear it leaking from her earphones.

Seth smiled and went back to a document he knew well, a United States federal report released in 2015 by the Government Accountability Office that pointed to weaknesses in air traffic control systems. The study suggested there was a small possibility that commercial jetliners may be vulnerable to having their computer systems hacked and hijacked remotely. Other experts disagreed with the findings.

The entire issue was currently a subject of some debate.

Seth considered the report rudimentary, but continued examining it as he worked. Seth examined the telecommunications infrastructure and the satellite-based Automatic Dependent Surveillance-Broadcast System, which used Global Positioning. He paused, swallowed more Shark's Blood, then studied the report on the En Route Communications Gateway and the Traffic Flow Management Infrastructure.

Full of holes, like Swiss cheese. I've seen gaming systems that were better designed.

A notification alert sounded on two of his laptops. The distinct tone signaled that a Kate Page story had just been posted online. Seth glanced at Veyda. The alert would override her music. He began reading:

A potential puzzle piece has emerged in the mystery surrounding the horrific crash of a jetliner at London's Heathrow airport and the near-tragic incident experienced by a New York–bound commuter plane.

Seth continued reading then shot Veyda another glance; she'd pulled out her earphones and was digesting the story. When he came to the first reference to Zarathustra he said, "There it is, babe."

Veyda's face lit up with the beginnings of a smile that soon vanished. "What's this?" She repeated parts of the story aloud.

"'It's not possible to hack into a system and take

remote control of a commercial airliner.' Wrong, wrong, wrong, wrong! Fifteen corpses in London say otherwise!"

"I don't get it," Seth said.

"And listen. 'In the end you'll find the boasts and wild claims made in the cryptic messages stem from a troubled and fantasy-driven mind. It's a sad fact that disturbed individuals who have such delusions create this sort of widespread, groundless fear.'"

Veyda clenched her jaw and lifted her head to the ceiling.

"This is so insulting, Seth. Kate Page held so much promise. This is not what we instructed her to do!"

Seth took a moment and read the story a second time.

"I'm concerned," he said. "There's something about the article, a subtext at play."

"What do you mean?"

"I can't help thinking that there's more to this story, that maybe they're getting close to us."

"No. If they were close, a SWAT team would be kicking down the door. They're clueless, Seth. Remember, we're dealing with the unevolved, linear thinking of ordinary people. As extraordinary people, we have the authority to punish Kate Page."

"What do you want to do?" Seth's keyboard clicked as he worked. "We could steal her identity, drain her bank account, create a blood test with traces of heroin and cocaine and send it to her employer anonymously. We could anonymously report her to police for child abuse."

Veyda gave his options a moment of consideration.

"They're good but rather mundane. They lack artistry. What I'm thinking of is bigger. We have to make an example of her."

Veyda concentrated on her laptop, shaking her head bitterly.

"Those worms. They have the audacity to say I have a fantasy-driven mind, that I'm delusional. Don't they know that we're extraordinary people, that we're elevating humankind? They owe us reverence!"

Veyda made a few keystrokes and their hundred-inch flat-screen TV came to life, displaying footage of the fiery Heathrow crash, then screaming passengers being tossed about on the EastCloud flight.

"We'll show them something the world will never forget."

Forty-Seven

Manhattan, New York

The infectious rhythm of Peruvian music kept time with the slap of skipping rope in Washington Square Park where Grace jumped double Dutch with street performers near the fountain.

As the music and ropes went faster, Kate and Vanessa cheered Grace on from a bench nearby. She kept pace until a misstep entangled her in the ropes, but the performers invited her to try again and as they resumed, Kate checked her phone.

It was Saturday, the day after Kate's story on Zarathustra had run. Kate and Vanessa both had days off. They'd taken Grace shopping in Greenwich Village before coming to the park.

But Kate's mind was on the response to her story—*Will it lead us to Zarathustra and the validity of the claim of hijacking jetliners?*

She hadn't dismissed Zarathustra's threat to her family, implied in the "we know where you live" line. While they no longer had Agent Hank Bradley staying with them, Kate and Vanessa were vigilant, keeping an eye on Grace and the nearest cop.

Everything was fine, under the circumstances.

On the response, Newslead had, so far, received about twenty emails or calls from readers offering advice. One reader offered her services as a "spiritual guide." Some callers had claimed to know Zarathustra, but then provided vague or useless information. *I think it's the cabdriver I had once, he was always quoting Nietzsche.* Or *It's a guy I met in a bar. He was talking about how we need to take down the government.*

Those were the responses for Kate.

As for the FBI, Varner had told her that in two instances, callers had claimed to be Zarathustra but had been unable to provide accurate information on the unpublished content of the email.

Kate was preparing to send Erich a message when Grace finished skipping. Kate gave her a five-dollar bill to drop in the performers' hat.

"Let's get a drink." Vanessa pointed to the nearest hot dog cart.

As they sipped their sodas on the grass in the shade of a maple tree, Kate's phone rang.

"Hi, Kate. It's Todd," the news assistant said. "I know you're off, but Chuck said to alert you if a reader called with something important."

"Sure, what's up?"

"I got this guy on the line. It's the third time he's called in an hour. He insists on talking to you directly, says he's got information that he wants to share with you."

"What kind of information?"

"He wouldn't say, only that it was critical."

"Did he give you his name, or his connection to the story?"

"No, nothing, and he refused to leave a message."

"Did he sound credible, or certifiable, Todd?"

"Hard to tell."

"Yeah, that's often the case. Okay, put him through."

"I'll connect him to you. Hang on."

While she waited, Kate turned to Grace and Vanessa.

"I have to take this. I'm sorry. Think about where we could go for lunch later."

Kate stood and walked a few feet away when her phone clicked.

"Hello?" a man said. "Is this Kate Page?"

"Yes."

"I saw you on CTNB with Reese Baker talking about the president's promise of technology to land passenger jets by remote control."

"Yes. First can I get your name?"

Silence.

The caller ID displayed the newsroom switchboard number because the call was bounced to Kate's phone.

"I'd like to know who I'm talking to."

"I don't want to say right now. First, I nccd to know if you protect sources."

"Yes, we do. I understand you have information?"

"On CTNB, you discussed the technology and debated its existence and use in the wake of 9/11?"

"Right."

"Are you aware of Project Overlord?"

"No. Hold on a sec." Kate muted her phone and

got Vanessa to search Project Overlord. It came up as some sort of video game. Kate rolled her eyes. "Is it something to do with video game programs?"

"No. It's a top secret government project to develop the technology to land hijacked commercial jets by remote control. Overlord is what the president promised."

"And how do you know this?"

"Listen, I was not, and am not, involved, okay?"

The way his voice grew nervous caused a shift in Kate's attitude.

"Involved in what?"

"Overlord."

"Okay."

"I was a contractor for various national security projects. I have a lot of friends in the business."

"Would one be named Erich?"

"No."

"How about Viper?"

"I don't know who you're talking about."

"You say you *were* a contractor on national security projects. What're you doing now?"

"Now? Let's say I'm something of an underground activist."

"Activist for what?"

"Letting the public know the truth about what its government is up to. With Overlord, the government worked with defense and airline experts to develop the technology to land troubled planes safely by remote control. It was called the Unhindered Autopilot System."

"We said on the show that the technology exists, that patents were obtained to develop it."

"You barely scratched the surface. Overlord was developed, but abandoned after the government feared it was leaked or stolen."

"You mean it's out there?"

"That's the fear."

"Then why haven't we heard more about this?"

"They don't want the public to know. It would destroy the airline industry and cripple the global economy."

Kate took a moment.

"I'm sorry but this is too fantastic to believe."

"I have documentation."

Kate caught her breath.

"Okay, send it to me and let me take a look at it."

"No. I'll give it to you only in person, if you agree to meet me."

"Are you in New York City?"

"No. California."

"Are you coming to New York?"

"No. You'd have to come here."

"To California? Look, I can't go to California based on your claim."

"Give me an email."

"What?"

"Give me an email. I'll send you a sample and you'll see. It's classified documentation I received from my sources, part of a file I've been assembling."

Kate gave him an email, a safe one that protected against viruses and malware. Twenty seconds later, her phone chimed, and she was reading a page on Homeland Security letterhead stamped Top Secret. It was less than a year old and had the grainy look of a document that had been photocopied several times. The subject headline was Project Overlord: Security Breach Concern.

Much of the content was redacted, blacked out, except the headline Project Chiefs. Some two dozen names and their affiliations were listed under it. Each name and affiliation was redacted. However, initials were penned next to some. Kate read: AU, JF, KS, RC, RM, SK, TH.

She got back on the line with her caller.

"How can I tell if this is a legitimate document? Besides, with so much blacked out, I'm not even sure what it says."

"It's real. I swear it's real. Little by little I've been getting leads on the names of the team members. I think one of them was suspected of a security breach and that person is your Zarathustra."

"How did you come to that conclusion?"

"I've been connecting the dots. That's what I do. And I heard through the grapevine that one of the experts had a family tragedy and became unstable. I have no idea which one. There are twenty-four. But I'm thinking that it's possible whichever one it was may be using the technology to exact some revenge for the project being canceled or something."

"That's a heck of a leap there."

"I know, but I've been working on this and watching your reports and I'm convinced this is your smoking gun. The incidents with the Shikra and EastCloud flights are the evidence. If you agree to meet me in person, I'll give you all the documents, the information, some of the names I have, everything."

"Why not go to the FBI or the FAA, or NTSB?"

"I'd be charged with possessing confidential national security documents. You, being the press, are protected by shield laws."

Kate looked over at her daughter and sister.

"Okay, I have to go. Let me think about this and talk it over with my editors. Give me a number to call you."

"No, I'll call you."

"I need a number from you."

"I can't do that. I'll call your news desk and I'll use the name Malcolm Grady. Tell them to put me through to you."

"Okay, very clandestine, like the movies."

"Yeah," he said nervously. "Like the movies."

Kate hung up and stared at nothing until she felt a tug at her arm.

"Mom?" Grace was loud.

"Yes, sweetie."

"I *said* can we go to the Shake Shack?"

Forty-Eight

"We've got to look into this," Chuck told Kate on the phone.

She'd reached him while he was at the Hemingway exhibit at the Morgan Library in Midtown Manhattan. After she told him about her tip regarding Project Overlord and sent him the attachment, Chuck said he wanted to meet at Bryant Park.

Kate, Grace and Vanessa took a cab there from the Shake Shack. Chuck was waiting at a table near the carousel. It was nice to see him without a button-down shirt and tie, casual in a navy polo shirt and khakis. But the expression on his face was all business. Vanessa and Grace lined up for a ride on the carousel, leaving Kate and Chuck to talk.

"We may have something here," he said. "But there are concerns. Is the document genuine, or are we being set up? Is this guy a nut, or the real deal?"

"I certainly had the same concerns."

"After you called and sent me the attachment, I sent it to Yardley at our DC bureau."

"What's he think?"

"We'll find out soon. He'll be calling me."

As if on cue, Chuck's phone vibrated and he answered.

"Laneer."

As he listened, Kate waved to Grace, who passed by laughing on a white horse. The carousel huffed out organ music as Vanessa took pictures.

"Okay, Tim, I'm putting you on Speaker." Chuck adjusted his phone and set it on the table. He and Kate leaned in to hear Yardley without increasing the volume. There was no risk of them being overheard above the squealing children and other sounds of the park.

"I've never heard of Project Overlord," Yardley said. "But there've always been rumors the government was working on something along those lines after 9/11."

"What about the document? Does it look real?" Chuck asked.

"It does, but there's no surefire way for us to test its authenticity without raising flags. If I started showing it to national security sources here, we'd tip our hand."

"We could take it to the FBI, see what they'll confirm?" Kate asked.

"No," Chuck said.

"But we've been doing well with them," Kate said.

"No, your caller's scared. He trusts you. No, you get to him first and get the records."

"I just thought we could leverage something from

the FBI because we're always pushing them to give us stuff," Kate said.

"That's how it is. That's our job. We traffic in information—that's our role. We're not police informants. We've already alerted them to the security and safety aspects of this story. We are not partners with law enforcement. They'll do a criminal investigation and we'll do a journalistic one."

"I agree with Chuck, Kate," Yardley said.

"What's your take on sending Kate to California, based on what we have?" Chuck asked.

"I'd send her to meet the source, get a read on him, get the documents. We can work on verifying them. If it goes south, all it'll cost you is the trip. Otherwise, if you fumbled on the real deal, someone else will score on you."

"Agreed. Thanks, Tim." Chuck hung up and looked at Kate. "I'll send you to California to pursue this, but with a few conditions. Go as soon as you can make arrangements with your source and our travel office. But you're not going alone. You'll go with a photographer."

"What? Why?"

"It's my job to watch out for you and put this into context. Look at all that's happened to you with this story. I'm not taking any risks."

"Neither am I. I'm a big girl, and I've been covering crime stories on my own for years. I can handle myself."

"Fine. You can fly out alone, but once you land you'll go everywhere you need to go with a photographer from our Los Angeles bureau. I'll advise our LA folks to line someone up for you. They won't like it. Bureau people are touchy about national staff working in their yard. Just so we're clear, my terms are nonnegotiable. And you'll check in with me at every step."

He looked at her for a long, serious moment.

"Is that understood, Kate?"

"It is."

"Good." He nodded to Grace and Vanessa. "You have two good reasons to be careful."

Chuck was right, Kate thought, while watching Grace's reflection in the subway window during the ride home to Morningside Heights.

She was sleeping on Kate's shoulder. Kate put her arm around her.

Vanessa smiled at them and took a picture.

Later that day, she took two more calls from "Malcolm Grady." Only after assurances that she hadn't informed any law enforcement or federal security agency about Project Overlord did he provide an address and a time for Kate to meet him.

The next morning Kate called Newslead's travel office, and they got her a direct flight that afternoon out of JFK.

Her flight was with American Airlines, the aircraft an Airbus A321—a great airline and a great plane. Nothing to do with Richlon-Titan. Kate had no fear of flying. Because of her job she'd flown many times, and it was about as stressful to her as crossing the street.

As the engines whined and the jet raced down the runway and lifted off, forcing her deep into her seat, a bad feeling began to steal over her.

Images of the terror inside the EastCloud flight and the fiery Heathrow crash blazed in her mind. Her jet climbed and she fought the fear mounting in her heart until she choked it off.

At last, the plane leveled.

Kate took a deep breath, letting it out slowly while searching the clouds and wondering what awaited her in California.

Forty-Nine

The faces of the dead haunted Jake Hooper as he and Pax rounded the corner at the east end of the pool at the National Mall.

It had been two days since he'd returned from London.

During his time there the *Daily Mail* had run a front-page gallery of photos of the Heathrow crash victims, six children and nine adults, inlayed over the wreckage.

The images were seared into Hooper's memory and weighed heavily on him as he tried to resume his routine. His early-morning runs with Pax at the Mall helped him organize his thoughts about his work and his life.

The night before, at their anniversary dinner, he'd given his wife, Gwen, the pearl necklace and earrings he'd bought in London. She'd given him a watch he'd liked and good news.

The vet says they're going to put Pax on an experimental drug therapy. It'll give him three to four more pain-free years. Isn't that great?

It was more than that.

Now, as Hooper finished his run, Pax's spirits seemed lifted. He panted happily as Hooper bent down and nuzzled him.

"Now we have hope, buddy. Now we have hope."

That was not the case with Hooper's work on the Shikra and EastCloud flights. The investigations were progressing slowly, though that was expected because they were always meticulous and exhaustive.

They had to be.

But recent developments had deepened Hooper's concerns about a possible cause.

When he got to his desk in NTSB headquarters at L'Enfant Plaza, he took out his copy of the *Daily Mail* and spread it across his desk. He stared into the faces of those who'd been killed and vowed to find the answers their families deserved.

Shikra, British, American and Kuwaiti investigators had examined a range of potential causes. Was it an irregularity in the computers controlling the engine systems? Was it an electronic malfunction? They'd studied weather systems and the possibility of a bird strike and they'd looked at radio interference.

All were ruled out.

But there were still hundreds of other aspects of the aircraft that they needed to study, and the investigation continued with plans for Hooper and other members of the team to return to the UK at the end of the month.

As for EastCloud Flight 4990, Hooper reviewed the latest examination of the fault logs of the Electrical Load Management System. So far their review had gone back thirty flights. No anomalies had emerged. They would go back another thirty flights. And they were still studying the quick access recorder. Meanwhile weather systems had found no indication of turbulence, nothing on radar. Bill Cashill and Irene Zimm were still pointing to human performance and crew behavior as the likely cause behind the trouble of the Buffalo–to–New York flight.

Hooper disagreed.

He believed the source of the cause in both incidents would be found in Richlon-Titan's fly-by-wire system, which was present in both planes. Underscoring his view was the increasingly disturbing aspect with the emails, the so-called Zarathustra messages, claiming responsibility.

The FBI had advised the NTSB that it was investigating and working on tracking the sender, which included the public appeal for help identifying the person behind them. Yes, investigators received crackpot claims of all sorts with high-profile incidents, Hooper thought, but they were rarely published. But the recent news story on Zarathustra and the FBI's approach took matters to a troubling level.

When Hooper went to the kitchen for a fresh coffee, investigators Jayden Kennett and Vernon Nall were having a heated discussion.

"What's up, fellas?" Hooper asked.

"Did you see Cal Marshall and Stuart Shore on CTNB last week?" Kennett asked.

"Yeah, I caught it online after it aired."

"We think Shore came close to identifying the technology with Project Overlord," Kennett said.

"Could be," Hooper said. "I don't know a lot about Overlord. I was never part of it. It was a long time ago and classified. You guys ever touch it?"

"No, I didn't have the clearance. It was beyond us," Kennett said.

"But you're thinking it's something we need to look into?" Hooper asked.

"I think so," Nall said. "Last night I went to the game with Cal Marshall."

"You know Marshall?"

"Our wives are cousins," Nall said. "Anyway, he told me he's hearing rumors on the grapevine about Overlord. Something's buzzing about it."

The lunchroom door closed behind Bill Cashill, who'd been standing in the doorway.

"Overlord was abandoned. It never happened," Cashill said. "So let's just kill any cockamamie ideas about it having any bearing on EastCloud and Shikra."

"Were you on the project, Bill?" Nall asked.

"No. It was a very select group back then, people from the military, industry, systems, FAA. There were two NTSB people on it—Elwood King, who died a few years ago of cancer, and John Carmody, who fell off a cliff last summer while hiking in New Zealand."

"Hang on, hang on." Hooper snapped his fingers at a memory. "I think a guy I worked with a few times from the industry had mentioned once that he'd worked on Overlord."

"Who was that?" Cashill asked.

"Robert Cole."

"Robert Cole? The guy who became a drunk and lost his marbles? The guy who calls us on every investigation with his wild-ass theories?"

"You know he worked with Richlon-Titan on their fly-by-wire system."

"So?" Cashill's face tightened. "Where're you headed here, Jacob?"

"I just don't think, given the current context, the FBI, the emails, that we can categorically rule out a cyber breach of the system in both planes."

"A cyber hack?" Cashill began shaking his head bitterly. "We've been down this road a dozen times. We know the systems. It can't happen. What you're suggesting is a distraction."

"It's our duty to be open-minded and investigate all scenarios."

"We have no real evidence!" Cashill raised his voice.

"But the emails," Nall said.

"The emails came out after the fact! They're post-incident claims!" Cashill said. "They're nothing but typing from a disturbed mind! The FBI's searching for the sender to charge them for making threatening claims, not interfering with flights, because that's impossible."

"Is it, Bill?" Hooper asked. "Do you know this conclusively?"

"Are you challenging me, Jacob?"

Hooper said nothing.

"Listen to me." Cashill held a finger near Hooper's face. "With EastCloud, everything points to pilot error, and with Shikra, everything points to errors in maintenance. I'm ordering you to stop this bullshit search for ghosts in the machine and to focus on reality. Is that clear?"

Cashill looked at his three investigators one by one.

"Now get back to work," he said before leaving.

At his desk, Hooper dragged his hands over his face.

He could not and would not let go of the real fear that someone had discovered a back door into the system or a wireless jump point—that they'd somehow found a way to override the plane's security software and gain access to the flight-critical system.

The faces of the Heathrow tragedy stared at him.

Then he noticed his discarded phone messages from Robert Cole.

Fifty

It's the coding.

Robert Cole stared hard at the screen of his laptop, then at the pages of notes and calculations spread across the dining room table.

It's the decision logic in the Omega Protection system.

In the days since he'd recovered his lost files from the second-hand dealer in Bismarck, he'd worked nonstop on repairing RT's fly-by-wire system. With his redesign he'd firewalled the vulnerability of the kill switch network, absolutely securing it against any attack. Then he'd checked and double-checked and triple-checked his work. Then he'd reviewed it again and again, until he'd been satisfied.

This is it. This will fix the problem in the control system.

Cole sat back in his chair, scratched the stubble on his chin, pushed back his hair that had curtained in front of his face, and downed the last of the tepid coffee in his cup. His next problem was getting his solution to the NTSB and convincing them that he was not the drunken shell of a man that they thought he was.

At least not anymore.

He'd go to Jake Hooper because he was the only person in Washington, the only investigator, with whom he had a slim chance of being heard. The truth was Hooper had never responded to his recent calls, but in the time after Cole had lost Elizabeth and fallen into the abyss, Hooper was the only one who'd acknowledged him, taking the time to speak with him, asking how he was doing.

Even when I called him drunk and out of my mind he was there.

He'd go to Hooper and beg for ten minutes, just ten minutes, and he would show him the problem and the solution. Cole had to do it. He had to make them understand before it was too late.

Before more people died.

Cole hadn't checked the news for the latest developments on the investigations into the London and New York incidents. He went online, scrolling through news sites from the United States and the UK. Finding a recent article from Newslead, he began reading.

A potential puzzle piece has emerged in the mystery surrounding the horrific crash of a jetliner at London's Heathrow airport and the near-tragic incident experienced by a New York–bound commuter plane.

Coming to the paragraphs concerning the FBI "examining cryptic communications made by someone claiming to have knowledge of what is behind both events," Cole read faster. His breathing quickened as he saw that the FBI was attempting to locate "a person or persons of interest."

Looks like a break in the case. They must have a lead, he thought, racing to finish the story, slowing when he read about the emails sent by "Zarathustra" to Newslead and the Kuwaiti Embassy in London. Cole read the excerpt in which the sender had written:

"…tell the ordinary masses that we are extraordinary people destined to soon achieve a monumental victory of a colossal scale, the likes of which the world has never seen. We will take civilization to unprecedented heights, lighting the way forward for all of human existence. We are Zarathustra, Lord of the Heavens."

Cole froze.

In a buried corner of his heart an alarm sounded, faint at first, telling him what he refused to believe—that the warning's words, the syntax and the meaning of the passage were familiar.

I know this. Where's it from?

But he'd no sooner posed the question when the answer hit him like a sledgehammer to his stomach.

"No, no, no!"

He searched helplessly among his papers, manuals and files spread on the table. He rushed to the other stacks of records he'd recovered from the second-hand dealer. He spotted the thick brown envelope from MIT, slid it from the stack and pulled out its contents, starting first with an old letter addressed to him:

Dear Mr. Cole:

Please forgive me for contacting you confidentially but I feel the need to bring a matter of concern to your attention.

I am your daughter Veyda's doctoral thesis advisor. As you may know, her thesis topic was to advance research in aircraft systems engineering. However, upon her return after the horrible tragedy your family has suffered—for which I offer my deepest and belated condolences—Veyda informed me of her intention to switch the subject of her thesis.

She subsequently produced a hastily pulled together work in another discipline. It was a rambling, nearly incoherent manuscript that bordered on a manifesto, calling for the Third Reich to be praised for its accomplishments. She also argued that Nietzsche's philosophy of supremacy without consequences should not only be worshipped, but applied in contemporary society in order to advance civilization.

Her thesis committee, supported by the graduate program chair, rejected her submission and suggested Veyda's tragic loss of her mother may have had a bearing on her emotional and intellectual state. The committee, with whom I concurred, suggested Veyda seek counseling.

At this writing we are unaware of her whereabouts or her welfare.

Mr. Cole, I hope you will understand that I felt a need to bring this matter to your attention privately out of concern for your daughter's well-being.

Sincerely,

Rachel Rinchley, PhD, Aerospace Engineering

Department of Aeronautics and Astronautics

Massachusetts Institute of Technology

PS—I've enclosed a copy of Veyda's thesis for your reference.

Cole recalled receiving the package when he'd been grieving Veyda's estrangement from him. He'd been in an inebriated haze when he'd first read it. Now, as he set her doctoral thesis before him, he exhaled slowly and began a meticulous line-by-line examination. With every sentence and every paragraph, the crushing realization soon overwhelmed him.

Veyda had written the emails quoted in the article.

The notes he'd made on her paper confirmed his fear. Chills shot through him as he read every reference to Hegel, Nietzsche and Dostoevsky; and the "extraordinary human whose achievements must be unfettered at any cost, take civilization to unprecedented heights, lighting the way forward for all of human existence." Then, "Without pain, without blood, there is no birth, no advancement for humanity."

He burned through the pages and the awful truth screamed at him.

Oh God.

Cole drew his shaking hands over his face to stop

the room from spinning as he struggled to absorb the implications.

If Veyda had written the emails, was she also responsible for the Heathrow crash and the East-Cloud incident?

News images of the bodies amid the fiery Shikra wreckage, the video of horrified passengers on the EastCloud flight, swirled before him.

Did Veyda cause this? Is my little girl a mur-derer?

He glanced at his photos: Veyda the diapered baby sleeping on his chest. Veyda on her bicycle. Veyda receiving academic awards.

God, please. No.

Maybe she'd written the emails but hadn't hacked into the RT system? The one he'd designed. But she was brilliant. She'd studied the engineering of systems much of her academic life. This could be Veyda's revenge for Elizabeth's death.

In killing my mother, you killed part of me. I no longer want you in my life. I never want to see you again. You are not my father and I am not your daughter.

Veyda's words hammered against his brain and his heart.

Cole had to do something.

I'll call the FBI. I'll tell them.

Suddenly he envisioned a SWAT team descending on Veyda, wherever she was. They could hurt her. Or she could hurt herself.

They could kill her.

No, he couldn't, he wouldn't, go to the FBI.

No, this is my fault. I created this monstrous sit-

*uation! I have to find her. Veyda's mind is broken.
She needs help. I have to find her, get a lawyer, surrender her properly and bring this all to an end.*

But how?

He held his head in his hands, listening to the
table making soft vibrations from his trembling as
he searched for an answer. He needed a drink. There
were bottles at the hangar. He could go get them,
take a drink, just one to help him think.

No. No. That's not what he needed.

He got up, washed his face, put on a clean shirt
and combed his hair. He sat before his laptop, activated his camera and microphone and made a short
video. After three takes he'd settled on one and replayed it, watching himself, tears in his eyes as he
pleaded to his daughter.

Cole knew full well the risks he'd face at every
turn if he released this video. But he had no choice.
Lives were at stake and time was running out.

Fifty-One

Hyattsville, Maryland

Veyda's monitor came alive with a blizzard of tiny animated planes representing the nearly six thousand commercial flights moving over the continental United States at this moment.

Look at them. Throngs of ordinary people speeding to their destinations.

She studied the living, breathing activity with the fascination of a self-appointed god looking over a thriving anthill. She was proud of the work she and Seth had done.

Now it's time we enlighten the world.

Veyda clicked and her monitor changed to show activity by specific airline. Another click and the screen showed flights in and out of specific airports and hubs. She sampled them, clicking on Atlanta, then Albuquerque, then Boston, Chicago, Dallas, Fargo, Houston, Jacksonville, Kansas City, Minneapolis, Omaha, Phoenix, Pittsburgh, Raleigh, San Diego and so on.

She clicked again and she saw flights by aircraft

make and model. Another click showed all traffic over each state. Another showed specific routes. Another click showed control towers across the United States. Then she clicked on radar approach facilities, then traffic control centers.

"It's a technological wonder—a beautiful, powerful tool, Seth!"

"We're set," he said, placing luggage at the front door. "Just have to lock on to the selection, employ our software, enter our codes and we're good." He surveyed the equipment on his worktable, deciding on which laptops he needed to take with them.

At her desk, Veyda leaned forward, staring deep into her monitor and thinking.

What about Kate Page?

Veyda hadn't landed on the punishment she wanted to administer to that insolent, insufferable Gamma girl.

We haven't seen any new stories. What's up with her?

Veyda's keyboard clicked and she browsed Kate Page's private information through the path Seth had created. Nothing new jumped out at Veyda until…

Wait…what's this? I don't believe it!

"Seth, come here and look at this!" Veyda tapped her monitor. "Look!"

Seth drew his face to the screen.

"Damn, she's just boarded a flight to Los Angeles. Wow!" he said.

"Can we adjust things to capitalize on it?"

"Let me see."

Seth moved to his desk and began working, clicking on graphs, charts and maps, making calculations while Veyda studied the new information. Kate Page had a round-trip flight from Kennedy to LAX.

Why's she going to California? What's that girl up to? Is she on to something? Working something with the FBI? It doesn't matter. We're too far advanced to be stopped. If anything, this is a gift, a golden opportunity.

"Okay, done," Seth said.

"So we can do it?"

"Yes, it was easy. We just need to fine-tune the coding, but it also means we're changing our plans."

"Great."

"We've got a little over two hours. Are you done packing?"

"Almost."

A chime notification sounded on one of Seth's laptops.

"What's that?" Veyda asked.

"I set up a notification alert for anything that comes up online with your name or my name."

Seth clicked on a new video posted online.

"Oh, no," he said.

"What is it?"

Seth moved so Veyda could meet the face of her father, Robert Cole. Seth looked at her. She blinked as her face tightened with anger.

"Play it," she said.

Her father's head and shoulders appeared and tears filled his eyes as he pleaded.

"Veyda, sweetheart, this is your father. Whatever you're doing or thinking of doing, please stop. We have to talk. I'm begging you. I want to help you, and me, too. You know how to reach me. You will always be my daughter and I will always be your father. I love you. Please call me. Please, Veyda."

For the last fifteen seconds the video showed a montage of photos: Veyda, the toddler, asleep on her father's chest at his desk; Veyda and her dad with her first two-wheeler; Veyda with her parents at the beach.

Then the video froze.

Nothing in the video identified the family name— but it wouldn't take long before someone somewhere zeroed in on it.

Veyda stared at the image, not moving. Her nostrils flared, her breathing deepening as emotion raged through her.

"Veyda?" Seth asked. "Are you going to be okay?"

Beyond Seth's worktable the large TV screen continued playing footage of the Heathrow crash and the EastCloud cabin video. The churning of passengers triggered Veyda's memory of the car accident that had killed her mother...

Oh my God, Mom, the winters in Cambridge are absolutely cruel...

Then their car was airborne... They were rolling... The screams... Glass shattering, metal crunching... Rolling...rolling... Her mother was pinned under the car...

Her father was shouting... *Elizabeth!*

Her mother screaming her name... *Veyda!*

Mom! She was crawling to them...blood webbing her face... *Mom!* Sirens...shouting...a helicopter... everything turning black...

"Veyda?" Seth was concerned.

Veyda was transfixed by her father's video, staring at the monitor as she spoke to it.

"I have a right. What he did. What he took from me. I have a right."

"Are you sure you're okay? We have to get going to catch our flight."

Another chime sounded on Seth's laptop, followed by a second.

"People are tweeting links to the video, Veyda. This one says, 'Hope this sad dad finds his daughter.'"

Veyda's face hardened.

"I am not his daughter and he is not my father. My parents are dead to me. You know what to do, Seth. Do it. Then shut it all down and pack it up. I'll be ready in five minutes."

Fifty-Two

Linthicum, Maryland

Down a labyrinth of corridors within the secured confines of the Defense Cyber Crime Center, Keith Dorling pursued his prey.

For the past few days he'd been struggling to identify the source of the potential threat arising from the Zarathustra emails.

The sophistication and artistry employed by the sender to cloak and preserve their anonymity was astounding. Dorling had followed the mazelike trail to servers around the globe.

His pulse raced when the path took a troubling turn to the Shanghai headquarters of the Chinese military's infamous Unit 68416. Dorling had feared the sender would be linked to signals intelligence, that the origin was a hostile action by a foreign government.

But he kept digging and soon he'd discovered China was merely a decoy; the trail bounced off satellites to domains used to control malware in Iran and the United Arab Emirates.

Now he saw that the sender had become complacent.

Didn't think anyone would last this long on your tail, did you?

His target's attempt to keep their identity secret had unraveled. After the trail left Dubai, Dorling tracked it with ease to Libya, then Bermuda, and finally...

"Bingo!"

He reached for his phone and called FBI Special Agent Ron Sanchez with the Joint Terrorism Task Force, who answered on the first ring.

"Sanchez?"

"Ron, Dorling at DC3. I've got Zarathustra and an IP address. It's here in the US. You better move fast to get warrants."

Fifty-Three

California

The words "Kate Page, Newslead" were printed in block letters on the paper sign held by the giant waiting for Kate in Arrivals at LAX.

"I'm Kate." She looked up.

"Devon Hill, Newslead shooter." He reached out to greet her.

Holy cow, Kate thought, as her hand disappeared in his, Chuck hadn't been kidding when he'd promised someone protective for the job from the LA bureau. Devon had to be six foot seven, with a muscular build.

"Let me take your bag, Kate. My car's this way."

Devon's car was a Jeep Liberty and he navigated it expertly through the airport chaos. While driving they made small talk about her smooth flight and California's weather until they stopped at the Holiday Inn where Kate had a reservation.

Devon waited in the lobby as she checked in and freshened up. She'd slept a bit on the plane and wanted to take advantage of the three-hour time difference and get to work.

"Good to go," she said, and they immediately headed out to meet her source, who lived in San Dimas.

"It's going to take us about fifty minutes or so," Devon said as they traveled east on the 105. "You sure you're up for this? I read all your stuff after Chuck Laneer assigned me to this job."

"Yeah, why?"

"Chuck told me that you've had some strange experiences and that your guy could be critical, or he could be a dangerous nutcase."

"We've come too far on this story. We've got to chase down this lead."

Devon nodded.

"So how'd you get stuck with me? Why do you think Chuck picked you for this assignment, Devon?"

He shrugged, smiling.

"My talent, or my size." He released a deep chuckle. "I was a second-team defensive tackle in college. But pro ball wasn't in the cards. Besides, I didn't like the concussion issues. So I followed my passion, photography. I worked on a few papers, like the *LA Times*, before I joined Newslead. Was a Pulitzer finalist for pictures of the wildfires up in Calaveras County."

"Sounds like Chuck picked you for your talent."

Devon smiled. As they left the 105 to go north on the 605, traffic was heavy, but it was moving. Eventually they got on the westbound 10 at West Covina, then north on State Route 57 to San Dimas, a small, pretty city, snuggled along the foothills of the San Gabriel Mountains.

"It used to be famous for oranges and lemons. Now the locals are big on horses. It's also a very white town—" Devon grinned "—according to the Census Bureau. I did a quality-of-life feature for the *Times* here."

They left the freeway for the Arrow Highway. Following his GPS, Devon made a number of turns until they were on a street that paralleled West Railway. It was a sleepy corner of San Dimas. He slowed to check address numbers along a stretch of modest, neat-as-a-pin houses with well-kept yards shaded by sycamore and oak trees. California fan palms towered over neighboring streets.

"Here we go," Kate said.

They stopped in front of number 213.

Paint blistered and peeled on the picket fence bordering the yard. The fence leaned inward and outward in places where pickets were missing. The garden beds were overrun with weeds that had trapped faded flyers and discarded fast-food takeout bags. Shutters were closed in all the windows. The sedan in the driveway was rusted and filthy. The rear was crumpled and the cracked right taillight was secured with duct tape.

"You sure this is your guy?" Devon asked.

"Well, according to the records check I did, the property belongs to Mavis Carlson, aged seventy-eight."

"She's your source?"

"No, it's a guy using the name 'Malcolm Grady.'" Kate checked her phone and the information. "This is the address he gave me and I told him I'd be here today."

Kate began typing on her phone.

"I'll send a message to let New York know where we are. Chuck's orders." Then she and Devon approached the side entrance of the house. It had a flimsy door; the top half was screen mesh and the way the sun hit it, Kate couldn't see inside.

She pressed her face to it, peering into the darkness.

She froze when they heard the soft electronic whizzing of a security camera that was tilted at them above the door. The lens turned to focus.

Kate knocked on the screen door.

"Hello, Malcolm! Malcolm Grady! It's Kate Page with Newslead!"

A few seconds of silence passed before a man's voice from the darkness said, "You were supposed to come alone."

"I never said that, Malcolm. The man with me is Devon Hill. He's a Newslead photographer. A reporter and photographer always travel together on significant assignments like this one. It's our policy."

"But I specifically said no names, which means no pictures. You assured me that you protect sources."

"I know, but we can talk about that once you let us in and let me assess the documents on Project Overlord that you promised. If you're changing your mind, or if this is some sort of hoax, I'll fly back to New York."

Silence followed.

"What's it going to be?" Kate asked. "I kept up

my end of the bargain. I came here on faith that you were the real deal."

Nothing. More time passed and nothing.

"Was it all just talk or are you the real deal, Malcolm?"

Several seconds passed before a man appeared at the door. He appeared to be in his late thirties. His curly hair shot, Medusa-like, from the sides of his balding head. He had a scraggly five-day beard, and his paunch strained his faded T-shirt, which bore stains and E=mc2 across his chest. He wore khaki shorts and sandals.

The hinge creaked as he opened the door.

"May I see your identification, please?"

After Kate and Devon held up their Newslead photo IDs, he nodded.

"Okay, come in," he said. "Don't mind the dark. My mother's sensitive to the light. She's ill, asleep in her room."

The air smelled of muscle ointment, baby powder and onions. They passed through the kitchen, where empty pizza boxes were stacked neatly in the corner. Plates, utensils, glasses and mugs had dried on the dish rack near the sink.

"This way." Malcolm led them into a living room, which was cluttered with a walker, a wheelchair and medical oxygen tanks. A flat-screen TV topped a shelf in front of two sofa chairs. A large desk with a computer filled one side of the room, and the other side held two large metal file cabinets and a credenza overflowing with files. Next to it was a bookcase, stuffed and overflowing with books stacked upon books.

Malcolm sat in the leather high-back chair behind his desk. Devon sat in a sofa chair, and Kate took another small cushioned chair near the desk and surveyed the bookcase. She saw books about conspiracies regarding Roswell, the Kennedy assassination, 9/11, and several titles questioning the lunar landing. When she spotted a ball cap lined with tinfoil she had to force herself not to groan.

Oh my God, he's a lunatic!

Kate turned and saw that Malcolm had seen what she was looking at.

"I know what you're thinking," he said.

"No," Kate said, "I just—"

"Your face doesn't lie, Ms. Page."

"Forgive me, I just—"

"It's understandable, given my appearance, and the fact I'm living here, taking care of my ailing mother. I'm sure I fit the stereotype of a nut, by your definition."

"I'm sorry, Malcolm. I mean, the hat and the books…"

He arranged the files on his desk.

"I have worked from time to time as a private subcontractor on classified government projects to help pay the bills. I'm not a nut job. I have a master's degree in astrophysics. I don't adhere to conspiracy theories, I debunk them. Much like you, I adhere to facts and use them to convey the truth. I lead a small group of investigators and we have a website."

"I apologize. On the phone you'd called yourself an underground activist."

"That's right. We blow away myths and conspiracy theories with the goal of letting the public know the truth about what governments are up to."

"Are those files—" Kate indicated the desk "—Overlord files?"

"They are. First, a primer. Yes, as your story correctly notes, shortly after 9/11, the president promised technology to land troubled planes safely by remote control."

"And some airlines got patents for it?"

"Back things up. With Overlord, the government worked with defense and airline experts to develop the technology known as the Unhindered Autopilot System."

"Right, so what happened?"

"Well most people know that variations of the technology exist. Drones can be operated remotely. Test flights in rocketry can be detonated remotely over the ocean. We've even seen the remote-control flight of jetliners by safety experts testing them for crash landings and other research."

"So where does Overlord come into the picture?"

"It was developed and was set to be applied but a number of issues arose. You touched on them when you were on CTNB. Some experts were skeptical about how well it would work. Pilots were concerned, security officials were concerned, so it was never ever applied."

"Then what? I know much of this."

"Well, there were reports. A number of top secret reports that showed Overlord was flawed, that it was susceptible to outside attack, raising the real possibility of remote-control hijackings of commercial passenger jets."

"Do you have copies of those reports?"

"I do. However, more recently, there have been rumors and theories flying around the contractor community about Overlord. Consequently, copies of classified documents have been coming to me from my sources."

"What sort of rumors?"

"Well, first there was the fear that Overlord technology had been leaked, and had made its way to North Korea, which might work in concert with Middle East extremist groups to hijack and destroy airliners."

"Damn," Devon said.

"We've found nothing to substantiate that, and trust me, we looked hard into that one. But as we did, another new thread emerged. Turns out one of the experts who'd worked on Overlord was an engineer with Richlon-Titan who pioneered the fly-by-wire system used in its aircraft and airliners around the world."

"The London and New York planes had RT systems."

"Correct. According to the rumors, this engineer had issues with the vulnerability of RT's systems. He had a profound disagreement with his corporation just before he suffered a terrible personal tragedy where his wife was killed, resulting in him having a breakdown, losing his position and dropping out of sight. We think he's the primary suspect for what's happened, that maybe he's acting on a vendetta."

"If that's the case, why not inform the FBI?"

"I told you, some of my documentation is classified. I could face charges for simply possessing it."

"What are your facts?" Kate asked.

"We're still working on them, but I can show you this."

"Munro!" A faint woman's voice called, interrupting. "I'm thirsty."

"Coming, Mother!" He looked at Kate. "I expect you did your homework on our address and know our family name is Carlson. Excuse me." He went to the kitchen, and Kate heard him fill a glass and take it to another room, where he murmured soothing words before returning. "Now, here." He positioned a number of files on the desk for Kate to look at.

Kate moved closer to see.

"Here you have a list of names of experts who worked on Overlord. Don't ask how I got these records. And here are a number of photos of the various teams, including the man I noted from Richlon-Titan."

"Who is he?"

He tapped a finger on the man identified as Robert Cole.

"This man, Robert Cole—he's one of the world's leading experts on flight systems. If I were looking into what happened to the New York and London planes, I'd consider Robert Cole a suspect."

Fifty-Four

California

Ten minutes after they'd left the house, Kate still felt adrenaline pumping through her.

Munro Carlson, aka Malcolm Grady, had just given her what could be the biggest break in the story so far—Zarathustra's identity.

Robert Cole.

Her challenge was to verify Cole's identity and find him.

"That was wild, Kate. Even if half of what that supernerd told you is true, you've got a huge story," Devon said, settling into a booth at the diner they'd driven to. He indicated the fat envelope of Overlord records Kate had set on the table. "It's like the story with that NSA contractor who leaked stuff a few years ago."

Kate fanned through the documents, stopping to study the stamps reading "Classified" and "Secret" on pages. They looked authentic to her but she needed confirmation. It had taken some doing but Carlson had agreed to give her copies of the records as promised, and had agreed to let Devon shoot him in shadow, obscuring his face, while Kate continually assured him his identity would be protected. In exchange, Carlson wanted Kate to say in her story that his anonymous blog, *Exposita Veritate*, Latin for "exposing the truth," had been the first to raise the question of an Overlord and Robert Cole connection to the London and New York cases.

It struck her that Munro Carlson could've been the mystery friend Erich had referred to. She sent Erich a quick message, then called Chuck in New York, who listened intently to her update.

"Good work," he said. "We need verification on all fronts. Can you scan the documents?"

"There are too many."

"Okay, then photocopy them and Fed-Ex them overnight to me here, and to Tim Yardley in DC. Make sure you watch the copies being made so nothing goes astray."

"Isn't this risky?"

"Yes, but we don't have many options. I'll get Yardley to study the records, to push his national security sources on Overlord, Cole and this Munro Carlson. I'll get Hugh Davidson to do the same here. Verification is critical on all fronts. You know what to do, Kate."

She set out to search for Robert Cole when she got a message from Munro Carlson with a link.

This just went up on YouTube—check it out. This guy really looks like Robert Cole. You've got to look into it.

Kate couldn't believe it.

What's going on? Is this really Cole? What's at stake here? I've got to find him.

She took a breath and worked with renewed urgency.

There were too many R. Coles in California, let alone the thousands across the country, for her to search for him alone. She studied Cole's face in the group photos in the documents and estimated an age range, then called the legal documents and public records agency Newslead used and got them to search for property and court records. Given that Richlon-Titan's headquarters was in Burbank, she reasoned that Robert Cole lived there and had asked for a search of the vicinity. If that failed, they could expand it to the surrounding communities of Glendale, North Hollywood, Toluca Lake and Griffith Park.

Their food came and they ate as Devon showed Kate the images he'd taken of Carlson. They looked good. By the time they'd finished eating, the records agency had called with an address in Burbank for Robert Cole, previously employed at Richlon-Titan.

Devon pushed his Jeep hard westbound on the 210 Freeway. During the one-hour drive, the agency also sent Kate court records concerning Robert Cole's vehicular manslaughter case in the death of his wife, Elizabeth, and injury of his daughter, Veyda.

Veyda. That's the person the man in the video is addressing. So that's got to be Cole in the video. What's Veyda's role here?

Kate resumed studying the case.

"This is so tragic," she said to Devon while reading the documents as greater LA flowed by.

The Cole residence was in Burbank's Hillside District, on a tranquil street. It was of mixed style, a ranch bungalow with a touch of Spanish influence—a low, broad house with stucco walls and a red-tiled roof.

A man in his late twenties came to the door.

"Kate Page, from New York. We're looking for Mr. Robert Cole or his daughter, Veyda."

The man shook his head.

"Nobody here by that name, sorry." He scratched his head. "Wait. I think that's who used to own this house before my mom and dad bought it."

"Did Mr. Cole leave a forwarding address?"

"I wouldn't know."

"Could we talk to your parents?"

"They're in Europe on vacation."

"Could you send them a text?"

"What's this about?"

"It's an urgent business matter and we need to reach Mr. Cole."

The man pulled his phone from his back pocket and typed.

"I think they're in Dublin. Not sure what time it is there." After sending the message, he looked closer at Kate and Devon. "Who're you with?"

"Newslead, the newswire service. We'd like to reach Mr. Cole confidentially. It's very important."

"This has got nothing to do with my folks, right?"

"Just Mr. Cole."

A chime sounded on the man's phone and he read the message.

"Dad says he doesn't have an address but thinks

that Cole moved to Idaho or Wyoming, some place like that. Maybe even Canada. Sorry."

"Thanks."

Kate and Devon tried a few other neighboring doors but it was futile. No one knew where Robert Cole had moved to.

"Let's try Richlon-Titan."

Richlon-Titan's world headquarters was in a ten-story glass building. Its dark blue mirrored windows reflected palms and the blue California sky.

"Kate Page, from Newslead." She placed her card on the reception desk. "I'd like to speak to Mr. Hub Wolfeson on an urgent matter."

The receptionist's eyebrows rose a bit.

"Mr. Wolfeson? Do you have an appointment?"

"No, but he should know who I am and it's urgent. Tell him it concerns Robert Cole, Overlord, and the recent aircraft incidents in London and New York involving RT systems."

The receptionist jotted a few notes. "Please, have a seat."

Kate joined Devon at a marbled wall of water. Next to it were huge portraits of RT airliners. Two minutes became five, then fifteen.

Kate tapped her notebook on her leg.

Wolfeson should indeed be familiar with her name, given all the crap with his nephew, Sloane F. Parkman. She hoped her unannounced visit made him nervous. Heels clicked on the polished floor and she turned.

"Ms. Page?"

A woman about Kate's age in a power suit and flawless makeup arrived.

"Shannon Bree, executive director of public affairs." She had an Australian accent. She didn't extend her hand. She was using both hands to hold a single piece of folded paper. "I'm afraid Mr. Wolfeson is unavailable. He's in Vienna."

"Well, I have questions on a number of urgent matters."

"Yes, we're quite aware of your reporting and I'm afraid given the circumstances of the ongoing investigations we can't comment. We do express our condolences to the families involved and we underscore that we're cooperating fully with officials in the United States and the UK. The safety of the flying public is our paramount concern."

"I have questions about Robert Cole and Overlord."

"Yes, but for privacy reasons we cannot comment on former employees or their past activities. I'm sure you understand. It's all here in our formal statement for you." Bree handed Kate the paper on RT letterhead, which echoed what she'd said. Then she offered a gleaming, officious smile.

"You made our cutoff by a whisker," the Fed-Ex agent said after accepting Kate's packages for Washington and New York.

After she'd shipped the documents, Devon dropped her at the hotel, where Kate kept working. She called Chuck and vented her frustration over not finding Robert Cole or confirming much more on Overlord.

"Did Tim or Hugh have any luck?"

"Not much. But don't worry about it. The trip's paid off," Chuck said. "We have a good foundation. You can pick it up when you get back to New York tomorrow."

Kate then called home and spoke with Grace, Vanessa and Nancy. Hearing their voices lifted her spirits. Afterward she took a hot shower then pored over the Project Overlord records. Much of it was technical.

Kate shifted her focus to read Robert Cole's court records on her phone, this time more carefully. *Dear Lord, this is so tragic.* After absorbing the details on Elizabeth Cole's death, Kate had to struggle to shove away the images of her own tragic car crash. She forced herself to keep reading. She paused when she came to sections concerning Robert Cole's daughter, Veyda, to replay her father's video plea, then resumed studying the records. Veyda was a doctoral candidate at MIT where she was working on aircraft systems engineering.

Veyda was following in her dad's footsteps. She'd know where her father was; maybe she'd know about Overlord, too. But Robert Cole's words from the video echoed in her mind: *Whatever you're doing or thinking of doing, please stop... I'm begging you...* Kate went online to try to find an email or some way to reach Veyda Cole.

No luck.

The sun was still high but Kate was exhausted as she continued her research. Looking again at the images of the Heathrow tragedy and the cabin video of the EastCloud flight, she was overwhelmed by the magnitude and horror of what had happened, and what was at stake.

Is Robert Cole Zarathustra? Or maybe his daughter is? They'd have the skills to attempt to interfere with the flights. If that's the case, then don't I have a duty to alert authorities to look at Robert Cole as their person of interest? Wasn't that the point of my last major story? But it's not my job to inform police.

Anguished by indecision, Kate raised her face to the ceiling.

What if something happened? What if another plane crashed? How could I live with myself?

She reached for her phone and called Nick Varner, hoping and praying she could talk to him. One ring and the line was answered.

"Varner."

"Nick, it's Kate Page."

"Hey, I really can't talk right now."

"I've got something important to tell you but you have to swear no one will know this came from me."

"What is it?"

"Swear to me, Nick."

"This isn't a good time."

"Swear, Nick."

"Okay."

"Your person of interest may be a former Richlon-Titan engineer with expertise on flight-management systems. He may have suffered some sort of breakdown and could be exacting revenge."

Varner said nothing.

"His name is Robert Cole. He used to live in Burbank, the Hillside District." Kate recited the address. "But he's moved. And he's posted a troubling video plea to his daughter, Veyda. This could be significant."

Varner said nothing, which Kate took as unusual. *Shouldn't he be asking me to tell him more about the Coles?* Varner's silence meant something was up.

"Nick, I'm violating my own ethical code to help you."

Silence. Kate looked at her phone, then pressed it back to her ear.

"Nick, are you there?"

"We're on the same track."

"You know about Cole?"

"We're on the same track and things are unfolding."

Kate sat straighter.

"Unfolding? What do you mean? Nick, where are you? What's going on?"

"I've got to go."

"Nick!"

Fifty-Five

After ending his call with Kate Page, Nick Varner continued looking through his high-powered binoculars at the house at the far end of the sealed residential block.

Robert Cole's home.

Varner reinserted his earpiece to resume listening to the whispered transmissions of FBI SWAT team members who'd taken up concealed positions near the house. He was shielded by parked emergency vehicles some one hundred yards away, where he was watching the operation.

Deputies from Bowman and Adams counties had already quietly evacuated all residents from neighboring homes that were in the line of fire and choked off all traffic at both ends of the quiet street.

So far, there was no movement or activity reported by SWAT members closest to Cole's building.

The task force cyber experts had traced the sender of the Zarathustra emails to a physical internet protocol address registered to Robert Cole of Clear River, North Dakota.

Investigators had immediately worked full-bore, putting in long hours without stopping. Further rapid investigation and expedited warrants revealed that Cole was a former engineer with Richlon-Titan who'd helped design its fly-by-wire system. Assistance from Homeland Security confirmed that Robert Cole was a member of the secret team that had worked on Project Overlord, the abandoned program designed to develop the technology known as the Unhindered Autopilot System, which would allow planes hijacked in-flight to be landed safely by remote control.

Robert Cole possessed the expertise to remotely threaten aircraft.

Varner had to give Kate Page credit. Once again she'd proven why he considered her one of the best journalists in the country. The information she'd obtained was solid.

The FBI's swift investigation of Richlon-Titan officials by agents from the bureau's Los Angeles division—and with support from the LA County Sheriff—showed that Cole's employment had been terminated after he'd become unstable following a traffic accident in which his wife was killed. There were indications that Cole harbored a grudge against RT over a disagreement on the flight-management system and that he blamed RT for his wife's death.

Varner agreed that the facts pointed to Robert Cole as their suspect.

The FBI had acted fast, securing arrest and search warrants for Robert Cole. They'd assembled a large operation, drawing on FBI agents from Williston, Minot and Bismarck. They were supported by FBI SWAT teams from the Salt Lake City and Minneapolis divisions.

The FBI had control of the inner perimeter. They were backed by tactical teams from across North Dakota who held positions at the outer perimeter, where Varner and other task force members waited.

Moments ago, another FBI team had moved on the hangar where Cole worked.

No one had been there.

Technicians from North Dakota's Bureau of Criminal Investigation Division were processing the hangar for evidence, but nothing significant had emerged so far.

The radio crackled with a dispatch from the command post.

"Heads up. Everyone's now in position," the team leader whispered.

"Hold," the commander said.

Varner dragged the back of his hand across his mouth as he watched through his binoculars.

"Holding," the team leader responded.

Several tense moments passed, the silence broken by birdsong and the barking of a dog in the distance. Then…

"Tighten your position!"

Heavily armed tactical members rushed from their covers with weapons drawn, moving quietly from behind trees, parked cars and house corners. One sniper was flat on his stomach on the roof of the house next door, his rifle scope trained on a bedroom window. Another sharpshooter used the hood of an SUV to take a line on a living room window.

Team members crept up to the house, taking positions at the front and rear. They were poised for a no-knock forced rapid entry.

"We're set," the team leader reported to the command post.

The SWAT commander nodded and used a megaphone to order Robert Cole to exit the house using the front door with his hands raised, palms showing, and surrender to the FBI.

He repeated the order for two solid minutes.

No one answered.

The commander then green-lighted his squad.

"Go!"

Seconds later the *pop-pop* and shattering glass sounds of tear gas canisters being fired echoed down the street. White clouds billowed from the main floor, followed by the deafening *crack-crack* and lightning flashes of stun grenades.

The SWAT team smashed through the front and rear doors.

Their helmet lights raked the acrid fog as they swept the living room and the kitchen. Then they stormed down the hallway then upstairs. Bedroom number one: empty. Bedroom number two: empty. The bathroom was empty. Closets: empty. The ceiling, floors and walls were tapped for body mass.

Empty.

On the main floor, team members completed the same inspection of all rooms and potential hiding places. The house was inspected three times before it was cleared and declared safe.

Once the air cleared, Varner was allowed into the scene in advance of the evidence response team.

He'd slipped on shoe covers, pulled on gloves, then stepped inside, coughing at the biting, ammonia-like traces of the tear gas. First, he moved from room to room, taking stock of Cole's home. It was plain, orderly and clean, except for the dining room.

What happened here? Looks like a couple of file cabinets exploded.

Layers of papers, files, reports, manuals and schematic drawings blanketed the table and the desk next to it.

Varner studied the material.

All of it related to Richlon-Titan's fly-by-wire system.

Varner picked up printouts of Kate Page's stories.

Paragraphs were highlighted, including excerpts of the Zarathustra email.

Varner swallowed hard.

We've got to find Robert Cole, now!

Then his eyes narrowed on a manuscript and the title page.

The author was Veyda Hyde.

Varner turned the cover to the first page with a gloved finger. At the top was a reference to Friedrich Nietzsche and Zarathustra. Varner blinked and flipped back to the title page.

Veyda Hyde.

Who's that?

Fifty-Six

Rachel Rinchley twisted and untwisted the strap of her briefcase as she rode the T from MIT to the downtown City Hall stop.

Maybe I'm crazy. Maybe I shouldn't be doing this.

She questioned herself repeatedly while standing across the street from the nine-story, crescent-shaped complex known as Center Plaza.

No, I have to tell them. They have to know.

Rachel entered One Center Plaza, passed through security, clipped on her visitor badge and went to the sixth floor, the location of the FBI's Boston Field Office.

She waited in the reception area until the agent she'd spoken with earlier on the phone, Kay Howard, came out and took her to a quiet office.

"We appreciate your coming downtown, Ms. Rinchley. What's the important information you wanted to share with the FBI?"

Rachel withdrew her copy of Veyda Hyde's troubling doctoral paper, passed it to Agent Howard, then proceeded to tell her why she was convinced that Veyda was the author of the Zarathustra emails.

"She's brilliant," Rachel began. "She used to be known as Veyda Cole, and she was originally researching aircraft systems engineering, computational engineering, controls, communications and networks, until her mother was killed..."

Fifty-Seven

In downtown Ottawa Tucker Ollenck rubbed his reddened eyes.

He hadn't slept since he'd read the news story online about the FBI's search for the people behind the Zarathustra emails in connection with that plane crash in London.

He knew exactly who that was. Problem was, he wasn't sure if he should alert the FBI.

He went to the window of his fifteenth-floor office in the Canadian capital, where he worked with a global IT firm, and stared at the Peace Tower for an answer to his dilemma. After a long, troubled moment, he returned to his desk, went to the FBI's website for the New York Field Office.

He scrawled the number on yellow note paper.

He rolled down his sleeves, slid on his jacket and told the office manager that he was taking an early lunch.

Tucker walked east across the Mackenzie King Bridge, over the canal to the Rideau Centre, the major downtown mall. He bought a disposable phone and a prepaid card. Then he went back outside to the bridge, and while gazing upon the canal toward the castle-like spires of the Chateau Laurier Hotel, he made an anonymous call to the FBI in New York.

After a few general questions he was put on hold. Several moments passed, and he was connected.

"FBI, Agent Brock."

"Sir, I've got information about your search for Zarathustra."

"Go ahead."

"I don't want to give you my identity."

"That's fine. Go ahead."

"I went to Stanford and became good friends with Seth Hagen. The guy's a computer engineering legend. He made a fortune developing video game systems, but he became something of a social recluse, said he didn't really like people."

"Okay…"

"He sort of dropped off the grid, but I kept in touch. I think I was one of the few people he talked to. Then he surprised me when he said he'd met this girl, Veyda, online. Seth never praised anyone, but he told me how she had a brilliant mind and he was in love. She was attending MIT, but dropped out. He said her paper about some wild theory on the philosophies of Hegel and Nietzsche had blown him away.

"He let me read it before I had dinner with them when I was in Washington, DC. I'll never forget it. The paper was chilling. It supported killing people to advance society. I got such a weird vibe off

Veyda. The woman struck me as being even smarter than Seth, but very, very scary."

"Scary how?"

"Her eyes. It was like she was dead inside. I honestly thought they had both lost their minds the way they were talking about extraordinary people, free will, the right to commit crimes without conscience. It was all kind of disturbing."

"Do you have a surname for the woman?"

"The woman's name is Veyda Hyde. The email excerpts could've been pulled from her paper. I swear that's her. Moreover, she was studying aircraft computer systems at MIT. See, it all fits."

"What else can you tell us?"

"The last I heard, they were living at Seth's place in Hyattsville, Maryland. I'll give you the address."

Fifty-Eight

Denver, Colorado

Veyda was behind the wheel of their rented Ford Escape.

Seth consulted the dash-mounted GPS while studying the storefronts as they rolled along Colfax Avenue.

They drove through menacing sections of the city with vacant lots bordered with wire fencing, abandoned buildings laced with graffiti and fortresslike liquor stores. But those areas eventually gave way to cafés, renovated businesses and new townhomes where Colfax Avenue had cleaned up.

They were taking the next critical step in their plan—a quick meeting and transaction with a man named Nash.

Before they'd boarded their flight to Colorado in Washington, Seth had hustled to work out the details for what they needed.

We did a lot of volunteer outreach at school, like computer seminars in federal and state prisons, Seth had told Veyda, while sending off messages in preboarding. *The aim was to help them stay abreast technologically for when they were released. I kept in touch with a few guys, because you never know when you might need their expertise. Here, I just got a response. A friend has arranged for a contact in Denver to help us get what we need. His name is Nash. Details to follow. We're good, babe.*

But now that they were here, they hadn't heard a word from Nash. And driving up and down the same blocks of Colfax was making Veyda uneasy.

Seth had done some exceptional work sending the Zarathustra emails through her father's computer, making his address in Clear River, North Dakota, appear to be the source point for Zarathustra. But with each passing minute, the video her father had put out was getting more hits and tweets. It lacked details, but sooner or later the police were going to be alerted to it. And that story Kate Page had written asking for people to contact the FBI could be problematic.

Veyda glanced at the time and bit her bottom lip while assessing the facts in their favor. They were so far along, so advanced in completing their plan, that the chances of anyone getting close enough to stop them in time were nonexistent.

Still, she kept an eye out for patrol cars.

"You're sure this is the right time and place?"

"Positive," Seth said. "Nash said to be in this area and he'd text me. There! Down the block on the corner. There he is, the guy in the checkered shirt. Pull over."

Seth dropped his window and Nash stepped up to it.

He was in his early forties. He wore a lumber-jack shirt over a white T-shirt and jeans. He was of medium build, had thin blond hair and a face ravaged by acne. He was holding a paper bag from a fast-food outlet.

"Are you Nash, Blade's friend?"

He nodded. "You Seth?"

"Yeah, and this is Veyda. Get in."

Nash climbed into the backseat.

"Have you got it?" Seth asked.

"I got it. Pull into the parking lot behind them golden arches up there."

Veyda drove to a far corner of the lot and parked. Seth got in the back. Nash withdrew a handgun from the bag and passed it to Seth.

"This is a forty-caliber pistol, very powerful. It's unloaded. Here." Nash tapped the gun. "This is the safety." He made it click. "See? This way—on. This way—off. Got it?"

Seth nodded.

Nash reached into the bag.

"Here's a magazine. I'm giving you three." He took the gun from Seth. "Slide the magazine in like this." It clicked. "Press here to release it and it drops like this." Nash demonstrated. "Try it."

Seth completed the action a few times.

"Good," Nash said. "Here's the chamber indicator to tell you a round is in the chamber ready for firing. So all you do is load the magazine, check the indicator, turn off the safety and fire. Got it?"

Seth nodded, tried the process a few times. Then he unloaded the gun, activated the safety and put everything in the bag.

"One thousand cash." Nash held out his hand.

"I was told it would be five hundred."

"One thousand, or no deal."

"Is the gun untraceable?"

"It is and I don't want to know why you want it. I don't give a rat's ass what you're up to. Do we understand each other?"

"Perfectly."

Seth reached into his pocket and peeled at a roll of bills, putting most of them in Nash's hand.

"It's all there."

"Good," Nash said. "Our business is done."

After Nash got out and walked away, Seth got into the front and put the bag under the seat.

"That was smooth, Seth."

"Very smooth, and we've got plenty of time to get to our point and set up. We have our insurance. We're ready for all scenarios. We're going to do this."

"Nothing's in our way now." Veyda reached out, taking his hand in hers. "Nothing's going to stop us."

Fifty-Nine

Manhattan, New York

The boardroom windows at the FBI's New York Field Office opened to a view of the Brooklyn Bridge and a jetliner on its approach to LaGuardia.

No one at the table was looking.

Agents were studying a one-page synopsis.

Developments were popping in the Zarathustra investigation. The credibility of a link to the Shikra Airlines crash at Heathrow and the incident with the EastCloud Flight 4990 was growing stronger with each passing moment.

Gil Morillo, assistant special agent in charge, chaired the briefing.

He made a quick roll call of those in the room and the people whose voices echoed through the speakers of the teleconference line. They included brass from the deputy director's office and the FBI's National Security and Criminal Cyber Response Branches at national headquarters in Washington. Nick Varner was on the line from the resident agency office in Williston, North Dakota, along with agents in offices across the country.

"Let's get to it, people," Morillo said. "First, we'll be taking part in another multiagency briefing with the FAA, the NTSB, the Transportation Security Administration, Homeland Security and the US Air Force shortly after this call."

Murmurs at the growing magnitude of the case rose around the table as Morillo continued.

"Okay, you've got the summaries. We've had some solid leads from tips called in. We've been expediting warrants and moving quickly. You have updated biographies on our persons of interest—Seth Simon Hagen, Robert James Cole and his daughter, Veyda Charlotte Cole, aka Veyda Hyde. Nick, can you update us regarding Clear River?"

"We're still processing the evidence found at Cole's residence, all of it related to flight systems. We've determined he boarded a flight at Bismarck to Minneapolis ending in Washington, DC."

"What's the status from the Washington office on locating him?" Morillo asked.

"Negative so far," Agent Harold Davenport responded. "He flew to Washington before becoming a subject. We've talked to American Airlines and the TSA. We're working with local agencies here to locate him or determine if he's taken another flight or mode of transportation."

"Baltimore," Morillo said, "what do you have?"

"We've executed warrants on the Hyattsville residence and on Hagen and Hyde," Agent Allyson Meeson said. "We're still assessing evidence from the house, which includes documents concerning flight operations and systems. We've just determined that our subjects flew from National in DC to Denver International. We've alerted the Denver office. Mitch, over to you."

"Right," said Agent Mitchell Butler in Denver. "Our subjects rented a Ford Escape at the airport. The rental agency confirms two people at the counter. We're now in the process of obtaining warrants to track the rental vehicle's location through its GPS and other devices."

"Okay," Morillo said. "Nick, can you get on a plane to Denver ASAP and support the office in locating Hagen and Cole?"

"Will do."

"Gil, it's Mary Ritter with the deputy director's office at headquarters."

"Go ahead, Mary."

"A few questions before I brief the deputy, who'll be briefing the director. Have we determined if a clear threat exists on a specific aircraft or flight?"

"Not at this time," Morillo said.

"And what is the FBI's assessment of a threat at this time?"

"Given events, the facts and evidence known so far, and the expertise of the people involved, we feel a very credible threat is evolving. Our priority is to locate and question the three people we've identified as potential suspects."

"Thanks, Gil," Ritter said. "This will top the director's agenda before he heads into his daily national security meeting with the White House."

Sixty

The memo from the NTSB chairman was urgent and terse.

All staff listed were to cooperate immediately and fully with the FBI in its criminal investigation into the emails linked to events concerning Shikra Airlines Flight 418 and EastCloud Flight 4990.

Jake Hooper's name was on the list.

He read it a third time, shuddering in disbelief. The memo validated the rumors going around the floor about incredible developments in the cases.

The FBI had found the source of the emails; the FBI had evidence pointing to interference with the flights; the FBI had suspects with a connection to the NTSB; there was a puzzling video posted by Robert Cole; the White House was involved. Finally, the rumors had turned to fact. FBI agents were here now, questioning people in Major Investigations Division.

"Jake?"

Hooper saw Anson Fox, his supervisor, at his door.

"The FBI's waiting to talk to you in Six Hundred D. Take nothing."

"Do I need a lawyer?"

"No, they need information, and they need it fast. Let's go."

In the room down the hall, agents Len Brock and Deacon Palmer waited on one side of the table for Hooper. They began by taking Hooper's information from his driver's license, then they showed him a photograph of Robert Cole and the short video he'd posted.

"Can you identify this man?" Brock asked.

Hooper said nothing.

"Mr. Hooper, can you identify this man?"

"Sorry, this is all— It's disturbing. Yes, that's Robert Cole. I've worked with him on several investigations."

Then they showed him photos of Veyda and Seth Hagen.

"I don't know them," he said.

"Can you tell us where Robert Cole is?"

"He lives in North Dakota."

"Do you know his location at this moment?"

"No."

"You say you worked with him. When did you last see him?"

"At his wife's funeral. That was a long while ago."

"When did you last speak to him?"

"About four or five months ago."

"By phone or email?"

"Over the phone."

"What was the nature of the conversation?"

"How he was doing. He also offered his insights

into investigations. After that, he called and offered his views on every ongoing aircraft investigation we had going. He was drinking heavily and not coping well. It got so I didn't respond. I felt bad. He left me messages in the wake of the incidents with the EastCloud and Shikra flights."

"What did they concern?"

"I don't know. His last one was a voice message. He was drunk, incoherent. I deleted it. It was tragic because he was a brilliant engineer and he ended up a broken man. I think he called to offer help because he wants to redeem himself for the guilt he carries for his wife's death."

"Do you think he's capable of remotely interfering with commercial aircraft, like the flights in this case?"

"Yes and no."

"Explain that."

"He helped design Richlon-Titan's fly-by-wire system and he worked on Project Overlord, the technology promised by the president after 9/11. You know about Overlord, right?"

The agents nodded.

"Well, if anyone would know how to attack a jetliner's controls remotely, Robert Cole would. So yes, he has the expertise. But I don't believe he has it in his heart to commit such an act, even with his personal problems. The man I knew was dedicated to safety."

The FBI agents exchanged a look then tapped Veyda's photo.

"What about his daughter? MIT told us she has one of the highest IQs in the country. She was studying flight systems engineering. Is she capable? What's the meaning of Robert Cole's video plea to her?"

Hooper looked at Veyda's embittered expression. Her eyes were pools of sadness and rage.

"I don't know."

"Mr. Hooper, we want you to alert us should Robert Cole, or Veyda, or Seth Hagen, contact you."

"I will."

"As a precaution, we're going to execute warrants on your phone and all devices to monitor them."

After his interview, Hooper left the room and passed Bill Cashill's office. The door was open and the man invited him in.

Cashill stared at his computer monitor, his face ashen.

"You just spoke to the FBI?" Cashill asked, keeping his eyes on his screen.

"Yes. Did you talk to them?"

Cashill nodded without looking at Hooper: "So you're vindicated, Jake."

"What do you mean?"

"I was looking at conventional causes in both flights. I focused on them because of my years in the business. I'm a linear thinker. I wasn't open-minded enough to even consider the possibility of a remote cyber breach of both planes. You were. For me it was out of the realm of possibility."

Hooper stepped in and closed the door.

"Bill, no one in the world could've suspected Cole, his daughter and this other suspect, whoever he is—"

"Boyfriend, according to the FBI agents who questioned me. Seth Hagen's her boyfriend, and some sort of computer wizard, too. The three of them are good if they're able to override the system. I mean, they just left us in the dust, except for you."

"Bill, we should urge Richlon-Titan to ground everything with an RT system now. We should issue an alert, get the FAA to put out an airworthiness directive."

Cashill dragged his hands over his face.

"I've been yanked off the EastCloud and Shikra investigations."

"What?"

"People are protecting themselves. This is moving fast up the chain. Reed Devlin's taking over as the IIC. He's with the chairman and the board right now. The chairman will take part in a national security meeting with the White House, the Joint Chiefs and the whole gang later today to assess the situation and give direction on the response to it."

Hooper leaned back and his shoulders thudded against the door. His mind raced with regret at not responding to Robert Cole's messages.

Could all of this, the deaths, the danger and the fear, have been prevented if I'd talked to Cole when he called me?

Sixty-One

That morning, the man next to Robert Cole in the communal shower ranted Scripture as he coughed and wheezed.

Cole didn't mind.

After he toweled off and found a free sink and mirror to shave, he considered the line of prayer from Saint Francis taped to the rust-stained wall: "It is in dying that we are born into eternal life."

There's wisdom in those words, Cole thought as he reflected on the reasons he'd chosen to stay in a homeless shelter near Washington, DC.

Yes, he believed that if police were looking for him, he'd stand a better chance of evading them if he stayed at a shelter.

But it was more than that.

He needed to get closer to the truth of what he'd become: a wretched failure and a waste. If he was going to be resurrected and redeemed, he needed to bury himself.

The night staff had asked no questions when Cole

had arrived requesting to stay at the shelter, which was an abandoned school. They'd accepted his cash donation, given him a piece of paper with the rules then escorted him, via a flashlight beam on the floor, to a lower bunk in the gym where dozens of other men had been snoring.

Cole was grateful, for he felt that he was undeserving.

Now he dressed in his best shirt, tie and suit.

One of the staff, a woman named Polly, was generous in letting him use one of the shelter's phones to check his number for any response from Veyda to his video.

There was nothing.

His heart sank.

He collected his briefcase and made his way to the Rockville station of the Washington Metro, blending in with other commuters.

He was destined for the NTSB headquarters to see Jake Hooper.

I'll see him and I'll show him what we need to do, if it's the last thing I do on this earth.

Sixty-Two

The president sat at the center of the mahogany table, back to the Rose Garden, facing the vice president and other officials who'd been called to the Cabinet Room.

Eighteen people, including cabinet secretaries, members of the National Security Council, Defense, FBI, Homeland, FAA, CIA and NTSB were at the table, while two dozen other experts flanked the walls.

The Zarathustra situation was allotted thirty minutes on the White House agenda for assessment and action.

The meeting began with the president giving the FBI director five minutes to brief the table. The heads of the FAA and NTSB were each given three minutes. The president then opened the discussion, starting with the transportation secretary.

"Given the situation, we recommend a national ground stop followed by a global ground stop," the secretary said.

"You want to ground all flights?" the commerce secretary asked.

"Yes, we believe that's the prudent step to take."

"I think under the circumstances it's an overreaction," the commerce secretary said.

"It's the best safety measure," the transportation secretary said.

"Yes, of course, but that hasn't been done since 9/11. And with 9/11 we were under attack," the commerce secretary said. "The economic impact of a ground stop today would be devastating, and I don't need to remind this table how fragile economies are in some parts of the world now. We must consider other options."

"Without this precaution, we risk lives until the suspects are apprehended and the threat is removed," the transportation secretary said.

"I understand that," the commerce secretary said, "but we haven't identified a specific target, have we?"

"Nothing specific," the FBI director said. "The two stricken aircraft had Richlon-Titan flight systems, and the suspects are linked to Richlon-Titan."

"Have the manufacturer and airlines been advised, or asked to ground these aircraft?" the Homeland Security secretary asked.

"Those discussions with industry are taking place as we speak."

"How close are we to arresting the suspects?" the president asked.

"We're tracking two in Colorado now, and we believe we're close. One is believed to be here in the Washington area."

"Washington?"

"Yes. We're going to make a public appeal shortly, with photos, and place them on our Most Wanted list."

"Do we have conclusive evidence confirming the suspects interfered with the flights?" the president asked.

"No, but we have mounting evidence that points to that conclusion," the FBI director said.

"We'll move into a higher stage of readiness," the president said. "I want the FAA to immediately put out alerts to the airline industry. In particular, advise commercial crews to be vigilant and to immediately report any anomalies. We'll have NORAD and the National Military Command Center stand by. I want State to advise other countries of our situation through intelligence protocols."

"What about a ground stop?" the transportation secretary asked.

"No ground stop will be undertaken at this point. We'll allow law enforcement time to apprehend the suspects and remove the threat. If stronger evidence surfaces to confirm direct interference with the flights, we'll take appropriate action."

The president took a quick look around the table.

"Finally, I want to be kept abreast of any developments. Thank you."

Sixty-Three

Mobile, Alabama

Some thirty-four thousand feet above Mobile Bay, NorthSun Airlines Flight 118 was a little over an hour out of Miami when a bell sounded in the cockpit, indicating a flight advisory.

First Officer Sam Zhang's brow creased as he studied the console screen.

"What is it?" Will Miller, the captain, asked.

"It's an alert from the FAA advising extreme vigilance concerning any control anomalies. We're to alert ATC if we experience any unexpected incidents beyond SOP. It arises from the Shikra crash at Heathrow and the EastCloud flight into LaGuardia."

"Let me take a look."

Miller had been a fighter pilot with the US Air Force prior to logging twenty-five years as a commercial pilot, the last fifteen as a captain. Zhang had flown cargo planes around the world before joining NorthSun, where he'd been a first officer for ten years. Miller read the alert on the screen, shook his head slowly then resumed looking into the sky.

They were flying on autopilot.

Their aircraft was the Brazilian-built Startrail AV600, one of the largest passenger jetliners in operation with a seating capacity of six hundred. Today they had a full flight, mostly European and Asian tourists who'd come off a Caribbean cruise for the second leg of their trip—an Alaskan cruise out of Seattle.

"So what's your take on the advisory, Will?"

Miller raised his shoulders in a subtle shrug.

"To be honest, I think they're overreacting."

"Really?"

"Yeah."

"There've been some recent news reports speculating on the causes. Maybe the FAA or NTSB's got new information that gives them reason to be cautious?"

"Maybe. But this stems from Richlon-Titan's systems and we know RT's a penny-pincher with a penchant for cutting corners. Anyway, my buddies in the UK are hearing that Shikra was a computer malfunction, not a cyber breach."

"What about what happened to EastCloud?"

"Word is that was clear-air turbulence and a distracted pilot."

"So you have no concerns?"

"No, I wouldn't say that, but our bird's a long way from anything RT makes. It's got a solid safety record, so I'd say we're okay, Sam."

Zhang nodded but failed to quell the slight twinge in his stomach over the advisory. He concentrated on monitoring readings on the flight deck, eyeing every parameter. The autopilot did its job, making minor self-adjustments for latitude, longitude, speed, course and direction as they continued their slow climb toward thirty-six thousand feet, the altitude they'd be at for much of the long flight.

Zhang took a soft breath.

All looked good.

Sixty-Four

Kate couldn't shake her sense of unease, feeling that somewhere, something major was breaking on the story.

And I don't know what it is.

Her anxiety had arisen from what Nick Varner had told her when she'd called to alert him to Robert Cole.

We're on the same track and things are unfolding.

What was unfolding? What had Nick meant by that?

Something was up. Kate could feel it in her gut, and it tormented her as she inched along the security lines at Los Angeles International Airport for her return flight to New York.

She needed more information from Varner. She'd tried contacting him again last night and today but it was futile. She'd also reached out to Erich for help but so far he hadn't responded. Her worry deepened with each passing minute because once she was on the plane she'd be incommunicado for at least five hours.

Maybe she should alert Chuck.

Alert him to what—my failure to advance the lead we got on Cole? No, I'll handle this my way. Once I get back to New York, I'll go flat out to find Cole and I'll press Nick to tell me what the FBI's doing. He's got to give me something. We put out the story with the appeal like the FBI wanted, and I told them about Cole.

At last, Kate reached the front of the line and the scanners, where she hefted her carry-on bag to the table, removed her laptop from its case and presented her boarding pass.

Once she'd cleared security and made it to the preboarding area of her gate, she immediately went online, checking for any reports on the story by other major news organizations.

Nothing so far.

But that did little to calm her feeling that the story was about to bust wide open.

Sixty-Five

At that moment, across the country in the Defense Cyber Crime Center, Keith Dorling's breathing quickened.

"Let's go over this again. Look at the bus crash." He was on the phone with a British cyber analyst working on the Zarathustra email that had been received by the Kuwaiti Embassy in London.

"See?" Dorling said. "There was a power outage in London."

Dorling read the notice aloud: "'A double-decker bus crash has caused a disruption of power southeast of Hyde Park for the Brompton Road area.'"

"The Kuwaiti Embassy is in the area on Albert Gate," said Lynn Utley, Dorling's colleague.

Dorling and Utley scrolled through supplemental information from the Kuwaitis.

"The Kuwaitis said that the crash caused the embassy's system to go down," Dorling said. "But the crash happened around midnight. Look at the time shown on the Zarathustra email and the date stamp."

"How did everyone miss this?" Utley said.

Dorling checked and rechecked.

"See? When power was restored, the system's time stamp failed to reset correctly," Dorling said.

"This means the email warning of pain and sorrow was sent *before* Shikra Airlines Flight 418 crashed at Heathrow and can't be a wild, after-the-fact boast," Utley said.

"Yes, they predicted the event. It means they had to have been behind it."

"We've got to alert people," Utley said.

"They're going to have to ground everything."

Sixty-Six

At LAX, Kate eyed the screen above the agent's desk at her gate.

Her flight's departure was still on time.

Good.

She resumed studying the TV monitor above the seating area, watching CTNB while focusing on the ticker crawling at the bottom of the screen. The news was about an economic downturn. Nothing on the flights had emerged.

Kate continued watching until her flight, Trans Peak Airlines Flight 2230, nonstop to JFK, was called. The plane was the largest in the airline's fleet, the five-hundred-seat Ultra Supreme 880. It had a stellar safety record. Kate had checked it to offset the nervousness rippling through her about flying today.

She remained locked on CTNB until her row was called.

Despite being a sold-out flight, the boarding process went quickly, Kate thought after she'd stored her bag in the overhead bin, settled into her window seat and fastened her seat belt. Some fifteen minutes later, the jetliner taxied into position and waited for clearance to take off.

The engines roared as the big plane accelerated down the runway, pushing Kate deep into her seat. Great, she thought, as it lifted off and climbed over Southern California. The sooner she got back, the sooner she could dig into Robert Cole's life.

On the ground, as the 880 disappeared from the sky over Los Angeles, the faces of Seth Hagen, Veyda Cole and her father, Robert Cole, appeared on CTNB.

News was breaking that the FBI had identified them as the most wanted people in the country.

Sixty-Seven

Weld County, Colorado

Veyda and Seth's SUV cut across a desolate stretch of the high plains.

They'd left Denver, heading north on Highway 85. After passing through Greeley, they were now traveling east.

"Not too much farther," Seth said.

While he concentrated on the GPS and his laptop, Veyda took in the miles and miles of flat, arid land. The farther they drove, the fewer cars they saw. It was spiritual here, she thought, loving how the sky met the horizon on even terms. She couldn't help but think of her father's video.

Veyda, sweetheart, this is your father. Whatever you're doing or thinking of doing, please stop... I'm begging you... You will always be my daughter and I will always be your father. I love you...

Her eyes stung and she shook her head.

You're not my father and I am not your daughter. She remembered how her mother had died. *No, you're not my father and I'm not your daughter.*

She saw her father's face, the kind face she'd once adored, saw his pain.

I'm begging you... I will always be your father. I love you...

She wiped her eyes.

No, I won't let you stop me.

She gritted her teeth, standing hard against the waves of sentimentality rising within her. Her knuckles whitened on the wheel, her blind determination killing any notion of doubt.

"Turn left at that gate post," Seth said.

He guided her along a secondary road that after several miles became an earthen path. Soon the main road had disappeared behind them in the small hills. The path was akin to a trail, undulating several more miles along a dry, uninhabited extent of treeless land.

"Slow it down. We're nearly here."

The SUV continued, gently twisting over the soft, grassy trail until they crested a gentle slope that swept down to a winding river and panoramic expanse.

"Stop—this is it. Let's get to work."

No other people or buildings were in sight as they unloaded their laptop computers to a thick patch of grass near the car and switched them on.

Their high-powered systems were equipped with wireless satellite technology, giving them optimum online access. For the next twenty minutes, Seth carefully entered coordinates, codes and other data into his system as Veyda watched over his shoulder, double-checking the process. Occasionally, they'd pause to discuss a code sequence, but their work proceeded swiftly.

Seth turned to Veyda.

"Ready?"

"Ready," she said.

A soft click sounded when Seth pressed the enter key, unleashing their greatest operation.

"It's done. It's in motion," he said. "Nothing can stop it. Soon everyone on the planet will be speaking our names."

Tears rolled down Veyda's face as she and Seth kissed, celebrating what was to come.

The gun waited on the grass beside them.

Sixty-Eight

Southbound on the Red Line Metro, Robert Cole closed his eyes and took another breath while mentally reciting what had become his mantra since boarding the train.

If they give me the chance I can show them how to stop the breach.

The train eased into Van Ness and, as he'd done at each previous station, Cole looked at his phone to see if he was connected.

He was.

He was going to check news sites, but first he went to his photos, almost smiling back at his wife who smiled at him from the screen. Staring into her eyes, he could almost hear her voice, inhale her scent and feel her skin.

I'm going to fix everything. This is my fault. I'm going to find Veyda before she hurts any more people, or the police hurt her. She's sick and she needs help. I swear to you, Elizabeth, I'll fix it.

The train began to roll out of the station and Cole

quickly checked the news. He went to the *Washington Post*'s online edition.

Shock shot through him.

His photograph, Veyda's and that of a young man he didn't know were displayed together under a breaking news banner:

FBI Hunts for American Trio in London Plane Tragedy.

Cole read the short news story before he lost his internet connection. His hand shook just as the train jolted and he lost his grip on his phone. It fell to the floor of his crowded car and he caught his breath. The woman seated next to him reached down and retrieved it for him.

"Thank you," he said, relieved the internet link had been lost.

"No problem." She smiled.

His heart racing, Cole put his phone in his pocket and subtly surveyed the car's commuters. They were reading, sleeping, talking, or looking at nothing. No one was looking at him. At least, no one that he was aware of.

Cole lowered his head, took documents from his briefcase and pulled them close to his face, pretending to read.

Take it easy. Take another breath. Remain calm. I just have to get to L'Enfant Plaza station and NTSB headquarters. It won't be much longer.

Cole exhaled.

Then somewhere before Cleveland station, the train slowed in the tunnel before coming to a complete stop.

Cole's heart slammed against his rib cage.

Two uniformed police officers had entered his car and were headed in his direction.

Sixty-Nine

An unmarked white Chevy Trailblazer, its emergency lights wigwagging in the grille, idled at Denver International Airport.

Nick Varner, who'd been alerted to his pickup, spotted it upon arriving after his ninety-minute United Airlines flight from Williston, North Dakota.

An FBI agent got out of the vehicle to greet him and take his bag.

"Mitch Butler. We met at the Chicago conference."

"Hey, Mitch. Thanks."

"Welcome to Denver, Nick." Butler opened the passenger door for him. "Let's get rolling."

The SUV pulled away with its lights flashing and threaded through traffic. In minutes they were speeding northbound on 85 as Butler updated Varner.

"Our subjects, Veyda Cole and Seth Hagen, landed in Denver. We tracked them to a motel on Colfax Avenue. ERT's processing their room."

"Anything?"

"Nothing so far."

"What about the GPS on the rental?"

Butler nodded big nods.

"Pay dirt. We've locked onto it and are setting up for a takedown."

"Really?"

"The signal shows they're stopped in the middle of nowhere in Weld County."

"Maybe they dumped the rental?"

"Maybe. We have no visual and no contact yet. We're in the process of getting confirmation. Here's the area." Butler handed a phone displaying a map to Varner.

"Who's in on this?"

"Everybody. We've got our SWAT out of Denver Colorado Department of Public Safety, State Patrol, and Weld and Morgan County Sheriff's Departments. We're still marshaling resources. We'll be joined there by experts from the NTSB's Denver office to provide immediate assessment of what we might find related to hacking flight systems. We're setting up for an operation in a community barn in Galeton. It's on the map there. That's where we're headed now. We should be there in an hour, give or take."

Varner studied the map.

"What could they do to jetliners out there in the middle of nowhere, Mitch?"

"Anyone's guess. There's nothing out there but a whole lot of nothing, except for the Minuteman missile launch sites."

"Missile launch sites? Are you serious?"

"But they're empty and inactive, so it couldn't be that."

Seventy

Camilla Rosa's eyes narrowed on her radar screen in the dimly lit room housed by the Los Angeles Air Route Traffic Control Center.

Ever since receiving the FAA's recent alert, Rosa had been functioning at a heightened sense of awareness at her station.

She was a skilled, conscientious air traffic controller, a ten-year veteran who was ever vigilant, but news stories about the FBI's search for three people related to the London crash and the troubled East-Cloud flight had every controller on edge.

The Los Angeles Center's reach of responsibility encompassed the southern half of California, southern Nevada, southwestern Utah and western Arizona.

Trans Peak Airlines Flight 2230, nonstop to JFK, was one of the flights in Rosa's sector. The flight had crossed over Las Vegas and was high above Lake Mead, Nevada. Soon it would be over southwestern Utah and out of her sector.

Rosa was preparing to hand off the flight to Denver Center when she felt a tiny ping of concern. Flight 2230's altitude was thirty-five thousand feet, the altitude assigned to the flight. But she'd noticed the aircraft was climbing to thirty-six thousand feet.

What's up with that?

Typically, east-to-west and west-to-east flights were assigned odd-numbered flight levels, while north-to-south and south-to-north flights were assigned even-numbered ones.

No immediate traffic was in Flight 2230's corridor, but the pilot had not requested to leave his assigned altitude, so Rosa radioed the aircraft.

"TP Twenty-two Thirty, LA Center. You're at flight level three six zero. Return to flight level three five zero."

"Twenty-two Thirty. Roger, LA Center. Stand by."

Rosa allowed sixty seconds. During that time she tended to other flights in her sector while keeping an eye out for 2230 to return to its assigned level. When it didn't happen, she radioed again.

"TP Twenty-two Thirty, LA Center. You're still showing level three six zero. Request you return to flight level three five zero as you're approaching Denver Center sector."

A full ten seconds passed in silence.

"TP Twenty-two Thirty, LA Center. Did you copy? Return to flight level three five zero."

"Twenty-two Thirty. Roger, LA Center. Uh, we're working on it but it seems we've got a system issue. Request you clear space until we can correct things."

"TP Twenty-two Thirty, what is your systems issue?"

"Twenty-two Thirty. LA Center, that's what we're trying to figure out."

Rosa scanned the vicinity near Flight 2230. They were clear in their space, but her unease had deepened, and in keeping with the FAA advisory, she pressed a button to summon her supervisor.

Seventy-One

Oklahoma

Five minutes after Seattle-bound NorthSun Airlines Flight 118 had flown over Oklahoma City, First Officer Sam Zhang blinked several times while scrutinizing their course readings.

"We seem to be veering slightly," Zhang said.

Captain Will Miller stuck out his bottom lip after appraising the figures on display.

"Just the autopilot adjusting. Give it another few minutes."

Five more minutes passed, and Zhang saw nothing change as the plane continued heading off course.

"Still veering," Zhang said.

"Maybe we've got weather up ahead and it's compensating."

"But we have no weather issues showing and no advisories."

Miller nodded and got on the radio.

"Kansas City Center, NorthSun One Eighteen. Have we got weather issues ahead?"

"Negative on weather, One Eighteen, but we show

you moving out of your assigned course. Please correct and advise."

"NorthSun One Eighteen, will do."

Miller turned to Zhang.

"Sam, see what you can do to adjust it and get us back on the straight and narrow."

Zhang made a number of inputs calibrating longitude and latitude. All were rejected. He reset and tried again. Nothing happened.

"It's refusing my adjustments."

"That's nuts," Miller said. "Let me try."

The captain's attempts met with the same result.

"How's our separation?" Miller asked, his tone betraying a degree of frustration as he continued trying to correct the course heading.

"We're still good," Zhang said.

"NorthSun One Eighteen, please adjust your heading."

"NorthSun One Eighteen here. Kansas City Center, we're on it. Seems we have a sticky issue. We request you clear space until we resolve this."

"NorthSun One Eighteen, identify your problem."

"NorthSun One Eighteen. Center, that's what we're trying to do. Stand by."

"Sam, take us off auto and I'll do this manually."

Zhang shut off the autopilot then Miller took control of the aircraft.

"All right, Sam, make the correction."

Zhang input the changes but nothing happened. Miller exchanged a glance with him then tried directing the plane manually.

His commands were refused.

"What the hell?" Miller said. "It's got to be a bug in the system."

Zhang's face was sober with concern.

"I think we should report an anomaly."

Miller was shaking his head.

"Let's run a diagnostic first."

"But that will take too long and who knows where we'll be then. Sir, I think we should first report an anomaly. We could still run the diagnostic."

Miller licked his lips and nodded.

"Okay. All right. NorthSun One Eighteen. Kansas City Center, we're reporting an anomaly with our flight-management system and request you clear space for heading…"

Seventy-Two

Washington, DC

Jake Hooper gripped his laptop computer under his arm like a football as he joined his supervisor, Anson Fox, and the new IIC, Reed Devlin, in running upstairs to the NTSB chairman's boardroom.

The alert that two in-air jetliners had confirmed flight-management control trouble moments ago had impelled top national security officials to convene an emergency teleconference to assess the facts and take action.

The NTSB chairman and several board members, along with chiefs from Major Investigations, Research and Engineering, and Aviation Safety were already at the large table. Hooper, Fox and Devlin found seats as the teleconference call got underway.

Speakers crackled on the line as the FAA led the teleconference with a short roll call. The same array of national security offices from earlier calls and meetings were represented.

"Here are the facts, people," Estevan Diaz, chief operating officer of the FAA's Air Traffic Organization, began with a lightning-fast summary of NorthSun Airlines Flight 118 and Trans Peak Airlines Flight 2230, nonstop to JFK.

"One Eighteen out of Miami is Seattle-bound. It's a Startrail AV600. The crew count is sixteen. The passenger count is six hundred. The second plane, Twenty-two Thirty out of LA, is headed for JFK. The plane is an Ultra Supreme 880. The crew count is fourteen. The passenger count is four hundred ninety-five. In total, we have eleven hundred and twenty-five souls aboard these two planes."

Diaz gave the course coordinates for each jet, which Hooper recorded in the notes he was making in his laptop.

"Given our current situational concerns, we believe that the flight systems of both aircraft have been breached. Both aircraft employ aspects of Richlon-Titan's fly-by-wire systems. We're also taking into account our new intel—that the Zarathustra email was sent to the Kuwaiti Embassy in advance of the Shikra Airlines crash, confirming that the suspects have the ability to undertake cyber hijackings. We've alerted NORAD and the National Military Command Center to the flights, as well as all national security organizations, and we're consulting the planes' makers and the airlines on the situation."

The White House national security advisor was the next to speak.

"So we have two remotely hijacked planes in two different regions of the country. Are there any others reporting trouble?"

"No others," Diaz said.

"What's the status of action to bring them down safely?" the White House advisor asked.

"Yes." Cord Bolton, office deputy director for operations for the military command center at the Pentagon, cleared his throat. "At this time we're scrambling fighters to the aircraft for escort or other operations."

"And our pursuit of the suspects?" the White House advisor asked.

"We're poised to launch an arrest operation near Galeton, Colorado, where we've located a vehicle rented by two of the three suspects," Kal McClure, with the FBI director's office, reported.

"How much time before we have an arrest?"

"I'm advised that we're within half an hour, maybe less," McClure said.

"And the third suspect?" the advisor asked.

"We're still in pursuit. We believe he's in Washington, DC."

"Any other actions before we brief the president?" the advisor asked.

"The FAA is recommending an immediate national ground stop of all nonmilitary and nonemergency aircraft," Diaz said.

"We'll brief the Oval Office. Anything else?" the advisor asked.

"Oh, no," Hooper said aloud.

"Excuse me? What was that?" the White House advisor asked.

Hooper, who'd been working as fast as he could making calculations, turned his laptop computer to Reed Devlin and whispered, "Reed, look. Of over five thousand flights in the air, only two have reported control issues. Given their present courses, these two aircraft will intersect somewhere over Galeton, Colorado, within forty minutes."

Devlin's face whitened and he tapped the shoulder of the supervisor next to him. Soon, the NTSB chairman spoke.

"Yes, this is the NTSB. Inform the president that our rough estimates show that these two aircraft are on a collision course that will end in about forty minutes over Colorado."

"You're certain?" the White House advisor asked.

The NTSB boss looked at Hooper, who nodded.

"We're certain," the NTSB chairman said.

"Deputy Director Bolton?" the advisor said.

"Yes?"

"What's the ETA before the fighters reach the jetliners?"

The director did a quick calculation then said, "They should reach the respective aircraft within fifteen minutes."

"We'll brief the president. If we can't restore control of the planes to the crews, we'll be forced to consider the option of engagement."

Seventy-Three

Weld County, Colorado

High above the vast reaches of the empty prairie, an FBI drone scoured the ground below.

It flew at a height that kept it invisible and silent from detection.

Equipped with high-powered video cameras and sensors, the small surveillance aircraft gave agents at the command post in Galeton a critical aerial view of the area where the GPS trail of their subjects had stopped.

The agent piloting the drone at a control console exercised the precision of a surgeon, carefully watching the video screen as she stabilized its position.

The camera panned, captured objects, then zoomed in.

The clear image of a lone vehicle emerged on the screen. Near the vehicle two people came into view, one male and one female, sitting on a blanket with laptop computers.

The camera pulled in closer.

"Is that the grip of a handgun by the male's leg?" asked Nick Varner, who huddled with other agents and SWAT team leaders near the monitor.

"We can't confirm," the drone pilot said. "But that's as close as we're going to get, sir."

"All right, let's go," Burt Young, the FBI SWAT commander, said. Then he instructed the drone pilot, "Keep us updated on movements because they're going to see us coming." Young confirmed coordinates with the other teams, who would each take a compass point for their approach, boxing in their subjects. Then he turned from the group and signaled to his team. They shrugged into their gear and climbed into the vehicles parked outside.

Varner strapped on a vest and helmet, checked his weapon and found a seat next to Mitch Butler, who had been on the phone.

"So what about those missile launch sites?" Varner asked.

"Just had it confirmed—they're empty and inactive."

Varner nodded. "Good. We can rule that out."

Engines revved and seconds later FBI, city and state SWAT teams moved out in a convoy of armored police trucks, along with two ambulances from Weld and Morgan counties, and two NTSB experts in an SUV taking up the rear.

They were braced for all eventualities.

Seventy-Four

The two police officers who'd entered Robert Cole's Metro car had moved past him without stopping.

Cole exhaled his relief but kept his face in his files until he got off at the Metro Center station, where he boarded an Orange Line train to the L'Enfant Plaza Metro station.

Anxiety surged through him during the short ride but he regained his focus on what he had to do as he stepped from the train, blending in with commuters as he made his way to NTSB headquarters. Suddenly, the enormity of his situation caught up with him, stopping him in his tracks outside the building's entrance.

How did my life come to this? I'm wanted by the FBI. Veyda's killed fifteen people and is planning to kill more.

He ran his fingers over his dry lips. He craved a drink. One drink.

No, you have to keep going. Cole tightened his hold on his briefcase. *Stop thinking of yourself. You have to fix this and you have to do it now.*

He entered the main lobby.

Streams of government workers and employees of companies in the building were using their ID badges to go through the security turnstiles. Non-government visitors had lined up at the security desk, where they had to show identification and provide the names of the people they were there to see. Their personal items were passed through a scanner and x-rayed.

I can't let it end here. I've got to see Hooper.

Cole licked his lips and fumbled for the ID badge he'd used when he'd worked on NTSB investigations long ago. He eyed the security officers while keeping his head down. His line moved steadily.

Remain calm and act natural. Calm and natural.

"Next," said the young female security guard, Atley, according to her nameplate.

"Robert Cole to see Jake Hooper with NTSB Major Investigations." Cole placed his ID on the desk.

Atley looked at it carefully, deepening his fear.

"It's urgent," Cole added. "I'm party to an investigation."

Atley looked at Cole, typed on her keyboard then reached for her phone.

Cole glanced at other security officers, momentarily eyeing their holstered guns. Then he looked back at Atley, not liking the way she was tapping his card on her desk while on the phone.

It telegraphed a problem.

Cole saw that one of the other security guards was taking a longer look at him. Cole looked away for several seconds, but when he looked back the guard was still looking at him—directly at him.

A collision course! Dear God, they did it. They've breached the system.

Jake Hooper rushed from the emergency meeting to his desk, stunned by the horror playing out over the sky, refusing to believe Robert Cole would engineer such devastation.

How can we stop it?

The nation's best experts with the NTSB, the FAA, the military, the airlines, the planes' makers, were all frantically searching for solutions that would release the cyber stranglehold that had locked the jets on a death course.

Nothing was working.

Jet fighters were getting into position to take whatever action the White House advised.

Impact was less than forty minutes away.

More than eleven hundred people would die.

The FBI was on-site in Colorado, minutes from moving in on Seth Hagen and Cole's daughter.

Is there time to stop what's been orchestrated?

Hooper racked his brain for a solution. It was futile. Whatever he'd thought of had already been conveyed to the crews by the Air Route Traffic Control Centers, and nothing was working.

Hooper glanced at the time: thirty-eight minutes to impact. His line rang and he seized it.

"Hooper."

"Security, sir. I've got Robert Cole at the desk for you."

"Who?"

"Robert Cole. He says it's urgent."

Hooper's pulse rocketed.

"Don't let him leave! I'll be right down! Hold him there!"

"Sir," Atley said to Cole upon hanging up, "your card's expired."

"Expired?"

"Yes, would you—"

"Let me take a look." The guard who'd been staring at Cole held out his hand for Cole's ID. He studied it, then the pages posted near the computer. His sharp blue eyes flicked to Cole, then to the pages, then to Cole.

Both men knew.

Cole's stomach clenched and he took a step back from the desk.

The guard very subtly shifted his weight while unsnapping the button strap of his holster.

"Sir, get down on the floor, on your stomach," the older guard said.

Cole didn't move.

In one smooth motion the guard drew his gun from his holster and leveled it at Cole's head.

"Get on the floor now!"

A woman screamed. People nearby backed away as Cole dropped to his knees, raising his open hands.

"Please, I have to see Jake Hooper! It's a matter of life and death."

"Atley, move your ass! Cuff him!" the older guard said.

"You don't understand," Cole said.

Atley rose from her seat and moved behind Cole,

pushing his stomach flat on the floor, and hand-cuffed his wrists behind his back. The older guard replaced his gun in his holster and spoke quickly into the shoulder microphone of his radio. Then he helped heft Cole to his feet and moved him around the security desk toward a small office, just as Hooper emerged.

"Jake!" Cole called to him. "Jake, it's my daughter and her boyfriend! They found a point of vulnerability! I can fix it!"

"Shut up!" the older guard said as his radio crackled a response.

"Hold on!" Hooper said. "I need to talk to this man!"

"No," the guard said. "He's wanted by the FBI. We've just alerted them."

"Where're you taking him?"

The guard nodded to the small office.

"Jake, please, let me help! I can fix it!"

More security people arrived, along with Reed Devlin.

"Reed," Hooper said, "Robert says he has the solution!"

Devlin's face tensed as he assessed the scene.

"This man's wanted by the FBI," the security supervisor said, "and we're holding him here. They're on their way."

"Reed," Hooper said. "Cole can help us and we're losing time!"

"Listen to me," Devlin told the guards. "We've got a crisis happening now and we need this man's expertise immediately. Please hold him in our operations room so we can talk to him. Keep him in custody and watch over him. The NTSB will assume responsibility but we must do it now!"

As the security supervisor shook his head Devlin stepped closer to him, enabling the security man to read the fear in Devlin's eyes.

"We have a thousand lives at stake! Do you want to be the guy history remembers as the one who stood in the way of saving them?" Devlin said.

The security supervisor's face whitened.

"We're in this together," Devlin said. "Let's do this now!"

The supervisor turned to the guards and nodded.

"Let's go. Take him up to the sixth."

Seventy-Five

"It's not working."

Beads of sweat grew on Lloyd Quinn's brow as he looked at Shawn Krenski, who was shaking his head.

Thirty-five minutes ago, they'd learned that their plane, Trans Peak Airlines Flight 2230 from LA to New York, was locked on a collision course with Seattle-bound NorthSun Airlines Flight 118. The time of impact was in thirty-one minutes.

Both crews had now been alerted and advised not to tell passengers of the situation so as not to risk chaos on the flight. Since the alert, Quinn and Krenski had made countless attempts to regain control of their aircraft.

"Anything happening with the autopilot?" Joe Brazak, the top engineer for the 880, said from Trans Peak's headquarters in Seattle.

"Nothing."

"Let's try that override again."

"Roger." Quinn nodded to Krenski, who issued a sequence of commands but to no avail.

"Nothing," Quinn reported, just as his headset beeped with a transmission from the ATCC.

"TP Twenty-two Thirty, Denver Center. No change to your course."

"Twenty-two Thirty. Roger, Center. We're working on it with engineering."

Quinn's headset beeped again.

"Try it again but with the reset," Marty Chan, the systems chief, suggested from Seattle.

Krenski wiped his sweating fingers on his shirt as he tried the reset without success.

"Okay," Brazak said, "try to reduce speed again."

"We tried again. Nothing."

"Try adjusting altitude."

Quinn made yet another effort, which failed, leaving him to curse under his breath and face the fact that they were trapped. Every command was shut out. He had no control of his aircraft as it cut across the sky thirty-six thousand feet above Grand Junction, Colorado.

They were moving at more than five hundred miles an hour, locked into a course that would end in a midair collision with a Seattle-bound flight in about thirty minutes.

Quinn looked to the corner of the console, where he'd placed a small photo of Maria, his wife, and Sophie and Ella, their two daughters. It was in keeping with a promise he'd made to himself long ago.

If ever he faced something impossible on the job, their faces were the last thing he wanted to see.

Quinn then looked at the sky ahead.

God help us.

Seventy-Six

Garden City, Kansas

Captain Will Miller's jaw muscles spasmed as he gripped the handles of the control wheel and battled his anger with engineering.

"We've run diagnostics three times now!" Miller said. "It's been futile! You guys have to give us something that works. We're running out of time!"

Seattle-bound NorthSun Airlines Flight 118 was high over Garden City, Kansas. Miller and First Officer Sam Zhang had worked in vain to recover control of the Startrail AV600. Engineers from the plane's builder in São Paulo, Brazil, and US operations in Houston had provided a line of possible remedies over the radio. Each one had failed.

"NorthSun One Eighteen, this is Kansas City Center. We see no change in your course."

"Kansas City Center, nothing's working for us."

"One Eighteen, we're handing off to NORAD. You'll find them on the emergency frequency. Good luck, One Eighteen."

One minute later, an F-16 appeared on Zhang's right side, while Miller saw one on his left side.

The two jet fighters were with the 140th Wing, Colorado Air National Guard out of Buckley Air Force in Aurora.

"One Twenty Tactical to NorthSun One Eighteen, this is Major Brennan. How do you read?"

"NorthSun One Eighteen, this is Captain Will Miller. Loud and clear, Major."

Miller took a deep breath.

It was now twenty-three minutes to impact with the New York–bound flight.

Seventy-Seven

White River National Forest, Colorado

Kate's plane was somewhere over Colorado.

She had no internet access, of course, underscoring her apprehension that she was missing something. Once she got to New York, she'd track down Robert Cole. She'd already started outlining her story but Cole was the most critical aspect.

I wish this jet could go faster.

She looked from her notes to the window, still troubled by Varner's cryptic response to her about Cole—that they were on the same track and things were unfolding.

What's unfolding down there?

A chime sounded and the seat belt sign illuminated. The in-flight beverage-and-meals-for-purchase service was abruptly halted. Attendants returned service carts with a sense of urgency.

Another chime sounded, and the captain's voice rang through the cabin. "Ladies and gentlemen, this is Captain Quinn." A long silence passed before the captain cleared his throat. "We request everyone remain in their seats with their belts fastened and refrain from using the washrooms. We have a situation with national security implications…"

Murmurs rose throughout the cabin.

"…and as a precaution, you may see military aircraft beside us momentarily. I'm sorry, but we have no further details that we can pass to you at this point."

An outcry of dismay, fear and anger erupted among the passengers.

"What the hell's going on?" one man shouted as attendants, with worry etched in their faces, patrolled the aisles to confirm all seat belts were fastened. One woman seized an attendant by the arm. "We have a right to know what's happening!"

"I'm sorry, but we only know what you know, ma'am."

"There they are!" a boy shouted.

Necks craned as people turned to the windows to see F-16 fighters flying off the wings on either side of the plane. The sight of the military jets a few feet from the jetliner hammered home the gravity of the situation.

"Oh my God!" One woman made the sign of the cross.

Attendants pinballed between the emotional trouble spots, comforting passengers, and soon a heavy, silent dread settled over the cabin as families held hands. Some passengers wept softly and others prayed.

Kate felt all the saliva dry in her mouth as she dropped her head back on her headrest and blinked several times.

Oh dear God. She gripped her armrests. *Is this tied to Zarathustra? Maybe they've taken control of the plane.*

Her stomach twisted at the surreal truth of her situation and she acted on the one clear thought she had. She took out her notepad, uncapped her pen and began writing.

Dear Grace and Vanessa. Right now, I don't know what's going to happcn, but I want you to know you are both the lights of my life…

Seventy-Eight

Weld County, Colorado

In the distance, the sun glinted off windshields and dust rose from the wake of approaching vehicles.

"They're coming fast," Seth said.

He was the first to spot the police convoys bearing down on them. They came in lines from the north, the south and the east, forming an armored horseshoe, for the west was a slope down to the river with no escape.

It didn't matter.

Veyda and Seth had no need to run.

"I'm surprised," Seth said. "They're faster than we expected."

"But not fast enough," Veyda said.

The armored trucks stopped within forty yards of them and spewed SWAT teams. Each member took up a shielded position and aimed at them in a C-ring of firepower.

"FBI! Stand up slowly! Put your hands above your head with palms showing! Now!"

Curtains of prairie dust floated over Seth and Veyda as they stood slowly and raised their hands.

"You're too late!" Seth called to them.

"What's done cannot be undone!" Veyda said.

"Shut up and walk slowly toward us!"

Seth turned to Veyda.

"We did it, babe. Yours is the power and the glory at thirty-six thousand feet above us."

Tears streamed down Veyda's face as she nodded and whispered, "We did it. We'll be immortal."

"Start walking now!" an FBI agent shouted.

"Are you ready?" Seth moved his hand slightly to touch Veyda's fingers.

"Yes, Seth. I'm ready."

Seth moved his hand quickly to his back, gripped the gun tucked in his waistband then shot Veyda, who dropped instantly, before he pointed the gun at the laptops, intending to destroy them before killing himself. But the law moved faster.

Gunfire exploded in a rapid, deafening volley and Seth collapsed on the computers next to Veyda.

In the peaceful silence, SWAT team members edged quickly to the scene. The paramedics were summoned and SWAT team leaders examined the aftermath.

Varner joined them.

The laptops were bloodied and one was chipped. Another had missing keys. Their last hope of undoing the midair disaster was gone.

Seventy-Nine

The president was in the Oval Office with a small group of advisors when the call came.

The chief of staff took it.

"It's the defense secretary with an update on the jetliners."

The president got on the line, absorbing the full weight of the situation. Two suspects had been shot in Colorado and a third arrested in Washington, DC. All attempts to recover control of the aircraft had failed. The jets were locked in a collision course. Impact was in twenty-two minutes. One thousand one hundred twenty-five lives would be lost over Colorado.

"However, if one aircraft is engaged—"

"Engaged? Call it what it is," the president said.

"If one of the aircraft is shot down approximately half of the total would be spared, giving us time to seek other options," the secretary said.

The president swallowed hard.

"The combat air patrols out of Buckley are in position," the secretary said. "We must fire upon the airliner no later than five minutes before impact to allow the debris field to clear."

The president's eyes closed at the thought of humanity and wreckage swirling in the sky... *Moms, dads, children, babies...*

"We need an order now," the secretary said.

The president knew the numbers. Six hundred sixteen souls were aboard the Seattle-bound jet, while five hundred and nine were on the flight headed to New York.

"Take out the New York–bound flight. More lives will be saved."

"Affirmative. We'll issue the order immediately."

The president ended the call, instructed the chief of staff to cancel the afternoon's political event in Virginia, then turned and gazed, hollow-eyed, out the French windows at the Rose Garden.

Eighty

Tears stained the pages as Kate wrote her farewell note to Grace and Vanessa.

Amid the anxiety that filled the cabin and her own anguish, she found the strength to convey what was in her heart.

> …I've been blessed to have you in my life because you are and always will be my world. I love you more than you will ever know…

Kate looked up to see that the woman in the seat next to her was offering her a tissue. The woman smiled weakly, and Kate saw that she'd been looking at family pictures on her phone.

"My name is Willa Neal, from Santa Ana."

"Thanks for the tissue, Willa. My name's Kate Page, from New York."

"You're about the same age as my daughter," Willa said. "May I hold your hand, Kate? Please?"

Kate took Willa's hand in hers and at that moment saw that the jet fighters were pulling back.

"They're moving away!" a man several rows ahead shouted. "What's that mean?"

"Maybe whatever's happening is over?" another passenger said.

Leaning forward and looking back, Kate watched the fighter vanish from view.

Maybe it's really over. God, please let it be over!

US Air Force Major Tom Garland shut his eyes for a second to block out the pleas from Captain Quinn of the doomed New York–bound jetliner.

"Trans Peak Twenty-two Thirty. Why're you pulling back, Major?"

Garland didn't respond. Captain Quinn repeated his query.

"Twenty-two Thirty. Why're you abandoning our escort? Please acknowledge, Major Garland!"

He couldn't lie and couldn't bear to tell the commercial captain the truth.

"For purposes of national security, I cannot reveal my orders, sir."

"Major, we have five hundred and nine souls aboard. We deserve an answer!"

"I'm sorry, sir."

"Major!"

Garland had been assigned command of the engagement operation on Flight 2230. He instructed his partner, Captain Ryan Taft, in the fighter on the jetliner's right side, to throttle back. The fighters were now a quarter-mile behind the jetliner. The pilots switched to a frequency that allowed them to speak freely.

"Our assignment's clear, Ryan."

"Yes, sir. I'm ready to carry it out."

Each fighter was armed with four heat-seeking air-to-air missiles and a 20 mm cannon. Garland eyed the controls used to fire a missile. Technologically speaking, taking down the jetliner would be as easy as pressing a button.

But morally...

Garland was hit suddenly with a crisis of conscience. He'd gone to work that morning like any other morning. He'd left his suburban Denver home, had kissed Angie, his wife, before she'd gone to her manager's job at the bank. Tonight they were supposed to be taking Troy, their son, out for burgers for his eleventh birthday. Garland grew furious that some deranged individuals had created a situation that would force him to kill five hundred and nine innocent people.

How will I face Angie and Troy after this?

"Ready to launch, sir," Taft said.

It was now fourteen minutes to impact.

Is this the only option?

Eighty-One

Sirens from the ambulances rushing Seth and Veyda to the hospital faded in the distance.

At the scene, the two NTSB investigators began examining the laptops.

Chet Meyer had established an open line to NTSB headquarters in Washington while Jill LaRose studied the damaged computers with the aid of the FBI, who'd quickly taken video records of the aftermath. Both devices were blood-splattered, cracked and chipped from the takedown.

But both were still in contact with the satellite connection.

"They're both functioning," LaRose said.

"Is there anything you guys can do to undo what they've done?" Varner asked.

"Depends," Meyer said, then, to LaRose, "Jill, can you read what's running?"

"It's— I don't—" She began looking at the open files and online links, struggling to decipher the complexities of the content and codes. "It's there, but it's so complex, Chet, I think it's beyond me."

Eighty-Two

Colorado

At fourteen minutes to impact, a serene calm washed over Major Tom Garland as his life blazed before his eyes.

From his dream to be a pilot while growing up in Toledo, to his marriage to Angie, then having Troy; then to enlistment, training and combat missions over Libya and Syria, to his time flying some of the most dangerous maneuvers ever with the aerobatic demonstration team.

It all passed before him in a heartbeat, culminating in a single, crystalline revelation: all that he'd learned, all that he'd done, all that he'd become, had been in preparation for this defining moment.

Garland knew what they had to do.

"Ryan, you know I flew with the Thunderbirds?"

"Yes, sir, but what's that got to do with—"

"We've got one god-awful, long-shot chance to save this plane."

"Our orders are to engage, sir."

"I know our orders, but we're going to get under each of his wings and lift him."

"Sir, with all due respect, that's crazy! With the upward flow, the weight, the speed, we just can't lift him! It's impossible and it's too dangerous!"

"Ryan, we have to try. Together we can do it. Look at our data. Both jetliners are at thirty-six thousand two hundred, exactly. Our opposing jet's tail height is sixty-three feet, and allow twenty feet for us. We've got nothing on our wingtip rail launchers. If we can get our guy up one hundred and twenty feet that should clear him and us."

"That's a big 'if,' sir, and a shave close enough to draw blood. We'd be disobeying orders. We'd face a court-martial if this went bad."

"That's the least of our worries. If this goes bad we pull back at the five-minute mark and engage. If it really goes bad, Ryan, we can eject. Look ahead. There are five hundred and nine people who can't. They're going to die in about thirteen minutes. We have to do what we can to save them."

Garland looked at his instruments and timer.

"Are you with me?"

Garland could hear Taft swallow hard.

"Yes, sir."

The F-16s throttled ahead to Flight 2230.

Eighty-Three

Seattle-bound NorthSun Airlines Flight 118 was flying over the Cheyenne Wells region when a cockpit advisory activated.

The jetliner's traffic collision avoidance system issued a "Descend, Descend," warning, indicating that an aircraft was intruding into NorthSun's airspace and the crew should be prepared to maneuver.

Captain Miller again attempted to control the plane and descend while First Officer Sam Zhang tried to get a visual on the opposing flight. Miller's efforts were futile, and the jetliner maintained its hijacked course.

"There's nothing we can do, damn it! We're locked at thirty-six two hundred!" Captain Miller dragged his hand across his brow and glanced at the jet fighters escorting him.

"NorthSun One Eighteen. Major Brennan, our TCAS has been activated. We can't pull out of our position to descend. Is there anything you can do to help us?"

"One Twenty Tactical to NorthSun One Eighteen. Negative, sir. An operation has been launched."

"What does that mean, Major?"

"I can't disclose details for reasons of national security, sir."

"Dammit, Major, you've got to be straight with us!"

"The operation will be completed shortly, sir."

The TCAS advisory continued telling Captain Miller and First Officer Zhang to descend. But it was futile. Frustrated and terrified, Captain Miller came to a decision and made an announcement to the passengers.

"Ladies and gentlemen, as you know we've been dealing with a situation with national security implications. Efforts to resolve it are ongoing and we're confident we'll have you safe on the ground in Seattle as scheduled. However, at this time, I would invite those passengers who are religious to consider prayers. For passengers who are not, you may want to collect your thoughts."

Shock, confusion and disbelief rolled in waves through the cabin.

It was now eleven minutes to impact with the oncoming flight.

The TCAS advisory had also activated in the New York–bound flight, just as First Officer Shawn Krenski glimpsed activity on his right.

"He's back, Lloyd! The fighter's back on my side and under us!"

"Mine's back, too!" Captain Quinn said. "What the—"

Quinn's radio crackled.

"One Twenty Tactical to Trans Peak Twenty-two Thirty. Captain Quinn, we're going to try to give you a little lift to get us all up over that speed bump ahead."

"Major Garland, that's noble but it's impossible."

"Doing the impossible is in my job description, sir. We have no other options and we've got very little time to do this. Please button everyone tight. It's going to get bumpy."

Garland and Taft very carefully began moving their jets up closer to the wingtips of the big Ultra Supreme 880.

"What's going on out there? Can anybody see?" one man shouted from the rows behind Kate.

Throughout the cabin, people began explaining what they saw, while others aimed their phones to record the jet fighters positioning under the wings of the jetliner. Some passengers made the sign of the cross as overhead storage bins began to rattle.

With an eye on instruments and the time, Garland and Taft inched their fighters meticulously into position.

"How's it looking, Ryan?" Garland asked.

"Doing all I can to break through the air flowing around his wing."

"I know it's going to take everything you got to keep it steady. You've got to massage it like a baby."

"Roger, sir."

"How's it going?"

"A yard out from contact, sir." Taft's voice was vibrating as he watched the gap of blue sky between his wing and the jetliner's close like a curtain. Then, a sudden scrape and a thud put Taft's left wing under and touching the Ultra's wing.

"Got it, sir!"

"Hold your position."

Garland drew on all his experience and strength to smoothly position his right wing under the jetliner's left wing.

"Okay, Ryan, we're set. On my count we'll lift, slowly and carefully. Too hard and too fast, something could snap. Ready?"

"Roger, sir."

"Okay, in five, four, three, two, one, lift!"

Using their elevators and throttle, Garland and Taft powered up gradually. Garland watched his altimeter and his heart sank.

"Well, we got five feet. More power, another five percent."

The fighters roared and the big jet climbed by another forty feet.

"It's working," Garland said. "We got forty-five."

In the Ultra's cockpit, a resolution advisory had activated, issuing the warning to "Climb now! Climb now!"

Captain Quinn and First Officer Krenski were helpless to do anything as another audio alert activated. "Increase climb now! Increase climb now!"

They were eight minutes from impact.

"Come on! Come on!" Garland said, knowing he and Taft were straining the elevators of their tail sections.

Seven minutes from impact, and they had the jet-liner up by sixty feet when his F-16 began shaking.

"Dammit!"

Garland's ride was getting rough.

"How are you doing, Ryan?"

"It's getting pretty bad, sir."

"I know." Garland swallowed drily. "We're now at seventy-five and we've got just under two min-utes until we need to engage. Increase throttle by another ten percent."

"Ten percent? But, sir!"

"Let's do it. We've got two minutes before we have to abort and engage, so let's do it. This is it, Ryan!"

Both jets throttled up.

As the fighter pilots continued the lift, something flashed in the distance.

The looming speck in the sky was the Seattle-bound flight.

"One Twenty Tactical. This is Major Garland to Major Brennan. Heads up, we're giving Flight Twenty-two Thirty a lift up, please descend."

"One Twenty Tactical, Brennan to Garland. Say again."

Garland repeated his message.

"Roger, but I don't believe it, Major! You're or-ders are to engage now!" Brennan's fighter team dropped under the Seattle flight.

Garland ignored Brennan and concentrated on his instruments, which were telling him that they'd raised the jetliner one hundred feet.

"Ryan, we can't pull out now! We've passed the

point of no return. We've got to do this! Give it another five percent!"

"Roger."

"Major Garland!" His commander came on the air. "Your orders are to engage! Fire on the aircraft now!"

Garland disregarded his orders.

Their aircraft growled, and all three aircraft shook wildly as the two fighters muscled the big jetliner higher. Thirty seconds to impact and they pushed it higher a few more feet at a time as the seconds ticked down.

"Come on!" Garland gritted his teeth as the big Seattle plane shot at them, growing larger with every second. "Come on!" One hundred ten feet, one hundred seventeen. "Come on!"

Four seconds to impact and Garland's instruments read one hundred twenty-one feet. His stomach heaved into his mouth as the massive Seattle-bound jetliner and two accompanying fighters streaked under them with a bullet's velocity.

Oh God! Thank you! Thank you! Garland sighed to himself.

"Break away, Ryan! Break away!"

The two F-16s dropped and pulled clear of the Ultra.

At that moment warnings began sounding in Garland's cockpit.

The stress the operation had put on his aircraft, especially his right wing, had taken a toll. A chunk was missing. Then another broke off as Garland's wing began tearing apart in small pieces, then bigger ones, before his wing was gone.

"Eject, Major! Eject!" Captain Taft, whose jet was undamaged, called. "Get out, Tom!"

Suddenly, violently, Garland's jet rolled, disorienting him as he reached for his ejection seat handles and pulled.

NorthSun Airlines Flight 118 continued, unscathed, on its locked position with its fighter escort.

Shaken, Captain Miller found his composure as he and First Officer Zhang resumed their struggle to regain control of the Startrail AV600.

In the cockpit of Trans Peak Airlines Flight 2230 to New York, a spectrum of alarms was sounding.

The big jetliner had not recovered from the vibrations encountered during the rescue operation, and its situation was rapidly deteriorating.

In the cabin, passengers, in shock over the near collision with another plane, began protesting and pleading.

"Please land this plane now! Get us down now!"

The jet bumped and jolted. Overhead storage-bin doors shook open, spilling luggage onto passengers as the plane shimmied and rocked.

Kate squeezed Willa's hand in one of hers while gripping the armrest with the other.

Suddenly the plane rolled hard, the left wing tipping upward. People screamed. The jet reversed its position, rolling right with the wings in a twelve-and-six-o'clock position.

Then the plane lunged violently to the left, dropping and banking.

In the cockpit, Captain Quinn and First Officer Krenski battled for control of their plane as it entered a steep dive.

Eighty-Four

A live radar tracking map filled the big screen at one end of the NTSB meeting room where security had brought Robert Cole.

In the screen's bottom-right quarter, a live video feed showed Jill LaRose and Chet Meyer working on Seth and Veyda's laptops in Colorado.

They were linked in real time to Reed Devlin, Jake Hooper and other top NTSB investigators, along with national security experts and air industry engineers, on teleconference. They'd been feeding calculations to Colorado in a frantic bid to unlock the cyber grip on the two flights.

One by one, each attempt had failed.

Robert Cole was handcuffed and under guard in a corner chair, but he was indicating that he needed his briefcase.

At that moment, four men in FBI Windbreakers entered the large room. One of the building's security people approached them.

At the same time, the joy over the miracle that

the two airliners had not collided died as NORAD's situational update was patched to the group. While Flight 118 and its escort were intact, one of Flight 2230's escorts had sustained damage in the cross-over maneuver, forcing the pilot to eject.

And more alarmingly, in the wake of the near collision, Flight 2230 had begun to experience excessive pitching and banking before entering into an uncontrolled vertical descent.

"With this angle of descent, terminal impact is in three minutes!" a voice warned through the tele-conference speakers.

"Jake!" Cole called out. "The codes you need to regain control of the planes are in my briefcase!"

Hooper seized the case from one of the guards.

The FBI, while being briefed by the security supervisor, watched coldly.

"The blue pages will undo the hack, Jake," Cole guided him.

"I've got them!"

"Tell your people in Colorado to submit my codes into—into my—" Cole choked on his emotion. "Did they find my daughter? Is Veyda okay?"

"Robert, I don't know—please, how do we submit the codes?"

"Focus on the decision logic of the Omega Protection system and mind the variables. Veyda found a back door into the kill switch network."

"Jill—" Hooper turned to the big screen "—did you get that?"

"Yes, we'll do it! Give us the coding!"

Hooper began entering the lines of code.

"Stop!" The lead FBI agent pointed at Cole. "That

man's wanted for threatening national security! The two planes missed each other, but he could be giving you information to sabotage your rescue! Everyone take your hands off your computers and end your calls, now!"

Hooper kept going, entering the last line of code before hitting Send. He lifted his hands from the keyboard when Jill LaRose in Colorado said, "Got them, Jake!"

Eighty-Five

Colorado

The jetliner's nose-down drop continued with increasing speed.

Kate gripped her armrests, the plane's momentum crushing against her as yellow oxygen masks dropped.

Passengers shrieked. Tears streamed from Willa Neal's clenched eyes.

One of the flight attendants suddenly smashed down the aisle. Passengers reached in vain to catch him before he hit a counter in the galley.

Laptops, books, coffee cups, soda cans and bags pelted the passengers and bounced through the cabin.

The jet was pointed straight down, rocking and shaking while plummeting. G-forces had turned Kate's body into a stone weight. Rivets came loose, popping like popcorn and hitting the cabin walls. The whining engines were deafening, mingling with the thudding against the fuselage as parts of it began tearing away.

Kate's stomach felt like a giant hand was forcing it through her mouth. Turning her head against the pressure, she grabbed hold of her most important thoughts and calmly braced for her death.

I love you, Grace. I love you, Vanessa. Thank you for a good life.

The cabin lights began flickering and one passenger screamed.

"Jesus, please help us!"

It was futile.

Battling the g-forces, Captain Quinn and First Officer Krenski submitted commands for control, but nothing worked.

They'd managed to pull on their oxygen masks, remaining conscious and alert as alarms buzzed and horns blared warnings. The console ignited with flashing lights; counters and dials went haywire.

Quinn and Krenski strained against the intense g-forces as the earth raced toward them with frightening speed.

"Twenty thousand!" Krenski shouted as the plane shook. "The VSI and the altimeter are going crazy!"

Quinn reached for the throttles, shoving them all the way down.

"Respond! Get your nose up you son of a— Dammit! Respond!"

"Fifteen thousand!"

Quinn held tight to the yoke.

"Twelve thousand! Lloyd, we're not going to make it!"

The immense Colorado plain loomed like a waiting graveyard as they rocketed toward the earth.

Quinn's knuckles whitened on the yoke.

"Eleven thousand! Oh God, this is it, Lloyd… Our Father who art in heaven…"

Quinn's arms vibrated against the bucking. He took one last glance at the photo of his wife and daughters, gritted his shaking teeth and begged God for mercy. That's when the lights of the instrument panel blinked then lit up with a different pattern, and the big jet's nose began inching up.

"Something's happening!" Quinn shouted. "Something's happening!"

"Ten thousand!"

The velocity shifted the g-forces, flattening Quinn and Krenski to their seats, quadrupling their body weight. Quinn summoned all of his strength, pulled back on the yoke and the nose continued inching up.

"We've got control, Shawn! We've got control!"

Quinn continued pulling the yoke back.

"Pull back on the throttles, Shawn. Easy!"

Slowly, smoothly, gracefully, the plane began leveling.

In the cabin screams gave way to gasps and sporadic cheers as the plane pulled out of its dive.

The speed decreased and once the jet leveled a funereal calm fell over the passengers.

Brushing tears from their eyes, Kate and Willa embraced. Most people were shaken, sobbing and trying to aid others when the public-address system was activated.

"Ladies and gentlemen, this is Captain Quinn. I'm happy to report that we've regained control of the plane. We've been cleared for a priority landing in Denver. We'll have you safe on the ground as soon as possible."

His words were met with soft applause before he continued.

"Please report injuries to the attendants. We request that anyone aboard who has medical training provide assistance and that everyone else please remain seated and belted."

A doctor and a nurse helped the injured attendant and the other passengers who were bleeding from being struck by falling items. Parents comforted terrified children, while strangers consoled each other. Observing the compassion of her fellow passengers, Kate acknowledged the palpable tension that was still in the cabin.

No one felt safe because they were still in the air.

Their trust had been shredded. The remedy was to be on the ground.

As the plane descended, Kate and Willa talked about their families while adrenaline coursed through them.

Only when Trans Peak Flight 2230 touched down safely in Denver did people cheer. Kate thrust her face into her trembling hands to cover her gasping sobs of relief. As the plane taxied she blinked at the ceiling, found a measure of composure, turned to the window and whispered her thanks.

Then she reached for her phone.

Grace would still be in school but Kate texted her.

I love you so much, sweetheart. So much! Can't wait to see you!

Then she called Vanessa, not sure if she was at work, at a class. When she got her voice mail, Kate said, "I love you, little sister. So much. We'll talk later."

Red and blue lights splashed in the cabin's interior. Kate leaned forward and saw ambulances, fire trucks and other emergency vehicles at the gate.

Pulling herself together she called the desk at Newslead.

"Laneer."

"Chuck, its Kate."

"Kate! All hell's breaking loose! Where are you?"

Suddenly she was at a loss, not believing what she'd just experienced.

"Kate? Are you all right? Where are you?"

She blinked hard, briefly cupped her hand to her mouth and took a breath.

"Chuck, I'm in Denver and I've got a story coming."

Epilogue

Once the crew of the Seattle-bound NorthSun Flight 118 regained control they were cleared to land in Cheyenne, Wyoming.

Two passengers reported heart palpitations, while several others had nausea. That was the extent of the injuries on Flight 118.

In Denver, thirty-nine passengers and crew from Trans Peak Flight 2230 required medical attention. Most serious was the attendant who'd fallen through the cabin—he'd suffered a concussion and broken ribs. Injuries to other passengers ranged from cuts to fractured fingers, hands and arms, as well as mild head wounds.

For her part, Kate had harnessed her shock, working fast. She'd reached Nick Varner, NTSB and FAA officials, collecting facts on the terror that had played out in the skies over Colorado.

After finding a quiet spot in the airport, she'd written a breaking exclusive on the cyber hijacking and near-midair collision of two large passenger planes collectively carrying 1,125 people. The incident, which investigators had told her was linked to the Shikra crash in London and the troubled East-Cloud flight in New York, proved that jetliners were vulnerable to hijacking by hackers. Had the cyber hackers, known as Zarathustra, succeeded, the Colorado event would have been the worst disaster in aviation history, she'd written, in what soon became one of the biggest stories in the world.

The events in Colorado, London and New York would become global news for days and weeks.

In that time, Kate had led a team of Newslead reporters in the United States and around the world to produce a multipart series that examined fly-by-wire systems, the secret Operation Overlord, Richlon-Titan, and Robert and Veyda Cole's connection to it all.

Cole had been investigated by the FBI but faced no charges. He was cooperating with all national security agencies in their investigations.

The challenge Kate had faced with the series was that Robert Cole had refused all interview requests. He'd turned down the *New York Times*, CTNB, *The Times* of London, the Associated Press, everybody.

Kate was frustrated but she understood, given Cole's tragic history.

Seth Hagen had died at the scene, but Cole's daughter, Veyda, had survived her gunshot wound in a Denver hospital, the location of which was not made public because the FBI was keeping watch to question her.

Kate's sources had told her that Cole had flown to Denver to be at Veyda's side, as her condition had been critical. On the third day of his bedside vigil she'd woken briefly, and as Cole had taken her hand, she'd said one word: "Daddy."

Veyda had died an hour later.

The next day Robert Cole had issued a statement.

To all those who have suffered from my daughter's actions, I offer my most profound apology. For the rest of my life, I will live with the irreparable damage and unending sorrow she has caused. Her evil actions are not those of the daughter I knew. I do not ask for understanding, nor do I seek forgiveness. Both are unconscionable in the face of the enormity of the crime. I pray that heaven helps you heal and find peace.

In the time that followed, reporters profiled Cole, Veyda and Seth based on public records and interviews with those who knew them. But nobody was going to get the whole story.

No journalist was going to get to Robert Cole.

The FAA had not ordered a national ground stop of all jetliners because, with the deaths of Seth and Veyda, the immediate threat had been considered neutralized. However, in the days that followed aviation authorities in the United States and around the world rolled out alerts and advisories to the industry for fleets to be grounded in a non-disruptive, scheduled manner to examine and safeguard their systems.

The world's top engineers analyzed what Seth and Veyda had done, while building on the remedy designed by Robert Cole. Plane by plane, airline by airline, security was strengthened on all commercial jetliners.

A number of federal investigations were launched against Richlon-Titan for failing to correct, and concealing, the problem with its systems. Several lawsuits were launched by airlines that had purchased RT systems or aircraft. RT's stock plunged and Hub Wolfeson was fired from his position with the board.

Sloane F. Parkman was disinherited from his wealthy family. Kate learned that he was supporting himself by working part-time at a clothing store in a mall in Albany, New York.

The NTSB and EastCloud had cleared Captain Raymond Matson of any suspected errors in the handling of the Buffalo–to–New York flight. Matson resumed flying with the airline in good standing.

At the NTSB, during Bill Cashill's retirement party, Cashill took Hooper aside and advised him to "Never stop doing what you do, Jake. You do it right. You keep an open mind. You're going to be one helluva IIC."

Some two weeks later, Kate was in the newsroom when a burst of dispatches from the police scanners made her think of how it had all begun.

Something overheard on the lowly squawk box.

At that moment her cell phone rang with a call from Nick Varner.

"Hey, Nick."

"Listen, Kate, we never had this conversation, okay?"

"Sure."

"Robert Cole wants to talk to the press. Says he

needs to get something out there because a lot of the stuff written about him and his daughter is inaccurate."

Kate sat up.

"You're not serious."

"I told him he should talk to you and he's willing to do it."

"Exclusively?"

"Only to you."

Kate alerted Chuck and while she was still uneasy about getting on a plane, she flew to North Dakota, rented a car at Minot and drove to Clear River, where she met Cole.

Kate shook his hand.

"Mr. Cole, I want to thank you for what you did at the NTSB in Washington. You helped save my life and the lives of more than a thousand people."

Cole didn't respond.

He was a haunted man; his eyes were pools of pain.

"I want to take you somewhere," he said. "There's something I need to do."

They climbed into Cole's pickup truck and drove across town, past the historic municipal buildings and storefronts that evoked another time.

"My wife, Elizabeth, grew up here," was all he said as he guided his truck south over the eternal rolling rangeland.

After a few miles, they took the narrow, paved road that curved to a grove of trees near a creek and stopped at the Riverbend Meadow Cemetery.

He got out, opened the storage bin of the console between the seats and, with care, removed a beautiful wooden box.

"This way." He motioned for Kate to walk with him through the burial grounds, stopping at the headstone that read "Elizabeth Marie Cole, Beloved Wife and Mother."

Cole got on his knees.

"These are my daughter's ashes. I want her to be with her mother."

Cole very tenderly emptied the box's contents, spreading them over his wife's grave.

"I didn't want to get a stone for her because I feared people would come and deface it, given what she did."

Kate understood.

Cole stared at the ashes and they began to lift as the wind tumbled across the plain.

"I'm to blame for her actions because I was not the father she needed," he said. "I'm going to tell you our story, the real story. I'm going to tell you everything the world needs to know."

But Cole didn't move.

The wind strengthened, lifting the ashes from the land, carrying them upward. Cole followed them, looking up just as the straight vapor trail of a passenger jet cut across the clear blue sky.

* * * * *

Acknowledgments
&
A Personal Note

The first thing you should know is that I have no fear of flying.

In fact, I enjoy flying and I believe it is one of the safest ways to travel. In crafting *Free Fall*, I looked at several aspects of the commercial airline industry and consulted a number of texts and final reports on accidents made public by investigative agencies around the world.

Still, I make no claim to being an expert or coming close to possessing any knowledge of aeronautical engineering, air traffic control or any other area of the industry. I apologize to the experts among you for the eye-rolling errors that would cause you to say "Things just don't work that way."

Free Fall is a work of fiction drawn in my imagination, where I exercised creative license and took liberties with technical realities, jurisdiction and the investigative process to present a drama concerning flawed human beings in an extraordinary situation.

I did benefit from the help of Ric Gillespie, a former aviation accident investigator and founder of The International Group for Historic Aircraft Recovery. Ric, a world-renowned expert, generously and graciously suffered my questions. For parts of the story that ring true, thanks goes to Ric. For the parts that don't, blame me for my transgressions as a fiction writer.

I'd like to thank Amy Moore-Benson, Brittany Lavery, Michelle Meade and the incredible editorial, marketing, sales and PR teams at Harlequin and MIRA Books.

Thanks to Wendy Dudley for making this a better story.

Very special thanks to Barbara, Laura and Michael.

It is important readers know that in getting this book to you, I benefitted from the hard work and generosity of many people, too many to thank individually.

This brings me to what I hold to be the most critical part of the entire enterprise: you, the reader. This aspect has become a credo for me, one that bears repeating with each book.

Thank you very much for your time, for without you, a book remains an untold tale. Thank you for setting your life on pause and taking the journey. I deeply appreciate my audience around the world and those who've been with me since the beginning who keep in touch. Thank you all for your very kind words. I hope you enjoyed the ride and will check out my earlier books while watching for my next one. I welcome your feedback. Drop by at www.rickmofina.com, subscribe to my newsletter and send me a note. I love hearing from you.

Rick Mofina

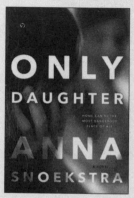

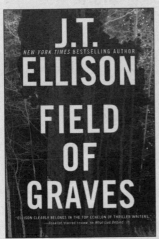

From *New York Times* bestselling author

HEATHER GUDENKAUF

comes a chilling page-turner about what happens when a woman uncovers earth-shattering secrets about her husband's family.

Sarah Quinlan's husband, Jack, has avoided returning to his hometown of Penny Gate, Iowa, since the untimely death of his mother when he was just a teenager—her body was found in the cellar of their family farm, the circumstances a mystery. But when his beloved aunt Julia is in an accident, he can hide from the past no longer.

As the facts surrounding Julia's accident begin to surface, Sarah soon realizes that nothing about the Quinlans is what it seems. Caught in a flurry of unanswered questions, Sarah dives deep into the puzzling rabbit hole of Jack's past. But the farther in she climbs, the harder it is for her to get out. And soon she is faced with a deadly truth she may not be prepared for.

Available now, wherever books are sold!

Be sure to connect with us at:
Harlequin.com/Newsletters
Facebook.com/HarlequinBooks
Twitter.com/HarlequinBooks

www.MIRABooks.com

MHGU1931TALL

RICK MOFINA

32948	IN DESPERATION	___ $9.99 U.S.	___ $11.99 CAN.
32901	SIX SECONDS	___ $7.99 U.S.	___ $9.99 CAN.
32638	VENGEANCE ROAD	___ $7.99 U.S.	___ $8.99 CAN.
31745	FULL TILT	___ $7.99 U.S.	___ $8.99 CAN.
31609	WHIRLWIND	___ $7.99 U.S.	___ $8.99 CAN.
31500	INTO THE DARK	___ $7.99 U.S.	___ $9.99 CAN.
31751	EVERY SECOND	___ $9.99 U.S.	___ $11.99 CAN.

(limited quantities available)

TOTAL AMOUNT	$_____
POSTAGE & HANDLING	$_____
($1.00 for 1 book, 50¢ for each additional)	
APPLICABLE TAXES*	$_____
TOTAL PAYABLE	$_____

(check or money order—please do not send cash)

To order, complete this form and send it, along with a check or money order for the total above, payable to MIRA Books, to: **In the U.S.:** 3010 Walden Avenue, P.O. Box 9077, Buffalo, NY 14269-9077; **In Canada:** P.O. Box 636, Fort Erie, Ontario, L2A 5X3.

_____ City: _____
_____ Zip/Postal Code: _____
_____e): _____

...ents remit applicable sales taxes.
...mit applicable GST and provincial taxes.

MIRA®

...v.MIRABooks.com

MRM0816TALLBL